SWORD AND PEN

Rachel Caine

Sword and Pen

THE GREAT LIBRARY

BERKLEY

NEW YORK

BERKLEY
An imprint of Penguin Random House LLC
penguinrandomhouse.com

Library of Congress Cataloging-in-Publication Data
Names: Caine, Rachel, author.
Title: Sword and Pen / Rachel Caine.
Description: First Edition. | New York: Berkley, 2019. |
Series: The Great Library; 5
Identifiers: LCCN 2019016968 | ISBN 9780451489241 (hardcover) |
ISBN 9780451489258 (ebook)
Subjects: LCSH: Libraries—Fiction. | GSAFD: Alternative
histories (Fiction). | Dystopias.
Classification: LCC PS3603.O557 S96 2019 | DDC 813/.6—dc23
LC record available at https://lccn.loc.gov/2019016968

First Edition: September 2019

Printed in Canada
1   3   5   7   9   10   8   6   4   2

Jacket art and design by Katie Anderson

To readers. To writers. To dreamers. To book lovers.
To librarians, with love.

ACKNOWLEDGMENTS

This book could not have been written without the love and support of these people:

R. Cat Conrad

Lucienne Diver

Sarah Simpson-Weiss

Anne Sowards

Joanne Madge

Zaheerah Kalik

. . . and many others who have given me astonishing insight, feedback, encouragement, and the precious gift of their time and passion for this project.

Also: to the Berkley art department, who has made these books so incomparably beautiful.

SWORD AND PEN

EPHEMERA

Text of a letter from Scholar Christopher Wolfe to
Callum Brightwell. Available in the Archive.

Mr. and Mrs. Brightwell,

It is with the utmost regret and sorrow that I must inform you of the
death of your son Brendan Brightwell upon this day in the city of Alexandria. I know that it cannot be a comfort for you in this moment of
grief, but perhaps it will ease your heart in the future to know that Brendan's courage in his final days and hours was exemplary, and inspired
every one of us who had the pleasure of knowing him. He was at his
brother's side for the battle, and I assure you that Jess is alive, though
laid just as low as you must be by this terrible loss. Jess was with him
as he died, and Brendan's passing was mercifully quick and painless.

He was instrumental in the victory achieved today in Alexandria
for the continued existence and protection of the ideals of the Great Library, and that is no small thing to remember. Brendan's loyalty to, and
protection of, his brother was extraordinary, and we will always honor
his memory.

I pray to my gods and yours that Brendan's soul finds peace, and
that you may also do so with this difficult news.

Funeral rites will be prepared for him, and once the immediate emergency is past I will write to you to finalize these arrangements. We will
welcome you to Alexandria for the honors the Great Library will give to
your sons—both the dead and the living.

With all my heart, I grieve with you. And I make you this pledge:
I will fight to preserve Jess's life with every ounce of strength I possess.
For though we believe that knowledge is all, still we value every life en-
trusted to our care.

Scholar Christopher Wolfe

CHAPTER ONE

JESS

Brendan was dead, and Jess's world was broken. He'd never known a moment without his twin existing somewhere, a distant warmth on the horizon, but now . . . now he shivered, alone, with his dead brother held close against his chest.

So much silence in the world now.

He's still warm, Jess thought, and he was; Brendan's skin still felt alive, inhabited, but there was nothing inside him. No heartbeat. No presence.

He was dimly aware that things were happening around him, that the bloody sands of the arena were full of people running, fighting, screaming, shouting. He didn't care. Not now.

Let the world burn.

A shadow fell over him, and Jess looked up. It was Anubis, a giant automaton god gleaming with gold. The jackal's black head blotted out the sun. It felt like the end of the world.

And then Anubis thrust his spear forward, and it plunged into Jess's chest. It held him there, pinned, and suddenly Brendan's body was gone, and Jess was alone and skewered on the spear . . . but it didn't hurt. He felt weightless.

Anubis leaned closer and said, *Wake up.*

When he opened his eyes, he was lying in darkness on a soft mattress, covered by a blanket that smelled of spice and roses. Out the window to his left, the moon floated in a boat of clouds. Jess's heart felt heavy and strange in his chest.

He could still feel the sticky blood on his hands, even though he knew they were clean. He'd washed Brendan's blood away. No, *he* hadn't. Thomas had brought a bowl of water and rinsed the gore away; he hadn't done anything for himself. Hadn't been able to. His friends had helped him here, into a strange house and a strange bed. He knew he should be grateful for that, but right now all he felt was empty, and deeply wrong. This was a world he didn't know, one in which he was the only surviving Brightwell son. Half a twin.

He'd have taken large bets that Brendan would have been the one to survive everything and come through stronger. And his brother would have bet even more on it. The world seemed so quiet without him.

Then you'll just have to be louder, you moping idiot. He could almost hear his brother saying that with his usual cocky smirk. *God knows you always acted like you wished you'd been an only child.*

"No, I didn't," he said out loud, though he instantly knew it for a lie and was ashamed of it, then even more ashamed when a voice came out of the darkness near the far corner.

"Awake, Brightwell? About time." There was a rustle of cloth, and a dim greenish glow started to kindle, then brighten. The glow lamp sat next to Scholar Christopher Wolfe, who looked like death, and also like he'd bite the head off the first person to say he looked tired. In short, his usual sunny disposition. "Dreams?"

"No," Jess lied. He tried to slow down his still-pounding heart. "What are you doing here?"

"We drew lots as to who would be your nursemaid this evening and I lost." Wolfe rose to his feet. He'd changed into black Scholar's robes, a liquidly flowing silk that made him seem part of the shadows except for the gray in his shoulder-length hair and his pale skin. He paused at Jess's bedside and looked at him with cool assessment. "You lost someone precious to you. I understand. But we don't have time to indulge your grief. There's work to be done, and fewer of us now to do it."

Jess felt no impulse to care. "I'm surprised you think I'm useful."

"Self-pity doesn't become you, boy. I'll be leaving now. The world doesn't stop because the one you loved is no longer in it."

Jess almost snapped, *What do you know about it?* but he stopped himself. Wolfe had lost many people. He'd seen his own mother die. He understood. So Jess swallowed his irrational anger and said, "Where are you going?" Not we. He hadn't yet decided whether staying in this bed would be his best idea.

"The office of the Archivist," Wolfe said. "You've been there. I could use help in locating his secure records."

The office. Jess blinked and saw the place, a magnificent space with automaton gods standing silent guard in alcoves. The view of the Alexandrian harbor dominating the windows. A peaceful place. He wondered if they'd managed to scrub the dead assistant's blood out of the floor yet. The Archivist had ordered her killed just to punish him. And Brendan.

Brendan. The last time he'd been in that office, Brendan had been with him.

Jess swallowed against a wave of disorientation and nausea and sat upright. Someone—Thomas, again—had helped him out of his bloody clothes and into clean ones. An informal High Garda uniform, the kind soldiers wore at leisure in the barracks. Soft as pajamas. It would do. He swung his legs out of bed and paused there, breathing deeply. He felt . . . unwell. Not a specific pain he could land on, just a general malaise, an ache that threaded through every muscle and every nerve. Shock, he supposed. Or just the accumulated stress of the past few days.

It might even be grief. Did grief hurt this way? Like sickness?

"Up." Wolfe's voice was unexpectedly kind. Warm. "I know how difficult that is. But there is no other way but onward."

Jess nodded and stood up. He found his boots   neatly placed at the foot of the bed—and slid them on. His High Garda weapons belt was nearby, with his sidearm still in place. Heavy and lethal, and he felt a bit of comfort as it settled on his hip. *We're at war.* It felt like he'd always been at war—his family had always warred with the Great Library, and then he'd fought for a place inside it. Then he'd fought to preserve the dream of the Great Library. And for the first time he wondered what peace would really feel like.

His hair was a spiky mess; he ran his fingers through it and ignored it when it refused to comply. "All right," he said. "I'm ready."

Wolfe could have said anything to that; Jess expected something dismissive and caustic. But Wolfe just put his hand on Jess's shoulder, nodded, and led the way.

The house, Jess thought, must have belonged to a Scholar—there was a cluster of black-robed Scholars around a wide table in the main room, anxiously chattering in Greek, which must have been the only language they had in common. A tall man with skin so dark it took on cobalt tones; a small, elegant young Chinese woman; another man, middle-aged and comfortably round, with distinctively Slavic features. There must have been a dozen of them, and Jess recognized only two of them immediately. None of his friends were here, which came as a vague surprise.

All the talk stopped when Wolfe approached the table. No question that he held authority here. "We're going to the Archivist's office," he said. "Thoughts?" His Greek was, of course, excellent; he'd grown up speaking it here in Alexandria. Jess wasn't as comfortable, but he was more than passable.

"Traps," the young Chinese woman said. "The Archivist was very fond of them. He certainly would have many waiting there, in case he lost his hold on power. Is there any word on where he is—"

"No," Wolfe said. "We assume he has loyalists who'll do anything to protect him. Our advantage is that the less savory elements of this city are firmly on our side, and without criminals to smuggle him out past the walls, he's trapped here. With us."

"Or we're trapped with him," said one of the Scholars—Jess wasn't sure which.

That earned a sharp look from Wolfe, and Jess knew the man could cut a person to ribbons with a single glance. "Don't think he's all-powerful. Without the apathy and passive consent of Scholars and High Garda, the Archivist would never have felt free to murder as he liked," Wolfe said. "We've taken that from him. Don't grant him more power than he ever earned."

"Easy for you to say, Scholar." That grumble was from the Slav, whose Greek was only lightly accented.

"You think so?" Wolfe's voice had gone sharp and dry, his face the color of exposed bone. "*Easy. For me.* Search the Archives. I was *erased* by him, like hundreds of others you've never even noticed missing. None of this is easy. Nor should it be. Killing a god-king ought to be *difficult.*"

It hit Jess with a jolt that the Archivist had another title: *Pharaoh of Alexandria.* The god-king. And no doubt the bitter old man took that deification quite seriously. *But we will kill him. Somehow.*

For Brendan, if for nothing else.

"Look for pressure plates under the floor," the Chinese scholar said. "He took most of his cues from the great inventor Heron, who built so many wonders of this place. The Archivist took his lessons seriously; his traps will be ingenious, but also quite conventional. He may also have a specific command you'll need to give to freeze the automata, should they be triggered for defense. I have no idea where you'd find that, but it should be your immediate priority." She hesitated. "Perhaps . . . you should let the High Garda do this, Scholar."

"Because their lives are less valuable than mine?" Wolfe shot back, and she looked down. "No. I know what I'm looking for. They may not. I know the old bastard better than any High Garda could. He was my mentor, for a good portion of our lives. I know how he thinks."

Jess tried to imagine Wolfe having the same relationship with the evil bastard Archivist that Jess had with Wolfe. He couldn't bring it into focus. For one thing, he couldn't imagine Wolfe as a young man. He abandoned the effort as a bad idea, and as he looked around, he spotted someone standing in the doorway, watching the discussion.

Dario Santiago.

Not his very favorite person in the world, but Jess felt much more comfortable about the Spaniard than he had before; they'd been enemies, cautious allies, friends, enemies again, but through all of that, Dario had been *present*. There was something comforting about that now, in this silent new world that lacked his brother. Jess walked over to join him. The young man had his arms crossed; he'd changed clothes, too, into a posh velvet jacket and silk shirt and finely tailored trousers. He looked rich and entitled, just as he was. But Dario had never pretended to humility.

"Brightwell." Dario nodded.

Jess nodded back. "Santiago."

They both watched the Scholars arguing for a moment. Odd, Jess thought, that though Dario was entitled to wear the black robes, he didn't have them on. He wondered if that had significance, or if it was just because Dario didn't want to take away from the cut of his jacket.

Dario finally said, "All right, then?" He rocked a little back and forth on his heels, as if tempted to move away from the question. Or from Jess. But he stayed put.

"All right," Jess affirmed. He wasn't, but Dario knew that already, and this was Dario's way of showing some kind of empathy. It wasn't much, but from someone like him it was a fair attempt. "Where's Khalila?"

"With Scholar Murasaki," he said. "They're helping to organize a full Scholars' Conclave. Word is we'll elect a new Archivist today. Tomorrow at the latest. We need an unquestioned leader if we intend to hold Alexandria independent; the nations sending their ships are all too eager to *help*." He shook his head. "They're cloaking conquest as rescue, you know. Their strategy is to sweep in and claim Alexandria as a protectorate. Once they do that, they'll pull us apart and squabble over the bones."

"We can't let that happen," Jess said.

"No. Hence the election of a new Archivist."

Jess felt the impulse to smile. Didn't. "And you're not in the running? I'm astonished."

"Shut up, Scrubber."

"Touchy, Your Royalness, very touchy."

There was something comforting about the casual insults; it felt like home. One constant in this life: he and Dario would always be slightly uneasy friends. Maybe that was a very good thing. He trusted Dario . . . to a point. And of course Dario felt the same about him.

"Your cousin's ships are in that fleet," Jess said. "I don't suppose you're feeling some family loyalty today?"

"If you're asking if I'm going to betray the Great Library to the Kingdom of Spain, then no. I won't," Dario said. "But I don't want to fight my cousin, either. Not just because I like him. Because he's a good king, but he's also clever and ruthless. He'll win, unless we make the cost of winning unacceptably high. And I'm not altogether certain what he'd consider too high."

My brother already died for this, Jess thought. *The price is already too high.* But he didn't say it. He swallowed against a sudden tightness in his throat and said, "Where are the others?"

"Glain and Santi are organizing the city's defenses. Thomas . . . God knows, most likely off tinkering with one of his lethal toys—not that it isn't worthwhile. Morgan is with Eskander at the Iron Tower; they're getting the Obscurists in line."

"And what are you doing that's useful?"

"Nothing," Dario said. "You?"

"Same, at the moment. Want to come with us to the Archivist's office?"

"Is it dangerous?"

"Very."

Dario's grin was bright enough to blot out Brendan's absence, for just a moment. "Excellent. I'm as useless as a chocolate frying pan at the moment."

"In that jacket?"

"Well, it is a very fine jacket, to be sure. But not *useful*." Dario's smile faded. He looked at Jess, straight on. "I really am sorry about Brendan."

Jess nodded. "I know."

"Then let's get on with it."

First Wolfe, now Dario. There was something comforting about their harsh briskness today. Thomas would be different, as would Khalila and Morgan; they'd offer him the chance to let his grief loose. But Wolfe and Dario believed in pushing through, and just now that seemed right to him. Eventually he'd need to confront his demons, but for now, he was content to run from them.

Wolfe joined them, took in Dario's presence without comment, and simply swept on. Jess shrugged to Dario and they both followed.

Off to defy death.

Seemed like a decent way to start the day.

The sunrise was cool and glorious, reflecting in chips of vivid orange and red on the harbor's churning waters; the massed fleet of warships that had assembled out in the open sea still floated a good distance away. The Lighthouse had sounded a warning, and it was well-known—at least by legend—that the harbor's defenses were incredibly lethal. None of the assembled nations had decided yet to test them.

They would, eventually. And Jess wondered how they were ever going to defeat such a navy. The Great Library had ships of its own, but not so many, and certainly if it came to that kind of a fight, they'd lose.

Dario was right. The trick was to make the cost too high for any-one to dare make an effort.

The residential district of Alexandria where they walked had a street that led directly to the hub of the city: the Serapeum, a giant pyr-amid that rose almost as high as the Lighthouse. The golden capstone on top of it caught the morning light and blazed it back. As the sun rose, it bathed the white marble sides in warmth. From where they walked, Jess could see the Scholar Steps, where the names of Scholars who'd fallen in service to the Library were inscribed. He'd never have his name there, of course; he wasn't a Scholar or likely to become one. But if there was any justice left in the world, surely one day Wolfe would have that honor. And Thomas. And Khalila.

Dario would no doubt believe he'd deserve it, and he might even be right.

"Jess," Wolfe said. "Heron's inventions. You're familiar with them, I would assume."

"Which ones? He had thousands. He was the da Vinci of the ancient world."

"The lethal ones."

"Well, I know as much as anyone, I suppose. Except Thomas, of course. He'd probably give you a two-hour lecture about it, and tell you how to improve them."

"A fascinating lecture for which I have neither time nor patience. This isn't a quiz, Jess. I will depend on you—both of you—to *think*. Because we go into extremely dangerous territory."

"Do you know how to reach the Archivist's office?" Jess had been brought there several times, but there were precautions: hallways that moved, a maze that constantly shifted its path. The Archivist would have had good reason to fear assassination.

"His private office? Yes. I know how to reach it." Wolfe didn't offer an explanation. "Then things get more dangerous. One doesn't hold power as long as he did without being prepared."

The city seemed so *quiet.* "Where is everyone?" Jess asked. Normally the streets were crowded with people. Alexandria pulsed with life, had a population in the hundreds of thousands: Scholars, librarians, staff, not to mention all of the people who simply called it home. But today it seemed silent.

"No one knows what's going to happen. They're staying inside, and safe," Dario said. "Sensible people keep their heads down. Unlike us."

He shared a grim smile with Wolfe. "Well," Wolfe said. "It isn't the sensible people who get things done in these situations, is it?"

That describes us perfectly, Jess thought. *Not sensible.* He imagined Brendan would have been right with him, eager to be reckless.

The walk was good; it drove the shadows back and made Jess feel almost human again. Sore, of course; the fight to survive had been hard, and he still bore the wounds. Someone—Morgan, he suspected—had applied some healing skills, or he'd have still been confined to a bed. But he felt loose, limber, ready to run or fight.

He wondered why Morgan had left him, but he knew; she believed her place was with the Obscurists just now. *It doesn't mean she doesn't care,* he told himself. But she hadn't been there when he'd awakened, hadn't been there when he needed her most to heal his broken soul, and he knew that did mean something.

It meant that he would never come first to her. *Be honest,* he thought. *If she came first for you, you'd have done things differently. You'd be with her right now.*

He wasn't sure what that meant and was too thin and tired inside to think it through. Better to focus on a problem he could solve, an activity he could complete. Leave the difficult questions for later.

They passed a company of High Garda troops—no informal uniforms there; every soldier was dressed sharply and looked as keen as knives. No one Jess recognized, but he nodded to the squad leader, who returned the greeting with crisp acknowledgment. A second later, he realized how wrong that was, and turned to Wolfe. "I should rejoin my company." He was wearing the uniform. The wrong uniform for the day, but nevertheless.

"You're seconded to me," Wolfe said. "Santi doesn't want you back with his company quite yet. You're more useful here." His mouth curled in a rare, non-bitter smile. "He thinks you may be able to keep me from my worst excesses of courting danger. I told him that was nonsense, you were as bad or worse, but he wouldn't have it."

That took a moment to sink in, too: Santi trusted Wolfe's safety to *him*. When he knew that Jess was running on emotional pain and grief. *That's why.* Because Santi was giving him something to keep him from wallowing in the loss of his twin. It was a brilliantly manipulative maneuver. It kept Wolfe with a semiqualified bodyguard, and at the same time gave that bodyguard a mission when he no doubt badly needed one. *And Dario?* Surely Santiago hadn't just appeared at random, either. He was the check to be sure Jess was operating properly, a second pair of eyes on their backs. Dario wasn't the best fighter of the group, but he was a strategist and a decent tactician, too, and that could be valuable on a mission like this.

By the time Jess had examined all that, they'd walked to the street that led in front of the Serapeum. The guard posts were manned by High Garda, and roaming automata as well; sphinxes stalked on lion paws, rustling metal wings and staring with red eyes in their sculpted metal human faces. One followed them a few paces, which made Jess nervous; he watched it carefully to be sure it hadn't been missed in the rewriting of how to identify enemy from friend. But it soon lost interest and padded away to sink down in a comfortable crouch, watching traffic pass.

"Thank God," Dario said. He'd noted it, too. "I loathe those things."

"You've stopped them before."

"And will again, I have no doubt. But I'm grateful for each and every time I don't have to fight for my life. I'm not as clever with them as you are. Or as fearless."

That, Jess thought, was pretty remarkable; he'd not heard Dario confess something like that in quite a while. Possibly ever. The Spaniard naturally assumed he was the best at absolutely everything, and even when proven wrong often insisted until everyone half believed him. It had taken some time for Jess to overcome his general annoyance and realize what a vulnerability that large an ego could be. He hadn't yet used that knowledge against Dario. He hadn't needed to.

But it was always good to spot a weakness, even in an ally and friend.

Scholar Wolfe hadn't been exaggerating; he did know how to reach the Archivist's office. It involved a journey past sharp-eyed High Garda, more automata—including an Anubis-masked god statue that made Jess flash back to his dream and the reality it had mirrored—down hallways that seemed different to what Jess remembered. "It's a self-aligning maze," Wolfe told him when he pointed that out. "There are keys. You look for them encoded in the decorations. The alignments depend on the time, day, month, and year. Rather clever. Heron himself invented the machinery." Jess almost turned to Thomas to comment on that, ready for the German's effusive happiness; Thomas worshipped Heron almost as a god himself. But Thomas wasn't with them. And it surprised Jess how much that dimmed his mood.

"Let's just get on with it," he said, and Wolfe gave him an appraising look, then nodded and led them on without more discussion. The path took them through the forbidding interior Hall of Gods, with all the giant, silent automata on their plinths . . . except for the ones who'd been dispatched to the Colosseum to kill the Library's rebels. Those had been hacked apart. If they were ever to be rebuilt, Jess thought, maybe it would be better to sculpt them out of stone or simple metal. Make them symbols instead of weapons.

But he'd rather not see them again, ever.

They arrived in a hub of halls that led out in spokes; those held the offices of the Curia. All of them dead now, or fled with the Archivist. The quiet seemed ominous.

"This is a bit tricky as well," Wolfe said, and showed the two of them where, how, and when to press certain keys on the wall to open the hallway to the Archivist's private office. "Elite High Garda soldiers would normally be in charge of this. Good thing they're all gone."

"Are they?" Dario asked. "How do we know they didn't flee here and fortify his office? There could be an entire company of the bastards waiting for us."

It was a decent question, and better warning. Jess drew his sidearm. From beneath his robe, Wolfe produced something else; it took a moment for Jess to recognize it, but the elegantly crafted lines gave it away. Thomas's work. That was a Ray of Apollo, upgraded and with better materials. Lethally concentrated light.

"Better to be sure," Wolfe said, and switched the weapon on. Jess made sure his own was set to killing shots, and nodded. When Jess looked back at Dario, he found the Spaniard had produced a very lovely sword, filigreed and fancied to within an inch of its life but no less dangerous for that in the hands of an expert. Which Dario was. He also had a High Garda gun in his left hand, the mirror of Jess's.

"You know how to use that?" Jess nodded at the gun. Dario gave him one of his trademark one-raised-eyebrow mocking looks.

"Better than you, scrubber."

Untrue. Dario could certainly kill him with a sword, but Jess was a *very* good shot. Unless the arrogant royal had been drilling in target practice with that likely stolen gun, he wasn't going to match any High Garda soldier.

Trust Dario to think he could.

Didn't matter, at least at the moment. Jess followed Wolfe into the hallway that revealed itself, and down the spacious, carpeted expanse. This, he remembered. The carpet alone was worth half a kingdom, and the recovered Babylonian walls with their Assyrian lions were just as impressive. An ancient Chinese jade vase as delicate as an eggshell glowed under a skylight.

And there was the neat, clean desk ahead. The desk of the Archivist's assistant, Neksa—Neksa, whom Brendan had loved. Who'd died for their sins.

Wolfe paused at her desk and looked at the two of them, each in turn. "Ready?" he asked. Jess nodded. Out of the corner of his eye, he saw Dario echo him. He felt the hot tension of his nerves, and that was good. Paranoia was a habit these days, but it also might help him stay alive today. *Might.* No fear, though. That seemed wrong, but temporarily useful.

Wolfe pressed a button on Neksa's desk, and the door behind it slid open. Wolfe held up a hand to stop them from rushing in, but he needn't have bothered; neither of them moved. They watched and listened from where they were. There was natural light streaming in from the expanse of windows that overlooked the harbor and the threatening mass of ships clustered on the horizon. Storm clouds were forming out to sea as well. That would complicate things.

Nothing moved in the office, and Jess carefully inched forward and flattened himself against the outer wall at an angle, the better to see into the far, shadowy corners within.

"There's no one," he said. He didn't relax. When Dario tried to move past him, he stopped him with an upraised arm. "Pressure plates?"

"Hmmm." Dario looked around. There was a statue of a serene Buddha in the corner of the assistant's office. The Buddha held a heavy jade orb in both hands. Dario went to it and carefully lifted the stone out of the statue's grasp.

He put the ball down and used his booted foot to roll it into the Archivist's office. As it reached the center of the carpet in front of the massive desk, the automata in the room came to life. Gods, stepping down from their plinths. Anubis. Bast. Horus. Isis. They stared at the inert orb for a long moment with fiery red eyes, and then stepped back up where they'd been. Inert.

"Their coding is still active," Dario said, quite unnecessarily. It was clear the automaton gods would cut them to bloody strips if they set foot in the office itself. "Scholar? I think this has to be your job. Since you have the weaponry to match."

"No," Jess said, and held his gun out to Wolfe. "Trade me."

"I'm not sure that's wise," Wolfe said. A frown formed, pulling his brows together. Jess knew that look. It was close to a glare, but lightened with a fair bit of concern.

He felt himself grin. "Don't worry. I don't want to join my brother. Someone's got to explain things to my father, and much as I'd like to avoid that, it should probably be me."

Wolfe didn't like it, but he allowed Jess to take the Ray of Apollo, and without hesitation, Jess strode into the office, came to a stop exactly in the center of the carpet, and waited for the automata to react.

They moved fast, but he was faster. He activated the weapon, and a thick, shockingly bright beam of coherent light jumped into being from the barrel; he held the trigger down and sliced it from left to right in an arc, severing Horus at the waist, then Bast, Anubis, and Isis. It took only a couple of seconds, a single heartbeat, and then there were inert mechanical legs and the statues' upper bodies toppling backward. Useless. By the time he released the trigger, he'd killed four gods.

It felt horribly wonderful. He stared at Anubis's face. The red eyes were still lit, but as he watched they faded to ash gray. Empty.

For you, he thought to Brendan. Not that any of these had killed his brother, but until he could reach the traitor who had, he'd take what satisfaction he could.

He'd dropped the last automaton in the same spot where Neksa had died here in this room, murdered by a mechanical's spear just to prove that the Archivist didn't make idle threats.

I'll kill Zara for you, brother, he thought. *And then I'll kill that old bastard. For Neksa.*

But he didn't say that. Not in front of Dario and Wolfe, who were stepping into the room and observing the damage. "Well," Dario said. "That is quite a thing Thomas has made. He frightens me sometimes."

"He frightens himself," Wolfe said. "Because he always worries how what he creates can be misused. And for someone with his particular genius, that's a very difficult trait." He held out his hand to Jess, and Jess gave him back the Ray. "Feel better?"

That was the moment when Jess's euphoria snapped, and he realized he'd let himself get complacent. *One trap? Just one?* No. The Archivist would have more. And they needed to be alert.

"Careful," he said as Wolfe approached the Archivist's massive desk. "It'll be trapped."

"Oh, I know." Wolfe dismissed it with an irritated wave. "I know his mind well enough. The old dog never did learn a new trick once he sat his behind in that chair."

"You hope," Dario murmured, and Jess echoed the sentiment silently. But he knew better than to stop Wolfe as he moved to the desk, looked it over without touching it, and then began to recite a nonsense string of words. Or, at least, it seemed to be nonsense. Jess kept his silence until Wolfe finished. It seemed like some superstitious incantation to him, and there was no sign that anything at all had changed from the recitation.

"*Careful,*" Dario said. He'd come to the same conclusion. "Scholar. Whatever you're doing—"

Too late, because Wolfe was sliding a drawer open and pressing a button. At the first flash of light, Jess whirled, ready to start shooting, but there wasn't any need. It was just ranks of glows turning on in the high ceiling, casting greenish arcs of light down the walls. "I disarmed his traps," Wolfe said. "He never changed his security. I knew he wouldn't. He never knew that I'd heard him recite it."

"When did you hear this?" Dario asked. Such a carefully neutral tone.

"Six years ago. Before he broke faith with me and stripped me of my honors. Before the prison."

"Long time," Dario murmured, for Jess's ears. Louder, he said, "And you remembered it?"

"I practiced it," Wolfe said. "Carefully. Yes. It was accurate."

Wolfe sounded all too confident, in Jess's opinion. Worrying. "Scholar . . ."

That's when an alarm tone sounded: a high, thin gonging sound that began to accelerate. They all instinctively looked up toward the lights.

A green mist was descending, drifting with deceptive grace in lightly coiling curls. And Jess's attention was caught by the door to the office.

Because it was sliding closed.

"Out!" Jess shouted. At the same time, Wolfe cursed and began yanking open more drawers, gathering handfuls of papers and stuffing them in the pockets of his robe. "Dario! Keep that door open! Scholar, there has to be an off switch! Find it!"

"Get out," Wolfe said flatly. He was opening another drawer, moving fast and with great assurance. "Don't let the mist touch you. *Go, boy!*"

"No," Jess said. He gritted his teeth. "I'm responsible for your safety."

Wolfe glared at him for a flash of a second, then turned his attention back to the desk. Jess crouched down, increasing the distance the mist would have to travel. The Scholar continued to ransack the desk.

Dario had placed his velvet-coated back against the sliding door, and now he said, "Uh, my friends? I can't hold this long." It was pushing him forward with relentless strength. He braced one foot on the opposite wall and pushed back. The forward motion slowed, but it didn't stop. *"Get out of there!"*

"Use your sword!" Jess shouted back.

"Swords are flexible, idiot!"

"To jam the track!"

Dario tossed it to him without a word—and certainly not an acknowledgment—and Jess threw himself flat to shove the blade into the way lengthwise, jamming the forward progress of the door. It might not last, but it eased the strain on Dario, at least.

"Do you know the history of that sword?" Dario said.

"Do you want to live to have heirs to carry it, Your Highness?"

Jess rolled back to a crouch. Wolfe was still at the desk. The mist was drifting just a handsbreadth above his curling, graying hair. "Scholar! *Now!*"

"One moment!"

"You don't have it!"

"Just one more drawer."

He was *not* going to explain to Captain Nic Santi how he happened to get Santi's lover killed on his watch, especially not when it was purely Wolfe's stubbornness putting them in danger.

So Jess stopped arguing. He rose, grabbed Wolfe by the back of his robe, and shoved him toward the door. When Wolfe struggled, he kicked the back of the man's knees and pushed him down under Dario's outstretched bracing leg. "Crawl!" Jess shouted.

Then he turned and ran back to the desk, because if Wolfe had been willing to die for whatever was in that last drawer, it was probably important.

EPHEMERA

Text of a letter from the Archivist in Exile to the head of
the Burners within Alexandria. Delivered by hand in
written form only. Available in the Codex only as a copy
from later collection.

*Hail, friend. I regret not using your proper name, but as I do not know
it, it is impossible. I hope you forgive this breach of protocol, as my prior
correspondence was only with the former leader. Opposed as the Great
Library and the Burners are, we have occasionally had common cause
together. And now, we do again.*

*I write to you now, in our most desperate hour, with an offer that
only I can make to you: absolute victory. Victory for your cause. If you
will join your forces with mine to retake the city and expel or eradicate
these upstart rebels who seek to take control of the Great Library, against
all tradition and sense . . . then I will personally guarantee a policy
change that will allow for the collection and preservation of original
works by individuals, unmonitored by the Great Library or its High
Garda. I will repeal the ages-old prohibition. I will strike down the law
that imposes a penalty of death for the hoarding of such originals, and
the sale and trade of them. I will indemnify your Burners from any and
all prosecution for the remainder of their lives for any acts committed before or after against the laws of the Great Library, including the murder
of our Scholars and librarians. You say a life is worth more than a book.*

Now I ask you to prove it.

Save our lives. Help us take this city back.

*Kill the falsely elected Archivist. Kill Scholar Christopher Wolfe,
Khalila Seif, Dario Santiago, Jess Brightwell, Thomas Schreiber, Glain
Wathen, and High Garda Captain Santi. Kill them and show me proof.
Then I will discuss additional payment.*

CHAPTER TWO

JESS

Jess stayed low and attacked the last drawer with a strong pull. It didn't open. *Damn*. The mist pressed down on him, and there was a smell that preceded it, like bitter flowers. It burned the back of his throat, a tingle that only grew stronger when he swallowed. Not the immolating stench of Greek fire, though that was what he'd feared. No, this was something else.

Possibly worse. Much worse. He had no idea of the kinds of terrible plagues and weapons the Archivist had kept in his storehouses. Few would. But they would be lethal.

Jess pulled his sidearm and fired it into the drawer's lock, shattering it, and then shoved his finger into the ragged hole and pulled until it yielded with a sudden snap. By then he was on his knees, and he couldn't remember dropping. The taste in his throat and the smell confused him. What was he doing? Why had he forced it open?

Papers. Grab the papers.

He folded clumsy fingers around the thick handful and tried to rise. Couldn't. His eyes burned. His throat felt numb and seared. Breathing was an effort. Easier to stay here, easier to just . . . wait.

Someone was shouting his name. *You need to move,* he told himself, but his body felt like an unfamiliar doll. He couldn't remember how to move, but slowly, agonizingly, he folded over and pressed his face to the soft carpet. The air was clearer here, and he gasped it in little bursts, a landed and dying fish.

The voices were coming from the doorway. He crawled in that direction. The mist pressed relentlessly down on him, heavy, *so heavy* he felt it like a steel wall against his back that weighed him down, and it was too hard to keep moving.

He was choking on the mist. It filled his throat like cement.

I'm dying, he thought. He felt some panic, but it was muted and at a distance. He pulled himself another scant few inches forward. It wasn't enough.

And then hands were pulling him forward with a sudden jerk, and it seemed like he was flying through the air and landing in a limp sprawl, gasping, spitting, a foul foam coming from his mouth. *I'm a mad dog.* It almost made him laugh, but then his stomach rebelled and he curled in on himself and tried to breathe. Couldn't without his throat closing up. Someone pried his mouth open and poured in something that burned; he spit it out. They tried again. This time, it scorched down his abraded throat and all the way to his stomach. He thought it was liquor until the fourth drink, and then he suddenly realized it was just water. Only water. The clear air bathed his brain in oxygen again, and now he could think, if clumsily.

"You stupid fool!" That sounded like Dario, but the voice seemed oddly unsteady. When Jess rolled over on his back he saw Dario kneeling over him holding a pitcher of water, now almost empty. The young man's hand was shaking, and so was the glass vessel. Dario set it down without comment. "Do you know how close you came? Do you?"

Oh. The Archivist's office. He'd gone back for the papers. Did he still have them? He raised his hands. No. He didn't. He felt a vast chasm of despair, and a huge spasm of coughing racked through him, pumping rancid green foam from his mouth again. His head pounded. He ached in every muscle. He shivered all over in convulsive tremors.

He'd failed.

"Sorry," he whispered. "Papers. Lost."

"Not lost," Wolfe said. "You held on to them. Somehow."

Jess looked up once his muscles unlocked again. The Scholar was fanning the documents out on the desk that once belonged to Neksa, studying them with great intensity. He looked pale. Beads of sweat ran down his face, but there was no mistaking the intensity on his face. Or the relief. "You found it," he said, and glanced over at the two of them. "Thank you. Both of you."

"Just tell me it was worth what it nearly cost," Dario snapped. "Because you almost had a second dead Brightwell to explain!"

Wolfe went still, and his expression blanked. Jess remembered a second later—only a second this time, a delay and then a deadly, detonating flash of knowledge—that his brother was dead.

He barely heard Wolfe say, "I'm aware of that, Santiago."

"What if he'd died getting those and it had turned out to be the Archivist's grocery list? *Think*, Scholar. Your stubbornness is likely to get us killed if you don't!"

Dario is . . . on my side? Jess didn't know what to make of that. Then he was a bit ashamed of his surprise. But only a bit.

"We should go," Wolfe said, and gathered up the papers. "Schreiber will need these."

Jess coughed out another mouthful of foul, green-tinted foam. Couldn't seem to take a breath without producing more. It hurt. "What are they?" he managed to ask. "The papers?"

That got both of their attention. He wiped his mouth and sat up. That brought on more coughing, but less foam. His lungs felt stuffed with cotton, but at least he was able to breathe now.

"They're records of the harbor defenses," Wolfe said. "And the process for activating them. It's a secret held by the Archivists for thousands of years, and we need it desperately now." After a short pause, he said, "This is to your credit, Jess."

"Thanks." Jess held out a hand, and Dario shook his head.

"Stay down there," he said. "Until you can get up on your own. You almost drowned in your own juices, fool."

"Who dragged me out?" Jess asked. Paused for another spate of coughing. "You?"

Dario shook his head and nodded toward Wolfe, who was rolling the papers into a tight scroll that he put into an inner pocket of his robe. "I was holding the damned door," Dario said.

"Don't forget your sword," Jess said. Four whole words without coughing, though he felt the threatening flutter deep in his lungs.

That got him a glare. "That reminds me. You owe me for a new sword. Though where you'll get enough *geneih* to pay for it . . ."

Jess shook his head. Didn't try to reply. He saved his breath for the effort to come, and with grim determination he grabbed hold of Neksa's desk and pulled himself up to his knees. Then his feet. He clung to the support for a long few seconds and felt dizzy with relief that he was capable of staying upright on his own. Running was a distant dream, but if he could stand, he could walk.

And he had the feeling that they needed to be on the move, without delay. He'd come very, very close to not leaving the Archivist's office alive, and he thought there was a more than good chance that there were more dangers to come before they were out of this place. "We should be on our way," he said. *Six* words in a row. He suppressed the cough.

Wolfe had been watching him with concern, but in the next instant he was back to the sour, dour man who had once greeted his class at the Alexandria train station. A black crow in a black robe, distant and dismissive.

"Very well," he said. "Keep up, Brightwell. We need to find Nic. He should be close by."

F inding Niccolo Santi was an easy task. He was at the Serapeum, standing near the base while a crowd of runners took orders from him and left. His lieutenants—Jess's friend Glain among them—waited patiently for their own instructions. There was a sense of calm, even in the chaos of people jockeying for position. Part of that was Santi himself, standing solid in the center of the storm and addressing himself to each person in turn with complete focus. He caught sight of Wolfe, Jess, and Dario as they emerged from the side garden and hesitated for only an instant before listening with full attention to the veiled lieutenant standing before him. He gave her a response, handed her a Codex, and saluted her with a fist over his heart combined with a bow. She returned the gesture and was off at a run.

Santi called a pause and pushed through the crowd to get to Wolfe. A quick embrace and he stepped back to study each of them. One second for each of them, and he said, "Jess? You look unwell. What happened?"

"I'll get him to a Medica. Here," Wolfe said, and handed over the sheaf of papers. "I'll go through the rest of what I gathered for strategic use, but this is the key to the harbor defense. Fetch Schreiber; he'll be most useful in this. It's unlikely to function as intended immediately; it's been so long since it was even rumored to be used."

"My God, I never thought we'd find this," Santi said. "I'll keep Brightwell with me, if you don't mind. I'll have a Medica look him over." He gave Wolfe a long, searching look. "And you? You're pale."

"I'm fine," Wolfe said. "I only got a mild dose of the poison. Jess breathed it deep. If you could see to his safety, I would be . . . relieved." He paused and looked around. Something seemed to dawn on him. "Isn't this the job of the new High Garda commander?"

"It is. The old High Commander stepped down. Don't look at me that way. Someone needed to make order out of this mess. It's temporary."

"Command looks good on you," Dario observed. "Perhaps you should keep the job."

Santi gave him a quelling look. "Have you considered that not everything needs your commentary, Scholar?"

"Ouch," Dario said, amused. "Let me think about it. Wait, I have. I disagree." He was bright-eyed and smiling and chattering, but there was something fragile beneath it. Jess was too tired to wonder at it. He wanted to sit and close his eyes and forget that feeling of suffocation. Of surrender. "Perhaps Scholar Wolfe intends to put his hand up for the position of Archivist later today."

"Me? Hardly," Wolfe said. "I have rather a lot of enemies even on my own side."

Santi's grin came suddenly. "No one's forgotten that. But you also have one of the best minds in this city."

"Debatable. And you're hardly impartial. I'm not meant to lead, Nic. Don't be ridiculous." He turned to Jess. "I'll leave you in your commander's capable hands. Rest. You've done well. And, Nic? Try not to get knifed in the back. You realize we have enemies masquerading as allies, don't you?"

"I do. That's why I'm here, to show that we are efficient, effective, and in control. I have troops moving to protect every critical security point in the city, and more roving squads to keep order in residential streets, and a special elite squad paired with automata to watch all approaches to the walls; the Russians have set up camp at the northeastern gate, and there's no sign they intend to move on. I've got High Garda ships dispatched to the mouth of the harbor as a temporary blockade. Thomas is, I believe, finishing with his fitting out of the Lighthouse beam. I'll send for him and have him tackle this information you've brought. It's well beyond me." Santi paused again and looked straight at Wolfe. "Let's survive this day, love. And raise a glass at home."

"At home," Wolfe said. "Until then, keep yourself safe."

"And you."

This, Jess thought, was the love he wanted in his life: a love of equals. Loyal and kind. He wasn't sure he had that yet. But it was something to aspire to.

That sent his thoughts spinning in Morgan's direction, and he said, "Captain?" That drew Santi's gaze back. "The Obscurists could help you distribute information more effectively."

"Yes, Jess, we've already worked that out. The Scribe there is relaying every order to the records, and from there it is disbursed out to the officer in charge."

That was when Jess realized that the statue sitting cross-legged on a plinth nearby wasn't merely decorative. It was, in fact, an automaton, one with a metal tablet in one hand and a metal stylus in the other, and as it inscribed words on the tablet's blank surface, they vanished into— he presumed—the Archives, where the Codex would then retrieve and distribute them as needed. All the orders would be coded with Santi's personal seal . . . or, Jess supposed, the High Garda Commander's seal, which was a role Santi now filled. The Scribe must have been tuned to Santi's voice, because it seemed to be transcribing all his conversations . . . including this one.

"Oh," he said, and felt more than a little stupid. *Of course Santi would have thought of it. How much of that mist did you breathe in, idiot?* The last thing he wanted to do was seem impaired in front of the captain. "Apologies. Where do you want me, sir?"

"In a Medica's office. Immediately. You look like you're about to drop."

Jess saluted him with a fist over his heart. "I'll go now, sir."

"In a carriage," Santi said. "That mist you breathed was no joke."

Santi was already raising his hand, and a lieutenant—Glain Wathen, tall and assured and strong in her uniform—was running toward them. She stopped and waited, hands folded behind her back and her gaze steady on the captain. Disciplined, their friend, so disciplined she didn't even glance at Jess. "Wathen," Santi said. "Get a rig for Jess, and accompany him to see a Medica, then to the compound and fit him out with a proper uniform. Get him back here safe if they judge him able to serve. No detours."

"Yes, sir." Glain's gaze slid toward Jess, then back again. "Will Brightwell be rejoining our company, then?"

"That depends on the needs of the day. The situation is fluid, since for the first time in recorded history the Great Library has no elected leadership. We have foreign navies in our seas, foreign armies on our borders. And if we don't defend ourselves, we will be torn apart in the teeth of nations." Santi paused, as if considering something he did not completely like. "Brightwell. Once you're cleared and fitted out, find Red Ibrahim's daughter, Anit. We're going to need her."

"You want to work with smugglers and criminals?"

"I don't think we have much choice," he said. "Can you find her?"

"I can make her find me," Jess said. He imagined Anit's face, and conjuring her up brought his brother's specter. "Has someone told my father about Brendan?" It was his responsibility, but he didn't want it. Couldn't imagine writing that message.

"Scholar Wolfe sent a letter while you were resting," Santi said. "He felt responsible for both of you."

"He wasn't, but I'll have to thank him," Jess said. "It's better coming from him." *Because Da will blame me,* Jess thought. He knew his father. Brendan was the heir and favorite. Jess was the spare. *Of course he'll blame me.* Didn't matter. He hardly expected an outpouring of emotion from his father, either grief or anger. It would be a silent kind of rage hidden in looks, turned backs, pointed mentions of what *Brendan* would have done. Da sometimes flew into a true, towering fury, but most often it was a death of a thousand shallow cuts.

So he had that to look forward to, he supposed.

Glain had waited patiently, but now she stepped forward and said, "If you'll follow me?"

No choice, really. And he was grateful for the ride.

The Medica was shocked he was still alive. Until that moment, Jess hadn't really believed he'd cheated death, but from the look on the older person's face, he'd pulled off a miracle.

"Here," the Medica said, and fastened some sort of mask over his face; it had a small symbol on the side, some alchemical icon that Jess didn't recognize. But that meant it had been activated by an Obscurist. "Breathe as deeply as you can. We must cleanse what poison we can from your lungs." Jess struggled to breathe in whatever it was the mask emitted; the gas smelled faintly bitter, but it burned hot going down. He obliged by taking it in as much as he could before coughs racked him, forcing it out; with it came another explosion of foam, and the Medica swiped it from his mouth and into a jar, for later study, he supposed. "Keep at it," the man told him. "You'll need an hour of that before you feel able to continue, but you can't exert yourself."

Jess pulled down the mask to say, "You do know we're in the middle of revolution, don't you?"

"I don't care. That doesn't change your situation."

"And what is my situation?" Jess coughed, and it became almost uncontrollable; he curled in on himself, fighting to breathe, and the Medica gave him some injection. He felt the burn of it but was too desperate for air to flinch. Whatever it was, it worked. His throat and lungs relaxed, and he was able to breathe in and out again. Almost as easily as before. "Thanks."

"Don't thank me," the man said. He looked grave. "The shot will keep you going for a while, but it will wear off. The treatment mask will help to a certain extent, but the more you rely on it, the less effective it will become. Take it easy for the next few days. If you don't, the consequences will be fatal."

"You're joking," Jess said. The Medica said nothing. "You're not joking."

"You're lucky to be alive at all. I'll be honest: I have no guess as to whether or not you will recover. If you do, I have no idea of how impaired you might be in the long run. Nasty stuff you breathed in. Most would have died in minutes."

"Lucky me," Jess said. He felt numb inside. He'd hurt himself before, of course; he'd been injured so badly that he thought he might die. But there was a large difference between a shot or stab wound that could heal and the thought of not being able to *breathe*. That was a horror he'd never really imagined. *Like half drowning every minute.* He'd never been afraid of injuries.

He was afraid of this.

The Medica left him to it, and he dutifully breathed, coughed, breathed more. After half an hour breathing came easier and hurt less. After an hour, he felt almost himself. Almost. He took the portable mask the Medica thrust at him when it was time to go, and promised to use it and return for more treatments and a better analysis of his progress.

Glain had waited. Jess wasn't surprised by that, or by how impatient she was. The last thing she'd wanted, he imagined, was to be his sheepdog. She could have been doing important things, he supposed. Instead, she was wasting time looking after him.

He wanted to tell her. But that seemed worse than just brooding over it on his own. Glain didn't have much patience with vulnerabilities. "Sorry," he told her as they left the Medica's station and took another steam carriage on to the High Garda compound. "I know this is shit duty."

"Oh, it is," she agreed, and gave him a look he couldn't quite interpret. "What did you do to yourself, Brightwell?"

"It's Brightwell again? I thought we'd made progress, Glain."

"You're my subordinate now. So it's back to Brightwell. And that's Lieutenant Wathen, to you."

"Lieutenant!"

She shrugged. "Field appointment. I'm sure I'll go down in rank as soon as the crisis is over."

He doubted that. Glain was among the very few people he'd met who were born to be soldiers and who accepted the hardships and responsibilities with ease. "Congratulations."

She nodded. "Back to my question. What happened?"

He told her. She listened intently, asked him about the mist with the analytical interest of someone whose business is in weapons, and he answered as best he could. She considered the matter for a few moments in silence, then said, "I know poisonous gases were among the inventions suppressed in the Black Archives. Some attacked the nerves; some killed almost instantly. Some smothered. It sounds like you encountered that last type. You were lucky to survive."

"I was lucky Wolfe and Dario were there to save me," he said. "I'd given up. I couldn't have made it without them." When he said it, he realized it was true. He owed both of them his life, such as it was at the moment.

It made him feel weak, and he hated it.

He turned his head toward Glain and fixed her with a look. "You seem to know a lot about it. Was that in one of the books we saved from the Black Archives?"

"It was in the Black Archives," she said. "But I left it behind. I thought it was better left undiscovered by anyone else. It must have burned in the fire."

"Good," he said. "Maybe the Archivists were right: some knowledge is too dangerous to be spread."

"Heretic."

"You're the one who chose not to rescue it."

She sighed. "Yes. But let's keep that between us, shall we?"

Going back into the High Garda compound felt like falling back in time for Jess. It hadn't been so very long since he'd first entered these gates and become a soldier, but he'd been a different person then.

Grieving Thomas, then intent on rescuing him from the trap he was in. But never dreaming that his actions would start a building wave of chaos and resistance that would come to a head here in Alexandria and force the most powerful man in the world to run for his life.

Strange how things had gotten so wildly out of his control, when all he'd meant to do was help a friend.

This place still felt oddly like home, though he hadn't spent much time in it. Jess stared at the gleaming Spartan automaton as they passed it; the statue's head turned to track and identify them, then went back to never-ending guard duty.

They walked slowly, out of deference for Jess's lungs; he felt impatient with himself, but he could not afford to push. He needed to remember that and not feel that he was holding Glain back.

But he *was* holding her back. He could sense it in the tension in her body, like a tiger poised to run. He tried walking faster. It woke an ache in his lungs almost instantly, and he felt abused tissues start to swell.

He slowed down.

Glain sent him a look. "All right, then?"

He nodded and didn't try to explain.

The entire High Garda barracks was mostly deserted now, all the clean and gleaming halls echoing with their footsteps. For the first time, Jess wondered what had been done with his room. He pointed toward the door. "Is my stuff still there?" Not that he'd had much. Growing up as he had meant being ready to abandon everything when the law came to call.

"Sorry. Your room was reassigned to another soldier. Your possessions were boxed up and sent back to your father. We'll kit you out of general stores."

"I liked that room," he said. "Good light."

"Are you going to stay a soldier? After this?" she asked him. Perfectly reasonable question, and one he honestly didn't know how to answer. When he hesitated, she turned her head toward him. There was real gravity to her stare. She must have learned it from Santi. "If you have to think about your answer, it isn't for you. You realize that."

"Yeah," he said. "I do. But what else will I be, if not that?"

"What do you *want* to do?"

"I don't know. Something useful."

"Jess. Your life doesn't have to be just *useful*," Glain said. "It's all right to have goals for yourself. Things you want."

Jess started to fire back that he always followed his heart . . . but that wasn't really true. He'd grown up knowing there were expectations of him, and he'd followed those as best he could. Rebelled when he couldn't. But all his life, he'd been reacting to something: his father. His brother. Wolfe. The Great Library itself.

But who was he—really? He had skills, but he knew he lacked real purpose. Glain had a clear vision of who she intended to be. So did Thomas. Khalila. Even Dario, in his way.

I'm more like Morgan, he thought. *She's exerted every effort to avoid her destiny. And so have I.*

"You should look into being a counselor," he said.

"Fuck off, Brightwell."

They'd arrived at a plain double set of doors with old Egyptian hieroglyphs inset with gold above the door and a Greek translation beneath. *General stores.* Glain pushed the doors open, and they entered one of the most intimidatingly vast warehouses that Jess had ever seen: racks that stretched three stories up, everything perfectly aligned and orderly. Crates and boxes neatly labeled. Clothing in crisply folded stacks. Glain didn't pause; she headed straight for a shelf that held battle uniforms and checked through them until she found what she wanted. She pulled out a protective vest, underwear, jacket, trousers, socks, boots, and weapons belt and unlocked the weapons cabinet at the back of the room to draw out a High Garda rifle and sheathed knife. She passed it all to him and pointed to a bench at the back.

"How do you know my sizes?" he asked her.

"Brightwell, I'm your lieutenant now. I know *everything*."

He caught the slight gleam in her eye, and a quirk of a smile tugging the corners of her lips. He gave her a full grin, which was hardly protocol, and as he turned away she planted a boot sole in his rear to speed him on his way. She, at least, wasn't going to treat him as damaged goods.

He dressed quickly, feeling exposed and cold in the cavernous space. Glain was, of course, right on the sizes, even down to the boots, which fit like custom-made. He checked himself in the full-length mirror, and the reflection startled him for a second.

Brendan stared back. And then it was just him, pale and unwell, an ordinary soldier in a well-fitting uniform with the Great Library's sigil gleaming on the collars and cuffs.

He fastened the weapons belt and eased the sidearm he already had into the holster. Extra charges on the weapons belt. He counted them out of reflex; the full ten. Exactly as expected.

"Stop admiring yourself and get a move on," Glain said. "Unless you want me to leave you here."

He couldn't tell if she meant that or only wanted to motivate him. With Glain it was very difficult to tell. She'd grown into a tall and fiercely handsome young woman in the last few months; when he'd first met her she'd been awkward and uncomfortable in her body, but one thing had never wavered: her commitment to the High Garda. The perfect soldier, Glain was. And he knew he'd never match that.

But it was a fine thing to see, really.

He came back to her, and she gave him a critical once-over. "Stand up straight," Glain said. "When you wear that uniform, you don't slouch, Brightwell."

"Yes, Lieutenant," he said, and saluted her. It wasn't mocking. He tried to do it well, and it must have been acceptable because she gave him a nod in turn. But then she stopped and met his gaze.

"I suppose I should say this. I'm sorry about Brendan," she said. "I didn't like him, but I know you loved him. Don't take any guilt for his death. Fact is, I doubt he'd have taken any for you."

He wanted to defend Brendan, but she was right; his brother usually cut his losses as soon as things turned against him, and Brendan had been pragmatic in a way that Jess knew he could never manage. And so he said, "Thanks. That must have hurt."

"You have no idea," Glain replied. "Tell anyone I showed you the slightest sympathy and I'll pull your liver out through your throat."

"Love you back," he said, low enough that she *could* ignore it if she was so inclined. She paused as she walked away and didn't quite turn.

"Glad to have you still with us," she said, just as quietly. "Let's go."

Jess settled the rifle sling around his chest and followed his lieutenant.

A roving patrol stopped them on the way out of the High Garda compound and checked their Great Library wristbands. Security was necessarily tight; Jess grabbed the sergeant in charge of the detail and said, "Post a guard on the stores. Pay special attention to anyone taking extra uniforms." Glain had used her badge to unlock the weapons cabinets, but uniforms weren't considered as secure.

The sergeant frowned at him, then nodded. He understood well enough what Jess meant; they had enough problems without potential saboteurs wearing High Garda uniforms and gaining access to easy targets.

Like the Archives, Jess thought, and felt a chill. He caught up with Glain. "Lieutenant," he said. "The Archives—"

"Yes," Glain said. "I was told there's already a plan in motion to secure the Great Archives. It's an easy target for Burners, as well as other enemies. We have to watch for anything. Don't worry, Commander Santi has it under control."

"Does he?" he asked. "I've met the old Archivist. I guarantee you that he'd burn the Great Archives to the ground himself rather than lose his power. And we know he must have loyalists still working for him. Until we get him, nothing's safe."

"I'll send word."

"Promise?"

"Yes," she said, and he believed her, though clearly she didn't put much stock in the idea that anyone who'd lived their life in the Great Library could contemplate the unthinkable: destroying books. Even though she'd been there when the Black Archives had been obliterated, she still didn't comprehend that heresy.

He could. The Archivist was the kind of man who'd murder his family rather than be rejected by them. And he'd destroy the heart of the Great Library for spite if he thought he might lose.

"All right. Then we move on to the next thing. Finding Anit."

She sent him a skeptical, analytical look. "Are you certain you're up to it?"

"Asking questions? It isn't hard labor."

"You're pale," she said. "And frankly, you look like you might drop in a strong breeze."

He hurt; he couldn't deny it. And he wanted badly to declare himself too weak to continue. But today wasn't a day for coddling himself, and he shook his head. "I'll be all right," he said. "The Medica gave me a mask to use to treat my lungs. I'll rest when this is done. Anit's got eyes and ears everywhere in the city. If anyone can help us root out the Archivist and his allies, she can."

"If she will."

"She will."

"Why?" Glain asked. "I'd think chaos among her enemies would be to her benefit." Anit's trade was the stealing, copying, and smuggling of books. And, yes, this did offer her opportunities, rare ones, but she needed a calm, orderly city to do her business well.

"Anit's practical," he said, and shrugged. "She'll help us because she knows we're better than the old administration. And she can earn some grace and favors."

Glain looked revolted at the idea of owing favors to smugglers, but less than she would have when he'd first met her; she'd come to accept that for everything prohibited, there would be an endless stream of people willing to cater to those who still craved it. And controlling those people was far better than attempting, uselessly, to completely eradicate a supply without also destroying the demand. "Fine. Where do we start?"

They were now outside the gates of the High Garda compound, on the hill that overlooked the harbor and the city below. A good vantage point, this one, almost at the level of the three major landmarks: the Lighthouse, the Serapeum, the Iron Tower. From here, a good commander could see all the approaches and defenses and most of the city's closed gates. Santi would be making his way here once he'd finished with orders at the pyramid.

It was going to be a long damned walk back to the Serapeum, and he felt a wave of weakness looking at it.

Jess pointed toward the docks. That journey he could manage. He thought.

Glain frowned. "Why the docks? No one's working today. No ships coming in."

"That's exactly why. Her men will be idle and drinking, and that'll be where they feel most comfortable. And most protected. So they'll be easier to approach there." *Hopefully.* Because Anit's men were hers by inheritance . . . they'd been loyal to Red Ibrahim, but she'd killed her own father. He wasn't sure of the allegiances just now. And if word had gotten around that Anit had killed Red Ibrahim to protect a pair of errant Brightwell boys . . . that would be dangerous.

Jess started for the path that led down the hill. Glain grabbed him by the arm. "No," she said. "Transport is leaving right now. We'll hitch a ride."

"I can walk."

"Save it."

She was right: there was a High Garda troop transport rumbling through the gates, and it slowed for them as Glain flagged it down. He climbed in with a real, humbling sense of relief. The troops inside were all grim and quiet; he exchanged nods with many of them he recognized, but no one said anything. Glain signaled to the driver to drop them off at an intersection of roads that led variously to the docks, to the Lighthouse, and around the curve toward the heart of town; she didn't help Jess down, and he was grateful for the trust. He wasn't *that* bad off. Yet.

The Alexandrian docks—like most docks around the world—were not for the casual tourist. It was the one place in the city where Scholars rarely visited, and High Garda went only on business, so it was a natural haven for the less savory elements, particularly smugglers and thieves. The ships crowded together at anchor in the harbor were a vivid reminder of just how vast the reach of the Great Library really was . . . red-sailed trading ships from China, massive multideck vessels with dragon heads from the cold reaches of Scandinavia. Sleek Roman ships rubbed hulls with ships hailing from Turkey and Russia and Portugal, those of the island nations of the Caribbean with the continents of North and South America. As many seafaring, trading countries as existed did business here . . . or had. Now they were all trapped in the harbor, awaiting the outcome of the most dangerous game the Great Library had ever played. Bored. And frightened. It was a bad combination.

There was, of course, a heavy High Garda presence here to keep order, but by common practice they left the bars, taverns, and brothels alone.

Jess headed to the closest and seediest bar he could spot. It didn't bother with a name, just an aged wooden sign swinging on a pair of hooks with a painting of a single mug with froth bubbling up. Efficient. Every language spoke it, even if every person didn't partake. He remembered the place. He'd found Red Ibrahim's representatives here more than once.

Glain stopped him a few steps from the door with a hand on his arm. "Remember, you're not going in there a Brightwell. You're in a High Garda uniform. It matters." She meant both *watch your back* and *don't embarrass us*, and Jess nodded to her.

"Stay here," he told her. "I mean it. Bad enough I swan in there dressed this way. With you looking official and disapproving, it's a useless effort."

"Five minutes," she said.

"In five minutes, I'll either have what I want or they'll be dumping my body and you'll still accomplish nothing by barging in," Jess said. "I'll be back when I'm done. Trust me. I know these places."

He did, but neither was he exactly sure of his reception right now. Still, nothing for it but to do the thing.

No one appeared to notice or care when he pushed his way into the room. It was—predictably—packed and sweltering with the heat of the bodies in it; the smell of the place was an earthy mix of sweat, fermented alcohol, and the sharp spark of heavily flavored meat cooking somewhere in the back. There were tables, but all of them were full to groaning with men and women packed on benches, and the clink of glass and metal was like heavy rain on a roof. The bar at the front was manned by no fewer than five staff, all of whom seemed overheated and overworked; Jess avoided the crush there and moved among the tables. No one met his gaze. He heard muttering from a huddle of African sailors; he didn't speak their language but he imagined that they resented being held here in the harbor for trouble that they had no part in causing. No doubt most of these crews felt that.

"You've got a nerve."

That direct comment came from a Greek—a captain, by the look of him—who drained the last of what was surely a long line of tankards.

He had a long pale scar across his tanned face and a belly the size of a wine barrel. He put both hands on the table.

"Just one?" Jess responded. The Greek was obviously talking to him, so it seemed only polite. "I hope I have several."

"This isn't your place, boy."

"Nor yours, unless you run the place. If you do, you shouldn't drink up your profits." Jess was talking just to be talking, because he was watching the man's hands. He wasn't certain what was happening here, but some instinct had stirred inside him, some memory he couldn't pinpoint.

Then the man's left hand moved. Three fingers curled down, and his right forefinger tapped the table twice. It seemed an odd gesture, and then Jess remembered. It was an old, old thing, this smuggler's code, used by spies and ne'er-do-wells for centuries before his time; his father had taught it to him, and his men had occasionally used it in situations just like this, to convey messages when there were too many eyes and ears around for safety.

It meant *beware*.

"High Garda bastards aren't welcome here," the Greek said. "Nor any fools who'll sacrifice *our* lives for *their* books."

His fingers were still moving. This time they indicated a word Jess didn't immediately understand. He finally parsed it down to *rival*. Rival what? Gang? Red Ibrahim had locked this city down in his day, but his day was gone. Rivals would have come up quickly, ready to seize their piece of Red Ibrahim's crumbling empire. Anit would have trouble, no doubt about that.

Jess grabbed the drunken old man sitting across from the Greek and brought him to his feet, handed him an Alexandrian gold *geneih*, and sent him stumbling toward the bar. Jess slid into the chair, put his hands flat on the table, and said, "High Garda's always welcome anywhere in our own city. You're just a visitor. Know your place."

Many were watching this, but Jess hoped that they were watching the obvious: a drunken captain insulting a High Garda soldier, who was taking it personally.

"You start a fight, you'd best be able to finish it," the captain said. His fingers signed *talk outside*.

"Oh, I can finish it," Jess said. "Outside. Not room enough in here to raise a glass, much less swing a proper punch."

"True," the Greek said. "But if I go out, I promise you this: only I walk back in. You, someone carries off to a Medica, or the Necropolis."

"We'll see," Jess said. He stood up and headed for the back door, a dim gray shape in the far corner. He waited a few steps, then looked behind. The Greek was still sitting there. "You coming?"

"If you're so eager to die." The man slammed his tankard down and roared, "Someone buy me a drink while I thrash this Library slave!"

Cheers broke out, and he waddled and weaved his way toward the back door. Jess went ahead. He was alert for danger as he stepped outside, and good that he was; he caught a flash of movement and ducked, and that saved him as a club whistled over his head and smashed into the side of the damp stone wall. He shifted his stance and kicked out hard; his boot connected with a sagging midsection and sent his attacker reeling backward. Not enough to take the man down, but enough to give him an advantage. Jess felt pain as he sucked down a deep breath, but he had to ignore it. No time for it. He ran at the wall, used it for leverage to twist and land another kick, this one in the center of the man's chest. It hit hard enough to crack bone, and the man went down gasping; his club spun out of his hand and went bumping unevenly down the hill. But Jess sagged against the wall behind. His lungs were burning, and he tasted blood. *This was probably not what the Medica meant when he told me to rest.* He tried to sound amusing to himself, but it wasn't funny. He felt real terror that he'd just damaged himself. Again.

No time to worry about it. Jess drew his sidearm and pointed it at the man's head. "Pax," he said, and fought off the urge to cough. "I'm not your enemy. I'm a cousin." *Cousin*, in the smuggling trade, meant that affiliation with one of the great organizations. The Brightwells. The Helsinki coalition. Red Ibrahim. The Li Chang tong in China. Or the Tartikoffs in Russia. Cousins didn't fight one another, not unless territories were involved.

"You're wearing a High Garda uniform, *cousin!*" The man he'd kicked down groaned. He was a big, overfed specimen with the rich copper coloring of a native Alexandrian, and he moved his hand toward his belt. Jess stepped on the hand, drawing a sharp outcry. He put a little pressure into it.

"Easy," he said. This time, he had to pause to cough, and he tasted more blood. Swallowed hard and forced a smile. "Let's not make this personal."

"You broke my ribs!"

"You tried to break my skull, cousin, so we're even." Jess looked toward the back door as it opened with a creak, and the captain finally stepped out. He was certainly not nearly as drunk as he seemed, because he took in the scene with a glance, glared at the man on the ground, and shook his head.

"Damned idiot," the captain said. "Can you please not break his fingers? He's useful."

Jess removed his foot and holstered the gun. It seemed a good faith effort was needed, and thank Heron it was rewarded; the big man got slowly to his feet and backed off. The captain leaned against the bar's stone wall and crossed his arms. He kept watching Jess, and there was something in the assessment that made Jess nervous.

"You don't look well," he captain observed. "Not sick, are you?"

"Sick of dealing with idiots," Jess shot back. "I'm looking for the Red Lady."

The captain's bushy eyebrows arched up, then down. "Ah. The girl."

"Might want to be careful about saying that too loudly. She won't take it well."

"She's got other troubles," he said. "When her father dropped and she threw her support behind *librarians* . . . well, it didn't settle well with some who felt she was betraying our own. Chaos is a time ripe for profit. Your Red Lady doesn't seem to understand that."

"There's very little she doesn't understand," Jess said. "You'd do well to remember that. Give her a year and your support and there won't be a thief or smuggler on earth who'd cross her—or you, if you stand with her."

"Not even your own father? I know who you are, boy. And how ambitious that man is."

The last thing Jess wanted to discuss was Callum Brightwell. The glancing mention brought up a deep, heavy wave of pain, and suddenly his hands felt sticky with his brother's blood. Again. He swallowed and said, "My father respected Red Ibrahim's territory, and he'll respect the daughter's just as much. Or he'll have me to deal with."

"Hmmm," the captain said, and rubbed a thumb across his gray-stubbled chin. "You're sure you want to find Anit, then?"

"I'm sure."

"Then let's strike a deal. We have three ships ready to sail in the harbor that hold precious cargo. We need them on the way before this damned war breaks out. Arrange that and I'll tell you."

Jess unsnapped the Codex from his belt and wrote a message. He waited for a moment, watching until the handwritten answer appeared, and then he turned it toward the captain. "Neutral trading ships will be released within the next hour," he said. "Including yours. No one wants them in the middle of any conflict."

"That easy, is it?"

"Yes." Jess had been lucky on that, but he'd been betting that Santi would want to clear the docks; having this many ships at anchor was a real risk of accident, fire, riot, a thousand other things. Best to get the strangers out of the way before trouble arrived. "Where is she?"

"All right. She's at the Temple of Anubis," he said. "Lie and tell her

I was loyal, while you're about it. Our ships had better sail soon. And if we lose our cargo . . ."

"You'll find me and kill me in horrible ways, yes, I'm sure." Jess sighed. "If you lied to me, you can count on the same."

"I haven't. You'll find her. Keep your word today and I'll consider supporting the girl against her rivals."

Jess nodded. "Done. And thank you. The Brightwells owe you a favor."

"I'll claim it someday," the captain said. "Titan Berwick, at your service."

"Captain Berwick." Jess bowed slightly. "Try not to kill any High Garda while you're about your business. If you do, you lose that favor."

"Now you're just being damned unreasonable."

Jess didn't smile. "That wasn't a joke."

He turned and made his way down the hill. He had to stop halfway around the building, lean against the warm surface, and struggle to breathe. It wasn't enough. He was weak and shaking, and his chest burned from the inside out. Felt like it was packed with burning cotton. He fumbled in his pocket, found the mask, and breathed through it for a few moments. It eased the pain, and when he rounded the corner he was steadier and stronger, at least for now.

Glain was where he'd left her, though she looked militant and poised to do real violence. She relaxed when she saw him. "About time. Did you find anything except trouble?"

"Trouble can be useful," Jess said. "Temple of Anubis. Let's go."

EPHEMERA

**A letter from the Archivist in Exile, blocked from
distribution on the Codex, archived for future review**

*To all within the reach of the Great Library of Alexandria: I summon
you to our defense.*

*Never before has the Great Library faced such a treasonous rebellion
from within its own ranks. I say to you now, as the rightful Archivist
of this vast and ancient institution, that without your action and un-
questioning loyalty, <u>the Great Library will fall</u>. The light that has
burned for thousands of years will be extinguished because of the petty,
selfish greed of a few disaffected rebels. The world will descend into
chaos, barbarism, and petty fiefdoms that squabble over the torn flesh
of an ancient wonder. It is within your power to prevent this.*

*I call on every Serapeum, every captain in the field, every citizen: de-
fend us. Send aid to Alexandria. Crush the rebels and restore order before it is too late.*

*Once any nation-state lands its forces on Alexandria's shores, or
crosses its inviolable borders, the Great Library ceases to exist.*

Be warned.

War is not coming.

War is here.

CHAPTER THREE

KHALILA

Scholar Murasaki stood next to the formal throne of the Archivist and touched her fingers lightly to the old, old wood. "I thought it would be more . . . ornate," she said. "And also perhaps more comfortable."

Khalila suppressed an urge to smile. This place wasn't meant for it. The Receiving Hall of the Archivist of the Great Library, a vast marble space with lotus columns marching into the distance. There was only one automaton here: a two-story-tall Horus standing behind the chair. It was an impressive, beautiful thing of black and gold, with bright turquoise eyes. Horus held a Scribe's tablet in one hand and a stylus in the other . . . but the stylus had a knife-edge and was the size of a sword.

The throne sat on a raised golden platform, which rested on the backs of golden sphinxes. There were seven steps leading up to it, a number sacred to the ancient Egyptians. Four burning braziers, one at each corner: another sacred number. The place smelled of bracing, aromatic herbs.

Through some trick of engineering, the air in this chamber felt cool despite the damp heat outside.

And Khalila knew she was observing to avoid her own sense of disquiet. She felt small here, which was by design; this was a place meant to make a mere human feel utterly meaningless . . . save for the one who sat in that lofty chair.

Though Scholar Murasaki—an elderly Japanese woman—seemed more than capable of dwarfing the chair, and the room. Which was what made her perfect.

"I don't feel I am worthy of this honor," Murasaki said. "I did not expect it when I was summoned here."

"You won by acclamation through Conclave," Khalila said. "Exactly as every other Archivist has been chosen throughout the millennia. There's no reason for you to hesitate."

"And no great need for haste," Murasaki said. "The Great Library has not survived by doing things in a rush. Even with the wolves at our door, we should take our own counsel and our own time." She had a bearing that reflected the gravity of the moment, and the office. Murasaki had accepted the Archivist's formal robes—cloth of gold and worked in silver with the eye of Horus—but rejected the elaborate Pharaonic headdress that came with them. Instead, in her gray upswept hair, she wore a simple diadem with the Great Library's symbol. She looked . . . magnificent, in Khalila's admittedly biased opinion. A true Scholar risen to the highest seat of the oldest institution in the world.

I could never, Khalila thought. She dreamed about it, of course; in her secret, most ambitious moments she imagined herself in this same throne room, conducting the Great Library's affairs, everyone bowing to her wisdom. It felt absurd now. Humility was the basis of her faith, and she trusted Allah to raise her up, if indeed she ever deserved it. But not now, in these desperate moments. She was grateful that Scholar Murasaki was here to bear this burden.

Even as she thought it, Murasaki heaved a long sigh and settled onto the Archivist's throne. She put her hands in her lap and said, "I'm ready."

Khalila turned toward the doors. She felt alone in this vast hall, but she wasn't; besides Murasaki, there were close to a hundred others already here, but in this vast space that felt like such a fragile, lonely assembly. There were many High Garda soldiers stationed in the shadows. Khalila gestured, and two of them opened the huge doors at the rear of the space.

And the rest of the Great Library's Conclave poured in. Thousands of black-robed Scholars. Ten times as many librarians and staff. Most had never been inside this hall, and, like Khalila, seemed struck with the gravity of the moment. Their steps slowed as they moved inside, and the crowd naturally flowed in to fill the space allowed. But the Scholars and staff present within Alexandria at this moment—those who were not stationed elsewhere, or who had fled with the Archivist—still seemed too small a number.

We are missing so many, she thought, and felt a deep stab of pain. *So many.* But her father and her brother were in the forefront of the crowd, and she clasped them both in her arms and wanted to weep in sheer gratitude for their survival. Her father was not well; he looked frail, and he shook with the force of his coughing. But he was alive.

Khalila framed his tired face in her hands and said, "Have you seen the Medica yet?"

"I will, my child. Soon. I promise." His smile lit her world. "But I would not miss being here today, not even if I had to be carried."

"Don't listen to him. He walked under his own power," her brother said, and picked her up in a hug that took her breath away. His smile was as broad as it had ever been, as if he hadn't endured prison and near death. "Khalila. Who knew my little sister could be so brave?"

"You should," she told him, and his smile moderated a little. "I was never afraid of *you*, after all."

"I'm not particularly fearsome."

That was a lie. Saleh was one of the most capable men she knew, and she knew a fair number of them these days. She decided not to argue the point, and instead cut her gaze toward her father. "Should he even be here?"

"Try to keep him away," Saleh said. "I'll be sure he sees a Medica. But give him this, sister. He needs to see the Great Library redeemed before he takes to his bed. So do we all."

Now that the Scholars had entered and found their places, the next rank to enter the hall was formed of High Garda: sharply dressed companies of soldiers, solemn and proud. At their head strode Captain Niccolo Santi. He looked grave with the responsibility, and as his troops took their spots at the edges of the huge hall, he advanced down the long white space. The black-robed crowd parted for him, and he walked to the foot of the stairs and went to one knee, fist over his heart.

"Your service to the Great Library is beyond price," Scholar Murasaki said. "As the elected Archivist, I thank you for your loyalty and vision, and I welcome you to this sacred place. Will you take your oath?"

"I will," Santi said. "I swear to serve the Great Library with body, mind, and blood for as long as it pleases the Archivist. I swear to defend it against all enemies, within and without. I swear to uphold the laws and covenants of the Great Library, and when ordered to direct and lead the High Garda in battle. I swear to protect knowledge and its servants wherever they may be threatened."

"Then, rise, Niccolo Santi, Lord Commander of the High Garda," Murasaki said. "Captains of the High Garda: do you affirm this elevation?"

Each captain, Khalila realized, stood at attention beside each block of troops, and one by one, they took a step forward, put fists to their hearts, and said, "I do so affirm." There were dozens of commanders here. The High Garda had united behind Santi.

Of course, not all the High Garda are here, she reminded herself. *The deployed companies, the local Garda in the cities and towns, they're not represented. And the High Garda Elite all broke for the old Archivist, and no doubt took some of the regular High Garda with them. How many, I wonder.* Santi would know. She'd need to ask him for the figures and details on the captains who were missing. Murasaki would need that information as quickly as possible.

"Khalila?" Saleh's whisper. She glanced at him and saw him watching Santi as he completed his ceremony and began to rise to his feet. "He is Scholar Wolfe's lover?"

"Yes," she said. "Though more than that. Partner for years, though I don't believe they have formally married."

Saleh nodded without taking his gaze from Santi. "Wolfe spoke of him," he said. "Well . . . not to me. I suppose better to say he spoke *to* him when Wolfe was . . . unwell."

"Unwell?"

"Prison was not good for the man. You should be sure he's coping." Saleh frowned and cast a look through the crowd. "I'd expected to see him here. Is he not?"

"No," she said. "He's hunting the Archivist."

Saleh looked frankly shocked. "On his own?"

"He has help."

"I hope *he* knows that," Saleh murmured, and she almost laughed because it was a very legitimate concern. Wolfe was absolutely capable of believing he alone was tasked with bringing down the world's most dangerous fugitive. That brought with it a stab of worry, belatedly; he had—she'd heard, at least—Jess with him, but Jess could just as often bring out *more* recklessness in people. The two of them together might well be a bad combination, especially with the grief that was bound to be consuming Jess just now.

She sincerely hoped Santi was aware of all that.

Murasaki seemed at home on the throne as she began the process of accepting the oaths of her High Garda captains. After that, the Scholars and librarians would renew their oaths as a body, along with the soldiers, and then the ceremony would be done—for them. Murasaki would have to receive the waiting body of diplomats, and then the Alexandrian Merchant Council. She had a very, very long day ahead.

Which meant, as her personal assistant, Khalila did, too.

As the captains finished their oath taking, Khalila embraced her brother again, kissed him on both cheeks, and said, "I have to go to her. Watch after Father?"

"Of course," he said. "Don't I always?"

Having a brother like Saleh was a gift, she thought, and she had never prized it as much as she should have done. She gave him a smile and he returned it tenfold, and she withdrew back to stand in the shadows near Scholar Murasaki's throne, where she could hear any requests easily.

The parade of captains had been a tense time; if the old Archivist had any assassins in their midst, that had been the best moment for them to strike. Khalila noted the positions of High Garda snipers up in the galleries; Santi had taken no chances today, other than the ones imposed upon him. She imagined the man was raw nerves, with Wolfe out exposed to danger and the threat of violence hanging in the air here as well, but when she looked at Santi she saw nothing but calm. Some might think it complacency. Khalila knew he was at his most dangerous like this.

The next phase was the mass renewal of vows from the Scholars, the librarians, and the High Garda rank and file. Khalila spoke the words with them. *In the name of sacred knowledge, in the eyes of every god in every corner of this world, I swear my allegiance to the Great Library of Alexandria. I swear to protect the knowledge of this world against all enemies, within and without. I swear to nurture and share such knowledge with all who wish to learn. I swear to live, teach, preserve, study, fight, and die in this cause.* The words gave Khalila gooseflesh, woke a breathless light within her. The thunder of thousands of voices together was powerful indeed.

Scholar Murasaki stood, and the cloth-of-gold robe she wore caught fire in the light. She raised her arms. "Knowledge is all."

"Knowledge is all," came the response, and then—though it wasn't part of the ritual—someone let out a wild cheer of victory.

And then they were all cheering, and Khalila was weeping from the force of it. *This* was the Great Library. Not the old Archivist's plots and schemes and cold-blooded power struggles. Not the heresy of his Black Archives, where he'd locked up forbidden knowledge. Not the prisons where he interred his enemies.

The soul of the Great Library was *here*, in this room, and in that transcendent moment with tears warm on her cheeks, she knew she loved it more than she would ever love anything or anyone else save for Allah himself.

Dario arrived late, just as the oath ceremony ended. She saw him slip into the room; he was wearing his Scholar's robes, and he made his way to her side to whisper, "Forgive me, my love, I had duties. The envoys are waiting under flag of truce."

"You didn't take the oath," she said quietly. The tears were dry on her cheeks; she hadn't wiped them away. She wanted to feel them there, always.

"I couldn't," he said. "Someone had to greet these ambassadors."

She understood that, but she also knew that on a certain level perhaps Dario preferred it this way. He did believe in the Great Library, most certainly, but like most politically inclined people he always had an eye for the main chance, and just now that trended toward the navies floating outside their harbor. He was of royal Spanish blood, and that would never change. She loved him. But in this one thing, she wasn't altogether certain she trusted him.

"Well, Wolfe wasn't here, either," he said, a bit defensively, and she realized her expression must have betrayed her doubt. "And neither were Jess, Thomas, or Glain. Don't single me out for doing my duty!"

"I'm not," she said, which was a tiny portion of a lie that she would have to make amends for later, but for now she couldn't spend time on the explanation. "Thank you, Dario. I'll let the Archivist know they've arrived."

He nodded and stepped back, taking it for the dismissal it was. She missed him acutely, wanted to follow him and stand with him and hold his hand, but she stayed at her post and moved to whisper the news to Murasaki. The new Archivist nodded, a single inclination of her head, and said, "See them made welcome."

Khalila told Santi, who signaled to his guards at the door. *Inefficient,* she thought. There were reforms to be made to this space. Perhaps the Obscurists could create some messaging system that would allow this process to be more effective. Or even more automata to secure this room.

It occurred to her then that not a single Obscurist had been here to take the oath. That alarmed her, set her heart to pounding heavily, and she took deep breaths to right its rhythm. *They haven't broken faith,* she told herself. Obscurists traditionally did not leave the Iron Tower for such ceremonies; instead, the Archivist made a journey to them to accept their oaths. But Eskander, the new Obscurist Magnus, didn't seem one to stand on such tradition. Perhaps there had been urgent things to be done and the Obscurists couldn't spare the time.

And, just perhaps, Eskander currently held far too much power—almost as much as Murasaki—and didn't wish to concede it. It was a worry. One that Khalila would have to resolve for herself, before a real threat emerged.

But for now, the only real threat was coming into the room.

She watched as the great doors swung open, and the ambassadors entered under the silken flags of their kingdoms. They were dwarfed by the majesty of the hall, even a hundred strong, but they carried themselves with the gravity and confidence of kings. They knelt as a body to the Archivist, who acknowledged them with a gracious nod and signal to rise, and then one of the ambassadors stepped forward.

She knew him. It was Alvaro Santiago, the onetime Spanish ambassador to the Great Library. He'd sheltered them in his palace, given them safety and support. But now he didn't spare her—or his cousin Dario, for that matter—a single glance. His attention was solely devoted to the throne.

"Honored Archivist," he said, and he had an orator's soothing voice without a doubt. "I am Alvaro Luis Honoré Flores de Santiago, ambassador to the Great Library of Alexandria. On behalf of His Majesty Ramón Alfonse of the great and sovereign nation of Spain, I bring congratulations on your appointment to this important and necessary position. May God grant you wisdom and strength."

"I appreciate your congratulations and prayers, Ambassador Santiago," Murasaki said. "Though not the presence of your fleet beyond our harbor."

He pressed a hand to his heart and bowed slightly. Very slightly. "The Archivist understands that with the chaos, the Kingdom of Spain felt it necessary to ensure the safety of the Great Library from incursions by other, less scrupulous nations. Change is necessary, of course, but change is also a moment of weakness. We brought our nation's strength only to ensure a peaceful transition of power."

"How very interesting. Such a noble cause, of course," Murasaki said. "And yet, as you see, our Great Library functions as it always has done, without pause or—as you said—chaos. Your concern is appreciated, most certainly. But I assure you that we neither need nor have requested your intervention. My sincerest thanks to your king, but I must now demand that you—and all the nation-states allied with you who stand at your side today—withdraw your warships and go in peace. I would also ask that before you go, you swear to renew the treaties your nations swore with the Great Library."

That woke some whispers among the diplomats. One in the front of the crowd said, "Your Majesty—"

"I am not a queen," Murasaki said. "Nor an empress. I am merely the most senior administrator. Please address me as either Scholar Murasaki or Archivist."

"Apologies. Archivist, we aren't authorized to renew treaties that our monarchs and governments have rejected. The criminal behavior that the Great Library has lately engaged in fully justifies this, I believe."

"Criminal behavior," she repeated. "I trust you are referring to the actions of our prior Archivist, who did indeed exceed the power vested in him. He should have been checked by the Curia of Scholars, except that he handpicked his allies to support him in most cases. But the Great Library itself has committed no such crimes, nor has it violated the terms of any of the treaties that have been in effect with most of your countries since the time of Julius Caesar. We have removed the offending person from his post, and I pledge to correct all the wrongs that he has done. What more can be offered?"

"Perhaps it's time the Great Library realize that we can manage our own affairs." The man who spoke was English, Khalila thought. Possibly Welsh. "And we can build and maintain our own libraries to fit our own needs. There's common talk now of a machine that can print thousands of copies of a document in a day. If true, the Great Library has outlived its usefulness."

It was a bold, shocking statement. It was also true, in some sense. It was what Wolfe had known, and Khalila had come to realize: that for the Great Library to continue, it had to change. It had to *adapt*.

Murasaki smiled. *Smiled.* "If you believe the Great Library is not useful, then I assure you, Ambassador, you have not studied nearly enough history to understand the import of what you have just declared. We will change to the needs of the world, as ever. But what we offer is not simply books on shelves. It is *commonality* of scholarship and knowledge. Without it, the world could easily fall into darkness and chaos, without a shared culture or understanding. And that, we will not allow. If you wish to withdraw from the Great Library's alliance, then you may do so. You may live in your small, dark corner and light a candle and pretend it is the sun; in time, you might even believe it. I certainly cannot stop you. But I will mourn for those you drag into the darkness along with you."

Khalila caught her breath at the elegance of that cut. The ambassador's face reddened, but when he opened his mouth to reply, Alvaro Santiago jumped in.

"Archivist, we may discuss treaties tomorrow, if you wish to do so. But today, we are gravely concerned for the state of this city and its vulnerability to attack. None of us can afford for the Great Library to be destroyed. So we ask your permission to enter the harbor, disembark our forces, and assign them to guard your most vulnerable treasures. Clearly, the Archives must be protected at all costs."

"All costs?" Murasaki's eyebrows rose. "You would advocate invading our city and taking ownership of our Great Archives to *protect* them? No, Ambassador Santiago. I am afraid that will not happen. *We* will protect the Great Archives, as we have for three thousand years. And no nation's army will set its foot on the streets of Alexandria while I draw breath."

If the ambassador was thrown at all, he certainly didn't show it. "I certainly did not mean to imply invasion. We only offer our help to enhance your security."

"An Archivist who stays in power with the help of foreign armies is not an Archivist," Murasaki said. "So I once again must decline your offer. Send your fleets home, and I will welcome you back to your establishments here within Alexandria, and we may resume normal diplomatic discussions. Refuse, and I will see your embassies permanently closed and your staffs exiled to their home countries. I trust I have made myself clear, Ambassadors."

For once, Santiago didn't seem to have an answer at the ready. A tall, regal woman beside him stepped forward and said, "Honored Archivist, I am Ceinwen Parry, ambassador from Wales. My king has directed that his troops assist in securing the Great Archives against any possible damage. We will never withdraw without seeing this done."

"Lord Commander," Murasaki said, and Santi stepped up to the foot of the steps, facing the assembled diplomats. "Instruct our guests what they may expect, should they attempt to enter this city."

"Yes, Archivist. Should your ships attempt to sail into the harbor, we are prepared to activate Heron's Guardian to defend the entrance. Should you somehow overcome this barrier that *no one* has ever defeated, be aware that we now possess a weapon which can set wooden ships alight at a distance—or melt metal to scrap. Should you evade both of these defenses, you will be met with the full force of the High Garda and the automata that defend this city."

Ambassador Parry didn't blink. "You should be careful of your threats, Archivist."

"Those are not threats," Murasaki said. "They are advisories. It is our duty to defend this city from invading forces, however well meant their stated intentions. We do not require your rescue. And we will not accept it. You have my answer, Ambassadors. You may take your places as honored diplomats, or you may go back to your ships and leave. But there is no third option that does not bring disaster to you."

"Archivist," Santiago said. "You badly mistake our intentions. We are here merely to assist in your struggle—"

"Look around you, Ambassador," Murasaki said. There was an edge to her voice now, and Khalila shivered at the sound of it. "We are not struggling. We have won. You may now retire to a room we will provide and discuss your options. When you are prepared to present a unified answer, I will listen."

It was a clear, cold dismissal, and the ambassadors all exchanged looks. All deferred to Santiago, who gave a cool, studied bow to the

Archivist and said, "We will discuss. My thanks, Archivist, for your time and consideration."

She nodded. "You will be provided with food and drink," she said, and Khalila immediately stepped forward. She felt rather than saw the Archivist's glance. "Scholar Seif will guide you to your temporary accommodations."

Khalila was trembling inside, but she kept her head high and face neutral as she led the party of diplomats and their guards out of the hall; she saw Dario watching, but he didn't attempt to join her. She was thankful for that, in a way, though she would have liked his company. As long as Spain had a stake in this, his loyalties were mixed.

The party passed through the massive doors and into the outer hall; she led them up an interior stairwell to a large, airy room with an open side facing the ocean to catch the cooling breezes. Light screens blew in the breeze and prevented the invasion of flies so typical of this time of year. There was a long conference table of polished stone with a dozen chairs of Florentine design, and couches and chairs nearer the windows for the rest of the ambassadorial party. Seating enough—she saw that at a glance. What they lacked was refreshment.

"Ambassadors, I will see you are provided with food and drink," she said. "You'll be assigned staff should you have any special requests. Is there anything else I may do for you?"

"Scholar Seif, may I offer my gratitude?" Alvaro Santiago said. "I am pleased to see you well, Khalila. Are your friends all safe as well?"

"All safe," she said, and smiled. *Be on guard. He's a clever one.* "Our sincerest thanks for your assistance to our ragged party of Scholars, Ambassador."

"Of course. It seems my assistance had a rather large impact. I am glad to see you well. And Brightwell . . . ?"

"He's fine," Khalila replied. *I hope.* "Unfortunately, his brother was lost in the struggle."

"All wars have losses," Santiago said, and she felt he meant more by that than a comment on Brendan's death. "And all wars are destructive. You should remind your new Archivist of that."

"I am quite sure she's aware of it, sir." Khalila nodded deferentially and left to order the promised refreshments from the busy Serapeum staff. Santi, she noted, had already dispatched soldiers to guard the room's sole exit. She approved.

The pyramid's middle level contained the staff services: cleaning and catering. Khalila headed there and found the area surprisingly understaffed; she sought out the beleaguered woman wearing the silver collar of a career servant of the Great Library and said, "Excuse me, but where are the workers?"

"They're worried," the woman said. She was a short, round woman with South Asian features, and a surprising number of scars on her hands. A chef, most likely. "Not sure everything is settled yet, and they don't want to be caught in the middle of things. I can hardly blame them, to be honest. There's panic in the city. They have families to look after. As do I, but my first duty is still here."

Khalila started to fire back a hot reply, but then took a beat to consider. There was no point in being angry; the woman's point was well made. Great Library servants were not all careerists; many signed on for limited contracts of a year, five years, ten. They had much to lose and little to gain in a conflict, and they weren't Scholars with a stake in the outcome . . . but they still had priceless value. It took vast numbers of people just like this woman, and the ones afraid to appear today, to make the whole city run. She needed to keep that in mind.

"On behalf of the Archivist, I thank you for your faithful service," she said. "May I ask your name?"

"Wadida Suhaila, Scholar." Some of the weariness disappeared from her face. She straightened her shoulders. "I appreciate the recognition, Scholar."

"Khalila Seif," Khalila said, and gave her a small, formal bow. "I know you are overworked, but might I ask you to provide what refreshments are available to the Seventh Great Room? We have a grouping of ambassadors there, debating their next steps."

"Of course. I will arrange it immediately." Wadida took a Codex from her belt and quickly made a note. "The kitchens will have it prepared, and I'll find servers to bring it up. Is there anything else?"

"Some tea for the Archivist, when you have time," she said. "In the Receiving Hall."

"Of course." Another note, and Wadida snapped the Codex closed and replaced it in its holder. She hesitated for a second, then met Khalila's gaze. "Scholar? If I may . . . Will we be all right?"

It was a simple question, but still hard to answer. Khalila settled for, "The Great Library survives. Always."

She took her leave, and hoped she had not told the lie of her life.

EPHEMERA

Text of a letter from Ambassador Marta Kuznetsov to the Russian emperor Vladimir Nikolaev III. Archived in the Codex.

The newly elected Archivist, Scholar Murasaki, is not as skilled in diplomacy as was her predecessor, but she is most straightforward, which is a useful trait in unsettled times. If she survives this strife, she will guide with a steady hand, and perhaps avoid some of the abuses that lie at the feet of the former occupant of the office. She has demanded a full retreat of the ships at sea. I am certain you expected nothing else.

I do not recommend we comply. This is clearly an opportunity for Russia to advance upon the world stage as a partner with other nations. Should the worst—or best—come to pass, we will split Alexandria in parts, and of course we should seek to control the Great Archives and the books within it, though the Spanish will almost certainly defend that to the death. Peace is clearly not possible without some test of the new Archivist's mettle and resolve; if she shows weakness or indecision, if we see that this city remains divided in its loyalties . . . then we have no other choice but to act in the interest of our crown and our people.

I am aware that the Archivist in Exile has placed a bounty upon the heads of many of those who engineered his downfall. This may be useful to us, whether we wish such a thing to succeed or to fail. I recommend that we say and do nothing, and see what strengths this New Alexandria possesses. And what weaknesses.

I remain, as always, your devoted servant, and await your instruction.

CHAPTER FOUR

JESS

The ancient sculptor who'd crafted the statue of Anubis in the temple—not an automaton, a work of carved stone, painted and gilded—had done an astonishing job of it. Jess gazed up at the god, whose head tilted down to consider the worshippers below. It stood on a golden plinth, one foot ahead of the other as if frozen in a moment of action. At each corner of the plinth sat a brazier producing pure blue flames that echoed the rich enameled ornaments of the god's clothing and headdress. The space wasn't vast in terms of floor, but it vaulted far, far up, and the god's upper body was cloaked in brooding shadow. The strength and power of this place wasn't mitigated by the small figure in priestess robes sweeping dust from the corners. Apart from the single priestess, the temple seemed deserted.

Jess knew better.

"Wait here," he told Glain. She stood watchful guard as Jess moved toward the priestess, one hand on her sidearm. No doubt she, like Jess, had calculated the depth of every shadow and the potential for every avenue of attack and escape. And that was fine with him, so long as she stayed where she was.

The priestess wasn't Anit; it was a plain young woman who watched him nervously as he approached. Jess stopped a respectful distance away and said, "Hello, Priestess. Are you in charge of the temple today?"

"I am," she said. It was a good attempt at authority, though she was at least two years younger than he was. "How may I help you, soldier?" She looked past him at Glain. "Did . . . did you come for devotions?"

"To make an offering of faith. A gift for the temple's maintenance, in memory of my brother."

She almost staggered, she was so reassured. "A recent passing?"

"Yesterday," he said. "In the Colosseum."

"Oh." She bowed her head. "Anubis will guide him on his way. Was he faithful to the gods?"

"Not to any god in particular," Jess said. "But he respected Anubis the most, I suppose." He had no idea if that was true, but he knew Brendan would approve even if it was a lie. "A thousand *geneih* in return for prayers for his safe journey into the afterlife. Where shall I make the deposit?"

"The al-Adena Bank," she said. "Or you may bring it here and ask for the treasurer. He is not in today, but I am sure . . ." She trailed off. Jess allowed himself a small, bitter smile.

"I am sure tomorrow might bring those less hardy back to the temple," he finished for her. "It's a real sign of your faith that you're here doing the work."

"I believe the Great Library will continue, sir," she said. "And Anubis will note my faithful service."

"I'm sure he will," he agreed. "But I confess, I also seek another power here. A quieter one."

The priestess raised her head slowly and gave him a long look. "Who are you?"

"Jess Brightwell."

"Brightwell." The young woman had suddenly taken on a far different stance. She knew the name. "Welcome, cousin."

"You work for her."

"I work for my god," she said. "But I am loyal to my friend, too. And careful of her safety, so you'll be wise to hand your weapons to your colleague."

Jess didn't intend to fight, and he wasn't in any real shape to in any case. So he drew his sidearm and kicked it to Glain, who picked it up. "Good enough?" he asked the priestess.

She nodded. "She mourns her father," the priestess said. "She's asked not to be disturbed."

"As much as I wish to respect that, I need to talk with her. Can you arrange it?"

The priestess started to answer, but a voice from behind the statue of Anubis, deep in the shadows, said, "She can't. But you can join me in our shared mourning."

Anit stepped forward. The shadows, he realized, hid more than just her; he saw the gleam of three more sets of eyes behind her. She'd dressed in a red pleated dress, as traditional as the priestess herself, and with kohl around her eyes and henna mourning inscriptions inked on both her arms, she looked like she'd stepped straight out of the time of the Pharaohs. She seemed older, and it wasn't just the makeup and clothing. She seemed to have aged years. Her copper skin looked richer, her hair a ripple of black silk left loose around her shoulders.

She was beautiful. It struck him hard, and he wished he hadn't noticed.

"Anit," he said. It was a ridiculous thing to say; she knew her name, and he didn't need to sound so damned surprised. But he'd expected to find an unnaturally clever child, and instead, here stood a dangerous young woman.

She raised one eyebrow. "Were you expecting someone else? Don't tell me you're here on account of your brother. I mourn him, too, but Brendan would laugh to think either of us was overly concerned for the state of his afterlife. He told me once that he'd always thought of you as his *shuyet*, his shadow-self. And I know you thought the same of him. But now his immortal soul stands before Osiris and the forty-two judges of his heart, and there we cannot help him."

"I couldn't help him in the arena, either," he said quietly. "Some shadow-self I am."

"Jess . . ." She shook her head. "Why did you come here?"

"You know why."

"The Archivist and his lackey, the one who killed Brendan. Yes. I expected you to be looking. But one glance tells me you're in no shape to exact any kind of revenge," she said. "And do you really think I know where the bastard is, and haven't taken action?"

"I'm fine, and if you don't know, you can find out."

Anit's eyes went cool and distant, like stones beneath running water. Far older than her years. "The old man is good at hiding," she said. "And his Elites stand with him. No good comes of putting your hand down a snake's hiding hole."

"No good comes of leaving a poisonous serpent where it can strike, either," Jess pointed out. He leaned against the dark stone wall and felt the chill of it through the thick cloth of his uniform. Suppressed a shiver. "And you know he will. Hard, and often. We can't let him take anything else from us. Not one more thing."

"Oh, I don't intend to," Anit said. "If I knew where he was, he'd already be begging Anubis to lead him to judgment. But I'm happy to let the Great Library take care of its own problems." She cast a glance toward Glain. "Fierce as she is, she's hardly an army, though."

"Help me bring him to justice," he said. "Common cause for killing a Brightwell."

She laughed. It sounded low and raw in her throat. "*Justice.* There is no justice for the likes of him that doesn't come slowly, with screams. And I know you, Jess. You're squeamish about such things."

"I'm practical. We can bring the bastard before the Conclave and let them decide his fate. He's a traitor to the Great Library. He'll get death, but it ought to be done in public, not in private. Justice isn't done in the dark."

"Come off your high ground, Jess. The shadows are where we live."

He didn't want that to be true, but somehow, he felt she'd just spoken an important truth to him. He *wanted* to be better than that. He *wanted* to be a Scholar, to live in the light. But he, like Anit, had been born in shadow, and she was right: he functioned better there.

But that didn't mean he had to like it.

"I won't assassinate him," he said. "But I will *find* him. And I'll bring him back alive, in chains."

She smiled. Not a nice expression, but a profoundly calm one. "Not alone you won't."

"Then *help me*," he said. "Unless you're pausing for your mourning period."

"Henna washes off," she said. "And I will be mourning what I did for the rest of my life, my cousin of shadows. But if we go together, you must understand this: your notion of bringing him to justice is quaint, Jess, but useless. He won't come quietly. He won't come at all, given any choice. He'll force his own death rather than endure trial and disgrace." Anit looked eerie just now, in the shadow of Anubis; she seemed almost supernatural in her calm. "This city will settle only when he's dead. Not before. Put him in chains, you risk riots and revolts, and that gives those ships and armies around us the opening to claim us as their own. Politics is a blood sport. The old man knew that when he started this. He's perfectly willing to destroy the Great Library and Alexandria without flinching."

Jess wanted to say what he knew Khalila would have said, something about mercy being greater than anger, something about rising above . . . but he knew this feeling too well. That growling, crimson rage that stopped him from reaching that high ground again. Because Anit was right. Taking the Archivist alive risked too much, whatever Wolfe intended.

"Fine," he said. It felt worryingly good to say it. "Then let's hunt him down. Together."

Anit said, "Only if you swear on Anubis that you will kill the old man if you can."

Jess walked over to the statue and laid his hand on the god's outstretched foot. "Before Anubis's eyes, and the Christian God, I swear to kill the former Archivist of the Great Library, or watch him die. Send me straight to hell if I lie."

"An interesting appeal to multiple faiths," Glain commented, "but since you don't practice either faith with any regularity, I can't see it matters."

"It matters," Anit said. "Devout or not, no one wants to break such a vow made in the presence of a god." She turned to Glain. "And you?"

Glain snorted. "I don't need an oath to want to kill the old bastard. It's my sworn duty. If you're done with the theatrics, can we please get on with it?"

He looked up at Anubis once more. There was a stillness here, as if the god stared unblinking into his soul. *Is this who you are? A killer?* That was his brother's voice in his head, and for once, it wasn't mocking. It sounded concerned.

Jess thought of his heart on the scales of Ma'at, a feather balancing it as the gods watched and judged.

I do what I have to do, he thought.

It wasn't a good answer, but it would have to do.

Anit led them to Red Ibrahim's house—not the same residence where Jess had originally met her, but another, more modest establishment in a quieter, more provincial part of Alexandria. An unassuming structure, if one didn't note the sturdy locks and the guards posted at every approach. On a normal day, they'd have blended with the common street traffic; today, they stood out like the uneasy sentries they were. In this quarter, as in so many others, families stayed indoors, awaiting whatever would happen next. Shops were closed, restaurants shuttered. None of the familiar scents of Alexandria, beyond the heavy salt of the sea; no baking bread, no spices, no tang of coffee. It felt like a terrified, breathless town today.

Jess struggled to keep up. Glain could tell, though Anit seemed oblivious; Glain deliberately held the pace back, and Jess felt both frustrated and grateful. *Just a little farther,* he told himself. *Then you can rest your damned lungs.*

The double doors of the house opened as they approached, and Anit quickened her stride. Her guards all seemed alert and relaxed, and her pleated dress, bloody crimson, floated in the fitful breeze.

One of the guards stationed near the building didn't look right, and Jess's gaze caught and snagged on him. A shorter man wearing a cap and old clothes, but he had the bearing of a soldier. The cap wasn't his own; it seemed too small, and the haircut beneath it seemed military.

Soldier recognized soldier. High Garda out of uniform, *today*? That wasn't good.

"Anit!" Jess shouted, and pointed at the man, who was positioned in a shallow, shaded corner. The soldier's hand lunged into his sagging coat pocket, and he came out with a glass globe filled with green liquid. *Greek fire.* He was looking at Jess and assessing the danger, and Jess saw the calculation come to an end. The man's focus shifted behind him, and he raised his arm, ready to throw.

There was no real defense against Greek fire. Only one way to stop it: keep him from throwing it at all.

Glain ran for the man, and as she did, she tossed Jess's sidearm back to him without looking. He grabbed it out of the air, aimed, and fired. Three shots, slicing a line diagonally across the target. The first missed. The second hit the man's elbow, an explosion of blood and bone. The third entered his stomach just left of his liver.

The elbow wound was the kill shot, because the man fumbled the glass globe, and it dropped at his feet and exploded, splashing Greek fire upward to cover his feet and legs. For one flash the man just stared in horror, and then the Greek fire exploded into flickering, ghostly flames that clung and grew like eerie green vines as they climbed his body in a rush.

Glain checked her run and veered away as the man flailed, burning. The would-be assassin screamed once and then stopped, though he continued to stumble forward, a human torch as the fire spread with unholy speed. Jess gagged on the bitter smell of the chemicals, then the sweetish reek of cooking flesh. The man's mouth still gaped open, but his throat must have been cooked, too ruined to form sound.

Glain looked back at Jess, and he read the order on her face. He took careful aim this time. The shot was fatal, directly through the man's brain, and he was dead before his burning body hit the cobbles. The reaction hit Jess in the next second, shakes and nausea and horror. He tamped it down quickly. *It wouldn't have been mercy to let him burn to death*. He knew that. It didn't absolve him.

The stench of the Greek fire and the burning body set off a round of coughing that tore at his already-raw throat and aching lungs. He tasted blood, again, and swallowed it down. He wanted badly to resort to that restorative mask, but not now. Not here. His breath came in shallow, liquid gasps.

Anit's guards were surrounding her and pushing her into the house now, and Glain rejoined Jess and shoved him toward the house as well. She had her weapon out, too. "Good job," she said. "Go on. It's not safe out—"

He didn't immediately hear the shot that hit her, but he saw bright blood spray the air from just below her ribs. A bullet had gone completely through Glain's back and out her front, and for a moment he thought it had hit him, too, but he felt no pain. Just shock. Everything seemed to slow down.

"Glain?" He heard himself gasp it. She was still standing, swaying.

"I'm all right," she said, and then she coughed, and a shocking explosion of blood came from her mouth. "Oh. I'm not?"

Then her eyes rolled back and she toppled forward into his arms. They were still ten feet from the door, and he found the strength—somehow, from somewhere—to drag her with him to safety, though a fuzzy darkness gathered in front of his eyes, and his body screamed for oxygen. He glimpsed the fresh, splintered mark on the doorway where the bullet that had felled her came to rest, but only as a flash, a point of information like the wide crimson swath Glain's body left in its wake. His boot slipped in her blood. He felt rather than heard the impact of another bullet cracking the stone next to his head, and then he was inside, easing her to the floor, and one of Anit's men was slamming the door shut and turning locks.

"Blessed Isis! Is she dead?" Anit asked. She crouched beside him. Jess checked the pulse at Glain's neck and found a rhythm.

"Not yet." His voice sounded oddly normal. As if the answer didn't really matter to him. Maybe it didn't. Maybe it couldn't. He felt numb at the moment, light and weightless.

"Jacket," Anit commanded, and he stripped it off and handed it over. She pressed the cloth firmly against Glain's wound in front and rolled her on her side. Blood was pumping from the hole in her back, too. "Fadil! Your shirt!"

The guard nearest to them stripped off his black shirt and handed it over without a word. Anit wadded it up and pushed it into the wound. She grabbed Jess's hand and put it against the cloth. "Hold that tight. Fadil, get our doctor. *Go.*"

The shirtless guard ran.

"Doctor," Jess repeated. Doctors were little better than hedge witches and herbalists, for the most part. "She needs a trained Medica!"

Anit said, "My physician *was* a Medica before we paid him handsomely to leave your service. Don't worry about Glain." She glanced at

Jess. Forced a smile. "You're lucky my house is made for events such as this. It's a fortress, my father's favorite bolt-hole, and fully staffed and stocked. Your friend picked the right spot to find herself wounded."

Jess knew he should feel more than he did at the moment; Glain was a friend, a *good* friend, but all within was silence. He'd shut himself down, the better to do the work that needed doing. He still wasn't healed from losing Brendan; he hadn't even faced it, really. And now Glain. *No.* He couldn't afford to feel it.

"Out of the way," a thin, reedy voice said, and a person in a dark silk robe effortlessly slid into the space Jess had occupied as he got to his feet. "I am Burnham, the physician. And who is this?" The physician, Jess realized, was speaking to Glain and ignoring all the rest of them entirely. Jess's first impression was the healer was male, and then the light shifted and he thought female, but it was clearly unimportant to the healer at all what others might interpret. *Glain's found a kindred spirit,* he thought.

"This is Glain Wathen," Jess said.

Shockingly, Glain started talking. When she'd come around, he wasn't sure; he couldn't see her face. Her voice came slow and almost dreamy. "Lieutenant of the High Garda. Captain Santi's . . . I mean . . . I don't know who my captain will be now. Jess?" Her voice suddenly sharpened on his name. "They won't make Zara captain, will they?"

"No," he said. "Not her." It was troubling that Glain even said it; Zara had betrayed them, left them, sided with the Archivist. Had killed his brother. She wasn't thinking straight. "Maybe Botha."

"That would be good," Glain said. Her voice drifted off, and she closed her eyes. "Botha."

"Soldier. *Soldier!*" No response. Burnham gave a frustrated, wordless growl, then said, "Mistress Anit, I'll need immediate assistance to move her to the surgery. Must close these wounds and repair the damage the bullet's done. And she'll need blood. A lot of it."

Anit snapped her fingers, and a guard stepped forward and scooped Glain up in his arms. He grimaced a bit—she was no lightweight.

Burnham nodded and walked quickly toward a hallway to the left. Anit stayed, watching Jess as he started to step back.

He lost his balance and fell back, gasping in surprise. The gasp turned into a cough that racked him almost limp. His vision grayed out. When it cleared again, he was sitting against the wall, and Anit's cool hand was on his forehead. He was breathing in shallow gasps. Her expression was worried, but she made an effort to clear it when she realized he was taking that in. "Well," she said. "I think you're another candidate for my doctor. What happened to you?"

"Gas," he said. He didn't have the will to lie about it. "Traps in the Archivist's office."

"Is it bad?"

"Bad enough," he said.

"Do you need anything?"

"Medicine." He fumbled at his pockets and pulled out the mask the Medica had given him. He fitted it over his mouth and nose and breathed deep to drag the treatment to the most damaged parts of his lungs. It burned, but he was getting used to that, at least. After a few moments, calm set in, and it didn't hurt as much. But he was no longer deluded enough to think it was healing him. Only time would do that, and rest.

Neither of which he had, or was likely to get.

Anit hadn't left. She sat on her knees, hands on her lap, watching. The household was in controlled chaos around them, and he lowered his mask to say, "Just leave me. You have things to do."

"No," she said. "Not yet. My people know what they're about. I have little to add. Put that back and breathe."

He obeyed. He didn't know why he trusted Anit, but he did. Likely that was stupid and reckless, but any kind of peace right now was better than none.

What was happening to Glain felt quite a great distance from him at the moment, and he wondered if he was in shock. No, he couldn't be. He was a soldier. He'd seen friends hurt and dead before. This was no different. Wasn't it?

"Jess?" Anit was saying his name. He realized he'd missed something. He wrenched his gaze away from the closed doorway and looked at her. "Do you think you can get up now?" she asked.

"Yes." He put the mask away and stood up. "I should get after the sniper."

"Don't be stupid. Come with me. Please."

He followed because he couldn't think of a better thing to do, in the end. Anit led him through the center portal of the entry hall; none of her guards followed. Beyond the door opened up a large, spacious indoor garden with a fountain spilling drops into a large pool. It held Japanese koi. He paused to stare at the lazily swimming fish. The garden smelled of herbs, with a quiet, earthy scent of the garden soil beneath. Lounge chairs were positioned in comfortable spots. On one lay an abandoned original book. He walked over to turn the volume faceup and read the title.

The Prince. Machiavelli. A forbidden work, on the restricted list in the Codex; the lending of it from the Great Library through the Codex was granted to a select few, and only for a limited period of time. If this volume were legally obtained, it would have been mirrored inside a Blank, but this was a hand-scribed copy, bound in blue leather with a carefully stamped gilded title. Funny, he knew the book almost by heart. He'd taken it from his father's storehouse when he was fourteen and kept it for almost a year, before he'd been found out. A rare volume. A dangerously illegal one.

He turned toward Anit, who had paused near the fountain. "Yours?" He held up the book.

"Yes," she said. "A gift from my father." He saw the flash of guilt and horror that came over her. "In better days."

"When are his funerary rites?" He put the book back where it had been placed. He wondered if she'd ever open it again without reliving the instant she'd killed her own father to save the lives of two foolish Brightwell boys.

"When things are settled," she said. "I've given him to the temple to prepare him for burial. He has a very nice mastaba ready to receive him. He invested quite a lot in it. I'll do my best to make his afterlife all he might have wished it to be. Just as he did for my brothers." Her voice trembled a little when she said it, and he saw the shine of tears welling up in her eyes. She took a deep breath and blinked them away. "You may keep the book if you like. I would be pleased for it to have a good home."

Her control broke. She began to silently weep. Jess walked to her and put his arms around her. "The gods must hate us, Jess. And maybe they should."

He couldn't think of anything to say in comfort, and didn't think she'd accept it if he did, so he simply held her and rested his chin on the top of her head and wished that he could find tears. Maybe it would be a release from the emptiness echoing inside. But he didn't have it in him. Not yet.

"Anit," he said, when the crying slowed and shaking subsided. She pulled back, taking deep breaths, and swiped at her eyes; it only served to smear the dark eyeliner she wore even further. She'd seemed so adult before, and now she was a child playing dress-up. She was now, what, fifteen? With the weight of a criminal empire on her shoulders. "I've lost a brother. You've lost your father. We can be each other's families now. If you'll accept that."

She considered it—that flash of adult, again—and then gravely nodded. "I would be honored," she said.

"I can't overly recommend the Brightwell family in general, but I can promise you: I will be a good brother to you." *Like I wasn't to Brendan.* He let himself find a smile. It was small enough, but real. "And together, we might just build something both our fathers would envy."

"Yes," she said, and took another deep breath. "I believe we could.

Thank you, Jess. I am sorry for . . ." She gestured at her tear-streaked face and laughed a little. "Wait here a bit. I'll make myself less of a disaster. Are you hungry?"

Was he? When had he last eaten? He didn't know. He shrugged. "I suppose."

"I'll send food," she said. "I don't have to remind you not to roam around this house, do I? My men don't know you yet. Accidents happen, especially in that uniform."

"We should be hunting that sniper," he said. "And the Archivist."

"You're in no condition. Sit. Rest. Eat. Read. The fight will wait."

She seemed supremely confident of her security within these walls. Jess hoped she wasn't overestimating that, but she was probably right: if her people were susceptible to being bribed, they'd have turned long ago and she'd have died in the road. She walked on alone out of the gracious, quiet garden room. He regarded the Machiavelli book for a moment, then sat down and began to read. *All states, all powers, that have held and hold rule over men have been and are either republics or principalities. Principalities are either hereditary, in which the family has been long established; or they are new. The new are either entirely new . . . or they are, as it were, annexed to the hereditary state of the prince who has acquired them.*

There was an entire chapter in *The Prince* devoted to the structure and weaknesses of the Great Library; it had been suppressed for Machiavelli's keen insight into the institution's vulnerabilities. The last thing that the Archivists of the past had wanted was to allow a mere prince or king to understand how best to overthrow what had been built at such great price. Like all nations and powers, the Great Library was built on sacrifice . . . some had gone to it willingly, others thrown screaming into the pit of an Archivist's ambition.

And what if this book hadn't been suppressed? Jess asked himself. *What if every single ruler of every single land had such information and insights? Maybe our leaders have been right to worry about dangerous ideas finding their way into the wrong heads.*

But he'd seen the consequences of caution, too. He and Thomas had almost died for even the idea of creating a mechanical press, and they'd been the lucky ones. At least a dozen Scholars before them hadn't survived the inspiration. They'd ended up buried in anonymity, their work lost, their lives destroyed.

And that was far more wrong than fearing what *could* happen.

It felt intrusive, reading this book that had been a loving father's gift to his child. Jess put it down and walked to the fountain. The koi swam toward him and lifted their gilded heads out of the water, mouths opening and closing as they begged for food.

Out of nowhere, it hit him: the image of Brendan in his arms, pale as paper, his mouth opening and closing as he gasped for breath against the truth of his dying body.

Jess sank down with his back against the cool stone edge of the fountain's pool, drew his knees up to his chest, and felt the ice inside break like a glacier in summer, shards and chunks heavy with their own sorrow. It hurt so badly he found himself trembling, and then he thought of Glain, of the bright red blood still smeared on his hands, and the smell of it overwhelmed him again. He plunged his hands into the cool water and scrubbed them clean while the fish scattered.

The door opened behind him, and he quickly stood up, ignoring his dripping hands, because it was Scholar Wolfe. *Wolfe. Here.* How . . .

Anit must have sent for him. That was an extraordinary move. Jess said, "It's not safe—"

"I know that." Wolfe brushed it impatiently aside. "I am in a den of thieves and smugglers and, yes, I am *most* uncomfortable that this is what I must do. But I couldn't allow you to do it without me. Not injured as you are." He glanced down at Jess's hands, and Jess followed the look. He hadn't managed to wash off all the blood. A dirty film of it still circled his forearms. Without saying a word, he dunked them again and scrubbed harder.

Wolfe said, "Whose blood?"

"Glain's," Jess said, and his throat threatened to choke off the rest. He forced himself to continue. "She was shot. Sniper."

He heard the tension in the Scholar's voice. "Is she—"

"If the last word is *alive*, then yes. She is," Jess said. "If you were looking for *all right*, then no. She is a long road from all right, but she's being treated now. She took a bullet for me."

"As is her duty. You'd no doubt take one for her," Wolfe said, but Jess wasn't fooled by the dry tone. He saw the worry in the man's eyes. "What sort of charlatan do they employ here as a Medica?"

"Looks competent enough," Jess said. "And getting her to a High Garda station was impossible." His hands finally looked clean. He sat back and shook them dry, then got to his feet. He staggered. Wolfe caught him by both arms and steadied him, and Jess pulled free with a jerk. "I'm fine."

"You are *not*. I'm sending you to Santi and telling him to confine you to bed."

"I can't rest. Not now. The Medica gave me something to treat it. I'm all right."

"Bullshit," Wolfe said crisply. "You breathed poison. And that has consequences. Stop pretending that it doesn't."

"I'm not. But don't pretend that the crisis will wait for me to heal, either."

"You know, we're too much alike in how we deny our own limits."

"I'll take that as a compliment, Scholar."

"It wasn't." Wolfe glared at him. "I didn't need your nefarious contacts to discover where the Archivist might be hiding, but we will need them to confront him. Don't argue with me when I tell you we wait for the cover of darkness before we leave."

"I won't," Jess promised. He was too broken inside to argue. "Where are we going?"

"To the afterworld. The Archivist took me to see his tomb once, in the Necropolis under the city," Wolfe said. "He built himself an absurdly large model Serapeum there to house his corpse for the after-life, a pyramid built underground. Ten rooms or so. Big enough to make a temporary command center for him and some of his commanders, at least."

The *Necropolis.* Jess steadied a little, because it was a place he'd only heard of, never seen, and he'd once been keen to tour it. The obsession of old Egypt was not death, but life; in death they'd been utterly sure they'd continue to live. Supplies, clothing, possessions . . . all of it went with them to the afterlife. A thousand years ago, they'd also begun building replicas of their homes in the Necropolis—smaller, but with all the familiar touches of their lives—so that on waking in the next world they would have the comforts of their mortal homes to orient them.

Leave it to the Archivist to build himself a massive pyramid instead of a modest miniature home. It reflected the size of his ego, and Jess winced at the wealth he'd looted from the Great Library's treasury to shower on his arrogance. *An emperor in all but name,* Jess thought. "He's living in a *cemetery?*"

"It's quiet and private, safely underground, and most avoid it," Wolfe said. "He'd have stockpiled all he needed there for himself and his loyalists. I'm sure living in a city of bones and corpses won't bother him as long as it keeps him hidden from High Garda eyes. Out of re-spect, Santi wouldn't necessarily think to include it in the door-to-door search."

"Or he'll leave it to last," Jess said.

"Might as well do it for him, then," Wolfe said. "I'm happy for you to remain here—I want to make that clear. This could be difficult. And dangerous."

"Since when has that ever stopped me?" Jess managed a smile, somehow. "Or you, Scholar? You're fresh out of a prison, your third in the last few years. Don't tell me it didn't affect you."

Wolfe's eyes narrowed, but he didn't answer immediately. When he did, it was to merely say, "Touché."

"And Santi would kill me if he knew I'd let you go off on your own without me."

"No, he's quite used to me doing as I please, thank you. And we both know you aren't worried about losing some chance of promotion. Your time in that uniform is temporary, we both know it."

Jess had grown to recognize that, in the past few months; however much he liked the physicality of the High Garda, his ability to follow orders was—at best—suspect. Yet he had no special calling to be a Scholar, either, or even a librarian, as much as he loved books. He was just surprised Wolfe had seen it, too. "True," he said aloud. "But we both have reason to find the old man. And Zara." Zara, once Santi's lieutenant, had thrown her lot in with the old Archivist. Jess's goal now was to make her pay for that mistake. "I don't want you walking out any door into the open. No one can protect you from a sniper with good aim."

"Not *very* good aim," Wolfe said. "He didn't manage to kill Glain."

"That reminds me. Why would anyone be aiming for *Glain*?"

Wolfe's eyebrows rose and drew together in the same motion. "Perhaps they see her as an important force in the new High Garda," he said. "Don't you?"

Jess was immediately ashamed. He hadn't adjusted himself yet to the idea that his friends, his contemporaries, were no longer ambitious students. They were now *achieving*. Khalila was rising ever higher. Dario was proving himself an effective diplomat. Thomas had always been a fiercely talented engineer, but now was recognized as something even greater. Morgan was the most talented Obscurist of her generation, and second in power only to the new Obscurist Magnus. Glain was likely to rise to the rank of captain, or even higher.

"You're right," he said to Wolfe. "They're all exceptional. Everyone except me." He smiled when he said it, just the way Brendan would have done. Self-assured and cynical. "My genius lies elsewhere. Or maybe I have none."

Wolfe said nothing. Just studied him with that sharp, unsettling focus Jess remembered from what seemed like half a lifetime back now . . . the moment a black-robed Scholar had assessed a confused, nervous gaggle of students fresh off the Alexandria train. It almost felt familiar now, that silent study; it never stopped feeling intrusive.

"I wonder if it was your father who made you think so little of yourself," Wolfe said, which was not at all what Jess expected. "Having met the man, I would believe it. But, Jess: don't believe what the demons whisper in the corners of your mind. We all have demons. You are not to be compared against any of the others, or against your own brother. You are yourself. And if I had not seen genius in you, I never would have kept you in the class. I don't coddle mediocrity."

Jess felt pressure building behind his eyes, and willed the tears away. *No. Not now. Not with him.* "You certainly never have before."

"Then take it for the approval it is." Wolfe continued to watch him. Jess avoided his gaze and became entranced with the fish again. He heard Wolfe sigh. "Your young friend Anit swears there is a secret exit we can use. We'll move at dusk. Until then, I want you reclining and resting and using whatever magic elixirs the Medica gave you. Understand?"

He didn't wait to confirm it, just swept out with his robe billowing behind like a storm cloud. Jess settled on the lounge chair and picked up the volume of Machiavelli again; he opened it to a random page and began to read, or at least run his stare over the cramped, precise handwriting. He understood none of it. Finally, he gave up the struggle and put the book down, sat up, and rested his head in both hands. He felt sick, hot, fragile, and he couldn't afford this now. He wasn't as good with waiting, alone with his thoughts, as he had been before. He needed to *do*, not think.

He used the mask again before he left the garden.

He found Anit in conversation with two of her own; both, he was mildly surprised to find, were women. Red Ibrahim seemed to have favored men in his gang of criminals, but perhaps Anit was changing that tune. All three of the women ceased their conversation when he entered, and two of them turned distrustful stares on him.

"I want weapons," he said.

Anit shook her head. "You think we have better than High Garda issue?"

"High Garda issue will get me killed if I'm seen on the street with them out of uniform," he said. "By either side. And I doubt your store-houses are any less well stocked than the High Garda's, Anit."

She hesitated only a second, then cut a look toward the taller of the two women—Nordic features, blond hair, brown eyes, tanned skin. The woman had her hair cut in a severely short style, which revealed a long scar that looped around the side of her head. At some point, she'd tattooed a striking snake over the scar. You could only see the image when she turned her head and it came clear. Effective. "Katja, take Jess to the armory. Let him have what he wants."

Katja clearly didn't favor that order, but she didn't object, either; she gestured sharply to Jess and walked away down a dark hall, through a doorway, down a flight of steps. Belowground now. The hall they walked smelled of dust and damp stone, and when he touched it the wall felt colder than he expected. An aquifer ran close to here, he thought. That was why Red Ibrahim had chosen this house; he would want a private, protected source of freshwater, too. No doubt this stronghold—modest as it seemed—had a wealth of hidden treasures to recommend it.

At the end of the hallway, behind a heavy locked door, lay one of them. Jess had been to the High Garda armory—well, one of many—so the sight didn't shock him. Anit didn't have the same volume of weapons stored here, but the quality was superb. *Not* High Garda guns, though he spotted some here and there that definitely didn't belong in private hands; no, these were clearly manufactured by civilian artisans to exacting specifications. He chose a long rifle; it settled warm and perfectly balanced into his hands, and he slung it over his shoulder and chose the ammunition that went into it. Long, elegant bullets. Anit's weapons weren't equipped with less lethal rounds. Good. He wouldn't need them, not for this journey.

"That's a good weapon," Katja said. "You're sure you know how to use it?"

"I'm trained High Garda."

She sniffed. "As I said."

He chose a sidearm, more ammunition. A knife. Considered a folding crossbow. "I like your tattoo."

"I don't care."

"You do know I'm a Brightwell, don't you?"

Katja looked him scornfully up and down. "All I see is a uniform," she said. "But if Red Anit says you're to be indulged, then I indulge. To a point."

Some darker part of him found her attractive. No, not just attractive. She stirred something primal in him, and he realized that since the arena, he'd hardly thought of Morgan at all. Before that fight, he'd worried over her, wondered if they had a future together, hoped they did. But right now, in this moment, he wanted something else. Something bitter and carnal and very far from love.

Katja met his assessing gaze and smiled. It was a cold thing. "Don't mistake me. I like a good shag as much as the next person," she said. "But I'm not interested. And if you know what's good for you, you'll stop looking at me like a sweet cake you want to devour."

Jess took a deep breath, let it out, and held her stare for a long few seconds. Not because he was trying in any way to threaten her; he knew that she was not someone he *could* threaten. Or beat, if it came to a fight. It would be foolish to even try.

But dear God, he wanted her. And he was ashamed and worried by that. "Sorry," he said. "I'm not sure what I'm doing anymore."

Katja laughed. It sounded like silk tearing. "Who is, Brightwell? Only fools are sure. The rest of us just do the best we can."

He picked up the rest of what he thought he might need, including plain, sturdy clothing and a particularly interesting armored jacket, and ignored her as best he could. It didn't work. She smelled like cinnamon and iron, a peculiar combination that made him want to know how she tasted, too. He hadn't felt this for anyone but Morgan for a while. What was it Wolfe had said? *Don't believe what the demons whisper in the corners of your mind.* His seemed to be particularly loud today.

He nearly flinched when suddenly her voice was at his ear, her breath warm against his skin. Nearly.

"If you're changing out of that terrible uniform," Katja said, "I might reconsider what I said."

He turned to look. She was smiling. It was pure, wicked invitation, and he felt heat rush through his body, and blood rush straight to his groin. *Damn her.*

It took every scrap of strength he had to leave.

And he knew he'd regret it. Fiercely.

EPHEMERA

Excerpt from the personal diary of Obscurist Morgan Hault. Archived to the Codex under interdict until her death.

I think I've been in love with being in love.

Does that even make sense? I care for Jess, of course. He saved me, and I've saved him in return; we're welded together in ways I can't even begin to explain. But am I __in__ love with him? I keep circling that question, but it remains just out of reach. I'd like to be in love with him. I want it. But . . . what happened in the Colosseum feels like an ending.

What's happened to us, been done by us and to us . . . it's changed us both. I am by turns exhausted, elated, terrified, dreadfully bored. Wild swings that hold no peace. And when I think of Jess . . . I realize that I think of him as comfort. But is love comfortable? I don't know. It feels like something's missing between us now.

Here I am, scribbling in my journal about love, while the world burns around me . . . but maybe that is what I ought to do. Maybe, in the end, love is all we have left, in peace or in war, to make the surviving worthwhile.

The Obscurist Magnus is calling for me. I must go. Another hard day ahead.

I hope that we survive it.

CHAPTER FIVE

MORGAN

Morgan sipped bitter, cooling tea and fought back a yawn. Her whole body felt on fire with exhaustion, and her eyes were starting to refuse to focus. But the documents that lay before her on the table were starting—ever so slowly—to give up their secrets, and she couldn't stop now.

Being exhausted could wait.

But if she could just rest her eyes for a moment . . .

"Morgan? Can you make out this part?"

She yanked herself awake, startled, and leaned forward. In doing so she nearly knocked heads with Thomas Schreiber, who sat across from her at the table. "Sorry," she said, and tried to get her concentration back. Predictably, he'd hardly noticed the near impact, so intent was he on the page in front of them. *Thomas* wasn't tired. He put a large but precise finger on a tiny line of faded Greek.

"There," he said. "Does that talk about the width of the chain?"

"Yes," she said, "but we already know the width of the chain. *Finding* the chain isn't the issue; that's clearly marked on the current maps. The problem is how to repair the mechanism that winds it. There's no information here on how to open the casing. No information any-where, in any of the records."

"True. But there is this." He moved his finger farther down the page to a string of symbols she'd read and dismissed.

"It doesn't even make sense," she said. "Unless my ancient Greek's worse than yours . . . ?"

"Not worse. Just different," he said. "This is shorthand among engi-neers. It may not make sense to anyone outside of the field, but we still use some of these notations. I believe these are instructions for opening the cas-ing, but it can't be done by one person, or even two; it's at the bottom of the harbor, for one thing. The ancients must have had automata to do this task; do the Obscurists have any record of them? The Artifex engineers must have partnered with Obscurists to make and maintain them."

Morgan's weary frustration turned to a sweet thrill of realization. "Yes! Or, at least, it's discussed as possible in some of the texts; I don't remember any of them describing the exact automaton used, only that it functioned underwater. It would need the two of us working closely together. I would have to bond you directly to the automaton; you'd see through its eyes and use its hands as your own. But I'm not so cer-tain that any automata we have in Alexandria now can do that sort of fine mechanical task."

"Scribes?" he suggested. The mechanical Scribes were able to write, so it seemed a logical enough question, but Morgan shook her head. She held up her hands and flexed her fingers.

"The Scribes' hands are made to hold a pen and reduce movement," she said, "to facilitate speed in writing. They don't even have functional legs to stand on. But . . ." She hesitated. It seemed faintly sacrilegious to suggest. "The hands of many of the god automata are fully articu-lated. They'd have the strength necessary and be able to move in the ways we'd need. What do you think?"

"I think there could be nothing more appropriate than to press one of our gods into the service of saving this city," he said. "Which one?"

Morgan considered it carefully. None of the automata she knew of were built to survive water for long, but it didn't have to be a particularly long job. Or so she hoped. An hour, no more. "One of the larger ones," she said, "in case we need leverage. This mechanism is bound to be very rusty."

"Not necessarily," Thomas said. "Heron was a master at designing mechanisms meant to stand the test of time. He was known to plate certain components with platinum and palladium to combat rust." He sat back and sighed, rubbing his neck. He looked thinner than she remembered, and more . . . honed, somehow, like a particularly keen knife. Then he smiled at her in that shy, distracted way he had, and it all melted away. He was Thomas. Still. "You're tired." He didn't make it a question.

Morgan gave him a weary smile. "Well, not all of us have the constitution of an ox and the brain of Heron himself, so . . . yes. I'm tired."

"I wish I could leave you to rest," he said. "But while I'm sure your Obscurist colleagues are good at their work . . ."

"They're not powerful enough to do this? Yes, except for Eskander, and you really don't know him. Plus you're right: we're friends; we can communicate better and faster. I can get a potion from the Medica to keep me alert." She yawned and laughed at the same time. "And I need one, obviously." Her smile faded as she looked down at the papers spread out between them. "We had to remove poisons from these papers before they could be safe to handle. Did you know that? The Archivist had the room trapped with lethal gas."

"I heard," Thomas said. "But they all came out alive, *ja*?"

"Jess was the one who got them." Her fingertips were just touching the page, and she felt a shiver run through her. "He was almost killed doing it."

"But only almost. And you know Jess. He cheats death almost every day, and for far less reason. Morgan? Are you worried for him?" Thomas's voice turned warmer. More concerned. She didn't look up. "Jess is a survivor."

"Until he isn't," she said, and took a deep breath. Forced a smile. "Forgive me. I get moody when I'm tired. And worried."

"You miss him."

"Yes," she said, though even as she said it, it didn't sound assertive. "I do."

"But?"

"But I have too much else to think about," she said, then immediately retracted that. "No, that's unfair. I'm wondering if he's all right, mostly. I—I should have stayed with him, Thomas. He needs . . . someone. After losing Brendan." *If you'd really loved him, you wouldn't have left him,* some part of her said. And she had to admit that was probably true. But she *did* love him. The question was . . . how much? For how long? How deeply? She'd been swept away by the breathless joy of being *seen,* being wanted. And so had Jess, she thought. But was that enough for the rest of their lives?

If you have to ask the question, you know the answer.

"Jess isn't alone," Thomas replied calmly. "He'll need comfort, but right now I think he needs structure. He has Scholar Wolfe for that. I think he is better with tasks to occupy him."

"Men," Morgan said. "You all hide your feelings too much."

"That is true, but not useful to want us to change, is it? We are as we were built."

"People aren't automata, Thomas. They *can* change if they want to do so."

"Ah, but can they change for the better? And who decides? This is why I prefer my machines. Far easier to fix a broken automaton than a broken person." His smile felt as warm as summer sun, and for a moment she forgot they weren't just two students, debating. But then he turned back to the paper. "Can you find me a suitable god, then?"

She knew it wasn't what he meant, but it was still a startling question. "I'll find one. But we shouldn't do this exhausted. It will take a lot of effort, at least for me. And probably even for you."

Thomas nodded, stretched, and yawned. Neither of them had slept in more than a day with the stress of what was happening, and she couldn't remember the last time she'd paused for more than a bite or two of food. Her throat was dry, despite the tea. She craved a large glass of water and her bed.

"Go," she told him. "It's getting late, and you and I both need the rest."

"May I sleep in one of the empty rooms?" There were plenty of empty bedrooms in the Iron Tower where the Obscurists lived; the population within had been steadily declining for a long time. "It saves me a walk back to the office I was given. I don't have sleeping quarters yet."

"Of course. Annis can see to it for you. And call at the kitchens, see if they can make you food. They should have plenty."

He placed a heavy hand on her shoulder and squeezed very, very carefully. She was grateful. Thomas's full strength could easily crack her collarbone. "Don't stay up brooding," he told her. "We are doing what we can do. What we can't do we must leave to others."

She nodded. Thomas's genius was legendary, but what most overlooked was the gentle care he took of his friends. Sleep would be relief, but she knew it might yet elude her no matter how much her body ached for the release. "I'll go to bed," she said. "Go on, Thomas. Annis is just outside. She'll see you settled."

When the big young man was gone, she felt cold. Alone. And although deeply tired, still agitated. Power sizzled in her veins, dark and glorious; she'd used so much in the battle at the Colosseum, and yet she felt bursting with it still. It wasn't the same power she'd grown up feeling; that had been a steady, slow trickle from the world around her, just enough to fuel the modest efforts at elemental manipulation, cleverly rewriting Obscurist codes, concealing herself from detection. She'd

spent most of her life in hiding, trying to erase her existence from the
Great Library's ever-seeing eye. But once she'd stopped hiding, once
she'd used the power she was born with . . . it had changed. Grown.
Darkened.

She knew how dangerous it was. Few Obscurists could reach the
power that she did, drawn directly from the universal fluid, the quintessence, of the world; the few who could died young and often took
others with them. Power always corrupted. It was a law of nature.

She sat back with a sigh and rubbed the sore spot on her lower back,
then stood. This was a spare workroom inside the vast Iron Tower; it
was little used and had a fine-ground grit on every surface. The clean-
ers hadn't visited in weeks, if not months. *I just made Thomas a vow that
I could bind him to an automaton,* she thought. *And I'm not sure what will
happen if I do it.* She remembered what she'd done on the arena floor,
and shivered. Her talents ran dark, no question of that. *No. I will just
have to be careful. So very careful.*

She blinked and saw a shimmering afterimage. There was power in
this room. Odd, hidden power. She closed her eyes and opened them
slowly, searching for the source of the glimmer. It came from a flagstone in the corner. Morgan walked to it, touched the stone, and felt it
move. Loose. She pried it up. Beneath lay a ring.

Not just any ring. This one was emblazoned with the seal of the
Great Library, gold set into an amber stone. Just by holding her hand
above it she felt the shimmer from it—not heat, but energy.

A voice from behind her said, "I hoped you'd find that when I told
you to use this room."

She looked around, startled out of her uncertainty. The Obscurist
Magnus Eskander stood in the doorway. He'd avoided the formal robes
of the office, unlike his unpleasant predecessor; he was dressed in a
plain workman's shirt and trousers, with boots that had seen years of
use. A lean, strong elder with long, curling gray hair. Scholar Wolfe's
father. Her honorary grandfather, in a sense.

"What is it?" she asked. He closed the workroom door and approached to stare down at the ring with her.

"What do you think it is?"

He was as bad as his son; everything, even the simplest question, had to be made into a lesson. Morgan resisted the urge to roll her eyes. "A ring?"

"Come, girl, you're not head-blind."

"Someone stored power in it," she said. "An accumulation from the quintessence."

"Not quintessence. Apeiron," he corrected. "Apeiron is a greater unification even than quintessence. It underlies the reality that we observe, and all other realities. But you are correct, the ring is rich in it."

"I didn't know it was possible to store it in a matrix like this."

"It's rare," he said. "But not unknown. This particular ring was created by the Obscurist Magnus Gargi Vachaknavi over five thousand years ago. Quite old. And quite dangerous."

"What's it doing *here*?"

"I put it here," he said. "I wanted to see if you'd find it. Which you did."

Another test. Morgan glared at him. "I thought you didn't want to be the Obscurist. You're acting like one."

"I don't want it," he said. "I want to be left alone. So training you to take my place seems the very best option I have to achieve that goal, wouldn't you agree?"

"I don't want to be the Obscurist!"

He waved that aside. "We don't always get what we want, and for as long as Obscurists are necessary to the proper operation of the Great Library we'll need a steady hand to guide them. We need to ensure that the automata and the Great Archives remain functional. You're the logical choice to take the job on. I've reviewed every Obscurist in this tower. You are, in fact, the only choice I can see that won't ultimately compromise the work."

"Annis told me you didn't give a damn for the Great Library. That you were brought here against your will and forced into service. Like me."

"Like many of us, and the ancestors of many more," he agreed. "But I don't do this for the Great Library. I do it for the memory of the woman I loved, who *did* believe in that cause. Whether I wanted the responsibility or not, it's landed on me. And it will land on you. Get used to the idea, Morgan. I know you're young for it, and rash, and frustrated. But the world looks to us for this. We can only look to each other."

"I never wanted it."

"I know," Eskander said. "Take the ring."

She hesitated. "The amount of power I used before—"

"I'm aware that you've overreached," he said. "Not the first time, nor I imagine will it be the last with you, though each time you burn so hot you shorten your own life. I trust you know that? The young feel immortal. But you're not."

Morgan took in a deep breath. "It's more than that," she said. "I can feel it. The power I can reach now . . . it's not pure. If I take this ring . . ."

"We don't know what will happen until you do," Eskander said. "Go on."

"What if I—"

"Take it."

She didn't like it. She was tired, and afraid, and sickened inside, but she stooped down and took the ring from its hidden spot. It gleamed soft gold and amber. There was a brilliant spot of red hidden in the stone, and as she turned it in her palm, it seemed to move. But that couldn't be true; amber was a stone made from ancient fossilized resin. Nothing could flow freely inside it.

"The speck you see inside is the blood of Gargi Vachaknavi," Eskander said. "She was the most brilliant woman of several dozen ages— famous enough that even the male-dominated courts of ancient kingdoms couldn't deny her honors. She lives on in that stone. And you are the one to wear it now."

"I'm not brilliant," she said. She felt humiliated, oddly enough. Small and fearful and unworthy. "Please take it." She held it out. He shook his head.

"You aren't Gargi," he agreed. "But you are something else. Something I feel certain that lady would find worthwhile to nurture. Put the ring on, Morgan."

"No!"

He put his hands on her shoulders and gazed down at her. His son had the same look. The same hidden warmth buried under layers of severity. "Put the ring on. I'm here. I won't abandon you."

She felt her tired eyes fill with tears. When those tears fell, they tasted bitter. "I feel so *wrong*."

"Then I will help you," he said. "Do you trust me?"

She did. Against her will. Against all her experience. So she nodded, took another breath, and tried to put the ring on her right hand. No, that felt wrong. It belonged on her left, on her middle finger, and as it settled against her skin she felt something wash over her. Not power. Emotion. *Welcome.*

The power came after, a wave that crashed in on her and buried her deep, screaming silently and rolling in the ocean of gold. Drowning in the deep, rich flood of something primal and powerful.

She felt it wash her clean inside. It burned, and it hurt, but she'd felt this before; she knew to hang on and wait for the relief. And it came, oh, it came cool as water through her veins. She flinched, shuddered, and looked down at the ring on her hand.

She hadn't imagined it. The red spot in the stone was *moving.* As if the honey under the surface remained liquid and sweet. She felt . . . free. Light. *Strong.* Strong enough to bring this entire tower down around her, to level cities, to burn out stars.

It was terrifying and wonderful.

"No one should have this power," she whispered. "No one." But she didn't want to give it up, either. There was a feeling that the ring itself had decided this and not her. That the ring believed in her, if such a thing was possible.

Eskander still held her shoulders, but he was looking at her completely differently now. There was a sharp assessment in his eyes, and a light frown between his brows. He was reading her on a deeper level than just the physical.

And he finally said, "The ring will help you with what you need. Whatever that may be. But don't underestimate it: it will judge your intentions, too. It's intelligent, in a way; it's also inherited Vachaknavi's loyalty to the Great Library. That's why this ring was put away . . . because the ring began to sharply disagree with the Obscurists Magni over the years about the course the Great Library was on. It will warn you first, then stop you, if it feels you are doing wrong."

"What if *it* is wrong?"

"Then you have to change its mind," he said. "But you can't take it off, Morgan. It's meant to be on your hand now. It will stay until it feels it's time to go."

"This isn't—this isn't alchemy. It's *sorcery*."

"It comes from a tradition that didn't see the distinction between the two," he said. "There's nothing to fear here. Now, go to bed. Rest. And help Thomas in the morning."

She intended to follow those orders, truly, but when she wandered out into the curving corridor, out to the central core with the lifting chamber that carried her to her old bedroom doorway—a bedroom that still contained things she'd left behind, full of past bad memories—she couldn't go in. She went to the kitchens and ate a bowl of soup standing up. The woman on duty was baking bread, and the rich smell of it made Morgan's mouth water even though her immediate hunger was sated.

Morgan took a hot roll with her up to the highest public level of the Iron Tower: the gardens. It was just as she'd last seen it, bursting with color and life. The singing of birds in the trees and the splash of fountains made something restless in her go temporarily still, and she stretched out on one of the long garden lounges, curled on her side, and finally allowed herself to sleep with the roll still clutched half-eaten in her hand.

I'm dreaming, Morgan thought.

She was floating in the ocean, staring up at a dark sky shot with stars. Watching comets streak across the blackness, trailing fire. She was happy.

And then she was drowning.

It felt as if a rope had been tied around her middle and a giant pulled her down. As if she was falling from a great height, the water rushing around her, her hands waving and grasping for the peaceful surface. She tried to hold her breath. Couldn't.

But when she breathed, she received air—fresh air that smelled of flowers and earth.

Then she was standing on the sandy floor of the ocean, which was also lit by a rising sun, and a young woman floated in the sea across from her with her legs crossed. She wore a bright yellow silk sari that fluttered in the water's ripples. "That's beautiful," Morgan said, and the words came out as odd little bubbles that somehow made sense, though she heard no sound at all.

The young woman smiled and studied her and said nothing. Then she held out her hand, palm up, as if she was asking for something. Morgan, uncertain, extended her left hand. The other woman's fingers closed around it, and she felt a shock like lightning striking. The water boiled and bubbled around them. The sun rose and fell, rose and fell, as if it was a toy on a string, and then it began to drift upward, and the two of them followed.

There was someone in the way.

The old Archivist looked down at them with his bitter eyes and seamed face and said, "Give me what is mine."

Gargi—somehow, Morgan knew the young woman traveling with her was Gargi Vachaknavi, whose blood inhabited the ring—said the first and only word she would speak. "No," she said, still smiling, and let go of Morgan's hand. Without being asked, Morgan stretched out and touched that same hand to the Archivist's face.

He blackened like the Philadelphia wheat. Poisoned. He turned to ashes and floated away on the tides, and Morgan looked at Gargi and said, "Was that right?"

Then Morgan realized that she, too, was rotting away. Flakes drifted off of her into the water. She cried out and reached for help, but the sun went out and then she was swimming desperately for the surface, but half of her was gone now, turned to ashes, and when she opened her mouth to scream, all that came out was a wet cloud of blood.

She woke up with a shock. Her heart hammered so fast it hurt. She slowly sat up and stared at the ring on her finger. *Did that cause the dream?* No, surely not. Surely the dream was only her own weariness and rage and pain coming back to haunt her while her guard was down. The ring couldn't cause nightmares. Couldn't communicate with her and give her orders, or warnings, or anything else. It was simply a storage device, carrying ancient energy.

If she believed anything else, even for a moment, she'd have to throw it into Thomas's forge to be melted down forever.

But despite the dream, she couldn't argue that the ring seemed to have helped her. She felt better. Stronger. More in control of herself and her power than she had in a long time. And though the opportunity to sleep had been welcome, she doubted that simple rest had worked that much magic.

When she consulted the view from the garden's windows, she was surprised to find it was still dark. The clock showed just after midnight. Odd. She felt she'd slept the day away.

The ring sat heavy and warm on her finger, and she lifted it up to the light to admire it as she brushed tangles out of her hair. The red spot moved slowly from one side to the other—not responding to the action of her hand, but traveling on its own. *Sorcery,* she thought again, and shivered a little. There had always been, in her mind at least, a hard wall between the ideas of magic and the rational, logical, reproducible effects of alchemy that drove the *seeming* magic of the Great Library. She could quote every philosopher and researcher on the similarity of all matter, on the transfer of energy, on every principle that allowed an automaton to follow coded instructions, or a Blank to fill with the contents of a recorded book. She understood these things. She understood why they worked.

But this ring felt . . . different. As if it was grounded in the same principles but it went farther, deeper, stranger, than anything she knew. It was terrifying. And intriguing. She knew of the legendary Gargi, of course; she was a woman who'd risen so far above other Scholars that no one, not even the most repressive of kings, could erase her brilliance. *And I am decidedly not her,* Morgan thought. *So why is this ring on my hand?*

Because it's needed.

She didn't know where that thought came from, but she accepted it as true without question. She felt healthy, steady, focused.

She also badly needed a bathroom, and her mouth tasted foul. Her hair was hopelessly tangled. Still the middle of the night, but she could at least try to seem presentable.

Morgan went back to her room and used the toilet, dressed, brushed out her hair. It was undeniable. She even *looked* better than she had in months.

As she readied herself to leave, there was a hard volley of knocks on the door. Agitated, frantic knocks, and she quickly threw it open.

Red-haired Annis stood there, mouth open, breathing hard. There were fierce spots of crimson in her cheeks, as if she'd taken several flights of stairs to reach her. "What is it?" Morgan asked. She was honestly afraid that something had happened to Eskander, as alarmed as the other woman seemed to be. Annis was fond of Eskander, always had been. She couldn't think what else might spark this kind of emergency.

But it wasn't Eskander. Standing behind Annis was Scholar Wolfe, looking tired and drawn. "Your friend is hurt," Annis said.

"*You're* hurt?" she asked Wolfe directly.

"Not me," Wolfe replied. "Glain was shot. The doctor with her has done the best they could, but Glain needs more," he said. "She's losing too much blood. She doesn't have long. I need you to come with me."

Morgan didn't hesitate. She stepped out of her room, shut the door, and said, "I'm ready."

If anything, Wolfe had understated the problem; Morgan knew that the second she saw Glain lying so still and quiet in the bed. The physician sitting with her rose when they entered and came to meet them.

"Any change?" Wolfe asked.

"None. She's bleeding internally, and I don't have the facilities here to open her and find the torn vessels. She'll die of shock if I try." The doctor seemed extraordinarily competent; Morgan took the diagnosis as complete truth. She moved to stand next to Glain's bedside and looked down on her. She'd never seen Glain this still, not even sleeping; the young Welshwoman was always in motion, eyes darting behind her lids if nothing else. But now she seemed pale and unmoving as her own funerary statue.

Glain's skin felt cold, as if the essential fluids of life had withdrawn into the core of her; Morgan called on a tiny trickle of power, and her friend's body came to shimmering life in front of her, mapped in flows of reds, blues, golds . . . and a steadily expanding darkness deep inside her.

Glain was dying. Fighting it, the way Glain fought all her battles—an absolute, unyielding struggle. But she was on the losing side of this one, resources depleted, allies gone. She fought alone.

No. Not alone. Not anymore.

But a little chill went through her, a vibration, a discord. And another voice whispered, *The damage is too great. You should not do this. Sometimes, death is inevitable.*

I can, she thought. *I will.*

Morgan looked at Wolfe, who stood nearby. "A chair," she said. "This will take time."

"Can you save her?" The physician seemed curious. "How?"

"I can't really explain if you can't see what I see," she said. "But I may be able to help her save herself." She smiled at Wolfe. "Don't worry, Scholar. Have you ever known Glain to give up?"

"Never," he said. "I'll get the chair."

She was settled in just a moment, and put her hands directly on Glain's bare shoulders. Took a deep breath and let herself *feel.*

The shock of pain nearly drove her back. The damage done inside of Glain was considerable, and growing worse as free fluid inside her crowded her heart and lungs. Her body was working too hard to survive, let alone heal. Glain's army needed reinforcements.

Morgan began by concentrating on the tears within two of the major vessels damaged by the bullet's strike; one was small enough to be closed with a relatively minor amount of urging. But the other was a gaping hole, half the vein torn away, and that was going to be difficult. Morgan tapped the vital energy flowing all around her and channeled it through the matrix of the ring; tiny amounts of quintessence were trapped in every cell of every creature, even in inanimate objects. Anything that came from the earth held quintessence. She felt the ring feeding her in a thick amber flow . . . and then guiding her to extract more from the human bodies standing in the room, and then the ones outside of it. Careful draws, light ones, nothing that would damage them in the least.

But it wasn't enough. She had fixed some of the damage, but it only slowed Glain's defeat; it couldn't prevent it. She sculpted the power, manipulated it into a tiny structural matrix and guided the tissues to build around it. The torn vein sealed. Morgan began breaking down the blood that had leaked into Glain's chest cavity, burning it into energy and feeding that energy back into the ring. Once that was done, and Morgan could see that Glain's heart was laboring strongly again, she went to the next challenge.

The damage to Glain's liver and lungs seemed grave, and so she set to work again, bit by bit. She hardly felt it when her own connections began to fail, when the energy she pulled began to flow more slowly. When its character began to shift. She *did* feel the ring pulsing on her left hand, a steady warning that grew in intensity as she ignored it and kept working, *had* to keep working because she could feel Glain's body sliding into shock from the effort to heal.

Morgan had a strong flash of her nightmare, of drowning, of darkness blotting out the sun, and she poured reckless amounts of energy through the ring, accelerating the knitting together of Glain's wounded organs, until she felt a sharp, agonizing stab of pain lance up her arm and into her brain, and broke free with a cry.

She was shaking so badly she almost pitched off the chair to the floor—would have done, if Scholar Wolfe hadn't been there to catch her. And she was cold, *so cold*, and his brightness shone like a torch to her.

She put her hands on his face and breathed him in like a gasp of pure, fresh air.

She took *life*.

You will not.

The ring caught fire on her hand, burned so painfully that she flung herself away and hit the wall. She sank down to a slumped sitting position, unable to do anything to prevent it. Wolfe had stumbled, too, and was now clinging to the bedpost for support. He looked wide-eyed and wild. Terrified in a way she couldn't remember ever seeing him. "Morgan, *stop!*"

She was still reaching for his brilliant energy, even at this distance.

Trying to consume it. And the ring was preventing her from doing any more damage.

She forced herself to stop, though it felt like falling into the deepest pit in the world, and leaned back against the wall to sob. She cried for the sin she'd just committed, or tried to commit, because now that she came back to herself she knew it *was* a wrong as great as anything she could have ever done. As the ring had warned her.

On the bed next to her, Glain let out a low, soft groan, opened her eyes, and whispered, "What happened?"

For a moment no one moved, and then Morgan stumbled to her feet. She looked down at the ring she wore. She could tell the glow was dim, the blood spot darkened. It needed recharging. It needed more than she could give.

Calm down, the ring whispered. *Breathe. Power flows around you. Power will come. Do not demand it.*

"I have to go," she told Wolfe. She felt sick and weak, but she didn't want to stay here. There was something about Wolfe, something shimmering inside him that wakened a hunger inside she didn't like. He was the child of two powerful Obscurists, and though he'd never manifested power of his own, there was a potential energy inside him that she could almost taste. It made her thirsty for the relief of it. "Thomas needs me today. I can't keep doing this, Scholar. Don't ask again."

"If I hadn't, she'd be dead," he said. "But you're right. Best you go, then," he agreed. "Morgan. Thank you."

She moved to Glain's bedside and clasped her friend's hand. Glain's color was better, and there was a shadow of strength in the way her fingers tightened. "Thanks," she said. "Apparently that was dramatic."

"A little," Morgan said. "You'll be all right now. Just don't—"

"Get in the way of another bullet? I'll try." Glain's eyes focused and searched Morgan's expression. "You're as bad as Jess, you know. Courting death when it doesn't come calling."

"It always comes calling. I'm popular that way." Smiling felt empty, but at the same time, it helped. "Take care, Glain."

"And you, Morgan."

Glain was already falling asleep when Morgan fled the room, away from Scholar Wolfe's too-bright presence and into the atrium of the house. There was a garden through the central door, and she went that way. Waterfalls splashed into a cleverly designed pond, and sleek, shimmering fish glided under the surface. She sat down on the edge and closed her eyes. Around her, the room was glowing in lines and surfaces; the fish were individual moving lights. Quintessence all around her, as the ring had promised. She opened herself and waited, and the power began to flow toward her. *Don't pull,* the ring whispered. *Allow nature to balance itself.*

It takes too long, she argued. The ring seemed utterly unmoved by the concept of time. *I have to hurry! I'm needed.*

You are unique. But not alone. And demands are not needs. I entered this ring as a frightened soul to escape my death, only to discover that death is hardly even the beginning of anything at all. We are so much more than flesh, Morgan. Allow yourself to feel this.

"I'm arguing philosophy with a ring," she said out loud, and surprised herself into a laugh. Her fingers were in the water, drifting like pale weeds, and a fish nibbled gently at them, then swam away when she moved. There was peace in this place. Maybe there was peace everywhere, if she'd slow down to look.

There was a sound of footsteps from the doorway.

It was Jess.

She rose to her feet when she saw him because for a startling moment she thought he was a ghost. His own brother's ghost. He looked starkly pale, *changed* somehow. And she could sense the damage from here. *No. No, not Jess . . .*

"Morgan," he said, and came toward her. The closer he came, the more she felt the sickness that had rooted itself deep into him. He was bleeding quintessence; she could *see* it like a cloud floating away from him.

And then he was embracing her, and she felt the ring taking his fog of escaping life. It wouldn't harvest from inside him, but this . . . this was different. The quintessence he was losing was being wasted. The ring was simply absorbing it.

Jess was *broken*. Cracked like a glass. It took her breath away, and she wanted desperately to help him. She reached for power.

Hit an unyielding wall.

No, the ring said. *Not for this.*

She'd healed Glain. She could heal Jess, too. Surely, she *must*. Because she loved him.

Jess's fate is his own. No one can change it. He lives or dies because of his own actions, not yours.

It felt breathlessly true. She had tears in her eyes, and they burned with that truth. Glain's wound had been inflicted on her. Jess's had been a conscious choice.

She couldn't take that from him.

"You're hurt," she whispered. She buried her face in his shoulder, and his arms tightened around her. "Oh, Jess. Why?"

"I'll be all right," he told her. "I've seen the Medica. Got treatments. I'm instructed to take it easy for a while."

"And will you?"

He laughed. It sounded grim. "Now? With all that's going on? How can I?"

"No!" She shoved him backward, which surprised him, and he caught himself as he staggered. "No, you don't get to kill yourself like this! *You will not!*"

"Hey! Hey, easy!" He held up both hands in surrender. "All right! I won't. I'll rest. I promise."

"Don't coddle me!"

"I'm just—"

"You're just humoring me and we both know it." She took in a deep breath. "How bad is it?"

He didn't answer. He slowly lowered his hands. Watched her.

"That bad?" She knew it already, but the fact that *he* knew . . . it hurt. "Jess."

"I had to do it," he said. "Wolfe would have killed himself trying. I had a better chance. I'm not sorry I did it. Wolfe said it was important."

She despised Wolfe in that moment, but she couldn't deny that it had been important. She and Thomas had found what they needed from it. "Do you want me to tell you what they really said?"

"No." He shrugged. "I have a chance. That's better odds than Brendan got."

Brendan. The brothers had been two stars circling each other in an orbit, and now that one was gone, the other had lost its anchor. Spinning wildly out of control. "I'm sorry about him," she said. "So sorry, love. He didn't deserve that." *You didn't.*

"He'd have never guessed he'd go out a hero."

"Well, you don't have to follow him. Rest. Please?"

"I will," he said. "You—why are you here? I thought you'd be at the Iron Tower."

"I was. Eskander set me to work with Thomas, but we both were so tired. Then Glain—"

"You came for Glain. Yes, of course you would have. You always come when we're in trouble." He stepped toward her again, and this time he kissed her, and she melted into it. His lips were firm and soft and sweet and she loved the way he held her, but it still felt . . . wrong. Empty, in a way, as if the bridge that had once connected them had fallen away.

He broke the kiss and pressed his forehead to hers. "I'm sorry." He whispered it, as intimate as the kiss. "I wish we were . . . you know."

"I—" She didn't know what to say. What to do. She knew in her heart that the two of them fit, and yet they didn't; they loved, and yet it was a patchwork kind of love with holes and gaps. He was what she *should* want; she knew that. But she also knew it wasn't enough for her. Or for him. "I wish we were, too. I'm sorry, Jess. I think we were right for a while."

"But not forever."

"No. Not forever."

The laugh he managed sounded mangled and rusty. "Aren't we *supposed* to be in love forever? Isn't that how it works?"

"I don't know how it works," she said, and she meant it. "Are you going to be all right?"

He stepped back, and she could *see* the armor go on. It wasn't his own; this had a brassy, brash edge that was all his brother's. "Me? I'm always all right," he said. "Take care of yourself, Morgan. I do care. I always will."

She nodded. She wasn't sure she could speak. There was a panic whirling inside her, a wild, off-balance need to make this right, to *fix it* and go back to the way things were, to safety and comfort, and what was wrong with craving those things even if there wasn't love along with them . . . ?

She forced a smile and said, "Good night, Jess."

There were tears burning in her eyes as he walked away, and she wanted to stop him. She wanted to *save him*.

But she knew that wasn't right, and she didn't need the ring to remind her of it.

"Good-bye," she whispered.

But he was already gone.

EPHEMERA

Text of a handwritten letter from Obscurist Vanya
Nikolin, smuggled from the Iron Tower and delivered by
courier to the Archivist in Exile. Indexed later to the
Codex as historical record.

I have succeeded in your requests to a point, Archivist, but it is becoming increasingly difficult to make the changes necessary without attracting the notice of the Hermit himself or his apprentice. I am working as quickly as I can, but I must be cautious. One mistake and I will be removed from the Iron Tower completely, possibly even imprisoned. I think I can avoid that by shifting the blame to one of my assistants, and I have seeded some damning evidence in their journals should this occur, but please understand that we must go carefully.

I have not been able to rewrite any of the automata likely to come into contact with the new Archivist. There is no possibility of assassination through that route, and as I've said before, I will not risk my life in the attempt. You have paid me to do quiet work, and this suits me. But hire assassins if you want someone to get their hands bloody. I will not.

I've recruited a few allies, carefully, and they have proven useful, but the more support I gather, the bigger the risk of discovery. We must be very, very aware of what is at stake, and not move too quickly.

I can't spend your money if I'm dead.

CHAPTER SIX

KHALILA

Khalila woke in predawn darkness, gasping and cold with sweat, and as she curled in on herself and tried to regulate her breathing, she didn't know what had made her wake in such distress. If it had been a dream, it was gone like morning mist.

But there was enough tension gathering to frighten anyone. She sat up and listened. She'd slept on a camp bed in a small storeroom in the Serapeum; she hadn't wanted to make the trip back to the Iron Tower and risk not being at the Archivist's side in an emergency. The Archivist's accommodations hadn't been much more luxurious than this, either.

Khalila rose, stretched, slid her feet into sandals, and realized that she'd have to leave the room and find a toilet soon. She brushed out her hair and coiled it beneath the same hijab she'd been wearing for the last few days. She desperately needed more changes of clothing, and a night in her own comfortable bed. And a bath, though she'd made do with basins and washcloths so far. She felt grubby, though once she'd found the toilet and availed herself, she checked herself in the mirror and found herself adequate, at least. She scrubbed down, then added eyeliner and a dash of color to her cheeks, took a deep breath, and told herself, "All will be well." She had to believe that. What choice was there?

The sun would be up soon. She went back to the small room she'd slept in, folded up the bed, and unrolled her prayer rug. Her prayers this morning were heartfelt. She badly needed Allah's protection today, with what the city faced. The peace would not hold. She felt that in her bones.

After prayers, she set about the business of the day. The fact that no one had summoned her during the night meant that the ambassadors had continued their talks. On finding one of the passing Scholars heading home for rest, she found that they'd requested, and been granted, sleeping quarters of their own, but that they'd risen early and were now gathered back in the large, spacious room where she'd had them settled.

Khalila knocked on the door and waited for permission to enter. It took a moment, and the High Garda soldiers stationed at the door exchanged looks with her. "They've been shouting," one reported. "It isn't good."

She nodded and took a deep breath. When the permission came, she opened the doors and walked inside.

Conversation stopped. The gathered ambassadors and their staffs seemed exhausted and ill at ease, and as she bowed to them respectfully, they all looked to Alvaro Santiago. The expression on every face was the same: grim.

Ambassador Santiago returned her bow. He looked ages older than he had just a day before. "Scholar Seif," he said. "I believe we are prepared to deliver our decision to the Archivist."

"I will send word," she said. "Is there anything you need, sir?"

"Nothing you can provide, unfortunately. Please, take a pastry from the lavish spread that's been provided. We have little appetite today."

She thanked him but didn't have any wish to eat; the atmosphere in this room felt heavy as lead. She wrote to the Archivist in her Codex and got a swift reply in Murasaki's fast, precise writing: *Bring them to me.*

She led the diplomats back to the Receiving Hall.

There were only a handful of people in attendance—the newly formed Curia made up of the Scholars Magni of Artifex Medica, Lingua, and Litterae, supported by a contingent of senior librarians. The Obscurist Magnus, Eskander, had already accepted his post and returned to the Iron Tower, so his place sat empty. Except for the Curia and the standing company of High Garda, the hall itself was cool and vacant. If anything, Khalila thought, it only made the space more intimidating.

The Archivist mounted the steps to her chair and nodded toward the diplomats. If she was tired or stressed, Khalila could see no sign of it. "Ambassadors," she said, and the words carried to every corner of the hall. "I hope that you have had a productive evening."

Khalila felt the mood shifting in the room like shadows, though there was no visible change on the Archivist's face. Her expression remained neutral. Waiting.

Ambassador Santiago stepped forward and bowed. The bow lingered until the Archivist gestured for him to straighten. "Honored Archivist, I have the privilege of having been once again chosen to speak for the group. We have spent many hours in debate and conversation regarding your proposals, and we are now prepared to render to you our combined answer." The pause felt torturous. "I must inform you that the assembled nations you see before you will not withdraw. You must face facts. You are new to power; you have enemies inside your city, and you *must* rely on allies to help you secure your position and protect the incalculable value of the Great Library to the world. There is simply no other choice. If you would preserve this great institution, you must allow us to help."

The Archivist let the boldness of that reply fall into a deep, waiting silence, and once it had taken hold, she said, "Allies do not force themselves on those unwilling. I believe that you come not as allies of the Great Library, but as shadow conquerors."

"Honored Archivist—"

"No," she said, and stood up with a rustle of glistening robes. "I have been patient. I allowed you time to deliberate. The Great Library has provided you with shelter and hospitality. But now you must go. Within the hour, you must be out of this city. Turn your fleets, Ambassadors. Turn them home. Or we *will* bring power to bear you cannot imagine."

Santiago didn't look at the others, which told Khalila how confident he was of the consolidation of opinion. "You're choosing a war that will cost us all dearly, Archivist. Better to make a peace you don't like than see your city burn."

"The moment the Great Library relies on foreign armies to defend it is the day it dies. I do not intend to serve as the last Archivist of this great city."

He held the stare of the Archivist and then slowly inclined his head. "Then let it be so," he said. "We will withdraw. The next time we speak, I hope that it will be to discuss peace."

"I hope that you survive to discuss it at all," she said. "Go. The High Garda will see you back to your ships."

It seemed too fast to Khalila; surely war could not be declared so quickly, with so few words. But the Ambassadors bowed, and then they were leaving, and she advanced to the foot of the throne to look up at the Archivist.

"May the ancient gods help us today," Murasaki said. "All of us." She caught herself and looked at Khalila. "Scholar Seif, I need you to find Scholar Thomas Schreiber and tell him to set things in motion. Immediately."

"At once, Archivist."

Finding Thomas proved complicated; she traced him to the Iron Tower, then to the Lighthouse, but he wasn't there, either. She continued to send him messages on the Codex but got nothing back, and she knew that time was running out. Out of sheer desperation, she finally went out to the terrace on the twelfth floor of the Lighthouse and looked out, as if she could possibly pick him out at this distance.

And impossible as it was, she did. That golden shock of hair, the way he stood a head taller than anyone else out on the street . . . it *had* to be him. She marked which direction he was going and ran down the stairs as fast as she dared, then held up her skirts to race around the point and to the harbor road where she'd seen him. By the time she arrived where she'd spotted him, she was panting and sweating in the storm-heavy air, and as she paused to take stock she felt another surge of despair. No sign of Thomas anywhere.

And the streets were awash with people staring out into the bay. Khalila realized that the last of the merchants who'd been waiting had pulled anchor and was sailing away; it was a mass exodus, leaving the docks ominously empty. More than thirty ships all heading away from trouble, as fast as possible.

The crowd thinned as people drifted away. Khalila shook herself and remembered her business.

A sailor in a Phrygian cap sat on the stoop of a closed business, whittling, and she went to him and tried to regain her calm. He squinted up at her. "Scholar," he said. "What do you want with the likes of me?"

"Have you seen a very tall young man pass this way? Blond hair?"

"The giant? Yes." He pointed down the road. It curved out of sight. "He seemed to be heading somewhere important. You might have to run to catch him."

"Thank you," she said, and bowed a little. He touched his cap with a grin. He was whittling a clever little sculpture of a dolphin jumping from a wave, she realized. Odd, she'd thought him a drunk who was just wasting time, but here he was, creating beauty. People were so unpredictably wonderful. "I like the dolphin!" She shouted that over her shoulder as she ran for the curve in the road, and heard him laugh, and then it was just the damp sea wind on her face and the feel of her feet on the cobblestones. She jumped a puddle and kept running, and finally spotted a blond shock of hair in the distance. *He's so fast!* Her lungs were burning, her legs trembling, and she thought with chagrin that she'd allowed herself to get soft. A turn or two around the High Garda training track wouldn't go amiss.

Finally, she was close enough to shout for Thomas to stop . . . but she couldn't gather enough breath to do it. She skidded to a halt, gasping and nearly sick to her stomach, and picked up a loose rock from the gutter. She threw it, half expecting to miss him, but it landed squarely in the center of his back. Not hard, of course, she had no real strength left, but it brought him to a stop, and he turned to look for who'd thrown it.

She waved, then braced herself with her hands on her thighs as she tried to slow her breathing. Thomas strode back to her. "Khalila? Are you all right?"

"Chased you," she gasped out. "Sorry. Catching my breath."

"Yes, so I see. Do you need to sit?"

She managed to shake her head and pull herself upright again. "We're out of time," she said, and managed to keep her voice more or less steady this time. "War's about to be declared, if it hasn't been already. Those enemy ships out there will be trying to enter the harbor any minute now, and we need to stop them. Can you do it?"

Thomas considered that, and his face settled into an expression she was all too familiar with: determination. "Yes," he said. "I can do it. But not alone. I need Morgan to bind me to an automaton as we agreed."

"I don't know where Morgan is!" Khalila said. "Is she at the Iron Tower?"

"I don't know. She was summoned away by Scholar Wolfe. You'd better send a message to him. He'll tell us where she is."

Khalila had already taken out her Codex. She unsnapped the attached stylus and wrote as quickly as she could, underlining the urgency. It would appear in Wolfe's Codex within seconds, and hopefully he would not ignore it. "Why didn't you answer *my* messages?" she asked Thomas as she closed the book and put it back in the case on her hip.

"What messages?" He looked startled, then chagrined, and clapped a hand to the pocket of his brown coat. Unlike her, he wasn't prone to wearing his Scholar's robes, though he was fully entitled to them; he simply found them annoying. His plain worker's clothing was better suited, she supposed, to the physical work he often did at forges and worktables. "I left it behind in the Iron Tower. I'm sorry, Khalila. That was careless."

Before she could ask him what he'd been doing in the Iron Tower, her Codex shivered to alert her to a reply, and she opened it to see Scholar Wolfe's neat, precise calligraphy. "She's not there," she said. "She left an hour ago, and he doesn't know where she's gone . . ." Her voice faded, because Thomas was looking beyond her with a warm smile. "She's behind me, isn't she?"

"Yes," Morgan said, and when Khalila turned she saw the young woman walking toward them. She was dressed in a plain outfit, like Thomas; she'd put away the Obscurist's robes, and now that she'd gotten rid of the collar that Obscurists had previously had to wear, there was no sign of her affiliation at all. *That's something for us to consider,* she thought. Obscurists needed to be offered the same structure as all others inside the Great Library: the choice to join for a contracted period of time as a copper or silver band, or to join for a lifetime as a gold band. Each came with benefits, of course. But Obscurists had been virtual hostages within that tower for so long that no one had even thought what would happen when they were free to come and go as they liked.

Khalila hugged her. It was impulsive, but it felt right. There was a sadness in Morgan's eyes, and in the shaking breath she took. "Are you all right?" Khalila asked quietly.

"Yes. I'm fine. Glain was badly injured by a sniper. Scholar Wolfe summoned me to care for her."

"How is Glain?" Thomas asked it before Khalila could, with a sharp edge to his voice, and moved to stand closer.

"Recovering," Morgan replied. "But it makes this thing we're about to do . . . harder. And possibly more dangerous for you. You understand this?"

"Yes," he said, and shrugged. "Dangerous *not* to do it. The navies outside of the harbor are determined to sail in."

"Then we have to raise the defenses."

"Now," he agreed. "Immediately. There is no time to prepare. Can you do it?"

"I have to get the Anubis statue here first to inspect the mechanism—"

"*There is no time.* We must trust the mechanism will work." He pointed at the harbor. At the rippling water. "You can bind me directly to it, can't you?"

"Thomas. *No.* And we don't even know if it's in working order after all this time! If I bind you to that and it *doesn't* work . . . I'm not certain I can sever that connection so easily. You could experience . . . terrible things. I don't know how this will affect you; it hasn't even been attempted since the time of Heron, as far as I know."

"Heron built these defenses," Thomas said. "If he managed it, then it can be done. Shall we proceed?"

"Give me a moment." Morgan looked worried, and Khalila didn't like it. At all. She started to say so, but Thomas looked at her and shook his head.

"No, Khalila, you won't talk me out of this, as eloquent as you are. Save your energy."

"What about the Lighthouse? I thought you'd want to be there," Khalila said. "You were installing the Ray of Apollo, weren't you?"

"The Artifex Magnus fully understands the mechanism. There's no need for me to meddle in her efforts. If you could send her word that we are about to attempt to raise the harbor defenses . . . ?"

"Yes. Of course." She didn't know exactly what Morgan and Thomas were planning, but to her it sounded ominously risky. *So, exactly what we usually do,* she told herself, and felt a little better for it. They'd been in many dire situations and come through. Surely this would be another exciting story to tell their friends afterward.

Surely.

But if Glain had been so badly wounded, Morgan must have worked a miracle to save her. A very dangerous and difficult miracle. Did she have enough left to do . . . this?

"I have a question," Khalila said. Both of them looked to her now. "Whatever it is you are attempting to do . . . Morgan, if you fail or collapse, does that sever the link between Thomas and these defenses?"

"I think so."

"But . . . you're not sure?"

"What we're doing hasn't been attempted in thousands of years," Morgan said. "It may not work at all. It may work for a moment. Or it may work *too* well. I just don't know until we do it."

"Thomas? Are you certain you want to—"

"Yes," he said. "We must. Right now."

They walked to the end of the docks. The harbor itself was starting to come to life, with workers arriving at stores and restaurants, bars and brothels. A city carrying on, despite the threats. As people did. *And now it's our responsibility to make them safe in doing so.* Now, as never before, that struck Khalila hard. Power was a nebulous, light thing until it lay heavy in the hand. Once it did, only the weak and corrupt found it easy to wield.

She turned to Thomas, hugged him impulsively, and said, "*In bocca al lupo*, Thomas." The mouth of the wolf. Always.

"*Crepi il lupo*," he replied. He would, as always, face the wolf and defeat it. It was the call and response for the miracle and terror of the Translation Chamber, but it worked equally well here. He was going into danger, and going alone.

She couldn't help him.

The preparations seemed simple enough. They all three sat down on the edge of the dock, feet dangling several feet above the water that lapped at the pier's concrete supports, and Morgan took several deep, slow breaths. Then she held up both hands palms up. For the first time, Khalila noticed her friend was wearing a ring, a large amber one inset with the seal of the Great Library. A flawed amber, with a spot of something dark inside. And was it moving? No. A trick of her eyes, or the light.

But Morgan wasn't much prone to jewelry, and the sight of that ring unsettled Khalila for reasons she couldn't begin to name.

"What do I do if you appear in distress?" Khalila asked. She meant it for Thomas, but it applied equally to Morgan. The two of them exchanged glances, and then Morgan shrugged.

"Leave it," Thomas said. "We won't get a second chance. The Great Library needs this to work."

Morgan disagreed, though only slightly. "Wait for half an hour," she said. "If by that time nothing has happened, then we've failed. Try to bring us out of it."

"How?"

"A sudden shock should do. Cold water, for instance." Morgan looked down at the lapping ocean water. "It should break my concentration and sever Thomas's link."

"I'm not pushing you into the sea!"

"Well, it would probably work."

"Do you even know how to swim?"

"Of course," Morgan said. Thomas, tellingly, said nothing.

Half an hour. Khalila didn't like the idea of that, not at all, but she had no better suggestion. She didn't dare sabotage this effort, not if it was as all-important as both her friends seemed to think.

She'd just have to use her best judgment. Power in her hand, again. Heavy and fearful.

She realized with a start that noon had struck, and as Morgan reached for Thomas's hand, and both bowed their heads, she got to her feet and moved back. Facing east put her at an angle to them, but she could see them well enough; she had a little flask of clean water that she habitually carried with her, and now she performed the ablutions, cleaning carefully as she did, but with no wasted motions. She could wait on her friends while conducting her *dhuhr* prayers with all the earnestness she could find; today, of all days, the prayers were vital. *Show us the straight path.* The words resonated strongly; they had never meant so much to her. Today would be the day of judgment for the Great Library. And for all of those who loved her.

As she finished, she added an extra plea to Allah for protection for her friends, and then she went to look at them anxiously. They were so very . . . *still.* Though as she watched, she saw that Thomas was moving very slightly: twitches of his big hands, his fingers, his chest moving in deep, painful heaves that were almost gasps. His face had gone quite pale and strained. Morgan, beside him, looked almost as strange.

Whatever they were doing, it was difficult. Very difficult.

And as she looked out to sea, she saw that the enemy navies were starting to move.

They were sailing for the harbor.

Khalila felt a sudden wave of dizziness and quickly grabbed for the protective rail to hold herself steady. *You should have eaten,* she chided herself, but there was no help for it now. She was tired, hungry, worried . . .

The dizziness hit again and it was worse this time; holding to the railing only helped her control her collapse to her knees. She breathed in deep, hungry gasps. There was a terrible sense of . . . injury. Almost as if she had suffered a wound and was now losing blood, though as she looked down at herself she saw no sign of such a thing.

But something was wrong. Very, very wrong.

It's Morgan, drawing power from my very essence. She knew it, *knew* it, and tried to rise. Could not find the strength, no matter how much will she put behind the effort. It felt like she was a piece of cloth being unraveled into ragged threads. Did Morgan even know what she was doing? Did she *care?*

Khalila let go of the railing, pitched forward, and managed to crawl a few feet before she lost the will to do even that. She felt loose inside, gray, exhausted. Oddly unafraid. She had done her *salat;* she had meant it. Surely Allah would be kind if this was her last day in the world.

No. I will not surrender.

She couldn't.

She wasn't sure how long it took her to move again—moments? longer?—but she began to slowly inch her way toward Morgan. *If I can only wake her, she'll realize what she is doing. How wrong it is.* It was agonizingly slow progress, but finally she could just touch the windblown fabric of Morgan's shirt. A few more inches, one strong push to plunge Morgan into the water, and this might end.

Or she might kill her friend.

Whatever Morgan was expending so much dreadful power to do, it wasn't working, and Khalila felt a tight panic spread inside as she realized that Morgan might actually kill her in this quest for—for what? She didn't even understand what they were trying to achieve.

Khalila made it to her knees, with an effort that felt like her last, and just as she did, the harbor's waters began to boil, as if they'd suddenly been heated over a huge stove. She paused, struck by the spectacle, and felt her strength ebbing more. *No. I have to stop this.*

Something told her to hang on. To wait. And she did, vision going gray, strength fading.

She saw a god rise.

The sharp golden points of its crown broke the surface first; it looked like a strange, sharp island emerging with seaweed dangling wet and green from its edges. Khalila stared as the head emerged: a massive riot of metallic bronze curls cascading down the automaton's back. It was dark from the sea, crusted with dead coral like bone jewels, and it *kept rising*, up and up and up, until it was taller than the Lighthouse. Taller than the Serapeum. It was *massive*, incomprehensibly huge, and as it turned its head toward them she felt a horrible urge to hide herself from that incandescent blue gaze. The human face seemed impossible at that scale, the prominent cheekbones and pointed jaw so perfect they blinded. Every muscle showed in definition on the automaton's neck, shoulders, arms, chest, legs. It was nude except for a rich golden loincloth, and the deep water of the harbor came only to its knees.

In one hand it held a three-pronged spear, a trident.

Poseidon had risen.

And it belonged to *them*.

Khalila felt the last of her energy sliding away. "Morgan!" Her voice was barely a thread, but she heard the desperation in it. "Morgan, *let me go!*"

She had no hope that Morgan would hear, or obey, but she felt the heaviness in her chest, the slowness of her heartbeat, and knew she was moments from death. If Morgan would not stop, she'd have to save herself.

The god strode forward, waves building before it with each step. It took it six strides to reach the wide mouth of the Alexandrian harbor, and then it reached down, bent almost double, and plunged its left hand into the water.

What it brought up was a chain. An ancient, massive chain that it held at about the height of a man above the lapping surface. Its action brought up pillars on either end where the chain was anchored, and there was a loud, audible snap as the chain pulled taut, shivering.

The harbor was closed. The chain would rip in half the hull of any ship that tried to ram it. By itself, the chain would have been enough, but now Poseidon stood with its trident raised above its shoulder, ready to bring it down on any who dared approach. Its feet were set wide, and its massive thighs blocked half the entrance. Between the god, the trident, and the chain, there was no possibility those ships would cross that boundary.

The leading ships in the fleet heeled sharply off their courses, and the entire invasion fleet began to turn like a flock of birds.

Defeated, for now. But that almost certainly wouldn't last.

Morgan broke from her trance with a cry, and Poseidon froze in place. Waiting. Khalila could only see it from the back; she didn't know if its eyes were still alight with that eerie glow she'd seen, but she hoped so. It would terrify the people on those ships even more.

Morgan fell backward into Khalila, and both of them went down. Khalila rolled weakly onto her side and just . . . *breathed*. She had never been so grateful to be alive. Her heartbeat was speeding fast, finally able to express her fear, but she treasured every panicked beat. *I'm here.*

They raised a god from the sea, and we're all still here.

Thomas hadn't quite collapsed, and he stumbled up and away from the edge of the dock before he suddenly went to his knees. He looked dazed, and altogether awestruck. He said something in German that her tired brain couldn't quite grasp for a moment, and then it came clear. *We have done it.*

They certainly had. She heard the screams and shouts and cheers from the city. She heard the alarms sounding on the ships out at sea as they rocked in violent waves propagated by Poseidon himself.

The harbor was secure.

"Thomas? Are you all right?" Khalila asked. He nodded. He still seemed lost in a dream, but he crawled over to her and put his arm around her. When Morgan groaned and stirred, he pulled her up to hold her close, too. She looked shockingly bad, worse than Thomas. Worse even than Khalila felt.

And Morgan was weeping. She curled in on Thomas, holding to him and rocking in her misery. As awful as Khalila herself felt, she could not help but feel her heart go out to the other young woman; she could not fear someone in so much pain. With much effort, she rose to her feet, walked to Morgan, and sat beside her. Put her arm around Morgan's trembling shoulders.

She and Thomas enclosed her in warmth, in love, in comfort, and Khalila thought, *This is the straight path.*

She stared out at the huge bronze automaton crafted so very long ago, and thought, *Surely they cannot fight us now.*

That was when the first volleys of Greek fire began from the Welsh ships.

EPHEMERA

Text of a late-period report by Heron of Alexandria (fragmentary) mentioning the city's defenses in a communication to Pharaoh Ptolemy Djoser VI

. . . Pharaoh's wisdom in appointing a special class of guardian soldiers for . . . Archives of the Great Library . . . nothing certain. We have ever been under threat for our . . . next we may expect invasion.

To this end, I have crafted in the metalworks an automaton the rival of any since great Talos . . . harbor. For a mighty construction such as this, partnership with . . . Pharaoh's priests and magicians . . . though I dislike . . . secret. A creature such as this could as easily be our destruction as our salvation.

. . . best hidden until it must be used. Instructions . . . Archivist's hands. There it must remain until a threat to the very . . . Library.

CHAPTER SEVEN

SANTI

It was the first quiet moment he'd had to grab a cup of hot coffee and find some solitude, and so it transpired that Santi sat on the highest steps of the Serapeum, just a few feet below the golden capstone.

He watched the foreign navies clustered there. The Portuguese had chosen the northern side, as far from the Spanish fleet as it was possible to be; the English, Welsh, and Japanese fleets made up a solid bulwark in the middle, the Japanese a calming force between the two ancient enemies. A formidable assembly, certainly. And one his troops would have to face, sooner or later, unless a miracle occurred.

My troops. He hadn't adjusted to it quite yet. He was comfortable as a captain, with knowing the names and faces and skills of every soldier in his command. But this? Lord Commander of the High Garda, responsible not just for taking orders but for giving them, not just for fighting the war, but for planning it. He did not feel ready. But he thought that every single Lord Commander in history—the good ones, at least—had felt the same on their first day.

Of course, they had not been forced to deal with the dethroning of an Archivist, a possible civil war within the Great Library, and a foreign invasion that could destroy Alexandria completely. It was rather a lot.

And he missed Wolfe's bright, sharp presence. And he couldn't allow himself that distraction. Not now. Not in this chaos.

Stay safe, my love, he thought, and he hoped Wolfe was sending the same back.

He'd just drained the last of his coffee and stood up to descend back to his strategy room when the water in the harbor began to roil and tumble, and he stopped to stare at it, barely daring to hope. From this height he couldn't make out individual people below, but he imagined that one small form, far out toward one end of the crescent-shaped harbor, had bright blond hair. *Thomas.* Was this his doing?

He watched in disbelief as the automaton rose out of the harbor, shining dully in the sun. Vast. Magnificent. *Dangerous.* How could anyone control such a thing? This was enormous. As familiar as he was with the mechanicals in all their deadly forms, this . . . this felt vastly different.

The size of it made him suck in a startled breath. He'd seen the drawings, discussed the dry, academic option of activating the city's ancient defenses, but he'd never imagined it would be like *this.* The thing—Poseidon?—stood tall, and the dizzying height of the top of the Serapeum only came even with the thing's pointed chin. It dwarfed even the most massive warships; the city, docks, and harbor looked like toys in comparison.

He watched it drag the chain up and freeze in place with its trident at the ready. No captain with any sanity would dare attempt a crossing. Not now.

And in the next instant he thought, *They don't have to.*

He dropped the cup he was holding and ran down the steps, heedless of his own safety. Every second passing was deadly. He could hear the city starting to react to the presence of the automaton guarding their city; some were shouting, many cheering. *No time, no time . . .*

He jumped the last three steps and landed running, flat out, shouting at surprised Scholars to make way. He arrived at the strategy room halfway down the pyramid and saw all his captains crowded together at the windows, looking toward the harbor.

"Shutters down!" he snapped, and pointed to the Obscurist who was standing nearby. She was a young thing, and he hoped to Heron she was competent. "Do it now! Emergency security for the Serapeum, the Iron Tower, the High Garda compound, the Lighthouse, and the Archives. Execute!"

She seemed dazed for an instant, then snapped upright and said, "Yes, Lord Commander," and stepped away. He had to trust it would be done. He had other concerns. As his captains turned toward him, the shutters began gliding down over the windows—solid metal, treated to resist Greek fire.

"Captains," he said. He sounded sharp and urgent, and in this moment he wanted that. "As planned. Tier one defenses, secure our approaches. Tier two, deploy into the streets with balm for the barrage of Greek fire we're bound to draw. They've had all the time of their crossing to map out their battle plans. Our response is in place. Stay loose, stay ready, and above all, defend our people and the Great Library from anyone, *anyone* who would threaten either one. If you need resources, all clerks are on duty to monitor the Codex for all requests; use the code previously issued. We will do all we can to support you. Expect the Obscurists to provide you with automaton support as soon as they can." He hesitated for one second, and said, "You know me, and I respect you. I trust every one of you to uphold your oaths and honor the ancestors who've guarded this city for five thousand years. Spend lives if you must. But make the enemy spend theirs *first*."

The sound of fists hitting chests made a palpable wave through the room. He saluted them back and watched his captains go. "Captain Botha," he said, and motioned his former lieutenant over on the way out. "I give my company into your care." Botha had command of his people now, and Santi was content with that. Botha nodded and allowed a thin, dangerous smile to emerge.

"Lord Commander, you've trained them well enough that no one could lead them wrong. We will prevail."

"I know."

They gripped hands for a moment, and then Botha was gone. The room was almost empty, save for the phalanx of clerks and Santi's newly minted aide, Senior Captain Nofret Alamasi. She stood calm and poised, waiting for orders. He had none to give at the moment, but he exchanged nods with her that told her to relax. She did with a visible sigh. "It begins," she said.

"Any moment now," he agreed. "May gods great and small be with us. We've word of the Russian infantry advancing fast from the north. The Saudis are standing firm in our defense, as are Turkey and India, but I don't like our odds if that fails. If Turkey or India turn to join the Russians . . ."

"I don't think that will happen," she said. "We all know without the Great Library they'd be at each other's throats. It must have taken all the diplomacy in the world to put English and Welsh ships within firing distance of each other, not to mention Spanish and Portuguese. How long do you think those truces will hold when bodies start to fall?"

"Excellent question," he said. "But unfortunately, not our greatest concern just now. I'd love to set our enemies against each other, but we have bigger problems."

She cocked her head, eyes narrowing. "Which are?"

"Something I'd rather not commit High Garda troops against. This is best done with misdirection, and I know just the person for that. Contact Dario Santiago and get him here. Quickly."

She took out her Codex and dispatched the orders. If Dario ignored the summons, he'd be met with High Garda escorts who would force the issue. The young man would come, like it or not. Almost certainly, he would not.

There was nothing about the current situation that Santi liked, either. He could at least spread the discomfort around.

The first wave of Greek fire hit only moments later. He knew it by the choking reek of the stuff that drifted in, and the alarms booming from the Lighthouse. *They'll be aiming for the Lighthouse first.* He hoped the Obscurists had enough will and power to defend their landmarks, both for the sake of history and to protect a vital strategic advantage. The Lighthouse wasn't merely offices, or the ancient beacon that had burned, in one form or another, for most of recorded history. Today, it became a weapon.

If Thomas's plans proved out.

"Updates," Santi snapped. Some of the clerks were coughing, unused to the stench of the firebombs. One stumbled to a corner and retched. "If you can't work, leave and send someone of stronger constitution. We can't afford gaps."

The clerk gulped, wiped his mouth, and nodded. He went back to his station. "Update from the Lighthouse, sir. The Artifex advises that the device installation is complete, but she can't guarantee it will work as promised."

"No time like the present to try," he said. "Alamasi? Direct them to fire it. Target close to the Spanish fleet, but don't damage any ships. Warning shot only."

"Acknowledged, sir, a warning shot," she said, even as she wrote down the instruction. "They advise two minutes to align and power the device."

He walked to the last set of windows and looked at the Obscurist. "Raise this set of shutters only. Alamasi, if I'm burned alive, then all this becomes your problem."

"Sir," she said reproachfully. "That's not the inspirational speech I need."

"I'm not in an inspirational mood."

The shutter rolled up, and he saw hell.

He'd watched the bombardment of Philadelphia under the orders of the old Archivist; he knew the devastation Greek fire could wreak, and he knew he'd hesitate to ever use it against a vulnerable target. But the Welsh—who had used it on London, heedless of civilian casualties— had no such qualms. They'd raised flags on their ships: black ones, with a red bar across them. The Welsh signal for *no quarter.*

So much for diplomacy. The Welsh, at least, intended to destroy whatever they could, reduce the Great Library to ashes if they had to. And the Spanish weren't turning on them. Weren't supporting their efforts, but certainly weren't demanding a stop.

The only saving grace was that the plans the High Garda had so carefully prepared were working. Stores of denaturing powder that could quell Greek fire were at every corner of every main road, and on many of the smaller ones, too. Special fire brigades were in place with dispensers to fire the powder over larger areas. So as many vile fireballs as streaked through the air toward the beautiful Alexandrian streets, few did more than land, spread, and be promptly smothered. Of course there was damage, unavoidably, but he saw only a few fires that were spreading, and those had plenty of attention.

So far, it was *only* Welsh ships firing ballistas. But if the other ships in that fleet joined . . . "They said two minutes," he said. "Is the Lighthouse aware of how much damage could be done by then?"

"Yes, sir. They're working."

As he watched tensely, one of the Welsh ships got the range and began to hammer at the Iron Tower. So far, it seemed unaffected. It was torture to stand here and watch the bombardment and deliver no answer. A barrage came at the Serapeum, hit the ancient stone, and slid away. The ancients had built their defenses well. *We rely on the past accomplishments far too much. Must do something about that.*

"Sir!" Alamasi's voice was vibrant with excitement. "Lighthouse signals ready!"

"Fire," he said. He hoped he sounded calmer than he felt.

A thick beam of red light cut from the top of the Pharos Lighthouse. It was as broad as a warship, as hot as the sun's fiery skin, and it sliced straight through the water in a line that only just missed the bows of several Spanish ships, including the one flying the flag of the ambassador.

Steam blew up in a blinding cloud, creating instant fog and confusion; through the mist, Santi saw one of the ballistas go wrong on the deck of a Welsh ship, and Greek fire exploded and spread. They'd have precautions, but the heavy, sudden fog did them no favors in organization. Ships drifted too close together. The crews were disoriented in the reduced vision. And the unholy green glow of the spilled Greek fire burned like angry spirits, creating a hellish vision of chaos.

The red beam cut out. Santi watched for a few seconds, and then said, "Senior Captain, please send a message to the Spanish ambassador. Tell him that the Welsh are to cease their bombardment immediately, or the next thing that the Lighthouse burns will not be seawater."

"Yes, sir." He heard the fast scratch of her stylus. Alamasi had a rare gift for quick communication matched with perfect script; he couldn't have done it himself. His scrawl would have been incomprehensible to the Spanish under this type of pressure. Much depended on precision.

The silence within the room felt heavy, overlaid by the distant screams and cries from the city below.

There were two more bombs fired toward the city, and then the bombardment stopped. The fleet sat quiet in the drifting fog.

And Alamasi said, "The Spanish ambassador writes as follows: *Our Welsh allies acted with reckless haste and have been reprimanded. We are willing to signal a truce and assist with the injured within the city.*"

"Thank him for his gracious offer," he said. "Should the fleet wish to remain against the orders of the Archivist and threaten our borders, we will respond with all weapons at our disposal to any hostile intention."

She was transcribing as he said it, and he felt a moment's light-headed weakness. *I'm no diplomat.* But in this moment, he did as he had to do, and he knew that was what the Archivist expected. Whatever mistakes he made would be discussed later, but for now, he knew weakness could only bring the wolves.

And the wolves would rip the Great Library apart.

Alamasi's pen stopped, and he waited. Long moments. The city's alarms still droned, warning the citizens to shelter, but now they fell silent, too. He saw flutters of bronze wings in the skies; the Obscurists had set the sphinxes in flight to circle above the city, ready to strike enemies with all the terror an automaton could bring. The lions were moving through the streets with the High Garda companies. Spartans and automaton gods would be stepping off their pedestals to patrol.

No one had ever succeeded in breaching Alexandria's defenses. And he would not have it happen under his command.

"Message to the Obscurist Magnus," he said. "Ask him how the Obscurists are holding up. We need those automata working."

After another moment, she said, "He reports that the workload is heavy, but they are managing. He recommends keeping a dozen sphinxes in the air for early detection of any threats. Save the dragon for emergencies."

"Good," Santi said. "Anything from the Spanish ambassador yet?"

She sounded regretful. "No, Lord Commander. But I do have a report that Dario Santiago has been found and is being escorted here."

That implied rather strongly that Dario hadn't come by his own will. Typical. Santi quite liked the arrogant little ass, but he knew how much Dario detested being told what to do. *Royals.* "Any updates from Scholar Wolfe?"

"I regret not, sir."

Santi clasped his hands behind his back in favor of balling them into fists.

Stay alive, Christopher.

And find that damned old man before he causes chaos on top of chaos. We can't afford to fight on two fronts.

Dario arrived under armed escort, and despite their professional behavior Santi could see it hadn't been an easy trip. The young nobleman was dressed in wine-red velvet, expensive and well made, though he probably considered his outfit quite plain. Not a jewel to be seen. Not even lace on his sleeves.

What he *did* have, which the High Garda soldier leading the escort deprived him of and handed to Santi directly, was a dagger. It was indeed jeweled, and it had a beautiful Latin inscription on the blade. *"Ego bibo alte,"* Santi read. "I drink deep."

"It works both for the blade and for me," Dario said. "May I have that back? It was expensive."

"In a while," Santi said, and put it aside on the table. "Come to the window."

Dario weighed his choices and wisely decided not to make it a fight; he came to the window, crossed his arms, and said, "What do you want, Lord Commander? I might be royal, but kidnapping me won't get you anywhere. The king of Spain has a lot of cousins."

Santi cast him a look that clearly told him not to push his luck. "Where is your loyalty?"

"Excuse me?"

"You wear the gold band of a lifetime Scholar," Santi said. "You've put it back on, I see that. But you've abandoned your robe."

"Not every Scholar wears one."

"Today they do," he said, "unless they have a compelling reason."

"Is this what you had me dragged here for? To critique my wardrobe?" Dario flicked an imaginary speck of dust from his jacket. But he was wary. Listening. Just putting up his usual rank of glittering defenses.

"I'm asking you where you stand," Santi said. "With the Great Library, or with your homeland and relatives. It matters very much at this moment."

Dario's face smoothed out into a blank mask. "Sir," he said, "I'm offended you should even have to ask—"

"Don't." Santi's calm, heavy tone put a stop to the foolishness. Dario rocked back and forth on his heels a moment before he answered.

"It's difficult," he admitted then, and Santi heard the ring of truth this time. "I love Spain. I love my cousins. And I hope they have the purest of motives—"

"They just *bombarded our city*."

"The Welsh did that!"

"Without the Spanish ambassador's complicity? Really? You're smarter than that, Dario. He used them to see what we'd do in response. Now he knows."

"He is an extraordinarily good chess player. But so are you, Cap—" Dario broke off and shook his head. "It's hard to break the habit of calling you captain."

"Imagine how it feels for me," Santi said. "I'm doing my best to protect and preserve this city, but my true and only duty is to protect and preserve the Great Library. I need help to do that."

"From me?"

"Yes. From you. If you're willing. And if you're loyal."

"I am," Dario said, and heaved a sigh as he looked up at the ceiling in frustration. "Dear God in heaven, I am loyal to this glamorous, miserable place, and I never thought I'd say that. I never expected it to force me to stand against my own, but here we are. It doesn't mean I have to be happy about it."

"Your happiness isn't required," Santi said. "I need something that comes to you as naturally as breathing."

Dario's dark eyebrows went up. It gave him a piratical look. "Which is?"

"Betrayal."

Santi didn't miss the fury that ignited in the young man's eyes, or the hand that went automatically to his side; if he'd had the fancy blade there, he'd have drawn it. Which was why it now lay on the table behind Santi. But Dario checked himself and said, "Be careful how you say that, High Commander. I'm loyal. Not a lapdog. What do you want?"

"I want you to tell your cousin that you need to borrow his spies."

The Archivist summoned Santi for a personal report after Dario was dispatched on his way, and she'd put aside her formal robes and headdress for a simple, clean kimono of pale green with pastel flowers. Murasaki looked calm and ordered, and she was gracious enough to allow him to sit as their tea was poured. It was a tea almost the shade of her gown, and though he wasn't prone much to tea, it drove his weariness away again. For a while.

"The reports tell me your preparations were effective," she said. "The damage to our heritage buildings is minor, and even in the unprotected streets your firefighting teams minimized the losses."

"Ten dead," he said. "Two of them librarians. Twenty-one injured seriously enough to summon Medica. I don't consider that minimized, Archivist."

"We're at war, in all but name. You must adjust your expectations. As must I. I have lived much of my life in Spain; I have served at the three largest Serapeums there, and I have a great love for the country and people. And my own home country has taken arms against us. It leaves me in a difficult position, but I will do what I must. As will you. Whatever the cost in lives and property, we have a greater responsibility—to knowledge. To the world."

He bowed his head. "Yes. I know that." He wanted to tell her about Dario's mission, but he didn't dare, not here. There were staff members around, and worst of all, Khalila Seif, who would not take this well at all. "I have a question, Archivist, if you would allow."

"Ask."

"Will you place this war completely in my hands? Trust me to follow a strategy, even if it seems wrong to you?"

"That is your position, High Commander. I would only overrule you if I saw imminent disaster."

"I need you to promise me: don't do it even then. We'll need our nerves steady, both of us, to do what I plan."

"And I suppose you will not tell me what it is?"

"I can't," he confessed. "Not because I don't trust you, Archivist. But because I am risking the life of someone who also trusts me. But I will tell you, I promise. When it's time."

Her gaze was cool, heavy, and assessing; she reminded him of Christopher in that moment. No fools suffered in this room. "Very well," Murasaki said. "But you know the consequences if this goes badly."

He toasted her with his cup of tea. "Are you telling me to return with my shield or upon it?"

"Thirty-six plans of how to win the battle are not as good as one plan to withdraw from it," she retorted. An old Japanese proverb. "But I will trust you. And you must trust me. Or we both lose."

He touched his fist to his chest—not quite a salute, but a suggestion of one, and she accepted it with a nod.

He had his approvals.

After thanking her for the refreshment, he rose to leave. The Archivist stopped him. "Distasteful as this is, we must discuss one of our own. My understanding is that Jess Brightwell is involved with the young woman who has inherited Red Ibrahim's shadow empire. True?"

"He knows her," Santi said. He didn't tell her that he did as well, if only slightly. It didn't seem a proper thing for a High Garda commander to admit.

"And Brightwell's father controls much of the illegal book trade of England and Europe?"

"Yes."

"Yet this boy was accepted to the High Garda? And we wholly trust him?"

"Jess is not his father," Santi said. "And his brother died fighting with us."

"But for what reason? I doubt his altruism." The Archivist had a very traditional view of book smugglers, and he couldn't blame her; he'd had the same opinions until Jess had introduced him to some of the players. Though he'd cheerfully knock Callum Brightwell flat any day of the week. As if she'd just read his mind, the Archivist continued. "His father has sent several messages demanding we hold an immediate funeral for his son, and that he and his wife attend. I am reluctant to admit him to our city, especially in this time of uncertainty. Or, frankly, at all. Your opinion, knowing all of these people better, would be welcome."

Funerals. Santi hadn't thought about them, hadn't even considered the need for them yet. But of course funerals would need to be held, particularly for those whose religions required immediate burial or cremation. He wasn't sure what religion the elder Brightwell followed. Or Brendan, for that matter. The Great Library always honored the traditions whenever possible. "And when is his funeral to be held?"

"I haven't yet decided," she admitted. "I would prefer to return him to his father in England for whatever rites are required, but . . . I think his brother should also have a choice in this."

"Brendan died for us, and his brother," Santi said. "I agree that having Callum Brightwell here is an invitation to chaos, but I will say this for him: he saved our lives during the Welsh conflict in London. And gave us shelter when we were on the run from the Archivist."

"And sold you out there, as well. Landed you in Philadelphia, at the mercy of the Burners."

"He had very little choice," Santi said. "But yes. Brightwell also connived with your predecessor because he realized an opportunity presented itself. He'd certainly be interested in profits, if there's some arrangement the Great Library finds beneficial. Times are changing, Archivist. There might be accommodations to be made."

"With *book smugglers*?" She sounded not so much horrified as disgusted.

"I know it goes against the grain," he admitted. "But consult with Thomas Schreiber. I believe he has an invention that will be vital to this discussion."

"The young man who just raised Poseidon in the harbor?" She nodded thoughtfully. "I will. Thank you, Lord Commander. I know you have a—I do not want to call it a war, but perhaps a campaign—to conduct."

He bowed. "My thanks for the gift of your trust, Archivist."

She nodded, and he left. Tom Rolleson was waiting for him in the hall; his younger aide seemed as if he'd aged years in the last few days. He was reading his Codex, and kept reading as he fell in step. "Sir," he said. "The fleet has moved back. They haven't departed completely, but they're putting some water between us."

"More likely, between that deadly cannon of Thomas's and their highly vulnerable ships," Santi said. "The Spanish ambassador's no fool. He saw Thomas make one of those weapons, and he'll know what they're capable of doing. But he's not one to give up, either. I imagine he'll test it periodically and see how long it can keep up its beam. How long can it, by the way?"

"No more than thirty-six seconds, sir. Then it needs to recharge for at least a few minutes."

"And they will quickly discover that. I need to talk to the Artifex Magnus and see what can be done."

Rolleson glanced up. "I'll arrange it, sir. What else?"

"There will be spies inside the city, likely part of the Spanish ambassador's ring that existed long before this."

"I'm told the Obscurists are looking for any suspicious writings in either Codex messages or private journals." Rolleson nearly missed a step. "Wait . . . how can they possibly read a private journal?" Santi recognized the scandalized worry in that question. He'd felt it himself when he'd first realized that personal journals weren't just for their intended purpose of adding to the history of the Great Library, but for surveillance by increasingly anxious Archivists. By slow, seemingly logical steps, they'd gone from pure motives to bitterly authoritarian outcomes.

"Let's just say that you probably shouldn't put anything in your journal you wouldn't want the Archivist to read over tea."

"Oh. But I thought . . . I thought they were to be locked until after our deaths." That wasn't scandalized; that was purely horrified. "Too late to burn it, I suppose?"

"Far too late," Santi said. "I've been making mine incredibly boring for many, many years. You might want to do the same."

"Yes, sir." Rolleson gulped and tried to regain his composure. "Sorry, sir, you were saying?"

"Orders. Post Captain Botha's company at the Lighthouse. I want his best defending the Ray of Apollo, but soldiers at all strategic levels and approaches, from the ground up. Some uniformed, some plainclothes. Spies will almost certainly come as Scholars. Check every band. Ask the Obscurist Magnus to divert two sphinxes to guard the door access to the Ray, and make damn sure we don't rely on them completely. Tell Botha to try not to kill any spies they find; I'd like them as trading chips."

"Yes, sir. What else?"

"Send a message to Scholar Wolfe. Ask if he has any word on the old Archivist. I need to know where the old man is and what he's doing."

And tell him to be careful, he thought, but didn't say. Sentiment would make Rolleson uncomfortable. And Wolfe wouldn't welcome his mothering right now.

But as they passed a statue of Isis, Santi sent up a silent prayer for his lover's safety, anyway. He wasn't a believer in the old Egyptian gods; he remained a staunch Catholic. But that really didn't matter so much at the moment; Isis was one of Wolfe's gods.

Surely, she'd look after him.

EPHEMERA

Excerpt from the text "Of the Imperishable" by
Archivist Gargi Vachaknavi

The ancient scholars, honored though they must be for their accomplishments, should not be deified with the belief that they were all knowing.
As wise a person as the great Greek physician Galen subscribed to the
notion that a woman's womb was not a natural organ, but instead a
living thing within the body that wandered from point to point. Aristotle mistakenly believed in many things, not the least of which are that
a vacuum cannot exist and that memory exists in a fluid. So we must
acknowledge that knowledge is ever expanding, ever changing, and so
we must also change with it.

This is my theory of the Imperishable, which the Greeks also named
apeiron: a force that is potential in all things, that exists and does not,
that underlies even the quintessence of force that makes up the basis of
all matter. The Imperishable exists beyond our understanding, and always shall; it transmutes the impossible to the possible, and we can witness the results but only rarely influence them.

Today, touching the Imperishable is impossible without losing one's
life in the process. But one day, a person will exist upon this earth who
can manipulate the Imperishable, the apeiron, and will redefine the
rules by which our very existence continues. On that day, that person
may no longer be a person at all, though we may continue to regard
them as such. And that is a troubling and difficult thing, that any
should be so close to godhood, and yet possess all the ignorance and base
impulses of our flesh.

I wonder if even the Imperishable could end.

CHAPTER EIGHT

JESS

Jess needed to sleep, but he lay awake, thinking about leaving Morgan behind him, thinking about the soft intake of breath she'd made. He'd almost turned around. Almost. But he knew there was no going back to where they'd once been.

She's better off without me.

One more lifeline, cut.

You're being morbid again, Brendan whispered to him. *I'm dead. You're only dying. Try to have a little fun.*

Shut up, Scraps, he thought, but his heart wasn't in it. He closed his eyes and tried to breathe, but his lungs felt stuffed with feathers again, and trying made him cough. He sat up and used the mask again; the Medica was right: the more he used it, the less effect it had.

But he couldn't rest.

He got up, showered, dressed, paced. Played dice with some of Anit's men and lost consistently; he suspected they'd broken out the loaded set to clean him out of his pocket money, but he didn't really care. It was something to do.

At sunrise, he checked on Scholar Wolfe, who—predictably enough—was arguing.

With Glain.

"No," he was saying when Jess walked in. "You are not going with us. You are staying here to recover, and that, soldier, is an order. If you want me to message Santi and waste his valuable time in confirming that—"

"Don't bother the Lord Commander," Glain said. "But I refuse to just lie about like some broken toy. I'm fine!"

She was, in fact, standing. And dressed in her uniform. She—or Anit's people—had washed the blood from it, and the bullet holes in it were almost unnoticeable. Almost. "You were inches from death yesterday," Jess said. "Just this once, why don't you admit it?"

"Why don't you?" She glared at him. "You've looked like something grave robbers dug up since you breathed in that gas. Why don't *you* rest?"

"I'm better today," he lied. "And the Medica cleared me." Only barely true. He hoped Wolfe hadn't checked. But Wolfe said nothing. He was studying Glain with those bitter dark eyes, looking for weakness. And even Jess had to admit that he didn't see much in her. Not yet.

"You can't leave me here in a nest of thieves!" she said. "No offense meant. Some of my best friends are thieves now."

He gave her a sharp-edged grin. "Too little, too late," he said. And realized that he was still taking on the mannerisms of his brother. He'd been doing it for survival here in Alexandria for long enough that it had become second nature. And, in truth, it felt . . . right. Maybe being a little bit Brendan would balance the darker shadows in his soul. "We should have gone last night, Scholar."

"No one was in shape to do that," Wolfe said. "And Anit needed time to gather her people. Today will do."

"We're targets, traveling in a group."

"We won't be seen."

Some Obscurists, Jess knew, could hide themselves from notice. It wasn't quite invisibility; it was misdirection. Morgan could. But hiding even one other person was a strain. Hiding groups? Even if Anit had the rare treasure of a rogue Obscurist, or an undiscovered one, he doubted Wolfe's assurance.

And then he didn't. "She's got tunnels," he said. "Yes, of course she does. I should have realized."

"They're extensive," Wolfe said. "I've gone over the maps. They'll take us all the way to the entrance to the Necropolis. They're normally guarded by sphinxes where they come out. I've put in a request for them to be coded to ignore us, but the Obscurists are obviously busy. Pity Morgan had to leave so soon."

"She was needed," Jess said. "Harbor defenses."

"Ah. Of course. I hope . . ." Wolfe stopped talking, which was unusual enough to make both Jess and Glain turn to look at him.

"Hope what?" Jess asked.

"Hope it goes well," Wolfe finished. And Jess knew that wasn't what he'd originally intended to say at all. "Glain. I'm not arguing with you. If you want to come, fine. But if you fall behind, we leave you." He turned a glare on Jess. "Same for you."

"Understood, sir," Jess and Glain said in crisp unison. Unintentionally.

"Get your kit together," Wolfe said. "Five minutes. Meet me in the atrium."

He left without waiting for a reply. The two of them looked at each other. Glain sat down on her bed. "You should move," she told him. "When he says five minutes, he means two."

"I know. I have everything," he said. He hesitated over what to say, and finally decided.

"I thought we'd lost you, Glain. I can't afford that. So if you're not up to this, don't risk it. All right?"

"You're worse than my brothers," she said.

"I'll take it as a compliment. I need more siblings."

She sent him a slightly horrified look. "I'm sorry. I didn't mean—"

"I know," he said. "It still hurts, and I'll still flinch when anything brushes that wound. If you want me to feel better, don't die on me, Glain."

"I promise," she said. "Let's make it a pact. I can't afford fewer friends, either. Hardly anyone likes me as it is."

"You'd be surprised."

"Don't get soppy, Brightwell." She held on to his hand, though, and met his eyes squarely. "Are you all right? Truly?"

He took his life in his hands and kissed her swiftly on the forehead; her reactions were slower than usual, and he got away with it. Barely. "Don't be late," he said, and escaped.

Wolfe was, of course, already in the atrium. He was huddled with a scarred older man talking in hushed tones. Before Jess reached them, the other man scuttled off, and Jess watched his departure, frowning. "Who's that?"

"Street beggar," Wolfe said. "Anit's put out word among the less legal Alexandria residents, and they've reported a number of sightings, not of the Archivist, but of some of his most trusted High Garda. And Zara Cole. Look."

He unrolled a map onto the table nearby, and Jess saw that he'd already inked in some colored dots. "What's the code?"

"Red for unconfirmed sightings of members of either High Garda Elite or individual Curia members. Blue for confirmed sightings."

"And black?"

Wolfe put his finger on the single black spot. "Zara. You notice anything about the pattern?"

The blue and red covered much of the city. Randomly distributed. He tried to make sense of it and failed. "I don't see it."

"Look at the one quarter of the city where they were *not* spotted.

Because I think he arranged for these sightings quite deliberately to confuse what he was planning."

It came into focus as soon as the Scholar said it: there was a single neighborhood of the city where absolutely no sightings had been registered. Jess studied it, but failed to remember anything remarkable about it. "What's there?"

"Dyers and papermakers, butchers and tanners," Wolfe said. He moved his finger to a particular anonymous street. "And the highly classified and secret High Garda workshop for producing and storing Greek fire."

Jess felt that go through him like an icy stab. "How much?"

"How much do you think the High Garda holds in reserve?"

Jess didn't really want to think. "But it's guarded."

"Of course. And Santi would have tripled whatever the normal complement would be. The Archivist in Exile will want to burn this city if he can't own it. That's the kind of man he is. Better the emperor of ashes than of nothing."

"You've warned Santi?"

"He's aware," Wolfe said.

"Shouldn't we—"

"No. Let Santi handle defenses. We must hunt the Archivist in his den, at the Necropolis."

They were lucky the old man hadn't managed to recruit any Obscurists to his cause, Jess supposed. If he had, the odds would have been thoroughly terrible instead of just overwhelming. Bad enough they were facing, by his count, at least thirty High Garda Elite—fewer, if some had since defected, which Jess profoundly hoped—who were all heavily armed and trained to be deadly to anyone, even to their own fellow soldiers.

He knew the old ex-Archivist wouldn't hesitate to kill, and order others to do it for him. His rule of the Great Library had been a long, bloody, brutal one. And even the cruelest dictators had allies . . . and could buy or compel more. Jess didn't doubt the old man had plenty of wealth he'd siphoned out of the Great Library's coffers. Money enough to buy his escape and permanent safety if they didn't find him, and soon.

"You're *not* wearing that Scholar's robe," Jess said. Wolfe allowed the map to roll up again and put it in a pocket inside the jacket he wore beneath the robe. Then he removed the robe, folded the thin silk up with practiced, expert motions, and slipped it into a small pouch that went in another pocket.

"I'll wear it once we have him," he said. "I want him to see the silk on my back, despite everything he's tried to do to rip it away."

And then the old man dies. For killing his innocent assistant, Neksa, if nothing else; the Archivist needed to know when the Brightwells held a grudge, they nursed it like a treasured child. He wanted that so much he was willing to die for it. Reckless, like his brother. Brave, like his brother.

Dead like me, too, he heard Brendan whisper. *You can choose your own path. You always have. Don't follow me into the tomb, Jess.*

Jess had never let his brother tell him what to do.

The tunnels they took were surprisingly clean, wide, and spacious, fitted with glows that kept them well lit. He'd seen far worse.

Anit had changed into trousers and a close-fitting tunic, a style borrowed from countries farther east; her tunic was matte dark blue silk, and the trousers matched. That particular blue, Jess recalled, was considered the best for moving unnoticed in the dark. He supposed that even though dawn had broken, they'd spend most of the day in the shadows. If all went well.

"You didn't need to come with us," he told her as they walked.

"I most surely did," she said. "In case my crew decides they don't like to follow the orders of a dusty old Scholar. Why, are you worried about me?"

"I think you know how to survive," he said, and coughed. They'd been walking nearly an hour, and his lungs were struggling now, swollen and tender. He covered the cough and tried not to see Glain's gaze, which was focused on him like Thomas's light gun. "Sorry. Dust."

"We keep our tunnels quite clean," Anit said. "Do you need to rest?"

"No," Jess said. "I'm fine."

She didn't argue, but she didn't believe him, either; he could see that from the glance she sent him. "Only about another twenty minutes," she told him. "We'll come to an intersection soon, then take the branch to the left. It's not far from there to the Necropolis."

"And exactly why do you have tunnels built to the Necropolis?" Glain asked.

Anit didn't answer that question, but Jess knew well enough. The Necropolis, with its underground city of tombs, was an ideal place to hide things; few ventured there after their dead were sealed away in their miniature houses. "Red Ibrahim had a false tomb built," Jess guessed. "Valuable books?"

"Very," Anit said. "The rarest of them all."

"And . . . where will you lay him to rest? Not there, surely."

"No," she said. "Another tomb, under a different name. He left instructions."

"I don't suppose you'd let me see the cache . . . ?"

She smiled a little. "Perhaps I will," she said. "Since I know we share a love of forbidden things. But not today. Today is for more serious things."

He nodded. Another cough threatened, and he swallowed it back as best he could. He could hear himself wheezing as he breathed, and hoped it wasn't as noticeable to anyone else. He couldn't use the mask here, out in the open; it would signal to everyone—including Wolfe—that he wasn't fit to fight. *I'll manage*, he thought. He slowed his pace a little, dropping back, and found that Glain adjusted her speed to match him. She wasn't looking at him. It seemed entirely coincidental.

"You're not well enough," she said.

"Oh, and you are?" In the eerie green glow, everyone looked faintly ill, but Glain's face was shining with sweat.

"We'll look after each other, then," she said, and he nodded. Together, they might just make it through. "And Wolfe, of course."

Always.

"How many know about these tunnels?" Glain asked him. Jess shrugged.

"No idea, but Red Ibrahim would have kept this one close to his vest. His most trusted lieutenants might have known about it, but few others."

"And what odds do you give that the Archivist didn't know about it?"

"Good ones," he replied. "If he had, he'd have seized the books. And probably wiped out Red Ibrahim and everyone who knew him. Those were his standing orders."

She didn't seem convinced, but she accepted that, and as they arrived at the turn, they'd fallen to the back of the company, away from Wolfe and Anit. Anit's picked crew consisted of about twenty, ten of them women who looked just as capable and focused as Glain. Mostly Egyptians, but a few drawn from paler lands, and at least a portion of the crew hailed back to origins farther east. Even criminals in Alexandria were cosmopolitan.

When the company paused, Jess and Glain caught up and pushed through to rejoin Wolfe. He stood with Anit at what seemed to be a blank, blunt end to the tunnel, and the gloom at this end—far from the last glow—made the situation seem even worse.

Anit pressed her small hands against the stone in a special pattern with her fingers spread. There was an audible *click* that rolled through the tunnel, and then the stone began to slide away to the left. It was almost silent, but almost, Jess thought, wasn't good enough. He unslung the rifle from his back and saw that Glain had already done the same.

Without speaking or even glancing to confirm, they moved out as a team ahead of Wolfe and Anit.

The Necropolis was dark. *Very* dark. The only light came from a single spot far above at the top of the chamber—a hole that poured light down in an almost solid stream. It was meant, Jess thought, to be bounced from a mirror; he could see other mirrors set on the walls of the cave, glimmering in the dimness. But someone had moved the mirror that caught the incoming light and distributed it.

The Archivist wanted to make this difficult for anyone who might come looking.

The problem was that this was a city of the dead; it was disturbingly quiet here, only a distant whistle of wind across the hole piercing the dome above to disguise their footsteps. He tried to step carefully. It was cooler in here than he'd expected, and there was a strong reek—not of decomposition so much, but of embalming chemicals. It clawed at his lungs, and he felt a surge of panic and held his breath. He could *not* cough. Not now.

He was so intent on that, he flinched when a tap on his shoulder signaled that Wolfe had joined them. The Scholar pointed toward one structure near the far left side, and once spotted in the gloom it was impossible to miss: a not-very-miniature pyramid with a capstone covered in gold. Jess signaled to Anit, who began to direct her people. She stayed back, which he appreciated. And she had a guard who stayed by her side. He glimpsed the distinctive haircut, though it was far too dark to see the snake tattoo beneath.

Wolfe was moving forward, and for an older man he still had an athlete's light, sure grace; he used the outer structures of the Necropolis for cover. Jess and Glain flanked him, ready to fire at the first sign of trouble. *I don't know why I always think of him as a Scholar,* Jess thought. *He moves like a soldier. Always has.* He'd spent a long time away from Alexandria out in the world, doing dangerous work for the Great Library.

Jess's lungs were on fire now, and he tried to breathe in the shallowest mouthfuls of tainted air possible. It didn't help. He shook with the effort to hold in the coughs, and tasted blood again. *No. I can't afford this. Not now!*

He should have been watching his footing. His boot landed on a stone, and the scrape echoed through the chamber like a shot.

Everyone froze. The others, he thought, didn't know he'd been the one to make the sound; it ricocheted off of tombs and walls and ceiling.

He heard whispers follow it. They weren't coming from Anit's people—that was clear; they knew better. No, this came from another group.

The Archivist's High Garda Elite were here.

Jess didn't catch the first flutter of movement, but Glain did; she raised her rifle and fired, and the flash illuminated the raw gray edges of tombs. In the next instant Wolfe flung himself behind cover, and a barrage of answering shots came at them. It was impossible to know how many of them there were, with the echoes in this chamber, but it sounded like a lot. Maybe as many as Anit had brought with them. Jess didn't think he was a match for even one High Garda Elite on a good day, and this wasn't one. He doubted Anit's band of mercenaries was, either. Glain *might* be. But even Glain couldn't best a crowd of them.

His mind was racing, and he was trying to think of some way around a fair fight. *I'm a liability. I shouldn't have come.* He knew that, and was enraged about it, but it was too late. He needed to use whatever advantages he could offer to save his friends.

It was far too dark in here to see properly; there was a very real risk of shooting allies. No way to tell if the Elites were wearing anything to identify them, but he'd memorized the faces of Anit's warriors. He just needed to be able to see them.

The lights.

Jess slipped off to the right, away from the fight. Tombs clustered thickly on this side, opposite the model of the Serapeum. He took shelter behind a tomb built to look like a gracious Egyptian home, complete with a stone garden in front, and used the mask in deep, convulsive gasps until the burning in his lungs calmed. Then he crouched and began a zigzag run between the tombs and toward the light at the center of the Necropolis.

The Elites hadn't destroyed the mirror, thankfully; they'd only tilted it down toward the ground. Jess stayed concealed behind a large granite statue of Bast and looked for any traps, any guards. Saw nothing. That didn't mean they hadn't thought of this, of course, but he hoped not.

The rolling roar of shots fired made him decide not to wait. Caution would get his friends killed.

He rushed forward with absolute focus on the mirror. Imagined exactly when to drop to his knees and spin the giant metal disc up on its metal frame so it caught the sunlight, then focus that light on the next mirror. With any luck, the Elites hadn't bothered to move the rest of the array.

He had to veer aside before reaching the mirror when what he'd taken for another inert funeral statue whirred to life.

Jess threw himself aside and rolled, but there was nowhere to go; his back collided with the side of another tomb and drove a wrenching cough from him that tore something inside. He spat blood and got a clear look at the thing coming for him.

It was a nightmare.

He'd heard rumors that the High Garda Elite had ordered special automata, but everyone he'd ever talked to had dismissed them as legends. He wished that had been true, because he was facing a Minotaur.

Even if he'd been standing it would have topped him by several inches, and it was three times as broad in the chest, with shoulders that bulged with cabled muscles. A bull's head with sharp, curving horns and glaring red eyes. It carried an axe, and it moved forward on metallic human feet with hardly a sound.

Jess scrambled upright and threw himself aside just before the axe buried itself in the ground and cracked the granite of the tomb he'd been lying against. The blow would have chopped him in half if it had landed. He darted for an open path but the thing was fast, and it was relentless; he veered away from a swing of its double-headed axe.

He backed away, and it followed. It was locked on him, and if he wanted to escape, he was going to have to stop it. No chance of getting close enough to it to look for an off switch, and somehow he doubted this automaton even had one. He'd never seen one quite like it. Not even the dragon had this much raw *presence*. Not even the gods. This was built to resemble a monster, and it moved like one; the fact that its bull's face had no real expression only made it worse. Even without the axe, the sheer power of those arms could easily pull him to pieces.

He just wanted to *run*, but he knew that was useless; his lungs wouldn't take it, and this thing moved so fast he was certain it would hunt him down, no matter what he tried. He tried his rifle, but the bullets glanced off the creature's armored skin. He needed Thomas's light ray.

He didn't have it.

How is it seeing me in this darkness? Because here, near the turned-down mirror, it was very black indeed, hard to see anything in any great detail. He ought to be nearly invisible in these clothes.

Because it can see in the dark, he thought. Of course it could. That made it extra-terrifying.

But if it could see in the dark, that might mean it wouldn't be well-adapted to the light. Not concentrated light.

Jess raced for the mirror. He reached it with the Minotaur pounding in pursuit just a dozen feet behind. He flipped the mirror to catch the sun and quickly angled it to shine directly into the thing's eyes.

It stumbled and veered away.

The mirror was on a rotating stand, he realized; he followed the Minotaur, drove it into a corner between two of the tombs, where it found itself trapped, unable to escape through the narrow opening between them. He kept the light pouring onto it, pinning it in place, and stepped back while he heaved in painful breaths and analyzed the thing. Very few vulnerabilities in it. But the eyes . . . the eyes might be the key.

He raised his rifle and aimed carefully, sent up a prayer to whoever was listening that the crafters who'd created this awful thing hadn't armored the *inside* of its eyes, and fired.

He missed. The bullet hit a protruding brow ridge and ricocheted, digging a deep gouge in the marble of one of the tombs. His heart was pounding, and his lungs throbbing in time.

Slow down, he told himself. *Relax. Focus.*

He fired again. One of the glaring red eyes went out, and the Minotaur gave a horrifying roar. It staggered forward. It lifted its axe.

Jess switched his aim to its other eye as it charged for the mirror. No time to be careful. He had to be *correct.*

The shot hit the right eye, and the Minotaur kept coming, flailing, wild, blind. Jess turned the mirror on its base to protect it, and the swing of the axe missed and sank the blade deep into the stone beneath. Jess kicked and landed his foot squarely in the chest of the Minotaur; it staggered back and lost its grip on the axe.

And then it flailed blindly at the air. It couldn't see and didn't know where he was. Jess stayed still, watching; it must be listening for any clues, but the wild hammer of gunfire from the other side of the Necropolis would be overwhelming for it.

The Minotaur ran at the side of a tomb and began to batter it, cracking marble as pale as bone.

Jess couldn't kill the thing, but at least it wasn't an immediate threat. He swung the mirror around and looked for the next bronze reflector; he aimed the beam of light at it, and instantly, the entire chamber illuminated with a bright glow as the array of mirrors lit up in series. It was oddly beautiful, this city of white houses and monuments and unmoving gods.

It was also a war zone. Now that the area was lit, Jess had a clear view of where the Elites had stationed their gunners, and he made his way in that direction, coming at an angle that put him at their backs. One was fully exposed in the light now, and Jess paused and aimed, fired, and saw blood splash in a shocking spray on white marble. The High Garda Elite soldier slumped. Down, or dead, didn't matter at the moment. The Elites wouldn't be able to tell that he was behind them, with the echoes in this vast cave. It was all a rattle of noise coming from all directions.

He surveyed the landscape of close-crowded buildings and found an easy approach to one of the higher tombs; even better, the tomb had a roofline that provided good cover. He climbed onto a simple mastaba, then jumped from that to a larger tomb, then made it to the roof of the last one. The effort made his vision go soft around the edges, but he made it; he rolled behind the protection of the small ledge around the roof and steadied his rifle on it. He saw four targets, and with methodical precision he aimed and fired.

He didn't miss.

He watched from his prone, resting position as the rest unfolded. Anit's crew swarmed one of the defended positions on the ground and took possession of the weapons after the Elites fell. Jess spotted Wolfe and Glain leading another band of mercenaries forward toward the Serapeum, where the last of the resistance was located. *I should be with them,* he thought, but it felt good here. Calm and comfortable. He could do more for them here.

And as it happened, that was the right decision, because a sniper wearing the Elite uniform crawled up to the roof of a tomb that had a good vantage point against his friends. The sniper had chosen— probably accidentally—a position that was partially blocked from his view by a statue of Anubis. Jess shuffled himself over as far as he could without tipping off the roof, and got a clearer angle on the Elite soldier.

But he missed. And the sniper whirled, searched for who'd shot at him, and Jess saw him aiming back.

Better not miss a second time.

He dropped his opponent with a bullet through the chest, and only seconds later realized that he'd killed a woman. He didn't know her, but she was younger than he'd expected, and it hit unexpectedly hard. But he'd had no choice. She would have gladly put a round in Wolfe's back, or Glain's. Or in his own head.

The firing reached a fever pitch, but it was all concealed from him inside the Serapeum; he watched tensely and finally relaxed when he saw Glain come outside and raise her fist. A sign of victory. She seemed all right, and Wolfe appeared a moment later, bloodstained but upright.

Jess climbed down and began the walk toward the Serapeum. He saw the blinded Minotaur still reeling and uncontrolled in the distance; it bashed holes in everything it touched, but it was easy to avoid now. Someone would have to put it completely down later, but it wouldn't be him, thankfully

He'd done enough.

He made it to within a few feet of the Serapeum before his vision grayed out again, and as Glain came toward him he said, "I think I need to sit down."

But he was already collapsing as he said it.

EPHEMERA

Text of a Codex message manipulated from within the Iron Tower to be hidden from observation, addressed from the Archivist in Exile to Callum Brightwell

Mr. Brightwell, I deeply regret the loss of your elder son; it is a great pity that the boy sided with his misguided brother instead of obeying your instructions, and if I could have saved him, I would have done so.

I have attempted, without success, to deal with your so-called cousin, Red Ibrahim's child, to negotiate a safe exit from the city; she has refused me completely. I hope you will be more reasonable, and will find a way to either prevail upon the girl's good will, buy her cooperation, or remove her and replace her with someone more willing. My work cannot be done here in a city that is both hunting me and under attack from outside forces. I plan to raise an army of my own to retake Alexandria and bring order back to the world, but I cannot do it from within these walls.

I will spare your younger son as part of this bargain, of course. And you may have your pick of the Great Archives on the day I triumph.

Advise me of a plan and the deal will be made.

Reply from Callum Brightwell, hidden from observation

Don't bother. You've promised me enough favors and ransoms that I should own the Great Archives, and the Great Library itself, four times over. If you're still lingering in Alexandria and not dead on a gallows by the time of my son's funeral, then I may yet hold you to account and get some value out of you.

Touch my other son and die.

CHAPTER NINE

DARIO

The first thing Dario did, after being released from Santi's zealous soldiers, was go back to his room in the Lighthouse to dress. It meant passing burning buildings with crews of firefighters, wounded being treated, familiar and beloved spots damaged by bombardment. That one there: his favorite shop for little cakes. There, the café where he drank morning coffee.

It made him angry and unsettled, and being shadowed by Santi's High Garda afflicted him with a rare dose of caution. He wondered what orders Santi had issued. He trusted the captain—*no, Lord Commander*—with his life for the most part, but in these unsettled times . . . well. Everything had become chaotic. Even the normally predictable Niccolo Santi.

Coming back to his room always made Dario feel warm and safe; it had a good view of the harbor and it was spacious and had plenty of room for his work desk and clothes closet. He stopped at the desk first, sat, and wrote in his Codex. He addressed the message to his cousin Alvaro Santiago; there was no indication that it would be reviewed by sharp-eyed Obscurists and High Garda, but he was certain it would happen. So he began with an entirely heartfelt entreaty to stop the bombardment of the city, invoking family loyalty as much as he felt would be appropriate, and after that, he used a particularly ornate curl of his pen. It was the signal, in the language of Spanish spies, to switch to a clever code, one devised by a mathematician who'd refused to study at the Alexandrian university or have anything at all to do with the Great Library. He'd been a rebel, that one; his writings were interdicted and difficult to find, even with a Scholar's clearance. But generations of Spanish diplomats had used his particular code, and as far as Dario knew it had never been cracked. The virtue was that it was not the words themselves that mattered, but the height and embellishment of each letter. It demanded precision on the part of the writer, certainly, but if executed properly it could be a nearly invisible and undetectable way to convey hidden information.

So while he wrote, *My loyalty is entirely to the Great Library, as you must surely know; I have been granted a gold band and a lifetime appointment, and this must direct my actions moving forward,* he knew that what he was actually conveying was *My loyalty is to Spain, and I seek an opportunity to speak with you. Send instructions.* He used the code only sparingly, for simple things like this, and he knew his cousin was sharp enough to spot it. Whether or not Alvaro would believe it, or comply, was another matter entirely. But it was possible. At the very least, Alvaro would want to explore the idea that they had a well-placed asset within the city . . . and one with the ear of the new Archivist. *And her new assistant,* he thought, and felt a flush of shame at what he was doing. Khalila might understand; she was, like him, a child of politics. But at the same time, he was very much afraid she might not.

He knew where his duty lay, and he could not apologize for it. He, of all of them, understood the fragility of the Great Library and the might of the kingdoms that surrounded her on every side. The only thing that had protected the ancient city was the legend, the glittering façade that covered rotten timbers.

But even that had tarnished now, and the only thing that could save this place was to make accommodations. Adjust. Adapt. Make Alexandria useful to the world in ways it had never been before. The Great Library could no longer command the unquestioned obedience and awe of the world, but it *could* make itself safe. And he would see to that.

Whatever others thought of him in the end.

He bathed and ordered food from the kitchens, only to find from the harassed copper band who delivered his meal that the circumstances of the day prevented anything heated. He settled for the bread, jam, and cold-press coffee, though not with any good grace, and went to choose his clothing carefully.

Brightwell had always accused him of being a peacock, and, yes, to be sure he liked rich fabrics and fine cuts, but today of all days advertising his royalty was inadvisable. He had in his stores a plain set of clothing, purchased secondhand; it was still decent quality, and very clean, and once he'd put it on he looked no different than any other Alexandrian. When he finished, he stood before the mirror and checked himself with exacting eyes. He'd put away all his jewelry, with the exception of his family signet ring; that, he turned inward so all that showed was a plain gold band. It was vanity to wear it, but, well . . . he was vain. The shirt, vest, trousers: all correct. The boots were a bit too good, but he imagined this alternate Dario Santiago had aspirations to better things, and besides, they were comfortable. He'd be wearing them for a long time, most likely.

He added a very plain, short dagger of Alexandrian design, and no sword; the lack of it made him feel a pang for the family blade he'd damaged this morning. He didn't actually regret doing that; it had saved Jess's life. But still. A loss. If he lived through this, he'd have to see about having it repaired.

Two steps away from the mirror he recalled that he needed to change his Codex. He'd purchased a new one and had it registered to the possession of a fictitious person named Bernado Allamante, an

immigrant from Granada. It had been used, but only for entirely innocent book requests and innocuous messages. A clean tablet, so to speak.
And one that wouldn't betray his movements, should the High Garda
choose to look into it.

He put aside his fancy jeweled Codex with regret. He'd grown up
with it, and it was precious to him . . . but not as precious as his life.
With any luck, he'd come back to retrieve it. If the Lighthouse still survived.

So much uncertainty.

He put on a plain Spanish leather hat to shade his face and disguise
him from casual glances, and nodded at his reflection. He didn't look
like a nobleman anymore, but he was about to do the work of one.
Bloody, terrible, cruel work that would cost lives. But that was why
people acceded to royalty; someone had to do it. And it was cowardly
to avoid one's duty.

Deep inside, he knew he wanted to run from this. Grab Khalila and
drag her off to live a quiet, anonymous life somewhere on a remote,
peaceful farm, growing—crops of some type. He didn't know how it
worked, really, but it sounded like bliss to him at the moment. It seemed
very real to him: Khalila next to him by a warm fire, children gathered
around.

A normal life.

You and that beautiful woman will never be normal, he told himself, and
settled his hat at a cockier angle. *She'd never cooperate for a moment in a mad
plan like that. You must accept that this is your destiny. And learn to like it.*

The second part of it would be much harder than the first, but he
came from a long line of people who had all done their duty . . . plea-
surable or not. He sighed, shrugged, and checked his old Codex when
it shivered with the arrival of a message. *Finally.*

His cousin Alvaro wrote back, *Of course I understand fully that your
primary loyalty must remain with the Great Library; Spain could ask nothing
else.* The code, however, said *Iberia Warehouse, dock seven. Go now.*

Dario took a deep breath and headed for the door. He'd almost reached it when he realized that there was one thing he'd forgotten, a thing so central to his life now that it seemed like part of his skin.

He opened his desk drawer, removed his gold Scholar's band, and placed it gently inside. Let himself feel the loss of it, and all it meant to him.

You can still change your mind, something whispered. *You don't have to do this. Put it back on. Forget this idiocy.*

Impossible.

He shut and locked the drawer, hid the key in his old Codex, and turned his back on all of it.

The Lighthouse security was extreme at the moment, but it was designed to stop and search anyone entering; he'd been subjected to that indignity on the way in. Going out, both the High Garda soldiers and the automata ignored him. Not a threat if he was departing. That was good. It also meant coming home, minus his Scholar's band, which guaranteed him passage, was next to impossible.

It felt like a book closing.

He walked around the harbor's long, sleek curve. All the fires were out, though smoke still curled up from one or two distant spots. The sun was shining, the sea shimmering brightly. Clouds still massed on the horizon, but the storm wouldn't arrive for another few hours. Hopefully. The day felt unnaturally hot, and the air heavy in his lungs. As clean as Alexandria was, the docks always had a taint of rotten fish to them, and it wasn't a pleasant walk . . . but it was a lonely one. Few had dared the streets after that bombardment, and fewer were out of High Garda uniform. The Scholars were all at work, he thought; the common folk were all hiding in their houses. It made him feel exposed and itchy, and the spot where his golden band had been seemed especially irritated.

He walked faster. Like almost everyone, he imagined, he spent much of his time gaping at the wonder of the automaton of Poseidon, risen from the sea to guard the entrance; it seemed impossibly large and threatening. The chain seemed like an impenetrable barrier, too. But he knew that the fleet out there would be considering new tactics. They might be down, but not yet departed.

Dock seven was on the far side of the harbor, and it was almost wholly deserted. The Iberia Warehouse was one of the smaller buildings, a long two-story structure of freshly painted white stucco with a tiled roof, and the seal of the kingdom of Spain embedded on the side. The door was locked, of course, but he tried it anyway; he knocked. No one answered. He knocked again.

This time, the door opened, and a hand pulled him inside, into the dark. The door slammed behind him. Dario put a hand on his dagger and turned, fast, to face the person who'd drawn him inside. The windows were shuttered, but a green glow kindled and showed him a tall young man. Eyeglasses that reflected the light in an eerie shimmer. "Codex," the young man said.

"Who are you?"

"*Codex.*"

There were others in the shadows, and Dario caught the glint of steel and eyes. All right. He was outnumbered. He slid the Codex from its holder and handed it to the young man, who checked it and nodded. He handed it back. "We wanted to be certain you remembered. And your band?" Dario showed him the spot where it had been. He received another sharp nod. "Good. Well thought-out."

"And exactly who are you?" Dario asked. He was fuming at the way he'd been patronized, but also knew better than to indulge his attitude just now. He kept his tone unsharpened.

"Cesar Mondragon," he said. "But you wouldn't know me. My trade is not being known."

"Spy." That got a slow smile in reply. Nothing else. "All right, I'm here. Now what?"

"Now you'll help us put the Great Library in a position where they have to see the patently obvious: they can't survive alone."

"Which means what, precisely?"

"We intend to take the Archivist prisoner," Mondragon said. "Your access and knowledge are important to this, and your willing cooperation." He stressed *willing*. Dario nodded slightly in acknowledgment. "Thoughts?"

"It's a stupid plan," Dario said. "The Archivist has a heavy guard. So will all the targets you've likely considered: the Lighthouse, the Serapeum, the Iron Tower, the Great Archives, and the High Garda barracks. You won't succeed in any of those places. And I can't make those odds any better."

Mondragon's smile vanished. "Then what use are you to us?"

"I can tell you the single most vulnerable spot you've never heard of," Dario said. "The one few even know about. If you do it well, you can take this entire city without a fight. That's what I'd prefer. I don't want idiots like you destroying it while saving it."

"Careful, Don Santiago," Mondragon said. "You may be royal, but you're not immortal. The king didn't order me to kill you. He didn't order me not to, either."

Young as Cesar Mondragon was, he clearly knew his business; Dario had to give him that much. He said nothing to that. Just waited. And eventually, Mondragon said, "Very well. Where is this magical place only you know? What use does it have for us?"

"It's where the High Garda produces and stores Greek fire," Dario said. "In a quiet, anonymous backwater of the city. Everyone believes it's made and stored at the High Garda compound, but that would be ludicrous; you don't keep volatile, potentially disastrous equipment like that in the same spot as your main fighting force. The liquid is made at a secret plant, stored nearby, and sent in small, regular deliveries to the High Garda compound for use. It's a well-kept secret. And once you take control of it, you can dictate terms to the Archivist, the High Garda, the Obscurists . . . everyone. The city will be yours."

"And you learned of this place how?"

"I've been traveling with Captain Santi for years now," Dario said. "He's careful with his secrets, but nobody's careful enough. Not constantly. I saw it in his private journal."

"How would you come to see his private journal?"

Dario smiled slowly. "The same way you would, in my position. Borrowing it when he was asleep."

"And why would you do that?"

"Because it might be useful one day. And turns out, it is."

Mondragon didn't altogether like his answer, but there was nothing to prove or disprove about it. Dario *had* read some private journals, including Captain Santi's, when he was still a student back in Ptolemy House and trying to understand the best strategies for survival in a hostile, competitive environment. He'd been searching mainly for blackmail material that he could use on either Scholar Wolfe or Captain Santi to ensure his elevation to full Scholar status. He'd found a great deal more than he'd expected. And he'd never used any of it, or admitted that shameful tactic to anyone until this moment. He supposed it didn't reflect well on his character. Not that he cared what Mondragon, or any of them, thought about it.

"Let's say I accept your idea," Mondragon said. "What exactly are you proposing to do with that information?"

"It will be guarded; it's always guarded," Dario said. "But if we can take possession of it, the Archivist will have to grant our request to open the harbor, land our ships and troops, and allow us to secure the city."

"Why would they do that?" Mondragon asked.

"Threaten to ignite the stores. If you do, the explosion will be . . . well. Like nothing this city, or indeed the world, has ever seen." He opened both hands from fists to palms, and Mondragon got the message. Eloquently.

"Surely the High Garda have guards, and safeguards to prevent just such an explosion."

"Yes, and yes. Automata and, of course, human soldiers. Probably triple guard posted, though they ought to be tired by now. And complacent, as much as High Garda can be." He paused. "As to the safeguards . . . there are alchemically treated doors separating the warehouse itself into smaller compartments that can be contained in case of fire. But once we take the complex, we can open all the suppression doors at will."

"Triple guards."

"There might be, yes."

"I don't like *might*," Mondragon said. "And I particularly don't like automata."

"Who does?" Dario grinned. "That's the point of them. But I know how to turn them off. Well, most of them. It's not easy, or safe, but it can be done. That just leaves the human guards, and I trust you can handle that."

"Probably," Mondragon replied. He swept Dario with a look, head to toe. "You seem prepared enough for the mission."

"I'd prefer a weapon," he said.

"Then you should have brought one." Mondragon's tone reminded Dario of Scholar Wolfe's at his most irritated, but the young spy snapped fingers, and one of the men in the shadows—all men, as far as Dario could tell—stepped forward and handed Dario a gun. He raised his eyebrows and examined it closer. It wasn't High Garda issue.

"Russian?" he guessed.

"Yes," Mondragon said. "Always nice to have allies who are fine weapons manufacturers. Don't lose it. You won't get another. Now, come on, we don't have time to waste. The storm that's approaching the coast poses a real danger to our ships and crews. We need to have them safely docked before it arrives." Mondragon unrolled a map and spread it against the wall. "Show me the location."

"Here." Dario pointed to the precise spot. Mondragon studied it and let the map roll up with a snap of stiff paper.

"Very well. Then let's move out."

Dario nodded and did as he was told. That included a trip through the warehouse to a side door that opened on a blind alley; there was a dilapidated steam carrier there with a large covered box rolling behind it. Big enough, Dario realized, for all of the Spanish team, which proved to be fifteen strong, including him. All anonymous. The most recognizable thing about any of them was Mondragon's eyeglasses, and those could, in a crisis, be discarded. He had no idea if Mondragon actually needed them at all.

There were not a lot of steam carriers abroad today, but Dario supposed there must be a few; life went on, even in a city under siege. This unremarkable carriage wouldn't be noticed. He sat with the others crowded in on the floor of the bare carrier box and paid close attention as they got underway. He had his own mental map of the city streets, and as the steam carriage made the necessary turns, he knew that Mondragon had taken him at his word. They were going to the right place.

And that was dangerous, even if it was what he wanted. There was a battle ahead, and it could be a bad one.

As the carriage slowed and the rumble of the wheels subsided, Mondragon said, "Santiago, you're in charge of stopping any automata. Villareal, you're backup. If Santiago fails, you succeed. Understood?"

"Yes," the man beside Dario said. He was older, and he radiated calm competence. "Time to come clean, Scholar. What's the secret to disarming the things?"

From his accent, the man was Catalonian. Dario felt a surge of homesickness. Now that he had no guarantee of living through the day, he had a sudden fondness for Madrid. For Barcelona. For food and spices he hadn't even missed, until this moment.

He cleared his throat and said, "If they're lions or sphinxes, under the arm, here." He pressed a finger to his armpit. "Most automata built with human or animal faces will have that installed. Not all, unfortunately. So be careful. Get in close, strike that button quickly, and move. It's the only way." He felt sick saying it. He'd just lied to the man, and with a smile, too.

Villareal didn't seem reassured. "I've seen these things gut men in less than a heartbeat. *How* quickly?"

Dario shrugged. "Well, if you miss the timing, you'll know."

"You're not amusing, *Highness*."

"You remind me of a friend of mine."

"You have friends?"

"Oh, now you *really* remind me of him." He wondered where Brightwell was right now. Probably lying in a nice warm bed, if the Medica had anything to say about it. He'd be all right. Jess was a survivor. Thinking of Jess was better than considering what he'd just done. It was a contingency only. He prayed he wouldn't have to see it triggered. "Good luck, Villareal."

Villareal nodded slowly. "You, too." He reached for the doors.

"Not yet," Mondragon said. "We've got a scout looking around." He opened a small peephole in the side, then checked his Codex. Wrote some words. From what Dario could tell, Mondragon had accessed the street plan for this area. He studied it carefully. When the message came back from his spy, Mondragon read it and frowned. "The property you indicated has closed gates," he said. "And nothing moving inside, as far as my scout can tell. It seems deserted."

"Of course," Dario said. "It would. High Garda would have this spot completely locked down. Nothing coming or going. Not even more High Garda." He took out his own Codex and a stylus and wrote a message. It was an entirely innocuous message to an entirely anonymous Codex, one that had been carefully erased from the system by no less than the Obscurist Magnus himself. He was careful about the height of the letters, the extra scrolling on the ends.

He wrote, *Difficult day here in Alexandria, and a storm on the horizon. Pray for us.*

The translation of the code was, *I'm here. Ready.*

The reply was immediate, though the handwriting was far too messy to read any letter height coding. *I will.*

The signal came a moment later—not from the Codex, but in the form of a scream and distant gunfire. Dario snapped the book shut, put it in its holder, and looked at Mondragon. "We should go now."

"Once we know what's—"

"Now!" Dario barked, and shoved the doors open. He jumped out, and the rest followed. Mondragon didn't like it, he could tell, but then, Mondragon was uncommonly smart. He was probably trying to work out what was happening and how the power had just shifted.

Dario didn't give him time to think about it.

One of the Spanish spies had a spray device that directed a thin, intense stream of Greek fire onto the lock of the gate; it was a one-use device because it self-destructed as it was fired, and he dropped the empty as he kicked the iron gates open. They creaked back, and Dario heard the shouts and screams and gunfire even more clearly. The sounds came from within the main building, which was made of thick stone and had thin vents near the roofline but no obvious windows. The doors were shut, and when he tried them, they were still locked. He gestured, and the same spy who'd taken care of the gates used another of his ingenious devices on the door. The lock melted, and a boot on the doors slammed them open.

Inside was a war zone. For a moment, Dario couldn't take it in, even though he knew what to expect; the sphinxes who guarded this place were ripping apart the men and women who had been set to hold it. Some of the sphinxes had already been destroyed or frozen in place; two were half-melted from Greek fire bombs, and as he stared, one of them clattered to a halt midattack and toppled over.

Blood dripped from columns, pooled on the floor, painted the walls in arterial sprays, and he shuddered involuntarily at the sight and smell of it. The stench of Greek fire coiled with the copper and set up a rolling nausea that he swallowed to contain.

There were three sphinxes still active, and at least twenty soldiers fighting them. After the shock passed, Dario snatched the rifle from the spy who was frozen next to him and began to methodically shoot targets. They were wearing High Garda uniforms, but that didn't stop him. He didn't let it, even though every face seemed to blur into someone he knew. Captain Santi. Glain Wathen. Jess Brightwell.

He killed as many as he could.

Mondragon's men were firing now, too, and in a murderous half minute, all the soldiers were down. The ones who hadn't died from the gunfire ended at the claws and teeth of sphinxes, and Dario turned away, sickened, so as not to witness that. He met Mondragon's shocked stare. "What is this?" Mondragon asked. "What just happened?"

"You saved the Great Library," Dario said. "And I'm certain you'll be handsomely rewarded for that, too."

The last muffled screams stopped, and the silence felt intense. Dario looked around. The two surviving sphinxes—one had fallen while he wasn't looking—settled into a waiting crouch, and their eyes dimmed from hell red to steady gold. The slaughterhouse was abruptly at peace.

He went to the first intact body and unbuttoned the bloodstained High Garda uniform collar to reveal the tattoo. It was the emblem of the High Garda Elite, with the inscription *nulla misericordia*—no mercy. They'd given none, and been shown none. "The old Archivist's High Garda Elite took over this place last night," he said. "They planned to blow it up in the event the old man was killed or taken prisoner. The last contingency of the desperate." He nodded to the back rooms. "You'll find the real High Garda soldiers' bodies back there."

"Why didn't the sphinxes protect the High Garda, then? Why go for the Elites now?" That question was from the spy who'd used Greek fire on the doors. He seemed nearly as sharp as Mondragon.

"The new Obscurist Magnus discovered this morning that the sphinxes here had been tampered with; the old man must have a captured Obscurist, or a rebel who's working with them. The damage was already done, and he couldn't guarantee that the sphinxes could kill all the High Garda Elite before the Elites decided to set fire to the Greek fire stores. Commander Santi needed a backup plan, and he was afraid asking his troops to fire on their own would be too much. So you were the perfect answer, Mondragon. Thank you."

Mondragon could have killed him in that moment; they were both well aware of it. Mondragon's gun was in his hand, and just to be certain everyone was clear about his position, Dario held up his right hand and, with his left, gave the rifle back to the spy he'd taken it from. Silent surrender. "You used us," Mondragon said tightly. "Lambs to the slaughter."

"Not a one of you is even injured," Dario said. "And you are more wolves than sheep, if you'll permit me to stretch the metaphor. But you can now safely go back to whatever your spymasters tell you to do next. Your role will never be mentioned. And the ambassador already knows of this brave action, and will reward you for it. It's not in Spain's interest to have this city in ruins."

"We occupy this place now. We can keep it for Spain," Mondragon said. Which was exactly what Dario had been afraid might happen. "Turn off the automata."

"No," Dario said quietly. "I will not. Shoot me and explain it to my cousin."

"No need for that," Villareal said, and stepped forward. "He told me the secret. I'll do it."

Dario pressed his lips together. He wanted to scream, to tell the man not to try it. He genuinely liked him.

He still kept his silence.

Villareal approached the first sphinx, and its eyes shifted from gold to warning to angry red. It came up out of its crouch.

He lunged for its armpit, and Dario averted his gaze. Not fast enough to avoid seeing the horror on the man's face as he realized he'd been tricked.

He managed not to look at what was left of Villareal once the sphinx had finished with him.

The silence in the room was profound. Dario shifted his gaze back to Mondragon, who looked pale with fury. Every gun in the room was pointed at him, and every trigger halfway squeezed.

"Conniving little princeling," one of the spies spat. Not Mondragon, who was unnaturally still.

"Yes, I am," Dario said. "Which is why you followed me in the first place. You're just angry that I connived for someone else instead."

"Tell me why I shouldn't kill you," Mondragon said.

"Because I'll be of use to Spain in the future. My cousin certainly thinks so."

"The ambassador would forgive me."

Dario didn't smile.

"I was referring to my other cousin," he said. "The one wearing the crown. Do you really believe he didn't know of this? And authorize what I've done?" Dario shrugged. "You may message him directly if you wish. If you have that access. And if I'm lying, I'm certain he'll order my execution."

This was, of course, a throw of the dice. He didn't know Mondragon; he didn't know if the young man actually had personal access to King Ramón Alfonse, or would dare to use it. He also, to be honest, wasn't entirely certain his royal cousin would back him up on it, either.

Mondragon finally lowered his weapon. He still looked murderous, and would likely make a very bad enemy in the future. But today, he nodded and glanced around at the others, who silently obeyed his lead.

Dario walked to the nearest dead man, crouched, and closed his staring eyes. "Rest now," he said. "Your duty is done." He stood and said, "Collect their Codexes and personal journals if they carried them.

They stayed loyal to their master to the end, and that deserves some recognition, at least. Their families should know they died bravely."

Mondragon didn't speak, but after a moment he nodded, and his spies began to circulate around the room. Once they were about their tasks, the head spy said, "I should add you to the pile. In this charnel house, who'd notice?"

"No one," Dario said. "But I wasn't lying when I said I will be of future value to Spain, and I can only do that if I'm still breathing. Are we understood?"

Mondragon nodded sharply. The tense muscle jumping in his jaw told Dario he was chewing on the facts, and not much caring for the taste. "What now, then?"

"I will do whatever the Great Library requires me to do."

"But not Spain."

Dario shrugged. "Well, not today. I told you my loyalty was clear. You only heard what you wished to hear."

Mondragon's men worked quickly, and within five minutes, Dario had a cloth bag filled with books. It was heavy, but manageable; as he heaved it over his shoulder he had a strange sense-memory and couldn't place it for a moment.

Then he could. The chemical reek of Greek fire, and the weight of books. The Black Archives. Not a memory he cared to relive, on the whole.

When he looked up, Mondragon was staring at him. The young man was still considering killing him, he could see that. Feel it hanging like a shroud in the tense, dark air. There was no getting around the fact that if the spies held this place and threatened destruction, they might very well win the day for Spain.

"You won't be able to," Dario said. "Even if you were willing to bear the consequences. This was Lord Commander Santi's plan all along. He had watchers posted. The moment the shooting stopped,

High Garda began to infiltrate the whole building; they'll have every suppression door closed and guarded by now. You're caught."

Mondragon's smile was more of a snarl. "You're a clever bastard, I'll give you that. I assume you're offering us safe passage out of here?"

"Absolutely. Go with God. As far as the High Garda are concerned, you broke no laws."

Mondragon didn't thank him, but Dario hardly expected that. He just turned and led his men out of the warehouse. The doors opened before he got to them: High Garda soldiers, visible evidence that this part, at least, hadn't been a bluff.

He sat with the dead, and the sphinxes, until Captain Liu approached him. "The facility is secured," he said. "Lord Commander Santi sends his thanks for a job well done."

"Nothing about this was well done," Dario said. He felt tired, and sick at heart. "It's a slaughterhouse, and I helped double the body count."

"Someone had to," Captain Liu said. "I'll call you a carriage to take you back to the Lighthouse."

"Don't bother," Dario said. "I'll walk." He needed to find a tavern, and a great and damaging number of drinks.

But he knew even that wouldn't erase the scar today had left. The slaughter, yes. But also the knowledge that Santi saw him for who he was, who he'd always been.

A deceiver.

EPHEMERA

Message from Obscurist Vanya Nikolin to the Archivist in Exile, hidden from observation

It may be of some interest to you that the search you had me conduct through the Archives has turned up a possible reference to the location you seek. It is not where we expected, at the very least; it's nowhere near the Necropolis, or even at the Serapeum, which is where I would have guessed. The good news is that it is easily accessible, and if you can find the right person to undertake entry through the trials, you may come up with assets like nothing we can imagine. The things that he left us are astonishing enough. Surely what he took with him to the grave must be worth more than all the power hidden in the Black Archives put together.

Here is the map to the location. I suggest you arrange for a distraction to draw High Garda and automata to the other side of the city. Perhaps there's finally a use for those Russians camped outside the walls.

I would attempt this myself, but if I leave the Iron Tower there will be no one left to cover for you and warn you of any actions. They already suspect, after discovering the rewriting of the sphinxes at the Greek fire armory.

I'm of more use here, for now. Until things change.

Reply from the Archivist in Exile, hidden from observation

We both know why you haven't left the Iron Tower. You're a coward, Vanya. But that makes you valuable to me. As to a candidate to undertake the trials . . . I think I know exactly who to get.

There is only one person alive in this city who understands Heron's work as deeply as Heron himself.

CHAPTER TEN

THOMAS

"No, not like that," Thomas said, and elbowed the Artifex Magnus aside. He was sweating, stripped of his jacket, and he hardly recognized that he'd just shoved a member of the Great Library's Curia out of the way until it was far too late. "Sorry," he mumbled, but not with any real regret. "We have little time."

"Yes, I know that, son," Artifex Greta Jones said. She was American, which was a curiosity in and of itself—a round, pleasant woman with more than enough talent at engineering for nearly any task set before her. A rich, slow accent like melting butter. "Easy, now. I don't think there's anything wrong with it."

There was no time to be polite, or easy. Thomas knew she was wrong. That wasn't modest, but it was true. He quickly unscrewed the bolts holding the gigantic crystal in place and gently lowered it to the worktable nearby. Everything *looked* fine, but he could read from the power consumption curve that it was not fine at all. "It's not performing as expected," he said as he unbolted the platinum casing that held the crystal. "The power cycle should have been longer, and recovery shorter. There's something—"

As soon as the casing was off, he saw it, and his heart sank. Something had been off in the measurements, just the tiniest bit, and the distribution of stress must have thrown the calculations off and caused vibration. Vibration had caused a flaw.

The crystal was useless. The crack within it was tiny, a speck that would have been meaningless for any other purpose . . . but not this one. It could be recut and the flaw eliminated, but he'd custom built the casing for *this* stone to exacting specifications. That had been short-sighted.

The Artifex looked at the crystal, and he could tell she saw what he did. "It'll crack straight through the next time we use it," she said. "You were right. I'm sorry I doubted you. We could recut it, but that will reduce power . . ."

"It will," he confirmed. "I'll have the jewelers cut more crystals while I make a different kind of casing. One that can adjust to different crystal dimensions, in case we must change them more frequently. Put this one back, reduce the power output, and pray that they don't force us to use it again more than once before the replacement is ready." The Lighthouse Ray was, in effect, a giant bluff, a gamble that he and the Artifex had decided was worth the risk when they embarked on it. Now it had become more threat than reality.

"I'm concerned that should the crystal shatter, the power released could destroy this chamber and even the top few floors of the Lighthouse," Artifex Jones said. "Look." She took out a tablet and quickly scratched out equations, a dense forest of variables and calculations that were impressive even by Thomas's standards. She finished and held it out, and as he took it and mentally recalculated, he nodded. She was right. There was a significant risk that if the crystal failed under use, the resulting explosion would create a deadly hail of fragments and shatter the Lighthouse's magnificent focusing mirror. It would destroy this chamber, possibly even cause damage down the central airflow chamber. The Lighthouse itself was built to withstand huge forces—floods, storms, earthquakes—but a single catastrophic explosion might even topple part of it into the sea. It was an enormous responsibility, and Thomas felt himself recoil. *I don't want to be the person who destroys the Pharos Lighthouse.*

But neither did he want to be the person who lost the Great Library because he couldn't mitigate the risk.

"It will hold for one more shot," he told her. "But only one, and then you must shut it down. I'll go immediately to the workshops."

"Requisition what you need. I'm giving you blanket authority." She'd already unsnapped her Codex and was writing the message by the time she finished the words. He refastened the casing to the flawed crystal, carried it back to the frame, and bolted it back in place. He adjusted the angle of it to be sure the alignment was perfect and then turned to the Artifex.

"Thank you for trusting me," he said. Her dark eyebrows rose at the same time she smiled.

"Why wouldn't I trust you?" she asked. "You're a brilliant engineer, maybe the best we've seen since Heron. Our business is one of careful steps, development, and revision until a thing is perfect. You can't predict that. Never forget: even geniuses make mistakes. It's not a moral failing. It's inevitable."

"We can't afford mistakes," he told her. "Not here, not now. We have to be perfect. And fast."

She nodded, but he could see the worry in her expression. He knew how he looked: tired, shadows under his eyes and lurking in them, most likely. He knew this had to be done. He just wished it was anyone else's responsibility.

"Go," she told him. "I'll arrange for the crystal cutting. Good luck, Scholar Schreiber."

He thanked her and left. Instead of using the lifting chamber that ran on cables from the lens chamber to the ground, he took the long, winding stairs. Physical activity helped him think and rid himself of the dark storm of anxiety that was still blowing inside him. By the time he reached the bottom he felt almost normal.

He'd managed to avoid thinking about the damage done to the city until he left the walls that surrounded the Lighthouse, but there was no missing it then. Still a dull smudge of smoke hung over the city, though the growing breeze blowing in from the sea was carrying that away. Mass warships still bobbed on the horizon. Poseidon still stood firm in its protective stance, trident poised to spear any ship that ventured too close.

The dark storm clouds looked like a wall, and the distant brilliant threads of lightning stitched through them. It was going to be a very dark night, and the ships out there would want—no, would *need*—to enter the harbor or risk being utterly destroyed.

The city of Alexandria had to survive that threat. It was up to him, the Artifex, and the entire array of Scholars working on the problems to ensure that happened. And the job of the High Garda to defend them while they worked.

He had a guard now, he realized; two uniformed High Garda soldiers followed him at a distance. He supposed Lord Commander Santi had decided he was important enough to assign protection, but it still made him feel uncomfortable. He decided to ignore them and continue on his business. Nothing else to be done. He concentrated on what was his to do: go to the workshop at the Colosseum. Work with his team of specialists to design and craft the reconfigured casing. If they worked at top, careful speed, they could have it ready within hours—plenty of time, surely.

"Sir," one of the High Garda said as they caught up with him at a jog. "We'd prefer it if you took a carriage. We'll fetch you one."

"Hurry up," he said, and didn't stop walking. Waiting was a thing he couldn't bear, not now.

It was just seconds before a carriage pulled up beside him, and he stepped aboard without waiting for it to glide to a stop. "The Artifex Magnus's forge," he said. "You know where it is?"

"Yes, sir," the driver said. She had on a traditional niqab, covered except for a slit that exposed her dark eyes. "I'll get you there quickly."

As he sat, his two guards piled in on either side. It was a tight fit.

"Sorry, sir," the one on his right said. "We're ordered to stay with you."

"Fine," he said. "Don't jog my elbow."

He was already jotting down notes in his Codex as he spoke, and he called up three books for reference and checked his assumptions as he sketched out the design. He was heavily absorbed in planning, so it was a surprise when he glanced up and realized that he didn't recognize the street they were on.

"Driver? Where are you going?"

No answer. He started to rise and rap on the ceiling.

The High Garda soldier to his right produced a sidearm and jammed it into his side. A second later, he had another gun pressed to his left flank.

"You make a large target," one of them said. "I'd be very careful, Scholar Schreiber."

He stayed very still. "I really don't have time for whatever you are doing. It's important that I get to the forge. Why would the Lord Commander prevent me—" He stopped himself as a grim realization settled in his stomach. "You aren't High Garda."

"Smart boy," the one on the left said. "Sit your clever ass down."

"What do you want?" The driver, he realized with a sinking feeling, must have been in on it as well; the carriage was still clattering along at a high rate of speed. Taking him . . . where?

"You," the soldier said. "And I'd like to keep you alive, but if that can't be done, then I'm just fine with the alternative. Are we understood?"

"You're very clear. Who do you work for? Not the Archivist, surely."

"Not the one you call Archivist, no." The man who was talking now had a cruel smile on his lips. The uniform made him anonymous, but Thomas memorized his face: long, narrow, pale. A vulpine sort of shape, with clever dark eyes and very dark hair. An accent that implied Russia, or one of the Slavic countries; it was difficult to say, since the man was speaking accented Alexandrian Greek. "Stay compliant and stay alive, Scholar. We have a long trip ahead of us."

"I don't have time for your games," Thomas said. "Please don't make me kill the two of you."

The two soldiers exchanged looks past him and laughed. "Scholar. Don't be stupid."

Must be fast, Thomas told himself. He mapped his movements out before he executed, the same way he planned an intricate machine, *this,* then *this,* then *this,* and by the time his hands moved with a snap he was already at the end of the equation, in which two High Garda imposters lay unconscious or dead.

But humans were not machines, and calculations were no guarantee of success, and he didn't anticipate that the men would have such fast reflexes. Or the instant agony that tore through his body, a shock like a lightning strike that left him utterly limp and helpless. *Move,* he begged himself; only sluggishly did his brain inform him that he couldn't. For a horrible moment he thought he'd been shot and was dying . . . but no.

He'd been hit with two High Garda stun rounds.

The men didn't waste time. One took out restraints and snapped them on Thomas's unresisting wrists. They tightened like constricting snakes, and as the man checked the fit, Thomas glimpsed a flash of gold from a Great Library insignia. It seemed to be embedded in the man's skin on the inner side of his forearm. He'd never seen that before, and even panicked and helpless as he was, he couldn't help wondering what it was, how it worked. It was definitely an emblem that would not be removed. A lifetime commitment, like a gold band, but . . . different.

"No games, Scholar," the soldier said. "Next time we use lethal force. I'll give you one rebellion. Not two."

He couldn't speak. Could hardly breathe against the continuing waves of agony that convulsed his muscles. All his size and strength meant nothing; he was being taken as easy as a rabbit in a bag. *Think,* he ordered himself. It was all he could do . . . but even as the pain subsided, he became aware that moving his hands caused the restraints to dig in deeper. And they had teeth, it seemed, because as he struggled to sit up and moved his hands, he felt sharp, biting pain under the metal. He winced.

"The more you fight, the more those cuffs will dig in," the other soldier said. He was a taller, darker man with shimmering dark hair and clever eyes entirely empty of sympathy. "I've seen them saw open veins. Not a pretty death, Scholar. Stay relaxed and you won't injure yourself."

"Who are you?" Thomas hardly recognized his own voice; it came out in a low growl, but it sounded vulnerable at the same time. Weak. "Not High Garda, though you wear their cloth." When they both ignored that question, he tried again. "Why do you want me?"

"Stop asking questions. The next time you open your mouth, I'll shock it shut. Be a shame if you bit off your tongue."

Thomas wished he could ask Jess what manner of soldier had access to High Garda equipment and also wore a Great Library symbol embedded in their skin. He wished Jess was with him for other reasons, too; his friend had a gift for twisting his way out of tricky situations. Thomas did not. He was large, solid, and occasionally lucky, but just now he was as trapped as a bull in a cage. *So what would Jess think about?* Not directly attacking, that much was certain. And when Thomas closed his eyes, he could almost hear his friend whisper, *Use your advantages.* But what advantages did he have? He was handcuffed, barely able to move. Wherever they were traveling, gravity had shifted him back in his seat. They were going uphill now, at a fairly sharp angle.

Then the steam carriage rocked a little as it passed over a bump in the road, and it came into his mind as clearly as if it was written in fire: *Schwingung.* Vibration. Oscillation. It was a common complaint that steam carriages, because of the height of their cabs above the ground, and the weight of their steam engines, were inherently vulnerable to toppling in high winds, especially on steep grades of roads. But how to take advantage?

First, get both the men on this side of the carriage.

Thomas was not an actor by nature, but he remembered how the stun round had woken convulsions in his muscles, and he did his earnest best to feign a relapse. He rolled his eyes back in his head and began to twitch and flail; he was careful about his hands, though he used his legs in the effort. One of them shouted at him to stop, but Thomas kept it up, seemingly unhearing, lurching and flopping and crowding the soldier to the right against the far wall. The other one finally moved from his left to take the seat opposite Thomas, shouting at him to calm down. He was over the centerline of the carriage, if not next to the window. It would have to be enough.

Thomas braced his legs against the opposite seat and stopped twitching and moaning, and tried to look very, very unconscious. He didn't flinch when one soldier leaned forward and checked his pulse. He was waiting.

The carriage hit another bump, a hole that rocked it from side to side as it rumbled forward, and Thomas came upright fast, throwing his weight in the same direction as the carriage's tilt, then quickly back, then up again, a motion that confused and surprised both soldiers, and in the few seconds it took for them to realize Thomas was doing *something*, the carriage's wheels began to bounce and twist. Thomas felt the entire vehicle shudder as it leaned. If the soldier on the far side of the carriage had the sense to move back to balance the load—

But he didn't; he tried to grab Thomas and hold him still.

Mistake.

Thomas timed his next move precisely. At exactly the height of the unstable side-to-side motion, he threw his entire weight to the right, and it sent the soldier tumbling as the carriage's oscillation passed the point of no return.

The driver yelled in alarm and jumped free as the carriage crashed over on its side, landed hard, and began to slide. The impact bounced Thomas's head off the steel frame as they landed. All the glass shattered, covering the three inside with sharp fragments. *The boiler,* Thomas thought. The risk was that in an accident it could explode; there were gruesome examples of such disasters, though the compartments were supposed to be shielded for that reason.

But he couldn't worry about that now.

It hurt—badly—but he rolled over the glass and on top of the stunned soldier nearest to him—the Slav—and brought his cuffed hands up and down in a precise slam that impacted the side of the man's head. He was careful. He didn't crush the man's skull. But he doubted the fellow would be objecting to anything else for a fair few minutes. The impact cost him as well; sharp teeth sank deeper into his flesh, and blood slicked his wrists and dripped down his hands. As much as he tried to move them in tandem and not twist or struggle against the bonds, he could feel the things digging. *Vile things.* He hated the engineer who'd designed them.

The soldier he'd hit was out and limp. The other one was bleeding badly from a head wound, also unconscious. Thomas quickly skinned back that one's uniform jacket sleeve and saw what he'd glimpsed before: a Great Library seal, but instead of being set into a bracelet, this was somehow grafted directly into the man's skin. Interesting in an intellectual puzzle, but disconcerting in the real world. Thomas gritted his teeth and touched the shackles to the man's skin seal, and felt the biting teeth of the restraints retract. The manacles clicked open.

Thomas used them on the soldier, who was starting to come around, then thought about that seal. No, better not to chance the restraints at all on him.

"Kiril!" That shout came from outside. The driver, coming back. "Are you all right?"

Thomas didn't look at his own wrists, though they were still bleeding; he assumed the flow of blood would be far worse if he'd severed veins. He grabbed both guns, stuck one awkwardly in his waistband, and checked the settings on the one he still held. He changed it to lethal.

While he was about that, the driver looked into the window.

Thomas aimed right at her face, and the woman flinched and dropped out of sight. Hopefully, she'd run away.

Time to go, Thomas thought. He shoved the pistol in his waistband and stretched up to grab the sides of the window. Glass crunched under his palms, and on the left side there was enough left to slice. He hardly felt it at the moment. No time. He heaved himself up and out, rolling off and down to his feet. He was not as fast or as graceful as some of his friends, but he was fast enough; the driver backed away, her niqab rippling in the strong breeze.

She was holding a gun.

"Don't make me," Thomas said, and he drew one of the pistols from his belt—the lethal one—and aimed. She hesitated, then dropped her gun to the ground. "Where were you taking me?"

Thomas stepped away from the carriage. The boiler's hissing seemed unlikely to result in explosion, but better to be safe.

The woman didn't respond, but she warily backed away from him.

He heard the scrape of footsteps behind him. More than one set. Several.

"Drop the pistols, Scholar," a calm voice said. "How exactly did you destroy the carriage? I'd like to know, for the future."

He slowly bent and put the weapon on the ground, dropped the other one still in his waistband, then turned to face her. "Zara Cole," he said. "The traitor."

Zara didn't seem nearly as tired or stressed as she should have been, he thought. Her fine dark eyes were clear, no shadows beneath or in them. Her hair lay in a neat, straight cap around her face. She wore a dark red uniform with gold embroidery on the shoulders: a High Garda Elite uniform. That settled, for him, the identity of the men in the carriage, and likely the driver as well. "I think we can debate just who's turned traitor at some other time, Scholar," she said. "You're going to help us take back what you helped steal."

Thomas's numb surprise vanished in a flash of rage. "No. I'm not going to help you. You killed Jess's brother."

"In all fairness, I thought I was killing Jess," she said. "But all book smugglers have an automatic death sentence. I only carried out a lawful execution in defense of my Archivist."

He calculated the odds of killing her. If they'd been even close to reasonable, he would have tried; she deserved that many times over. But she had a full squad of Elites filling in behind her, all heavily armed, and another carrier parked on the side of the street—they were on a street, he realized, but one full of derelict buildings, and no help of any kind in view. He realized with a sick churning in his stomach that he'd waited too long to escape. Five minutes earlier, and he'd have made it away.

"On your knees," Zara said, and nodded to her squad. Three of them moved toward him, and Zara's aim never wavered. "Twitch and I'll kill you and find another engineer. Understood?"

"You chose me because it would hurt Wolfe," Thomas said. "Correct?"

She shrugged. "Let's call that a bonus. Is that bitter old fool still alive? I'd thought he would have died in the arena."

"We're going to win," Thomas said, as another set of restraints settled and tightened around his wrists. "And you're going to die."

"That last is a certainty for everyone. But winning?" She gave him a slow, secret smile. "I think that's going to be harder than you think, Thomas. Much, *much* harder."

He lifted his head and fixed her with a look; she stared back, completely at ease. "I won't work for you."

"No," she said. "But I think you won't be able to resist this job." She paused, then shook her head. "And all of this is your fault, you know. You are the root of all this evil. You and your *printer*."

"*Tota est scientia*," he said. "Knowledge is all. It either is, or it isn't; you can't say some knowledge is evil because it's inconvenient for you. And anyone who claims differently has no understanding at all of what the Great Library represents."

"We'll debate this another time," she said, and looked at her soldiers. "Get him. The Archivist is waiting."

The Archivist.

Thomas swallowed a ball of fear that mixed poisonously with rage.

He would wait until they underestimated him.

Eventually, someone would.

The ride was short, and all Thomas could think to do was to bide his time, observe, *wait*, no matter how much that grated on him. He was surrounded by enemies, and not just people he disagreed with, but ones who had actively harmed him. Put him in prison. Tried to murder his friends. He had to be very, very careful.

He was also horribly aware that time was running out. If he didn't gain his freedom and build that casing . . . the whole situation at the Lighthouse would quickly become a disaster. How long before anyone realized he'd gone missing? Hours, probably. Far too long.

There were no windows in the steam carriage, so he had no idea where they'd gone, and before the doors opened Zara slipped a heavy canvas bag over his head. Hands grasping his arms moved him into what sounded like a hallway—one just barely wide enough to accommodate his bulk, plus minders on either side—and he was almost certain it was made of stone. Low ceiling; he felt his head brushing against the top. It certainly hadn't been made for someone of his size. His forehead hit the top of a doorway, and he staggered and stooped to fit underneath. When he straightened again, he felt he was in a larger chamber. He heard the echoes of the room. *Underground?* He couldn't tell. There was a damp coolness to the air, and a smell of earth.

But when the canvas was pulled from his head, he realized he wasn't underground. Just in a large, cavernous old building, a deserted space that must have once been used as a warehouse of some kind. Part of the roof was gone, and pigeons roosted in the rafters, murmuring.

There were at least a hundred High Garda Elite gathered here. Or, at least, he assumed that was what they were; only some of them were in the distinctive uniform. Many wore the outfits of laborers, but their bearing was pure military. There were some in Scholars' black robes—surely those weren't actually Scholars who'd followed this dark, ugly path? He didn't recognize any of them, but it was a horrifying possibility.

"What is this?" he asked Zara.

"A staging ground," she said. "Not our whole force by any means."

They had automata as well. Many of them. *They have an Obscurist. Must have.* He supposed that shouldn't come as a surprise, if Scholars had come over to the old Archivist's side. Surely one Obscurist would turn sides. "Staging ground for what? You can't take the Serapeum. You know that."

"No," she agreed. "Nor the Iron Tower. Nor the Lighthouse, not immediately. It won't be a short battle, or a bloodless victory, but I will put the Great Library back in the hands of the man who's guided it for half a lifetime."

"He's a devil!"

"No. He's a leader. People like you, people like Wolfe . . . you all think that governance is clean and fair. It can't be. Dissent is chaos, and it must be controlled. Knowledge is all; that's our guiding force. And sometimes, knowledge must be protected at the cost of lives."

"Innocent lives?"

"If necessary," she said.

"The old saying is that knowledge is power. But power has thoroughly corrupted the man you follow now. You have to know that."

"You're a dreamer. You believe you can make the world. You can't, Thomas. The world makes you."

She was a cold one, Zara Cole. Ruthlessly good at her job, but Thomas didn't understand her any better now than he had the first moment he'd met her. He was mostly glad of that. "What do you want from me? You know I won't cooperate."

"Oh, Thomas. I know you *will*. Because you're a good servant of the Great Library. Follow me. Make any move to attack, or escape, and I'll have you hamstrung."

He believed her. And followed without tempting fate. But he was taking it all in: the soldiers, the configuration of the warehouse, the positions of guards. The stocks of supplies and weapons.

There was a large tent set up in the far corner of the room, and the concentration of guards grew higher as they approached it; Zara was stopped at the outer perimeter and told to wait by a cold-eyed High Garda captain who clearly did not trust her as much as she expected. Interesting. Thomas was searched so thoroughly they took away the nub of a pencil in his coat pocket, a bag of birdseed he kept there for pigeons, and a half-eaten wrap of cheese. "You missed the knife," he said, and enjoyed the doubt on the face of the soldier.

The soldier wasn't amused. "Strip," he said. "Down to skin." Thomas shrugged and lifted his manacled hands. The guard turned to Zara. "Unlock him."

"Don't be ridiculous," she said. "He doesn't have a knife. He's been searched three times."

"I'm not letting him in to see the Archivist without making sure.

You can afford to be careless. I can't." There was something unspoken hanging in the air. *They don't like her,* he realized. Maybe because she'd been elevated to their company by the Archivist's decree. Maybe because they knew she'd betrayed her own once before.

"I said—" Zara's voice had gone cold and sharp as a frozen blade, but she was stopped when the tent's flap pushed back, and the Archivist—former, Thomas reminded himself—stepped out.

"Let them in," he said. "Schreiber won't kill me. It's not in his nature."

He doesn't know me very well, Thomas thought. That was useful.

The Archivist wore a golden robe, but it was simple, not ceremonial; maybe he hadn't had time to loot the Great Library's treasures during his escape. He seemed older than Thomas remembered. And less well kept. Unbrushed, tangled, oily hair. Deep, dark bags beneath his eyes, and weariness cut so deep into his face the lines looked like wounds. He hadn't slept easy, if at all. *He is an old man,* Thomas thought. *Fragile. I never thought of him that way before.*

The soldier didn't like it, but he stepped aside and let Zara take her prisoner into the tent. There were, of course, more guards within, standing silently at the four corners, but these were automata. Spartans, with shields and spears and expressionless metallic faces beneath their helmets. They all turned toward him, eyes kindling red.

"If you've actually got a weapon concealed on your person, Schreiber, you have seconds to say so," the Archivist said as he walked to a small folding desk. It had an equally plain folding chair behind it. Hardly the opulence to which he was accustomed, Thomas thought. "Unless you'd like your little joke to be your epitaph."

"I'm unarmed," Thomas said. That didn't change the red eyes, or the focus the Spartans kept on him. Perhaps they could smell his rage. He felt it hissing in his veins like venom. "I don't need a weapon to kill you, if I wanted to do that. And certainly *she* couldn't stop me."

"Couldn't I?" Zara pressed a knife to his back, just above his kidneys. "I think I could. But you're too smart to try."

He was. But all his thinking, analyzing, observing . . . it was all to control his anger. *I have engineered my rage,* he thought. Focused in, like the Ray of Apollo, to turn it lethal and beautiful. And one day, this tired old man would know that.

But not when there was no way to survive it. *I'm needed,* Thomas thought. If he didn't get back to his duties, if the Ray of Apollo failed in the Lighthouse . . . that would be the beginning of the end. He hated to think of himself as indispensable; there were many competent engineers, designers, mechanics. But he was the one with the vision, and that had to be preserved through this crisis. After that, he would be relieved to be just another engineer. Just another Scholar.

He fixed the old man with a stare and said, "What do you want from me?"

The Archivist restlessly moved a pile of loose papers from one corner to the other, as if it irritated him merely by existing in his presence. "I started out like you, bright and overly optimistic about the world. I thought knowledge could solve every problem, heal every wound. But we flawed, foolish humans have to decide how to use knowledge, and we rarely choose for the better. There is no absolute good. No absolute evil. Every cure can also kill."

"So killing you will not be evil," Thomas said. "That's good. I was not worried, but—"

"I'm trying to explain to you how we got to this point. Don't be impertinent."

"Oh, I understand," Thomas said. "I made a weapon that can kill thousands in the blink of an eye. I installed it in the Lighthouse today. I know about the dangers of excusing anything to reach a goal, but you? You took an oath to protect and distribute knowledge. Instead, you killed Scholars rather than see their work shared. You upheld a system to hide inconvenient discoveries. Everything you've done is to keep yourself in power. I know."

The old man shook his head. "You understand *nothing*. Every year, I meet with the heads of every kingdom and country, high and low. I convince them once again to pledge their loyalty to the Great Library. What does the world look like without that, Thomas? It's a burning wreck, fueled by madness, sectarian violence, ignorance. *I save the world.* Every year."

"You make it in your own image. There's a difference."

"Thomas—"

"I liked it better when you were calling me by my last name. If you're trying to convince me to help, you're just wasting breath."

The Archivist sat back and stared at him, and the cold glitter in his hooded eyes put Thomas on guard. "Very well. Here's what I want from you, *Schreiber*: pick some locks for me. That simple. Once you've done it, I'll even let you leave alive."

"I'm not a thief."

"Well, unfortunately, your lock-picking friend Brightwell is busy dying at the moment, so I can't ask him. You'll have to do." It was a blow delivered carelessly, but intentionally, too. Thomas felt himself go tense and hot all over, and he leaned forward. He had to resist the urge to smash through that flimsy desk and grab the old man by the throat and demand answers. He also knew it was suicide.

"What happened to him?" he asked, and tried to make it sound as if he didn't care so much it tore him apart. He thought he failed. *Not Jess, no . . .*

"Blame Wolfe. He dragged Jess into my office, searching for secrets. Jess breathed in Dragonfire. His time on this earth is limited."

"I don't know what that is," Thomas said. He didn't. He wasn't involved in the making of High Garda weapons, if it was one.

"No reason you should; the formula for it burned up with the Black Archives. A demonic sort of weapon, one that rots you from within. There is no antidote, and very little chance of survival. So I suppose that is the end of the Brightwells, so far as their dynasty is concerned. Good riddance. Smugglers and book thieves deserve to be wiped from this earth."

Thomas rocked back on his heels, feeling it like a real, physical blow in his stomach. *Poison.* Jess had been poisoned. And there was no cure. No, surely there must be something. Anything at all. Morgan could heal him. She would.

"Jess is no longer your concern, or mine," the man said. "Wolfe soon won't be, either, along with whoever he drags into his hapless efforts to kill me. He'll be the death of more than one of your friends in the end. And accomplish nothing. By the end of today I will hold the Great Library again and impose order. I'll have to execute all the traitors, of course. I will do so because that is the hard thing, the *necessary* thing, that ensures the Great Library's survival. But not you, Thomas: you can help me. I can spare your life if you help me."

Thomas didn't blink. "Kill me," he said. "I'd rather be a useless corpse than a useful fool."

Maybe it was the bleak certainty in his voice that made the Archivist look to Zara; Thomas felt rather than saw her nod. She believed him. The Archivist sighed. "Then we'll have to make this more difficult," he said. "Zara. Show him."

She walked to a tall cabinet in the corner—a heavy cedar thing, with the Great Library seal worked in gold on the doors—and opened it. Inside was a large silver mirror. The Archivist rose and touched the ornate frame. "I had this made a long time ago," he said. "Another hangs in the office of the High Garda Lord Commander. One in the office of the Obscurist Magnus, one in the Lighthouse room of the Artifex Magnus. Do you know what it is?"

Thomas didn't answer. He watched the surface of the mirror ripple like a troubled sea, and then it settled again, took on a reflection—no, not a reflection at all, an image—of a map of Alexandria. Detailed and perfect, down to what seemed to be every building, every street and alleyway.

The Archivist touched a part of the map, and the image changed. Bright red dots appeared. He touched one of them, and the image sharpened again, into what seemed a brightly lit cavern full of white houses.

No. Tombs. The Necropolis of Alexandria. The view was moving, as if they were gods looking down on the city of the dead. Thomas stepped closer, because he saw *people*. This was not an image. It was something else, as immediate as the connection of writing in one Codex and the precise text appearing in another. He could see people moving, and as the image sharpened, he even recognized a face.

Glain Wathen. She stood beside someone with his back turned to the view, but the posture was familiar. Scholar Wolfe. Glain was speaking with a young woman in a dark blue tunic and trousers. He knew her, too. Little Anit, Red Ibrahim's daughter. *Safe. They were safe.*

Then he saw Jess. His friend sat on the ground, propped against the wall of a tomb, and his color almost matched the pale stone. He looked ill and miserable, and he had some sort of mask over his face.

But he was alive, that was clear enough, and some of the awful tension in Thomas's gut eased. He glanced at the Archivist and realized this was *not* what the old man had expected, or wanted to show him; the fury in those faded eyes burned like acid.

"They're alive," Thomas said. "What did you think you were going to show me? All my friends, lying dead?"

The Archivist glared at him. "Watch."

The circling view suddenly began to change. As if the watcher was falling out of the sky, plummeting down . . . toward his friends. Thomas saw a flash of metal feathers and realized what the Archivist had, what this view in his mirror showed.

They were looking through the eyes of a sphinx that had been circling quietly overhead, and now arrowed down straight for Glain.

"No!" Thomas shouted, and lunged forward, but two Spartans were there before him, spears crossed, shields joined. He ran into the barrier, and the Archivist held his ground. Smiling.

Thomas watched helplessly as Glain realized, too late, that she was in danger. The sphinx landed on her back, slammed her down to the ground, and pinned her there with a clawed paw on the back of her neck. Blood sprang from where the knife-sharp claws dug in.

"Five seconds, Thomas," the Archivist said. "You have five seconds to agree, or her head comes off."

There was so much blood. The claws dug deeper. Glain was writhing, trying to break free.

"Two seconds—"

"Stop!" Thomas couldn't control the word—it burst out of him in a desperate rush. "Stop this!"

"Agree! One second!"

"Yes! I agree! *Stop!*"

The sphinx suddenly launched back into the air, spiraling up, and in the view as it rose, Thomas saw Wolfe rush to Glain's side. There was no sound, but Jess was kneeling beside her, too, and others were moving to help. Bright pops from weapons, and the sphinx shuddered and veered.

Thomas tasted bile and swallowed hard. His hands had clenched into thick, painfully tense fists.

The Spartans still stood between him and the Archivist.

"Two things I know about you, Scholar Schreiber," the Archivist said. "First, you care about your friends more than yourself. And second . . . you don't break your word."

"You do," Thomas said. "Easily."

"I've made you no promises, except that I wouldn't kill your friend in that moment, and I've kept that. Now you must pay your debt. I need you to open the locks on Heron's Tomb."

Heron's Tomb.

Thomas closed his eyes, and to his great and abiding shame, he thought, *I would have done that for nothing.* He'd dreamed of being inside Heron's Tomb, surrounded by the astonishments that were rumored to be hidden there. Every Scholar did.

You can't let him have what's inside, he told himself. *You don't know what power Heron asked to be hidden there. You can't let the Archivist be the first to use it. Your curiosity isn't worth the world.*

The Archivist said, "The sphinx has the taste of her now. It can track your friend anywhere in the city. Kill her at any time I please. Cross me, and Glain is dead. And Khalila. Dario. Morgan. Wolfe. Santi. That I guarantee, and you may rest assured I won't break *that* promise."

He didn't mention Jess, Thomas realized. That was because he thought Jess was going to die, anyway.

"I'll keep my word," Thomas said. "Why me? Why didn't *you* open it?"

"No one who's attempted the Trial of Seven Locks has ever lived," the old man said. "And I know I'm not the one to win that distinction. But you? Maybe, Scholar Schreiber. Maybe you will. And I know you love a puzzle. You'll do it for the sheer challenge of it."

The awful thing was that the old man was right.

EPHEMERA

Text of a letter from the last Archivist of the Library of Pergamum to the Archivist of the Great Library, shortly before the final destruction of Pergamum

My great friend and rival, I greet you in the sight of the gods and the name of knowledge, which we both have pursued so hotly over the years.

War is coming to our doorstep, and I fear that our library will not survive it this time. With every scroll lost, the world grows darker. Our lives are harder and shorter. I greatly fear that all that we have built is too fragile, too temporary, for it to last in a world of violence and greed.

When we are gone, remember us. Rise to meet the challenge we have set: become the greatest protector of knowledge in this world. Not for power, not for glory, not even for your Pharaoh's pride. Do it for future generations who must build the world. The foundations must be solid. Don't let it all fall to ruin.

When death comes to us here in Pergamum, I hope to die with honor. No doubt most of us will defend our scrolls to our last breaths, but there are always cowards. Always false friends. Always those who look to advantage and better opportunities. I have already found books missing from the collection, stolen by those who should be holding them closer than ever. So beware of that, should you find yourself in similar circumstances, may the gods forbid.

I know you, my great enemy and great friend, will defend your own library to the end should the world ever come for what you hold dear. Whatever our differences, we have that in common.

Hail and farewell.

Knowledge is all.

CHAPTER ELEVEN

MORGAN

"I can't find Annis," Morgan said, and Eskander stopped writing in his Codex, but only for a few seconds. Then he continued.

"Annis is still inside the Iron Tower," he said. "I'd know if she'd left it."

"What if she removed her collar?" That was both likely and, at the same time, unusual; Annis hated the collar, but she'd worn it for so long that she'd confessed to Morgan that she felt uncomfortable without it. So she *might* have removed it, but she wouldn't have left without it, either.

"Even if she did, I'd still sense her crossing the threshold," he said, and sat back. He put his pen down. "Why are you looking for her?"

"I need her help with a book. She's fluent in Assyrian, isn't she?"

"I wouldn't say fluent, but she's literate in it, yes." He thought about that a moment. "Don't tell her I said she wasn't fluent. She'll take it personally."

"I won't," Morgan promised. "Can you tell me where she is, then?"

Eskander looked tired. They were all tired, of course; she was trembling with exhaustion, but rest would have to wait until she finished the translation of the passage that she needed. Thomas would require the information locked away in that obscure text if he was going to understand the inner workings of Heron's Poseidon statue. There was every possibility that if the combined navies outside the harbor concentrated Greek fire on the statue, they might breach its coated exterior. That text contained the specifics of exactly how much damage it could endure and still function.

"I can't find her," Eskander said. "I'm not a tracking hound, girl, I'm the Obscurist Magnus. Find her yourself; you know her almost as well as I do. Likely she'll be in the kitchens, or the library."

He sounded irritable, and she knew why: Eskander had never asked for this power and didn't enjoy the responsibility, either. He'd spent too many years a hermit to gladly bear regular interruptions. Especially now, when so much hung in the balance.

She nodded and left his spare, dusty office; he'd set up his desk in an old storeroom instead of the silk-and-velvet nest that generations of other Obscurists Magni had used. The only spectacular thing in this place was the view from the wide window, but just now it only showed growing, oppressive clouds.

Annis was not in the kitchens (which was, indeed, a good guess), and the workers there hadn't seen her recently. Nor was she in the Iron Tower's library room, though a few other Obscurists were there, taking comfort in books while they rested from one difficult task and prepared for another. Everyone worked today. Everyone.

Which was why it was strange she couldn't find Annis.

Perhaps she's with one of her lovers, she thought, but rejected the idea immediately. Annis did have a number of them, but she also took her duties seriously. This wasn't the time or place.

After checking in every busy workstation, Morgan was even more concerned. Why would Annis be hiding? She wasn't ill, or in her rooms, or anywhere else she ought to be.

Morgan set out to look in the unlikely places.

It was in the twelfth room that she found her: a dusty old laboratory that had been long abandoned. It was crowded with old and broken equipment, discarded furniture, trunks of personal belongings from long-dead Obscurists.

Morgan heaved a sigh of relief when she caught sight of Annis's flood of curling red hair from the back. It looked as if the older woman was bending over to look at something on the floor. "There you are," Morgan said, and came into the room. "I was worried, you know."

No answer. And no reaction. Annis's hair swayed a little in the cool breeze from a fan vent above, but otherwise she was completely motionless. Why would she be standing in that awkward position? What—

It all came together for Morgan in a terrifying, frozen moment. Annis was upright because she was tied to a strong wooden post. The only things that stopped her from collapsing to the floor were the ropes wrapped around her body and the ones securing her wrists behind the post.

"Annis?" Morgan's voice had gone soft and strange. *"Annis?"* She felt robbed of breath, of energy, until it all returned to her in a terrific jolt of fear. Her heart, which had hardly seemed to beat, began to hammer painfully, and she fought against a wave of instinct to run from this place. She couldn't. Her friend needed help.

But she knew she was too late. She knew even before she carefully pulled back Annis's hair and saw her death pallor, the gaping wound in her throat. The blood that had soaked down the front of her Obscurist's robes and pooled thickly around her feet. Strange that she hadn't seen the blood until *after* the wound, as if her mind simply wouldn't allow her to notice.

Morgan pressed trembling fingers to her friend's throat.

Her pulse was quiet.

If I scream, no one will hear me in here, she thought, and then dismissed the thought because fear was useless; fear was a distraction. Annis had been murdered. In the *Iron Tower.* Why? By whose hand? *Why?*

She heard the door swinging shut, but when she whirled to look, it was moving on its own. No one there. But she felt the aura of power, and *saw* it next, a shimmer like glitter dropped from the air to cluster around the edges.

Then a burst of raw energy, and the door changed to a wall.

She was trapped.

She turned as another sunburst of power ignited behind her, and saw a doorway being created this time—a stone arch, darkness behind it. And an Obscurist stepped through it.

She recognized his face—how could she not, as scarce as the Obscurists were these days, barely a few hundred in this vast tower—but she didn't *know* him. He was ten years or so her elder, a thin, balding man who was utterly medium in all aspects. Medium brown hair. Medium skin tone that could have been traced to fifty different ethnicities. A forgettable arrangement of features, eyes the color of dried, dark mud. Even his height and weight were average.

But one thing about him seemed exceptional now. He'd concealed his power. She'd never had the impression of real force from him in the small interactions they'd had, but it took expert manipulation of quintessence, and prewritten formulae, to reconfigure walls. Especially in the Iron Tower.

He didn't speak to her at all. He just came for her, and she backed up quickly, glancing around for a weapon and finding none . . . but as she dodged his grasping hands, she remembered that Annis commonly carried a knife strapped to her forearm, even at home. She'd always claimed it was for cutting fruit and trimming threads. But the important thing was that it was sharp, and it was *here*.

Morgan lunged for her friend's body and ripped her sleeve in her haste; she had a wild urge to apologize, a flash so out of place it nearly blinded her, and her fingers grazed a leather sheath. She grabbed for the knife.

It wasn't there.

It was in the hand of the nameless Obscurist, who was lunging at her.

She slipped in Annis's blood and fell backward, and it was a lucky thing; the knife cut air half an inch from her throat as she lost her balance. Morgan fell into a stack of glassware and sent it crashing around them, but one thick vase-shaped vessel—*alembic*, her mind automatically supplied—rocked but stayed on the table. She grabbed it by the neck, turned, and shattered it against the man's head with as much force as she had in her body, and he staggered sideways and dropped to one knee.

She kicked that knee away and then followed that with a boot to his head in the same spot she'd landed the first blow, a stunning impact that jolted all the way up her hips and through her spine and seemed to explode out of her head. It hurt. But it worked. His head snapped sideways, and he toppled to the floor with a dull thump. Unconscious or dead, she didn't know which; regardless, she grabbed up the fallen knife and cut strips of cloth from his own robe to tie him tightly. Then she dragged him to the heaviest desk in the room and tied him to that as well.

Only then did she allow herself to feel the horror and terror of the attack. She crouched down, panting, face in her hands. She smelled sweat and fear, and blood and tears crowded in her throat, but she forced that away. Tears could come later. Right now, she needed to know why he'd done this.

She found out when she snapped loose his Codex. She could sense the difference in it from standard as soon as her fingertips touched it; he'd rewritten the scripts that powered it, just as she had her own, so that messages went unmonitored and unrecorded.

He was working with someone. She flipped to the messages; he'd wiped most of them away, but a few remained. One was about rewriting codes for specific automata, but they were all referred to by numbers, and she had no knowledge of what that meant. *That's who he is.*

One of the specialists who retasks automata. It was a trusted position, requiring exacting and expert skills to make automata function properly with changed instructions.

As to *who* he was working with, that was a mystery . . . at least until she saw a particularly eccentric loop to a letter in a reply, and remembered seeing it before.

The old Archivist. That was his handwriting; she'd seen it on orders. Gregory had brandished those like weapons in front of her many times.

The man she'd felled was the old Archivist's spy within the Iron Tower, and she needed to tell Eskander, at once. She unsnapped her own Codex and wrote a message, waited for a response, but saw nothing. Her heart sank. Sometimes he ignored Codex messages when he was concentrating on other things. She'd have to go directly to him to get his attention.

There was no going back through the door she'd originally entered, so she'd have to use the newly created exit to the adjoining room. She knew the Tower well enough; there was no real risk of getting lost. She grabbed a glow from the wall and whispered a little power into it, and the light spread beyond the doorway. Just another room, this one thoroughly abandoned except for spiderwebs and husks of insects.

She opened the far door, thinking it would reveal the main curving corridor, but instead she walked into yet another room. This one wasn't deserted, and she felt such a wave of relief that she nearly dropped the glow. There were four Obscurists here, and a High Garda soldier in uniform, and she said in a rush, "Thank God, I need your help, Annis has been killed!"

None of them seemed surprised.

"Take her," the oldest one said, and the High Garda soldier advanced on her. Horror turned her cold, but she knew she had to get through. No going back. She showed the knife in her hand then, and he checked his progress and drew his gun. "No, don't kill her. She's Eskander's new pet. We can use her."

"The Obscurist knows," she said sharply. "I've already told him."

That rattled their composure, but only a little. "Told him what?" the High Garda asked. He was a big young man, blunt-featured, with eerily clear blue eyes. "About the dead woman?"

"Yes," she said, and blurred effortlessly into the lie. "And about the messages in the traitor's Codex. Your plot is being uncovered right now. You should give up before you're killed."

They couldn't know what their colleague had written; reading others' Codexes and journals was a social sin so deeply ingrained that none of them would have tried. She hoped her bluff would panic them into immediate retreat.

It didn't.

"If that's true, we have to move quickly," the eldest said. "Bring her. Stun her if you have to, but we need her as hostage to be sure we get to the Translation Chamber safely."

She wasn't about to go quietly; they knew that. And the ring on her finger knew it, too.

Be at peace, the ring said, which caught her off guard and wasted a vital second, because in the next instant one of the Obscurists had seized her wrist, and another was reaching for her. But the ring just repeated it. *Be at peace. You are not in danger.*

She let go, and power rolled through her in a massive, warm swell that ignited the air around her with a shimmer. The Obscurists let her loose and backed away; they weren't hurt, only surprised. But when the High Garda soldier aimed his pistol, it transmuted effortlessly into its constituent parts, rattling in fragments to the floor. "You can't hurt me," Morgan said. "And I won't hurt you if you give up all thoughts of escape. You won't leave the Iron Tower. Not unless the Obscurist Magnus releases you. You've all committed treason against the Great Library."

"We stayed loyal to it," one threw back at her. "When *you* stole it away from us."

One of them—the biggest of them, the High Garda soldier—came directly for her. He smashed into an invisible shield that threw him backward and into a wall with such force he hit the ground, unconscious.

She wasn't doing *any* of this, not consciously; it was the ring defending her. But why now? Why not before, when she'd been about to be killed?

Because you did not need the help. But you are outnumbered now, the ring said. *And so, I help.*

Morgan forced a smile. "Anyone else want to try?"

No one seemed to, but then she felt a little shiver, a waver in the power in the ring. It had only a limited reserve. It would refill itself from the latent power of quintessence floating in the air, but not quickly.

She couldn't wait here.

Before the Obscurists could move, she dashed for the doorway, threw it open, and ran out into the corridor. Deserted. She made for the long spiral of stairs, heading down toward the more occupied levels. She tried to shout, knowing it would echo through the central corridor, but one of the Obscurists had managed to dampen sound around her. It was a simple enough prewritten code; they probably had an entire volume of them, all designed to keep themselves safe and undiscovered. But Annis *had* discovered them, and they'd killed her trying to find out how. Or she'd chosen that death instead of telling them. That would have been more like her.

Grief burned, and Morgan found herself gasping against tears as she plunged on down the steps, feet silent, not even her sobs making a sound.

She missed a step and almost fell, and forced herself to slow down. She saw people moving two floors down. If she could reach them . . .

Something hit the wall beside her, raising a puff of dust and an explosion of sharp fragments. It made no sound, but when she looked back she realized that one of the Obscurists had found another gun and was firing it at her. They no longer wanted her alive. They just wanted to stop her from telling anyone else.

A clap of sound so loud it deafened her brought her to a sudden stop; she felt as though her skull had shattered. *Am I shot? Am I dead?* She didn't know until she lowered her hands from her head and saw no blood . . . and then saw the shape striding up the stairs toward her. The thunderclap had been an internal Translation within the Iron Tower.

And the man coming toward her was Eskander.

She opened her mouth to scream at him to take cover, but though she felt the strain of trying, the sound just . . . vanished. She didn't know how to dismantle the effect, and there wasn't time to try.

But Eskander didn't need her warning. He plunged past her on the stairs, heading up, and she felt him slashing at the altered reality in a way she couldn't even grasp as he moved.

Sound snapped back into being. His footsteps on the stairs. Her breath heaving in her lungs. "They're armed!" she shouted, and a fraction of a second later she heard the shot. It seemed to echo through the Iron Tower like a scream, and she caught her breath as she saw Eskander stagger and miss a step.

No. No, that could not be.

He went to one knee.

Go, the ring told her with a decisive snap. She lunged forward and reached for some line of defense, something, *anything,* and the ring's whisper said, *Be calm. Feel the air.*

The air.

She shifted the density of the air in front of Eskander into a thick block, a shield made of nothing, and as the second shot rang out, she saw the bullet hit the block and slow. It was as if it moved through thick gelatin, and when it finally tunneled its way through, it simply dropped to the stairs and rolled away, all its force spent.

Morgan pushed that shield back as she ascended the stairs. She extended it and formed it into a bubble that trapped the Obscurists inside, battering uselessly at the milky barrier. *Will it hold?* she asked the ring, and felt a warm pulse of approval. The power had come from the walls of the Iron Tower, from the generations of powerful Obscurists who'd been born, lived, worked, and died here. The barrier was anchored in that power. It would not break, and it wasn't likely these traitors had the skill to rewrite their formulae to remove it.

She went back to Eskander. He'd gotten to his feet, and he was a little shaken, but when she said, "Show me," he pulled his hand away from his side to show her the wound. "How bad is it?"

"It missed anything vital," he said, and groaned. "Not entertaining, but I've had worse in my youth." He smiled at her briefly. "Sorry I didn't read your message immediately. It's a busy day."

The smile vanished as he looked at the Obscurists she'd trapped on the stairs. There was a dangerous light in his eyes. "They killed Annis."

"Yes. She must have found them doing something they wanted to keep hidden." She took in a deep breath. "They're working with the exiled Archivist. I think they've been sabotaging our control of the automata and hiding the changes. We'll need to do a full review of all of the machines to be certain what's been compromised, and what it means."

"I was already aware of some of these changes," Eskander said. "But I'd asked Obscurist Salvatore to investigate." He pointed to the eldest of the trapped people. "*That* is Obscurist Salvatore." He sounded angry, but she thought it was mostly frustration with himself. "I chose the guilty to investigate the crime."

"You couldn't have known—"

"It's my business to know," Eskander said. "Now more than it's ever been for any other Obscurist in history. And I've failed. Annis is dead because I did." She saw the flash of real grief in his face, but like her, he had to put it behind him for now. "Your job is to take Salvatore's place and review the entire inventory for compromise. Test them all."

"Sir, that might take days," she said quietly. "We might not have days."

"Start with the ones that pose the most threat and work down. But we don't have time to waste."

Shouts had broken out below them, and both Obscurists and High Garda soldiers were rushing to the rescue. Good. As the first High Garda met them, Morgan said, "The Obscurist Magnus has been wounded. Find someone to take him to the Medica floor. Go up three floors; you'll find another High Garda who's knocked unconscious. Arrest him for treason."

The soldier—a tall, capable-looking young woman—hesitated only an instant before looking to Eskander for confirmation. When she got the nod, she began issuing orders to those arriving. Morgan wasn't good at reading rank, but she thought this woman must have been a sergeant, at least. She had the bearing and authority.

Two Obscurists and two High Garda were assigned the task of taking Eskander to the Medica. He paused before leaving. "Start now," he told her. "We're out of time already."

She bowed her head, and swallowed her worry as she descended the stairs. She was halfway down when the High Garda sergeant called, "Obscurist Hault? We can't get through this—barrier."

Without pausing, Morgan raised her hand and pushed the air back to normal density. She heard a sharp *pop* and felt the rush of wind ripple past her, but she didn't look back.

She had work to do.

Obscurist Salvatore had his own office on the fourth floor. The entire level was dedicated to automata control; there were more than fifty Obscurists working constantly on monitoring and rewriting commands, but Salvatore's office had only two others in it, both assistants.

Morgan didn't know them. And couldn't trust that they hadn't also turned traitor. "Out," she snapped to them, and when the middle-aged man began to protest, she looked at her High Garda escort, and without a word spoken, they were both taken away. "I'm going to need food, water, and Obscurists Chowdry and Salk. They'll be assigned here for now." She knew both of them, and they were competent, solid, loyal people. "Take the Codexes and journals off both of those two who were just taken out of here. Review them for any signs of disloyalty or deception."

"Yes, Obscurist," the sergeant said. She'd joined Morgan after seeing to the arrests, and from her posture she intended to stay.

"What's your name?" Morgan asked her.

"Sergeant Mwangi," the woman said.

"Thank you, Sergeant Mwangi."

Mwangi inclined her head just the slightest bit and left the room for a moment. Morgan opened the cabinet in the corner of Salvatore's office and found more than fifty volumes shelved there; each had the classification of automata on the spine. There were seventeen volumes just for sphinxes, ten for lions. More than twenty for Scribes.

This would take a long time, and she already felt the ache building behind her eyes. She pulled the first volume and carried it to Salvatore's desk. He had a bookstand, and she placed the volume there. The entries were orderly, but it was the wrong order for what she needed, and she requested them differently; the contents revised, and she had groupings of sphinxes in the highest-risk spots in Alexandria, starting with the Serapeum.

She started with the first and pressed her fingers to the entry. She felt an answering tingle of connection. *Storeroom in the Serapeum*. She called up the complex formulae that formed the basic program for this type of creature and overlaid it on the code she called up from the patrolling sphinx. It fit perfectly. No meddling.

She placed a verification code on the entry and moved on.

Ten entries on, she felt rather than saw the two Obscurists she'd asked for take their places, and she paused to instruct them on how to proceed. They didn't need oversight, which was why she'd requested them; both had written countless scripts for automata. They understood how to find even clever digressions. She had Salk take the lions, and Chowdry the less common models: Spartans, gods, monsters of all types.

She found her first compromised sphinx nearly a hundred entries on, blocked the malicious commands, and marked the automaton as compromised. That one patrolled the Serapeum's gardens, but so far, no one had activated its more sinister functions. She continued, moving faster, and located two more before her headache and exhaustion forced her to pause for food and water and to rest her eyes. She put up a map of Alexandria on the wall and marked where she'd found compromised machines; the others added their own discoveries. She found only two tampered with at the Serapeum, but there were six inside the Great Archives. Six inside the Lighthouse. *All* the sphinxes inside the Greek fire facility, but those had been discovered and their malicious commands erased by someone else. Eskander, most likely.

She finished the first volume and went to the second.

She wasn't even certain how far she'd gone when something odd dragged her out of her iron concentration. Her brain wouldn't put it into the right box, since it was so fixed on the problem in front of her . . . and then she knew what had distracted her.

Screaming.

She looked up. Sergeant Mwangi was still in the doorway, but she was writing in her Codex, and as Morgan focused on her the sergeant said, "I'm locking you in here for safety."

"No!" Morgan jumped to her feet and ran out. "You two, keep working!" She crossed the threshold, and Mwangi locked the door behind her. From the corridor, she could hear the sounds more clearly. "What's happening?"

"An attack," Mwangi said. "Companies are responding."

"What kind of attack?" And how had anyone gotten into the Iron Tower? Obscurists could enter and leave, but anyone else coming in required specific credentials. She hadn't checked the Iron Tower, but she knew Salk's list would have covered the automata downstairs at the ground level, and there were none higher, not here.

Or were there? She couldn't remember if Gregory had installed one in his opulent office, the one that Eskander had refused to use. But if so, that door was locked and couldn't be opened by anyone except the current Obscurist Magnus.

"What's happening down there?" Morgan asked, but she asked it on the move, running for the stairs; it would be faster than the lifting chamber. "What kind of attack?"

"Obscurist, *stop!*" Mwangi ordered, but Morgan didn't obey. She kept running. "There are two traitor Obscurists! *Please stop*, I can't let you go down there!"

Morgan came to a sudden halt at the landing and looked down. There were two of them; they had already set the sole automaton guardian ablaze with Greek fire, and it was melting into a horrifying skeleton as she watched. The High Garda were shooting, but the two Obscurists—young men, both of them—had some kind of alchemical protection in place. She caught her breath as she saw one of them throw a glass bulb toward the sheltered High Garda soldiers. They saw it coming, but there was nowhere for them to go.

Morgan reached out her hand and hardened the air around the globe. She lowered it gently to the flagstones, then, with a puff of air, rolled it quietly back toward the Obscurists. The one who'd thrown the globe was still staring where it should have landed, waiting for the virulent green flames to erupt and set the soldiers alight . . . and he didn't notice that the globe he'd thrown was bumping toward him until it bumped his boot.

He drew back his foot to kick it away toward the High Garda.

Morgan couldn't let him have a second try at killing more people.

She quickly denatured the components inside the globe, and by the time his boot hit it, it was filled with nothing more than sludge that would leave a stain but couldn't burn if they put a match to it.

But there was something else; she could feel it. Something shrouded in Obscurist formulae, something *not right here.*

Then she saw it, an apparently abandoned bag sitting in the exact center of the floor on top of the mosaic seal of the Great Library. It looked anonymous, but inside . . . She struggled to understand the complex whirl of formulae waiting to be triggered. That one would create a violent updraft of wind, something strong enough to reach through the central open space of the Iron Tower all the way to the top. The layer entangled with it ensured that fire burned hotter, a simple enhancement used in Artifex forges.

Beneath that was a bundle of Greek fire bottles waiting to be broken.

The last layer, the trigger layer of commands, was a single word that would crush the bottles.

Morgan realized with a wave of sick horror that what was intended here was mass murder. With a single spoken phrase, these two rogue Obscurists would unleash a whirlwind of Greek fire that would spiral up through every floor, trapping innocents in an inferno from which there would be no escape. The High Garda's denaturing powder wouldn't be enough.

She had to stop it before it started.

One of the two men opened his mouth, and she saw the feverish light in his eyes. This was it. He was going to ignite the bomb.

She used the same trick they'd used on her. She had no prewritten scripts to help her, but she didn't need them; she'd spent years perfecting the ability to hide, and that meant hiding any sounds that might betray her, too. She could play the same games.

He shouted, *"Tota est scientia!"* The motto of the Great Library, used as a weapon.

But she'd already stilled the air around him, and the sound never left his lips. He was effectively mute.

He tried again, and again, looking desperate now, and when he realized it was useless he fixed on her with pure hatred.

He threw another Greek fire bomb at her, and she fought the urge to panic. *No. Stand. You have to keep him silent!*

While maintaining his imposed silence, she reached out to catch the glass globe as it fell toward her.

It was the only thing she could do, and it was a horrible risk; if she fumbled, she'd burn. If she cracked the glass in her terror, she'd burn.

But she caught it like a dropped egg and held it in her trembling palm for a long few seconds until Sergeant Mwangi rushed over, grabbed the innocent-looking thing, and lobbed it with deadly accuracy back at the two Obscurists.

They were not prepared. One of them attempted the same catch, but it fell between his outstretched hands, struck the pavement at their feet, and splashed liquid in a thick pool around them.

Then they burned.

"Put them out!" Mwangi shouted, and turned to Morgan as the squad rushed over with denaturing powder. One of them seemed like he might live. The other, by the time the powder was applied, was a blackened, burning nightmare.

She realized with a flinch that she was still imposing silence on him, but when she released her hold on the air, he didn't scream.

His throat was too seared to make the sound.

"Obscurist?" Mwangi grabbed her arms as she wavered. "Obscurist, are you all right?"

"Yes," she said, but it felt awful and hollow. She turned away to avoid Mwangi's glance. Tears burned in her eyes, but she fiercely blinked them back. *I did what I had to do.*

The ring said nothing. But as the burned man lay dying on the floor of the Iron Tower, the ring began to gather the quintessential fluid rising from his body.

"Bomb," she managed to tell Mwangi. "In the bag. Be careful, it's deadly. I can make it safer, but I need time."

Mwangi looked doubtful, but she nodded. "What do you need?"

I need the Obscurist Magnus, she wanted to say, but Eskander had already saved her once today. He needed to rest.

She took a deep breath and said, "Time."

Then she set to work unraveling and erasing the work of madmen.

It took the better part of an hour before she was certain all of the tricks the Obscurists had built into the bomb were disabled, and she was covered in sweat and exhausted when she finished . . . but the bag was safely removed, and the Iron Tower secured under heavy guard.

"They intended to kill as many as they could," she told Mwangi as they took the lifting chamber back up to the office where they'd left her assistants. "Maybe even destroy the entire Iron Tower; I'm not sure even this structure could hold up under that kind of Greek fire attack from inside."

"But why would they?" Mwangi asked. She was very shaken, underneath that professional calm. "Surely not even the old Archivist would want to destroy the very foundations of the Great Library!"

"I think he wants to destroy as much as he can, and build from the ruins," Morgan said. "Wars have casualties. And he knows we sided against him."

"He took an oath!"

"And as he probably sees it, he's keeping it," she said. She was so tired she wanted to weep. "I hope this is the worst he tries."

But somehow, she didn't think it was.

When Mwangi unlocked the door, both Chowdry and Salk were

crowding at the threshold, talking at once. Mwangi pushed them back with a frown. "It's all right," she said. "The crisis is—"

"Morgan, there's a pattern," Chowdry shouted over her. "We know who was behind the ring of traitors here. It was Vanya! Vanya Nikolin!"

She frantically tried to remember the faces of the Obscurists who'd been caught or killed. Vanya hadn't been among them; she would have remembered. Eskander had given him important tasks. *I trusted him, too,* she thought with a sinking heart. *I should have been more careful. He always did favors for Gregory. Leopards hardly ever change spots.*

"Is he still inside?" Even as she asked that, she checked her Codex. "The record says he is, but—"

"He's not," Salk confirmed. "Chowdry saw him leave in a hurry earlier, and while you were gone we noticed that he had altered the records. He's also removed his collar, so we can't track him with any accuracy. But that doesn't matter. We know where he's going, we think."

"It was the Spartans and the gods that tipped us off," Chowdry added. "Those are the ones that he's positioned to guard a particular path."

"What kind of path? To where?"

The two men looked at each other and said at the same time, "We think he's found the Tomb of Heron."

EPHEMERA

Text of a letter from prior Archivist Alfred Nobel to his Curia, interdicted from the Codex

Scholars Magni,

Since the French rebellion that cost so many lives and precious volumes, I have given much consideration to the preservation and protection of the Great Archives themselves. The Archives structure, while unquestionably secure and almost impossible to breach, still represents the single greatest attraction for potential enemies and would-be conquerors in the city—perhaps even the world. As long as our enemies believe it is possible to seize our wealth of books and control it for themselves, the Great Library exists in constant peril.

I would much prefer to install within the Great Archives a fail-safe, one that will make even the most audacious and power-mad ruler pause.

We would never use this system, of course, but it would act as a great and terrible deterrent. The secret of the system should be kept rigorously, and a threat to use it issued only in the event of an upstart kingdom or country vowing to take the Great Archives by force.

I believe that the threat of wholesale destruction, of worldwide intellectual suicide, will cause any would-be intruders to retreat and leave us in peace.

Obviously, this secret must stay in the hands of the Archivist; no other, not even the Lord Commander of the High Garda, should be entrusted with its activation key. It is a responsibility so great, and so terrible, that I would never put the burden on another.

The only option is to make any attack on us so costly to the entirety of humanity that war itself becomes unthinkable.

Should you concur, we may start construction of this system within the month.

CHAPTER TWELVE

KHALILA

"Hello, my desert rose."

Khalila straightened but she didn't turn; she had just put down her Codex on the small table that she was using for a desk. "Dario." Her tone was carefully neutral. "Are you all right?"

"You heard." His hands touched her shoulders, but he didn't try to turn her around. Good. She was still angry with him, and perhaps he could sense it. "No *well done* or *you were so brave*? You break my heart, beauty."

She did turn after all, because she wanted to see his face. On seeing it—the not-quite-right smile, the bleakness in his eyes—she abandoned all effort at anger and silently came into his arms. She felt him take a sudden, deep breath that seemed more like a shudder, and then he relaxed against her. Heavy in her arms. He smelled like death and alcohol, but she ignored that and pulled him closer. She put her lips close to his ear and said, "Well done, my prince."

"You know what happened?"

"I was told," she whispered. "Oh, Dario. Why didn't you tell me Santi—"

"There wasn't time. From the moment that Santi found that the Elites had taken the Greek fire facility and had control of the automata, the clock was spinning. His forces were already stretched thin. He needed a . . . creative solution."

"And that was you."

"I am good at deception," he said. "Growing up in my world, that's considered quite a strength."

She pushed him back a little and met his gaze. "You don't fool me," she said. "It was worse than we were told, wasn't it?"

"If it was, do you think I'd ever tell you? However would I maintain my image as—what was it Jess called me once—a right bastard?"

He had his defenses up, gilded and sharp. She decided not to test them. She kissed him instead, and his response seemed desperate to her. As if he couldn't quite believe it was real. His lips tasted bitter for a moment, and then bittersweet as heartbreak and moonlight. But warm, so warm. So *wanting*. Her fingers trembled against his face, and she thought she might break from longing. Today of all days, she needed to feel love.

And so, very evidently, did he. She could feel the feverish longing in him, and something else, something so desperate it took her breath.

"Easy, *querida*," he whispered when they separated just enough to breathe. "I don't want to forget my promises. Or your duty."

There was such a terrible bitter weight on the word *duty*. She felt him trembling. "Dario," she said. "You can tell me what happened. You know you can."

He shook his head. His smile seemed desperate to her, and then it crumbled like a falling wall. He caught his breath on a sob that took him by surprise, and it took all his strength to try to hide that pain again.

"No," she whispered, and put her hands on his face. "My love, there is no shame in tears for a terrible thing. However necessary it might have been."

He almost let go. Almost. But then that glittering, feverish smile rallied. "Ah, *querida*. I will weep when this is done. For now, I will move to the next moment, and I want to spend that with you, not bad memories." He took a breath. "If I'm honest with myself, I want to spend *every* moment with you." No jests now, no defenses. "I asked you to marry me. I truly was not joking, Khalila. Choose the day, and I'll write the marriage contract."

He was so serious, so vulnerable, that it frightened her. She kissed him again. And again. And when she felt that wound in him had sealed a little, she whispered, "I would say today, if I could. You know that."

"But soon, yes?"

"Soon," she confirmed, and smiled. "And what will you give as a *meher*?" She was teasing him, really. The *meher* was an ancient practice, tradition and symbol now instead of the bride's compensation as it once was.

"My heart, for the token," he said. "And half my wealth, if you'll have it."

He *wasn't* joking. She had to check twice to be certain of that. "Dario! I don't need your money. Surely you don't think—"

"I don't. But what is mine is yours, flower. And always will be. Marriage contract or not. Formalities or not. That's what I believe."

She kissed him again. Gently this time. "Soon."

"Name the day."

"Quiet, you," she said when they finally parted, and led him to a padded sofa someone had dragged against the wall. It was serving as her catnap spot; she couldn't imagine having a full night's sleep anymore. Not as things were. "Sit and rest. Have you eaten?"

Dario shook his head. He bent forward and ran his hands distractedly through his wavy black hair. "I just realized that I stink like a pig farmer," he said. "I'm sorry. I just . . . needed to see you."

"I'm glad. I'll find you food. For now, lie down. Rest."

"Lie down with me?" he asked, and then smiled at her raised eyebrows. "You know what I mean. A little comfort, that's all."

"It's never that simple with you, Dario."

"Are you suggesting that I am not a gentleman?"

"Never. But you certainly pretend not to be one to everyone else."

He shrugged. "They see what they expect to see," he said. Their hands fell close together and automatically entwined, fingers yearning for each other. "Khalila—" He was trembling on the edge of that memory, that darkness that he was trying to escape. She sat down beside him. "I did things today, saw things—I don't know. Is it worth it? What we're doing?"

"It has to be," she said. "If the Great Library comes to pieces, what's left? Warring kingdoms fighting over the bones, dragging apart the Archives, hoarding and hiding knowledge? Do you want to live in *that* world?"

"No," he said, and took a deep breath. "But I'm afraid we may inherit it, anyway."

She left him asleep on the couch and went to find Archivist Murasaki. The older woman was standing in the conference room that had so lately housed the fleet's diplomats; it seemed large, silent, and lonely now. The vast windows offered a view of the bay and the storm that swept black clouds ever closer from the north. The winds were already blowing. The storm wasn't far off now, and the ships out there would have to make a quick decision: seek shelter, or attempt to ride out the weather. "They're too close together," Murasaki said as Khalila came to join her. "When the storm hits, they'll be their own worst enemies."

"You're thinking of allowing them harbor."

"No. I'm thinking of asking the pasha of Tripoli to allow them emergency shelter. I don't want unnecessary deaths on our conscience."

"They're our enemies," Khalila said.

"Until recently, with the exception of France in exile, they were signatories to our treaties. Partners in our great work. If this is handled properly—and it *must* be—then they will be our allies again. We can't war with the world if we intend to also teach them, Khalila."

That, Khalila thought, was a difficult thing to achieve: saving one's enemies from their own folly. But she nodded. "Shall I send a message to the pasha?"

"I'll do it," Murasaki said, and sent her a sudden, warm smile that lit her serious face in wondrous ways. "I'm not yet settled in my throne to the extent I can't wield a pen for myself." The smile lingered, but it dimmed. "I'll also send messages to the respective governments, urging them to order their captains to safety."

"I can help with that, Archivist."

"I have other work for you," Murasaki said. "I am concerned for the Great Archives. It's the most vulnerable jewel of this city, and I am not satisfied that we have secured it completely. I would prefer some plan to protect that information more thoroughly. Message the Curia and present the problem. I want plans and suggestions in the next hour."

"Yes, Archivist." Khalila was already taking out her Codex and marking down the names of the Curia. As she wrote, she said, "Perhaps you should consider the invention that Thomas and Jess created? Not for this crisis, but for the future. Surely having additional printed copies of the work would help preserve it in case of . . . disaster."

"Heretic," Murasaki said, but gently, and with a stroke of humor. "Well. The world is changing; that much is definitely true. And we can either change with it or be left behind. I will evaluate this machine of theirs and see how the Great Library may use it to our advantage."

"You won't try to suppress it?"

"Here is where I part ways with prior Archivists. Progress will come. It is our job to be sure we remain of use even as it overtakes us. No. Suppression is not our policy, not while I am Archivist."

That woke a wild streak of hope inside Khalila, a feeling that the world was, at last, cracking open. Changing into something new.

If they could survive to see it.

She finished her rapid message to the Curia, and by the time replies began to appear, the Archivist said, "The pasha indeed offers shelter to the assembled navies. I am sending this information to Ambassador Santiago. I hope they are not stupid enough to remain."

"Maybe they won't be," Khalila said. "But also, maybe they'll try for our harbor."

"Against Poseidon? And the anchor chain? That would be folly."

"Even Poseidon can't withstand sustained Greek fire bombardment," Khalila said. "And if they decide to go that direction . . ."

"Then we will fight them," the Archivist said calmly. "The Obscurists have other automata that we haven't shown them yet. Between that and the storm, I do not think they'll like their chances."

But she was wrong.

As she and Khalila began organizing the room for the arrival of the Curia, the Lighthouse siren sounded, a dire wail that vibrated up Khalila's spine like a poisonous snake. They both rose from where they sat, and the Archivist looked at Khalila for a long, frozen second before they both turned to look out to sea.

The fleet was coming.

They weren't running after all.

The first Greek fire hit the Poseidon automaton glancingly on one shoulder; the metal god simply brushed the fire off, and though the skin beneath was a little darker, it seemed undamaged.

But the next volley hit it squarely in the center of its body, multiple ballistas targeting at once, and the fire clung and glowed hideously in the growing dusk. It was beautiful in a way, the explosions, the green flames outlining the sea god, but it was also deeply terrifying to watch their most visible, most ancient defense under attack.

But the automaton wasn't without its open offensive capabilities. Poseidon lifted its trident and threw it directly at the ships; the massive weapon smashed through three of them like toys, speared three more on its points.

The sheer devastation was horrifying, and Khalila covered her mouth to hold in her gasp. She couldn't see the blood, the torn bodies, the dead and drowning, but she knew it would be appalling. Violence at a distance was still horrific, and should be felt just as deeply.

The bombardment continued. Intensified, if anything. Hundreds of Greek fire bombs, all aimed at the giant figure of Poseidon. The blaze completely enveloped the automaton, as if it had combusted; where its legs met the waterline, steam erupted and billowed to create an eerie fog.

Not every bomb landed on target. Some sailed past to the docks. Some landed farther in on Alexandrian streets and buildings. Lives were being lost here, too.

The shutters began to close as a security precaution, but Murasaki made a notation in her Codex, and these shutters stopped their descent. "Archivist—," Khalila began, but the older woman shook her head.

"I need to watch," she said. "You may go if you wish."

It was a risk, staying in front of this open window; a lucky ballista shot could sail inside, turn this entire room into a nightmare of flame. But if Murasaki stayed, Khalila would as well. She had to.

She heard running footsteps behind, and then they slowed. She whipped around, pulling the knife she kept at her waist for emergencies like this, and felt an immense rush of relief to see it was Dario. Just Dario, breathless and pale.

High Garda followed just a step behind. "What are you doing?" she snapped, not at Dario but at the soldiers. "Your job is to stop *anyone* who approaches the Archivist who isn't on the approved list!"

"With respect, Scholar . . . he is on that list," said one of them. "We were only escorting him. He just pulled ahead."

"I added him," Murasaki said. "Khalila, if you trust him, so must I."

That was a shock. And a compliment. And a worry, too.

"My thanks, Archivist," Dario said, and tried for a bow. He wasn't steady enough for it to have as much grace as usual. "You should—"

"Shut the windows? Yes, young man, I'm aware what I should do," Murasaki said, and there was unmistakable flatness to her voice that warned him off the subject. She leaned forward a bit, hands flat on the surface of the marble railing. "It's moving."

She was talking about Poseidon. Dario joined Khalila, and their hands twined together, but her attention was fully on the automaton.

It was *walking*. Lifting one burning leg out of the water and stepping over the harbor chain. Then the other. The burning giant strode forward, pushing tremendous waves ahead with every step.

It sank down to its thighs as the water deepened. Then to its waist. The Greek fire continued to burn underwater for long moments before it guttered out, but from the waist up, Poseidon was a flaming green torch. Terrifying and relentless, it advanced on the fleet. They were packed too close in waters shallow enough for it to stand above the surface, and as the ships began to break and try to move away, it grasped hold of one and simply crushed it. Khalila cried out. Murasaki's hands tightened on the railing. Dario said nothing, but Khalila felt his grip on her fingers grow crushingly hard. She didn't protest. Pain was something that kept her from weeping as she watched the metal god remorselessly slaughter every single ship it could reach. Hundreds dead with every single swing of its hand. Greek fire dripped from its burning arms and set other ships alight, too. It was a nightmare like nothing she could have imagined.

"No," Dario said. "Stop it. You have to stop it!"

"I can't," Murasaki said flatly. "Heron put these commands in place. I can't stop it from defending the city."

It had torn its way through the British and Welsh ships. It was approaching ships flying the Spanish flag now, and they were fleeing but not quickly enough. Not nearly quickly enough.

"The Obscurist Magnus, then!" Dario demanded. "You can't let this happen!"

"Eskander's been injured in an attack at the Iron Tower. And as difficult as this is, *should* we stop it? Your kinsmen came here intending to take control of our city."

"They're trying to run!"

They were. It made Khalila sick to see it. The bombardment had ceased; the fleet wheeled like a flock of birds. The British and Welsh were virtually destroyed. The French had already broken off and sailed toward Tripoli. The Japanese were turning toward home.

The Spanish, the central bulk of the force, were trying to maneuver toward escape, but the seas were turbulent, and the god's pursuit relentless. Waves broke over the chest of Poseidon, but it kept up its chase. Snatched up two more ships and crushed them. Dario let out a low cry. "Khalila, Morgan! Get Morgan!"

She fumbled for her Codex. Surely it was enough now. Surely this had to end. Morgan might not be able to help, but at least she could *try* . . .

And then, suddenly, Poseidon stopped moving. The automaton stood burning, just chest and head above the water, with one hand outstretched toward a fleeing Spanish ship . . . and it no longer moved. Waves slashed at it, washing away the Greek fire in guttering ribbons.

What was left was just a melted, unformed *thing*, with exposed, frozen clockworks and tubes. In time, it would rust earth brown, become a home for coral and fish. Become an island that no one remembered was once a god.

Poseidon would never rise again.

But it had done what it had been designed to do by Heron so long ago: it had destroyed an invading fleet. Protected the Great Library. *At what cost?* Khalila realized she was still shaking only as Dario put an arm around her shoulder. She tried to seem braver. Surely the Archivist would want that.

"Today is a day of mourning, not victory," Murasaki said quietly. "I think I begin to understand the weight that these robes carry."

It took Khalila a moment to realize that the Archivist was crying, despite her calm and steady voice.

"Your cousin's ship—?" Khalila turned to Dario. He shook his head.

"I couldn't see," he said. "God help this city if he's gone. King Ramón Alfonse will never agree to peace if Alvaro is dead."

They watched the Spanish fleet gather together and turn in a large, solid wheel.

Headed back for the harbor.

"No," Dario whispered, "no, *no*, you fools, don't—"

The Lighthouse's droning alarm suddenly cut off, leaving an eerie and echoing silence, and Thomas's Ray of Apollo kindled into fierce, solid life as thick as one of those Spanish ships. It burned a line through the water only meters away from the leading ship's bow. Another warning. A very pointed one. It transformed water to superheated steam where it sliced, and after just a few seconds it went out.

Murasaki said, "Scholar Seif, send a message to the Spanish ambassador. Tell him to make for Tripoli with all speed, or prepare to meet his god."

As Khalila wrote the words, black clouds swallowed the last of the day's light, and a bolt of lightning shattered out of the heavens and struck the Iron Tower. Shimmers of power radiated down it and bled away into harmless sparks. It was as if Allah himself had decided to emphasize the message. When she finished writing, she realized that she'd used the Arabic alphabet for the city's name. Instinct and habit. But Santiago no doubt knew Arabic as well as Greek, English, and half a dozen other tongues. All the ambassadors did.

Khalila stared at her Codex tensely until the answer appeared in tight, angry words. "Message acknowledged. They're turning," she said, and looked up to be sure. *Yes.* The Spanish ships continued their turn, avoiding the Alexandrian course and locking in for the shelter of the docks at Tripoli, and the assurance that the pasha of Libya would protect them from reprisals. They'd be safe there, if given a chilly reception by the pasha, the sooner to send them back on their way to their king. "The ambassador writes that the Great Library stands or falls alone now. They will do nothing to help or hinder our fate."

"He *is* angry," Dario said. "Alvaro's usually much more pleasant. But his better sense will come back as soon as he cools off. I'll send my cousin Ramón a message. Spain won't destroy our long relationship so easily as that." He sounded confident. Khalila hoped he was right. But for now, tonight, at least it was one less worry.

The storm's wind arrived in a sudden gust that jerked at her hijab, and she quickly put a hand to it to be sure it held firm. The first spits of rain hit the marble, and there was an edge to that wind, a chill that seemed foreign to her. A wind that had raced halfway around the world, gathering cold and violence as it went to deliver its vengeance here.

"Close the shutters," Murasaki said, and Khalila went to the manual hand crank and turned it to finish the job. A boom of thunder shook through the walls, the floor, her flesh and bones. The storm growled, and a low wail of wind rattled the closed window. "I need to speak with the Curia, then with the Lord Commander. We must understand what's coming this evening, and I need an update on the search for the rebel Archivist."

She was already in motion, walking toward the two guards standing at the door, and Khalila saw them exchange looks. Khalila moved to follow the Archivist, and Dario came with her, saying something she didn't catch because she was distracted by another violent boom of thunder.

She didn't see it happen, to her horror and shame. She only saw Murasaki suddenly stop, sway, and then turn toward them.

Then she saw the blood on the Archivist's robe. *Something's wrong.* She felt cold, numb, utterly incapable of understanding this because why would the Archivist be bleeding, what—

The Archivist looked at Khalila, opened her mouth, and said, "You must—"

She was shot again, in the back, and folded at the knees. She landed on the floor, tangled in her bloody robes, and Khalila screamed. Everything went suddenly, icily clear. The thin smoke curling from the barrels of High Garda guns. Dario, lunging forward.

Assassins.

She drew her knife and didn't hesitate, not for an instant. She had practiced this motion so many times as a child, as a young woman, drilling and drilling for hours, and the second the knife left her fingers it arrowed straight for the right eye of the man on the left, the one who was smiling.

Because he was smiling.

It buried to the hilt, and he was screaming. His dying flail knocked his companion's arm, and the shot meant for Dario went wild and gouged a white wound in the marble column behind him.

Which meant that Dario's dagger punctured him just under the armor, angling up. It drove the soldier backward, gagging on the pain, but whatever he might have done to fight back no longer mattered, as Dario withdrew the blade and used it again. It was a pretty thing, patterned with emeralds.

It slit a throat with ease.

It took a few more seconds for the soldiers to die, but it was just stubborn bodies refusing the inevitable; Dario kicked their guns away as Khalila knelt beside the Archivist and searched for a pulse. She felt something, but it was weak. "Dario, go for help! *Now!*"

He didn't want to leave her, but he obeyed and ran past the two dying men. *Were more High Garda compromised? How had this happened? Did the old Archivist command even now, even here?* Khalila was cold and shaking and hot all at the same time, a sickening sensation made worse by her own rapidly beating heart. She pressed down on Murasaki's wounds as best she could, but she could see that it was a desperate situation.

Blood flowered and flooded between her fingers, shallower with every pulsebeat. "Archivist? *Archivist!*"

Murasaki's lips moved. They'd gone a pale, unnatural color, but her eyes were fierce and dark, and her hand gripped Khalila's wrist and held it tightly.

"You must get to Wolfe," she said. "I trust no one else now. He must serve."

"He won't!"

"He must," Murasaki repeated, and let her head fall back to the bloody floor. She closed her eyes and whispered something in Japanese. Khalila didn't catch the meaning.

"Archivist? I didn't hear!"

Murasaki, with a huge force of will, opened her eyes and said, "Codex."

She was *dying*, and she asked for a Codex. Khalila, confused, handed hers over and opened it to a blank page. Put the stylus in the Archivist's shaking fingers.

And the Archivist wrote. Just three lines, and then the stylus fell from her fingers and she put her head back down and let out her last breath in a long, quiet sigh.

Khalila bit her lip to hold back tears and retrieved the stylus, then looked at the words Murasaki had written. Her eyes blurred. The graceful kanji written there looked like music.

It was her *jisei*, her death poem. An achievement the great Japanese poets aspired to make in their last moments.

> *Desert rain runs clean*
> *Green chains shatter in lightning*
> *I run warm at last*

She felt Dario beside her and said, "She's gone." Her voice sounded soft and lonely. His arms closed around her. "Dario, *she's gone*."

"I know, love." He took a deep breath. "More High Garda are on the way. Honest ones, I hope. God knows how much *geneih* it took to buy these men."

She wiped her tears as he helped her to her feet. "This should never have happened. *Never!*" She felt ice-cold now, and full of fury. "We shouldn't have killed them both. Now they can't answer for what they've done."

"Revenge can wait," Dario said. "Are you all right?"

"Yes. Unwounded. You?"

"I'm fine," he said. Her Codex buzzed, and she reached for it, then hesitated. Her hands were still bloody, and she wiped them on her dress before opening the book.

Dario watched her read the message. "What is it?"

"Santi's coming in person," she said. "He's angry."

"He should be. These are *his* people. It's an outrage."

"Dario. Did you hear what she said?"

"When?"

"Before she wrote the poem. Did you hear?"

"No."

She took a deep breath and let it out. "She wanted us to find Wolfe. She wanted Wolfe to be the next Archivist."

And that meant drawing a perfect target on the back of the man she had grown to love as much as her own father.

EPHEMERA

Text of a letter from the Russian ambassador, destroyed before delivery to the Archivist in Exile

As you asked, we sacrificed our two most precious assets—High Garda soldiers assigned within the Serapeum, in striking distance of the False Archivist. Though it cost their lives, they were successful. I am pleased to report that she is dead. Confusion will now set in. And with it, we now have our chance. Tonight we will attack the northeastern gates, and your inventions you sold us will no doubt strike real fear into the High Garda. I marvel that you've never used them for the defense of the Great Library. Unless you know something I don't.

Tonight is your chance. Seize it! It will not come again.

If you survive, we will of course allow you to take the throne of Alexandria once more.

But the tsar of Russia will be the true ruler of this place. That is the bargain. We will hold you to it by whatever means necessary.

CHAPTER THIRTEEN

WOLFE

The Necropolis was more of a cemetery now than ever, as the bodies were lined up and casualties counted.

Anit's criminals were unpleasantly good at killing. The High Garda Elites had given a good accounting of themselves, and the fighting within the miniature Serapeum had gone on for hours, but they had never expected to be trapped inside it. They'd thought to fight in the dark and strike before Wolfe and his team had any warning.

Jess's trick with the mirrors had robbed them of their stealth, and his accuracy with a rifle had robbed them of their most valuable snipers. From then on, it had been straight combat, and good as they were—and High Garda Elites were *very* good—they were rarely challenged in any meaningful way. They'd always had the architecture of the Serapeum to defend them, and the automata, and their own legend. The only automaton here was the Minotaur, and Jess had blinded it. It roamed the tombs like a ghost still, lost and dangerous.

Wolfe made himself a note to ask Morgan to see to stopping the thing. But that would be a low priority, he suspected, in the chaos of the day.

Anit's losses were also considerable; once the tally of the dead and wounded was complete, she'd lost ten and sent five to be treated by the physician, Burnham, who'd come with them on this grim adventure. The High Garda Elite's fatalities numbered forty-six, and the remaining four had finally surrendered. Wolfe would have to find some deep hole to throw them in—but not one they'd ever guarded before and might know how to cheat. That would be a challenge. Maybe expulsion from the city would be the best possible answer . . . No, that would just give their enemies outside the walls useful allies and information. It was a terrible thought, but he knew it would have been a simpler problem if they'd just killed them all.

"And still no sign of the Archivist," he said to Glain as he closed his Codex. She was bloody, but only a little of it was her own; she'd fought like a woman possessed. She looked pale and strained now as the adrenaline departed.

"No, sir," she said. "It seems likely he was never here at all. All this was set up to kill *you* when you came looking. They meant it to be a deathtrap."

"And if I'd come with just you and Jess—"

"We'd all be dead," she said. At his look, she smiled. "I'm good, Scholar. Nobody's *that* good."

"Well, perhaps you're—"

"Sir!" Glain was moving suddenly, and he went immediately on his guard for whatever was coming . . . but she was running toward Jess Brightwell, who was in the act of slumping to the ground with his back against the gunfire-chipped door of a tomb.

Wolfe followed. He didn't see any wounds, but the boy was pallid, sweaty, breathing in strangled gasps. His lips had taken on an unsettling violet tinge. "He can't breathe," Glain said. "He's been like this since—"

"I know," Wolfe said. "Didn't he see a Medica?"

"Yes. He said he was all right. They gave him a mask of some kind—" She dug in Jess's pockets and found a small, formfitting device of flexible rubber that fitted over his nose and mouth. It seemed to work, after a tense few moments; his breathing eased, and his color improved from grave gray to sallow. Color back in his lips and fingernails, at least a little.

"He's not well," Wolfe said quietly. He'd been afraid of this. Afraid that his obsession, his lack of sensible caution, had finally cost a life. Worse still, the life of someone he cared for. Brightwell was in his charge, and he'd been reckless with the boy. "He should be in a Medica treatment hospital, not here."

"If he hadn't been here, this might not have turned out as well as it did," Glain observed. "He's tough. He'll be all right." Her words were brusque, but the way she smoothed his hair back from his face was far more telling. Glain had a soft streak in her. In that she reminded him of himself. Rather strongly.

"He's waking up," Wolfe said. The boy's eyelids were fluttering, and they finally raised on a blank stare that seemed utterly unaware for a few long seconds before he blinked and focused on Glain's face.

"Welcome back," she said, brisk as ever. "Good job you didn't do this in the middle of the fight."

"Well, I try to time my collapses conveniently," Jess said, which almost made Wolfe smile. Almost. The young man's face looked sharp, as if the skull under the flesh showed through. Unnerving. His skin seemed far too translucent. "Scholar, you're all right?" He tried to get up. Glain pushed him down and placed the mask back over his face. He tried to bat it away. She speared a commanding finger at him, and without a word exchanged, he surrendered and breathed as deeply as he could. It did not seem deep enough to Wolfe. *I've killed him.* The thought struck deep, and it hurt so badly he drew in a startled breath. *A death in slow motion, but nevertheless, a death.* He wondered what exactly the Medica had said. Surely not that he should be back on duty, doing what he was doing. And he knew Jess would never tell him.

"I'm fine," he told Jess. "Fine work, Brightwell. You blinded the Minotaur, I understand."

Jess managed a shrug, and a hint of a smile behind the mask. He pulled it away to say, "Best I could do. The damn thing's almost invulnerable."

"Breathe," Glain scolded, and shoved the mask back in place. She looked at Wolfe, and he saw the same bleak knowledge in her eyes.

He nodded. "Don't make me nail this to your face, Jess. I will if you don't use it when you're in need."

"It works less every time," he said quietly. "The mask won't help too much longer."

"Well, as long as it does, *you use it.* We're going back," Wolfe said. "I need to talk to Santi, and get a better sense of where the old man's been sighted. And you, Jess: you're going straight to the Medica facility, where *you will stay.* Understand?" He could only pray the medical branch had tricks up their sleeves they hadn't yet tried.

"Sir? There's news," Glain said. She pulled out her Codex and flipped pages, then showed him a High Garda message from the Lord Commander's Scribe. *The Greek fire production and storage facility was compromised last night, and High Garda security killed. The situation is now resolved and the production facility is once again safely in our control. No further action is required.* "This had to be the Archivist's handiwork. But I doubt he was actively on the scene. He's not one to risk himself that way."

"True," Wolfe said. "That's why I expected to find him crouching among the dead like the coward he is. But he's seen me coming, and gone somewhere else. He failed to capture the Greek fire storage. Where else would he try to strike?"

"Serapeum?"

"No, too difficult, though he'd try to disrupt every location vital to the Great Library, if he could. Suicide attacks at the Iron Tower. Lighthouse. Serapeum. Santi would have thought of it already, even if he's unable to prevent every one of them."

"Can the old Archivist open any of the gates? The northeast, perhaps?"

It was a serious suggestion, and Wolfe considered it. "Where the

Russians are camped? Certainly he could try to let them inside, but again, Santi would have thought of it. He'll have a concentration of forces there, and at the second choice of gate as well. No, the Archivist isn't so much of a strategist; he leaves that to his experts. He'd be looking for something no one else considers. Something that will give him a real advantage."

"Such as . . . ?"

It was on the tip of his brain but refused to come to him. Something glimpsed from the corner of the eye that vanished in full view. He almost knew. Almost. But there was a missing piece, something that would tell him definitively where the old man would shift. Until he saw that, he wouldn't be able to find the answer.

And then it didn't matter, because the Codex in his hands shivered and a new message arrived. He handed it back to Glain; manners dictated that he not read her correspondence, but he couldn't help gleaning the meaning even from the unintended glance. It was confirmed when Glain said, "Santi's summoning us to the Serapeum. I don't know why. Maybe he's got new information."

"Or maybe it's something worse," Wolfe said. "All right. We'll need to head back through the tunnels—"

"He's sending a transport," Glain said. "To the front of the Necropolis. We're to meet him there. I don't think the criminals are invited."

"Hey," came Jess's muffled protest. "I'm still going."

"I didn't mean you, idiot. I meant—" She gestured at Anit and her clustered forces, who were preparing their injured and dead to be taken home. "You know what I meant."

Anit must have noticed Wolfe's glance toward her, because she walked to them, touched Jess's sweaty head, and said, "All right, my brother?"

He removed the mask. "Yes, I'm fine. Sister." There was something there, Wolfe thought. He'd always thought the smugglers only referred to one another as cousins in the business of crime. This seemed . . . more. "I'm sorry you lost so many."

"They knew the risks," she said. "And I'll pay the Library price."

"Library price?" Glain asked.

Jess smiled. Not a very comforting expression, given his gaunt pallor. "The tradition is that for every one of our cousins that falls fighting High Garda, we pay a large sum to their families, and sponsorship for their children."

"Same as the High Garda does for its soldiers," Glain said. "Clever, if reprehensible."

"Well, the High Garda started the fight."

"You *are* High Garda, in case you've forgotten."

"I haven't," Jess said. "But we both know those days are coming to an end, Glain."

There was a certain chilly certainty to that, and Wolfe felt it down his spine. He made his tone especially bitter when he said, "Enough chat, children. Anit, you may call on me for favors. Two or three of them, *not* to include any books from the Great Archives. Understood?"

"Yes, Scholar. I accept. If you need more help, well. More favors. You understand."

"I do." He offered her his hand, and she took it. "Thank you."

It was only in the awkward way she nodded that he saw her youth, just a flash and then gone. She walked back to her own, giving Jess one last look. He nodded in farewell, then—with Glain's help—got to his feet.

"Can you walk to the entrance?" Wolfe asked him. "No egotistical nonsense. It's a direct question."

"Yes," Jess said. He looked down for a second. "Not much further. I need rest."

"Obviously. And you're going to get it if I have to have the Medica put you in restraints."

The fact that the boy didn't argue worried him. Deeply.

He'd just turned away when he felt the shift of air above them, heard the impact. Wolfe whirled back and saw the sphinx throwing Glain hard to the ground, its weight grinding her down. Its claws flexed and ripped bloody furrows through her uniform cloth, armor, and skin below.

He shouted and reached for his weapon, but then he froze as the sphinx turned its head to regard him. It hissed in warning, and the claws sunk deeper. Glain twisted and cried out, and he stopped and raised his hands. "Let her go." He didn't know why he said it; surely the sphinx wasn't going to respond to him. But he could draw its focus, at least, while Jess moved in on it to turn it off. "Please. Let her go."

He had the weird sense that this sphinx *listened*, that the menace he felt coming off the thing wasn't simply mechanical programming but something almost human. An intelligence looking through its eyes.

Jess didn't need instructions. He approached carefully, and Wolfe moved a little, trying to hold the thing's attention.

It didn't work. It moved its head to stare at Jess and freeze him in place, and clawed deeper into Glain. *Gods.* Wolfe swallowed a bubble of horror and tried to keep everything calm. All around them, guns bristled, and all were focused on the sphinx, but even if they all fired at once, the sphinx could easily rip the young woman's spine out before it was disabled. They had to find a way to turn it off without risking Glain's life any further.

Wolfe moved to his left, fast, and the sphinx's head snapped around to follow him. It was an opening for Jess, if he was well enough to take it . . .

But it wasn't necessary.

Inexplicably, the sphinx suddenly *smiled*. It was an awful expression, completely inhuman and horrifying, and then it launched itself straight up into the air, gliding away on golden wings that extended with a snap. Moving too fast for shots to land properly, and dodging away from the mirrors into the shadows far overhead. It would be impossible to hunt the thing.

They needed to get out. Now.

Wolfe rushed to Glain, along with Anit's physician, Burnham, and Jess, who was already kneeling at her side.

"I'm fine," Glain said, and batted away attempts to look at her back. "It's not bad. I'll get it seen to later. We can't afford to stay here." Brave, but he saw the pallor on her face. It was almost certainly worse than scratches. "We need to *go*! Now!"

It was going to come after them again. That much was absolutely certain.

They were halfway through the Necropolis when Jess said, "It's coming."

Glain—who was being helped along by Jess, or perhaps it was the other way around—looked sharply around the silent tombs. Anit's people had already disappeared through their now invisible passage; they'd taken the Elite prisoners with them. Except for the distant stumbles and roars of the Minotaur, they seemed to be the only ones still alive in the whole vast cave.

"Where?" Wolfe asked without looking up.

"Up and left," Jess said. Now that he focused, Wolfe could hear the metallic whisper of wings overhead. The sphinx had been silent for a while, but now it was flying high above them in the shadows.

"Get your weapons ready. Jess, you're in no shape to attempt any tricks; use your gun and stay out of reach. I know where the switch is located. If I can, I'll get to it. But we'll need it to land first."

"I'll aim to damage the wings," Jess said. "They're the most vulnerable at the joints," Jess said, and took his rifle from his shoulder.

Glain cast a lightning-quick look at Wolfe. "Sorry," she said. "I'm not in fighting shape, but I'll try."

"Leave it to me," he said. He readied himself and then looked up, directly at the sphinx. "Come on, if you're coming," he said. "Theo." He knew the old Archivist was looking at him. Could *feel* that. And the use of his first name—a name Wolfe hadn't used in ages—would goad him.

The sphinx glided closer and caught the light in an elegant, terrifying metallic shimmer. It let out its unsettling war cry.

Jess's shot hit its right wing just at the joint, and though it didn't come off, it flopped loose and out of control. The sphinx tumbled toward them and managed to land on its lion paws. Snarling.

"Scatter!" Wolfe shouted, and grabbed Jess, who was trying to fire again but had begun to cough uncontrollably. He shoved the young man into a corner between two tombs and stood in front of him. "Glain!"

She knew what to do, and peppered the flank of the thing with rapid gunfire. It turned, snarling, and Wolfe lunged forward for the switch beneath its jaw.

He was too slow.

It caught his arm between its sharply pointed teeth, and its red eyes blazed as if with joy. He had on an armored jacket beneath his shirt—Santi's insistence—and the teeth did not *quite* penetrate. The crushing pain was breathtaking. An instant later Jess was there jamming the butt of his rifle between the teeth and levering up to provide some temporary safety. "Hurry!" he shouted. His voice sounded raw and stark. The rifle wouldn't take the strain long, not from the inhumanly strong clench of those jaws.

Wolfe groped for the switch one-handed. He still couldn't free his arm, not until Jess's rifle was out of the way, but the rifle was keeping him from serious damage. It was an awkward stretch, and he felt a sharp twinge in his shoulder that warned him he was neither as athletic nor as limber as he'd once been, but his fingers found the button and pressed it.

Nothing happened.

He pushed again, harder. And again. The sphinx clawed at him with a razor-tipped paw, and he turned to avoid it. The claws caught in his jacket and ripped it from neck to waist. "It's not working!" he shouted to Jess and Glain. "They've disabled the fail-safe!" The jacket's mail had protected him thus far, but for how long? If those paws caught him on an exposed limb, a major artery . . .

"Can't use Greek fire," Glain shouted back. "You'd both be burned!"

"I have an idea," Jess said. He sounded oddly calm. "It's risky."

My arm is in the mouth of a sphinx that's only a moment from ripping it from the socket. Risky sounds quite safe, Wolfe thought, but he didn't say it. Too many words. "Tell me!"

"Work your arm free," Jess said. "Run. Make for the Minotaur. If you can make them fight each other—"

Risky wasn't the right word for it. *Suicidal* was far more on point. But Jess was right; it *could* work. If he was fast enough. If he was lucky. If, if, if. He liked certainty. It was rare enough in life, but completely absent now.

The sphinx shook its head, trying to dislocate his arm; he grabbed hold of its neck with his free arm and rode the motion, though it made him dizzy and sick with the pain. Jess's rifle slipped, and he jammed it back in. His face had gone taut with effort, his eyes black with concentration. No room for fear here. None at all. The boy was the runner of the three of them, but he couldn't do it this time. He simply wasn't capable.

It's up to me.

Wolfe took a breath and pulled at a hard angle. He scraped an inch of arm free, and the sphinx screamed and tried to claw him again. Shreds of cloth flew from his jacket, and the thing narrowly missed his right leg. *Don't think about the arteries that might have been sliced. Now or never.* He set his teeth and pulled, *hard*, and got himself free. Jess jammed the rifle in harder, holding the sphinx in place.

Wolfe ran. He was no athlete like young Brightwell, no trained High Garda like Glain, but he'd survived a long time in a dangerous world, and he knew what was coming. *Stay alive. Stay alive for Nic, if not for yourself.*

Dying in a graveyard seemed like the most ignominious end of them all. He wasn't having it.

Run, don't think. He heard Jess's raw shout behind him and hoped to all the gods that the sphinx hadn't turned on the boy, but there was no time to check. He twisted around a looming gravestone, ducked beneath a low, carved arch. The path was clear but hardly straight; it wandered between stark monoliths and carved monuments, miniature temples and houses full of the dead. The reek of this place seemed almost familiar now, but it was tainted by his own fear. His desperation. He heard the Minotaur's dull bellow; it was ahead and to the left. The path turned again, and now he heard the metallic crunch of the sphinx's paws on the path behind him. It couldn't fly, but it could leap if it chose, if he left it an opening. If it landed on him, it would sever his spine with one bite.

The path twisted right. He plunged on left, weaving between narrow spaces he knew the sphinx's bulk couldn't manage. This was a risk, a huge one; in spots the tombs and monuments were thick as teeth, and if he got slowed down, caught in that trap . . . He dodged a thicket of cenotaphs and around a looming statue of Anubis, whose palms held eternally burning lamps. Did it just move? *Could it?* He had no time. He ran in the direction of the Minotaur's frustrated cry.

The sphinx had kept to the path, and as he burst out ahead he saw it just coming around a turn. His lungs burned, his legs felt light and fragile, but he forced more speed from his body. The Minotaur couldn't be far. On his right, mirrors flashed at the center of the spiraled array, and he averted his eyes from the glare.

He nearly missed the Minotaur's approach as it blundered out of a blind alley of tombs with its thickly muscled arms scything the air. Searching for a victim. He ducked and avoided it, rolled clear, and right on cue, the sphinx shrieked as it came on after him.

The Minotaur turned toward the sound, and the sphinx leaped past it to get to Wolfe. Well, tried to.

The Minotaur's searching hands brushed a wing, grabbed, and *tore.* It smashed the sphinx out of the air midleap to roll on the ground, and as the wounded automaton scrambled to get up, the Minotaur grasped it by the neck.

As Wolfe caught his breath, it struck him that the Minotaur was treating the sphinx like an intruder. *Why, if it's on the side of the Archivist?*

And then he realized that the Minotaur wasn't, or at least, wasn't anymore. Jess's bullet must have damaged something in it more than its eyes. It had reverted to base instructions: kill intruders.

And the sphinx wasn't meant to be here.

The battle was horrific. The sphinx gouged long, ragged scrapes into the Minotaur's metal skin, severed cables, bit at exposed tubing. One of the Minotaur's legs stopped moving—frozen in place. The fight was a blur of claws, teeth, battering fists, and then the Minotaur finally got a good grip with both hands on the sphinx's neck. It applied brute strength to twisting the sphinx's shrieking head relentlessly around until the noise stopped, and then ripped it completely away from the body in a spray of pale fluids and snapping cables.

The bull-headed monster raised the head in one hand as the sphinx's red eyes faded to black. It bellowed its defiance in a shocking roar.

Wolfe backed away slowly, careful to make no sound as the Minotaur tore pieces away from the metal corpse. He finally felt safe enough to run again, and wove through a thick forest of memorials to where the path came clear again. Walked the rest of the way as the fear subsided, and shock began to sink a chill into his skin. His arm ached, and when he stripped off the jacket he found a hand-span red bruise starting to ripen. Lucky bones hadn't shattered.

Lucky in general.

Jess and Glain were coming down the path, which didn't surprise him; they saw their duty as his guardians, and he saw his going in the opposite direction. Good they could meet in the middle, he supposed.

Glain, always reserved, stopped and nodded after giving him a thorough sweeping glance. "It worked," she said.

"Must have," Jess said, "since he's not dismembered." But Jess looked tired and worried. "Did it? Really?"

"More or less," Wolfe said. "Word of advice: in a battle between those two automata, do not bet on the sphinx. Now let's leave this palace of bones before one of us ends up staying."

Coming out of the main entrance of the Necropolis—not the massive marble gates cranked open only for grand funerals, but the smaller side door that locked from the outside and required a Codex authorization to open—felt like being reborn, and Wolfe thought about Orpheus emerging from the underworld. Had Orpheus also emerged into darkness, rain, and slashing lightning? Perhaps he had. *By no means am I looking back and tempting the Fates.* He ushered his two young High Garda ahead of him, just for superstitious certainty, and as Glain had promised there was an armored High Garda carrier on the road, with two armed soldiers standing next to it in rain gear. The downpour was breathtaking in its intensity and chill, and Wolfe was sodden and cold in half the distance.

One of the soldiers skimmed back his hood and stepped forward. Lieutenant Tom Rolleson. Troll, to his friends. "I see you've had adventures," he said. "Tell me all about it, Scholar."

"Not here," Wolfe growled, as he watched Glain help Jess into the carrier. Then finally accept help herself. Walking wounded, both of them. "What news?"

"Didn't you see?"

"See what?"

For answer, Rolleson pointed toward the harbor, which was barely visible from this spot on the hill. Lost in darkness until a bolt of lightning shot across the sky, and Wolfe realized what was missing. "Poseidon?" He felt a real stab of alarm. "The fleet?" He tried to look out to sea, but the rain was slanting from that direction, and he could make out nothing but mist and waves. "What's happened?"

"Poseidon went to war and died for it," Troll said. "The fleet's dispersed. We're safe at the moment, thanks to the storm. Inside, Scholar, this rain isn't doing either of us good."

He was right, of course. The relief of the warm interior of the carrier unleashed a wave of weariness that Wolfe pushed aside. He leaned forward and fixed Troll with a stare. "Why did Santi summon me back?"

"Sir, I don't know," Rolleson said, which Wolfe sensed was at best half-true. "But I know he wants you there *now*." He banged on the partition, and the driver in front began to move the carrier on at a high rate of speed. The Necropolis was a fair distance from the Serapeum, but Wolfe supposed there would be little traffic. Who'd be foolish enough to be out in this rain?

No one, apparently. He slid back a window cover and looked out at the city as it flashed by. "Did the fleet attack again? Is that why Poseidon left position?"

Rolleson shrugged. "They tried to destroy it, and it took issue. We'll have a job of recovering bodies from wrecked ships tomorrow. It was a shocking sight. I imagine the survivors will remember it a long time."

"I imagine," he agreed, and closed his eyes. "Quite a cost for all of us."

"Still better than our supposed *friends* taking control of our city. You know that once that happens, we'd never get it back."

Wolfe nodded. He knew. But he also knew what a balance this was. How delicate and imperfect. The Great Library seemed so ancient that few in modern times could imagine how the world would look if it fell . . . not even those who *wanted* it to fall. But it was always, always poised on the knife-edge of goodwill and strength. Disaster and daring. It was the *gamble* of it he loved, more than anything else: the pure will of those ancients who'd understood that without knowledge, there could be no truth.

He would die for the Great Library. Despite everything it had done to him, he would, without question. He just asked that it be as many years away as possible. He'd come very close the last few days. He could still hear the strangely gruesome crunch of the Minotaur twisting the head of the sphinx away from its body. The almost plaintive cry of the dying automaton.

Could have so easily been him, and he suddenly wished for *peace*, for the days and nights he'd spent traveling with Nic on the way to some dire crisis or other—days they spent talking, or not talking, making love or just lying together, reading. Playing a nightly game of chess, or Egyptian *sennet*, or the board games of ancient Ur. Something with history and meaning.

He'd underestimated how much peace meant to him. Never Nic, but the still, quiet moments . . . those seemed precious to him now.

Wolfe shook himself out of his musings and forced himself back to attention. The city seemed quiet, but it wasn't peaceful. The storm battered at walls and towers and the sides of their carrier. The Serapeum, as they approached it, seemed to be a flowing fountain of water down all sides. The street was a river. Rain was rare here, and flooding nearly unknown, except for ocean-driven tempests like this one. Storms always shut the city down.

The carrier went underground to the High Garda's stronghold below the Serapeum, and from there, Wolfe, Glain, and Jess took the main tunnel up to the garden level. He ordered them both off to the Medica and made sure they actually went before he proceeded with Rolleson. Security was tight, and their identities were checked, and checked again, at every level they passed. The grim silence of the sentries made Wolfe's skin prickle.

Wolfe was directed to a conference room, and as the two of them entered the room he found Nic was there, gazing blankly into the distance. The sight of his lover's face was like a beacon back to home, and he basked in it for an instant before he noticed the rest of those assembled.

That included the full Curia, or as many as could be spared; he didn't see the Artifex Magnus, who must still be manning the Lighthouse. There was no sign of Archivist Murasaki, which was . . . curious. Only Khalila, her assistant, who stood silently at the corner of the long table. Slowly, the Curia rose to their feet. Wolfe stopped, staring at the scene. It made no sense to him.

"Nic?" he asked. His voice seemed odd to him. He was aware there was something in this room, something heavy.

"Archivist Murasaki is dead," Santi said. His eyes were bleak.

Shattered. Wolfe felt a real jolt of horror—not so much for Murasaki as for the pain he could feel radiating out of his lover like fever. "I failed in my duty." He didn't elaborate, which wasn't like him; he just stated the fact and stepped aside with his head bowed. It was terrifying. Santi *did not fail. Not like this.*

"Dead," he repeated numbly. "How? What happened?" *Why the hell am I here?* The question had real dread, real weight.

Khalila stepped forward, such a small young woman to hold such a dense gravity of purpose. "Scholar Wolfe, the Archivist was assassinated by traitorous High Garda soldiers," she said. Her voice was steady, but he saw the tears glittering in her eyes. "Men bought off by the exiled traitor. Her last words were that you must take the post until a new Archivist can be elected and confirmed by the Curia. We cannot be without a leader. And she asked for you."

He stared at her. His eyes burned, and for a moment he thought it was with tears, but no, *no*, it was *anger*. He couldn't speak. Could hardly breathe for the pressure of fury building in his chest.

He turned to Nic, but Nic would not meet his eyes, or even look up.

Christopher Wolfe stood alone, the center of the world, and he *hated it.*

He finally found his voice. "Surely the Curia has a better suggestion."

"We don't," said the Litterae Magnus—Carole Vargas, a large, dour South American woman with a breathtaking instinct for language and a deadly gift for insult. They'd come up in Ptolemy House together as students. They'd never been friends. "As difficult as this is, none of us wants the role, not in these dangerous times. You were named. You must serve."

"As what, your sacrificial goat?" Wolfe snapped. *"No."*

The head of the Medica branch said, "Archivist Murasaki named you for a reason. You know the old man, after all. You're his bitter enemy. Who better?"

"That's exactly why I'm not the right choice," he said. His tone was

hard as diamond, and it cut deep in his chest. Carried to every corner
of the room. "By all means, give me orders to chase after him, run him
to ground, bring him to justice. But don't ask me to sit on a throne and
decide the fate of nations. I can't lead. Too many wounds, too many
scars, too many enemies. You know that. Half of you only want me in
the role because you think, like Murasaki, I'll end up slaughtered; the
other half will start the next hour scheming how to remove me and replace me with a more palatable choice. *No.* Let's save each other time
and energy by naming someone else now."

"You have to be the one." Khalila held something, a folded pile of
cloth, that glimmered in the light. Archivist's robes. "Please, Scholar
Wolfe. Please do this. She trusted you. *I* trust you."

He hesitated, then took what she offered. The weight was astonish-
ingly light for something so important. Cloth of gold, woven so finely
that it felt like silk. He held the robe by the shoulders and let it shimmer in front of him in the light, and for a brief, disorienting moment
he imagined himself in it, sitting on the Archivist's throne in that great
hall.

The Archivist and Pharaoh of the Great Library.

It made him want to laugh, but he knew it would come out as half
a sob. What a sour joke this was, that the same colleagues who'd looked
the other way when he was dragged off in the night, when his work
had been scrubbed from the shelves and his body broken in the cells in
Rome . . . those same colleagues now wanted him to be their shelter.
Their scapegoat. Their great and fearless leader.

He knew what he had to do.

"Very well," he said. "I accept." But he didn't settle the robe around
his own shoulders. He walked around Khalila, turned, and put it
around *her* shoulders.

Her gasp went through him like a knife, and she turned, eyes as
wide as saucers. "What are you doing?"

"Retiring," he said. "And naming you my successor. Scholar Khalila

Seif, will you accept my nomination as the Archivist of the Great Library of Alexandria?"

"I—I—" Khalila, never at a loss for the right words, had nothing to hand, and that made Wolfe smile just a little.

"Don't say *I can't*," he advised her. "Because I know you, Khalila. Your family history goes deep in the Great Library. Your level of scholarship is exceptional. Your ability to navigate the difficult politics is a skill that can't be taught, only refined. And you will have time to learn."

Litterae Vargas said, "But she's a *child*!" She sounded as shocked as Khalila.

"She's young," Wolfe admitted. "But hardly a child. And if you want to fight an old man who wants to drag the Great Library into the past, appoint a young woman who looks to the future. That is my recommendation, and I believe with all my heart it is the right one." He swallowed hard and looked at Santi. "Nic?"

Santi slowly raised his head. The bleakness in his eyes was still there, and it broke Wolfe's heart. "I knew you'd refuse. The Litterae is right. She's just a child. But you're also right; she's the most intelligent, thoughtful, strong young woman I have ever met. Charm and skill and the right streak of ruthlessness. I have no objection."

"Thank you. The Obscurists are not represented but—"

"They are," Morgan said. She seemed to emerge out of shadows that hadn't existed a moment before, and the power that took, the raw talent, struck all of them silent. "My apologies. Eskander was injured, but he's better now. We had—we had an incident in the Tower. Assassins tried to—to kill many of us. But they failed." She seemed well enough, but there was a bright shimmer to her eyes that Wolfe recognized, and it put him on edge. She was exhausted, and exhaustion in an Obscurist like her was deadly to those around her. He still felt the unnatural, unnerving pull of her at his life-force. She'd tried to unravel him like an old sweater before, and even now he felt the black need gnawing at her control. His Obscurist talents were blunted, but not entirely absent. He knew.

"You've proposed Khalila for Archivist," she said. "Eskander agrees." She smiled, and Wolfe was struck with how much older she looked now than her years. Beautiful, but fading like a winter rose, and seeing that hurt. *I failed her,* he thought. But he knew he couldn't have helped her, either. Sometimes there simply were no good choices to be made. Only costly ones.

"Morgan—" Khalila looked breathless, but then she steadied herself. Wolfe *saw* the change, the way her body shifted to fill that draping robe, the way her chin lifted and her breathing slowed. "I am humbled and honored, Scholar Wolfe, but I am still little more than a student of the Great Library. I'm not worthy of this—"

"Oh, quiet, girl, are you not a full gold-band Scholar? Were you not granted a lifetime appointment? You meet the requirements," Vargas snapped. She tapped her stylus restlessly on the desk and studied Khalila with sharp, predatory eyes. "And you're not ignorant of politics, which is the main requirement of this particular posting, I'll allow you that. I agree with Wolfe; he hasn't the inhuman patience necessary for the job. Neither do I, Christopher." She sent him an unexpectedly cheerful smile, and he found himself nodding back. "Greta, our Artifex, is brilliant but quite raw in social skills; it seems to be a theme in that field. So that leaves Medica. Chen Shi?"

The Medica Magnus was a younger man, in his early thirties most likely; Wolfe didn't know him. But he smiled and said, "I have absolutely no desire to be Archivist, and I wouldn't be good at it. Let me do my own job. I do it well."

"And Lingua?"

"No," the old man in that seat said. Him, Wolfe recognized. Achim Ben David, a man of his father's age who'd studied in the Great Library his entire life. He'd never taken a single posting beyond the borders of

Alexandria, but that didn't hold him back from being the single most learned man in the room. "I would not take the chair unless I was the last Scholar in Alexandria. I'm terrible at politics. From all accounts, even Murasaki relied on the girl for advice. To each their strengths."

"I believe Archivist is the sort of job that disqualifies anyone who wants it," Vargas observed. "But your point is well made. Lord Commander?"

"I've surrendered that title," Santi said.

"And we've rejected your surrender. If the new Archivist wishes to take your resignation, then you can rejoice, but for now you are still the Lord Commander of the High Garda, and I need your answer. Do you want to serve as Archivist?"

Wolfe didn't miss the revulsion that flared in his lover's eyes. "No."

"Do you support the elevation of Scholar Khalila Seif to the position of Archivist of the Great Library?"

Santi's vote, like it or not, would carry the room. Wolfe knew it. They all did. Nic took his time, choosing his words, and finally said, "I wish it wasn't necessary. In time she'd have risen to it, I have no doubt of that, but we're out of time. I'd rather not place this heavy weight on her, but . . . yes. I support her elevation."

"So say we all?" Vargas made it a question. One by one, the Curia nodded. "Then it's done except for the ceremonies. Archivist Seif, you may have the shortest tenure in the Great Library's history—"

"Except for mine," Wolfe murmured. Vargas's eyes flickered, and her lips twitched as if curving toward a smile.

"But for tonight, at least, you are the Archivist. Tomorrow, if the city still stands, we will see what can be made of that. I would say congratulations, but I don't think they are much in order. We have the Russian army massed at the northeast wall. We may yet have the Spanish in our harbor once the storm clears, gods know. We have traitors in our midst, and the former Archivist planning to retake his power. A city to protect. Treaties to repair." Vargas tapped the table again with her stylus, a sharp exclamation point to her remarks. "And now we await your orders."

This, Wolfe thought, was the moment. The moment that would make or break his student. And it was a rare privilege to be here to witness it.

It also terrified him, because there was nothing he could do to help her.

Khalila was silent for a few seconds, and then she walked to the head of the table where a seat had been left vacant. The whole Curia rose to their feet. Even Vargas.

Wolfe leaned against the wall and crossed his arms.

Khalila sat and nodded to the Curia, and they took their chairs. After a brief hesitation, Santi sat down as well. His demeanor had changed. His back was straight, shoulders square. He hadn't come to terms with his failure—that, Wolfe knew, would haunt him forever—but he was prepared to carry on.

"My colleagues," Khalila said. "'Thank you' is inadequate to the trust you've put in me. Let's take a moment to remember our first duty: to preserve the knowledge that has been put in our keeping. That means the Great Archives. Is there any chance that they could be breached?"

Morgan replied, "Speaking for the Obscurists . . . we've locked down the Translation functions within the Great Archives. Nothing comes in; nothing leaves. There's no risk by any alchemical means."

"And if the old man has his own Obscurist?"

"Even then, we've blocked the access to the base script. Only Eskander himself can unlock it—or me. But no one else can open Translation within the Great Archives. Even a rebel Obscurist can't do that." She hesitated a moment. "I have a suggestion, if you don't mind."

"Please." Khalila nodded.

"I think we all have to agree that the Great Archives is our most fragile resource. Having those manuscripts as the source of all our knowledge makes us dangerously exposed. It always has, but especially now."

"I agree," Khalila said. "And I intend to authorize the Artifex Magnus to incorporate Thomas's marvelous print machine into the Great Library's plans, but that will take time. Do you have a better solution?"

"For the moment, yes. How many Blanks do we have in storage?"

"Litterae Vargas?"

"Several hundred thousand," Vargas said. "Why?"

"How many books can each of them hold?"

"Depends upon the size of the book, and the size of the writing of the Scribe. Ten? Twenty?"

Morgan turned back to Khalila. "Then I propose you allow us to take those Blanks, task all the Scribe automata to immediately copy every book—or as much of the Great Archives as possible—and as each book is filled, set an Obscurist to disable the script that allows the contents to erase."

"Rendering the Blanks as originals?" Khalila asked. She understood immediately. And the whole Curia looked various shades of uncomfortable. "How long would it take?"

"If we devote all the Scribe automata to the job? A day. Maybe more. But at the end of the day we have copies that the Archivist doesn't know even exist. And they will be in a completely separate location."

"Which can then be sold, stolen, destroyed—" Achim Ben David seemed repulsed by the idea. "We have *always* maintained originals. Never copies!"

"Not true," Khalila said calmly. "In the earliest days of the Great Library, copies were made. Sometimes as many as a dozen. The Serapeum, the daughter libraries—those held copies, if you remember. It's not without precedent."

"It hasn't been done since the Great Archives was first copied into Blanks for lending!"

"And it's time to reconsider our approach." Khalila nodded to Morgan. "Proceed, Morgan."

"Yes, Archivist. We'll start immediately." And with that, she was simply . . . gone.

Wolfe suspected she'd already started without any such permission, from the curve of her smile. Clever girls, both of them. And Morgan, at least, had never been too concerned with the Great Library's rules.

"Before I issue any further orders, I'd like a full report of the city's defenses," the Archivist said. "Lord Commander? If you please. I depend on your wisdom."

"I'll leave you to it," Wolfe said, and headed for the door.

Her voice stopped him. "Scholar Wolfe."

He turned. That was not the voice of his student. It was the voice of his queen. He bowed slightly. "Archivist."

"Do you know where the former Archivist is hiding?"

"No," he said. "But I intend to find out."

Khalila took out her Codex. "There may be something just as important. The Artifex Magnus reported in shortly before Archivist Murasaki was killed that Thomas couldn't be located; Artifex Jones was expecting him back at the Lighthouse some time ago. I know he sometimes loses himself in his work and ignores his Codex, but—I wonder if Thomas is in trouble. Please look into it. We can't afford to lose him."

He nodded. "Yes, Archivist. I'll find him."

Thomas might have simply plunged himself so deeply into his work that he forgot the world; it wouldn't be unusual for him. But at the same time, Thomas knew the dire needs of Alexandria. Schreiber wouldn't just ignore all summons. Not for this long.

He was worried for the boy.

EPHEMERA

Text of a letter from Jess Brightwell to his father,
Callum Brightwell, never sent

Da,

I suppose they've told you of Brendan's death. I have nothing to add except that he died with honor, not that I think you value that. I suppose, too, that you blame me; without me, he'd never have thrown his loyalty to my side, and gotten himself killed for it.

I loved him. Without measure. And I accept that blame.

I have to tell you that when they shot him, his killer probably believed he was me. I don't know if that makes things better or worse, but it's the truth.

Here, at the end of things, I wanted to tell you nothing but truth. I don't know if I'll ever send this letter, but if I do, I want it to be honest. You've taught me to survive, and without meaning to, to love books; I can give you that much. But what you also taught me was that every friend and every ally is temporary, every trust is there to be broken to an advantage. I hate that I see the world through eyes you crafted. Maybe no matter how much I try to avoid it I'm still a Brightwell.

You once ordered me to the Great Library to be your spy. It's the kindest thing you ever did for me. I've found my feet, my soul, my voice, my strength, my friends. And I'm grateful.

I'm dying, Da. They haven't come out and said it yet, but the Medica's words are too careful. I'm to "conserve my strength" and other such nonsense, but I'm getting worse, not better. Anyway, no time for rest now. Better I die for something, even if it's nothing you'd believe in. Loyalty's just a word to you. It's real for me.

I'd like to say I love you, but I promised truth. I've feared you, admired you, hated you, maybe even worshipped you. But I know what love feels like now, and we never had that.

Tell Ma that if I love anyone, it's her. She's always been quiet and distant, but I think that's because she hates you and I'm collateral damage. I wish I'd known her without you. I think we'd understand each other better.

Good-bye, Da.

Go to hell.

I hope I'm not there waiting.

CHAPTER FOURTEEN

THOMAS

The Tomb of Heron had always been a myth. His entire life, he'd read about it in books, a fabulous hidden storehouse full of unseen and unknown wonders, but no one had ever found it. The official records said that Heron had died and been cremated, by his own wishes. That there was no such thing as Heron's Tomb.

But here it was.

"How did you find this?" Thomas asked. He was manacled at the wrists and ankles and had no less than three High Garda Elite guns at his back. Their weapons would be set on a nonlcthal choice, he imagined; they'd not want to spoil the Archivist's plans. That gave him a decided advantage.

They were in a faded ancient temple built to Thoth, god of many things, including technology and magic. It seemed in poor repair, but the fires were still lit by the altar, and the statue of Thoth—just a stone statue, not an automaton—had been kept painted and patched where time had worn at its surface. It stood near the western wall of the city, surrounded by brickworks and dye shops that had grown around it and dwarfed its modest presence. There was a temple to the Greek god

Hephaestus not far away; Thomas had visited it, since inside was one of the earliest automata that still survived. The bronze god inside hammered ceaselessly in his forge. The iron hammer had been replaced every year, as had the anvil, but the automaton still worked on and on. A marvel beyond price.

That should have covered Heron's Tomb. Not this dusty, rigid statue.

"I collected the clues," the old man said. "It's never been opened. Never looted by hungry smugglers. There are seven locks, and the theory is that no one has ever survived past the third. But I'm betting that you, Schreiber, you will be the first."

"I'd like to disappoint you."

"I'm sure you'll contain your disappointment if it means surviving."

Unfortunately, the old man was right. Thomas had no choices, or at least, no good ones. He could refuse to try, but he remembered the circling eyes on Wolfe, Jess, Glain. Certainly the Archivist would have assassins who could go anywhere, kill anyone they chose—if they were prepared to die for it. He couldn't risk the lives of his friends.

Risking his own life wasn't something he relished, either, but since raising Poseidon's avatar from the hidden cavern beneath the harbor, he'd felt . . . different. Steadier. More his old self, as if the god's shadow had healed something inside of him that prison had broken. He wasn't the same. But where he'd been welded together again he felt . . . stronger.

"So where is the first key?" Thomas asked.

The old Archivist—pale, seamed, sharp-faced, seemingly so frail—smiled and placed his hand on the plinth where the god stood, and a piece of decorative stonework slid aside. "It will only open for someone with a Scholar's band," he said. "Simple enough."

Inside it was a lock. "And is there a key?" Thomas asked.

"Of course there is." The old Archivist made no move to hand anything over.

"Long lost?"

"Precisely so. But every thief and smuggler passed this part of the test. I assume you will, too."

That was a good hint, even if the old man didn't intend for it to be; Thomas held up his cuffed hands. "I can't work this way," he said in a reasonable tone.

"Certainly not." The Archivist nodded at the Elite captain who stood nearby, scowling. "Unlock him."

"Archivist—"

"Do as I say. Scholar Schreiber won't betray me now. He knows the price. And he wants to see inside this tomb as much as I do, don't you, boy?"

It was true, shameful as that was; Thomas just held out his wrists for the unlocking. His ankles came next.

"Careful," the captain said. "I'll shoot you down if you make any move I don't like. Understand?"

"Oh yes," Thomas said. "You'd better hope you don't miss." He made it cheerful, which he thought was more disturbing. It seemed to work from the change in the older man's expression, and the step he took back. "I'll need two pieces of wire, please."

Someone handed him what he asked for, and he inspected them, then twisted them into the angles that he wanted. Jess was extraordinary at this, and Thomas had learned by watching and trying it himself when no one was looking; it seemed a useful and intriguing skill to have. He wished his friend was here. It would be comforting to have Jess's humor and practicality at his side.

Thomas closed his eyes and *felt* the lock as he worked the tension lever and rod, probing at the rudimentary, stiff mechanism until he had it mapped in his mind in elegant detail. Opening it was a simple lever operation, and as he turned both the wires he felt the tumblers turn and fall.

Click.

With noiseless elegance, the entire statue of Thoth rolled backward on the plinth and revealed a narrow staircase leading down. The air that breathed out of that chamber smelled ancient and stale. Thomas didn't move, though every impulse demanded he charge recklessly down toward the secrets that Heron promised. "How many died of bad air?" he asked.

The Archivist touched his fingertips to his chin, as if trying to remember, though Thomas knew he must have every fact memorized. "A few," he finally said. "But since you've asked so nicely . . ."

The High Garda Elite captain held a mask. It shimmered with some kind of coating, a chemical that was probably also alchemical, activated by an Obscurist's work. Thomas took it, strapped it on, and was pleasantly surprised by the fit of the thing. It felt perfectly balanced, and when he breathed in, the air seemed fresh and clean.

"We use them for fighting fires. This will last two hours," the captain said. "If you aren't out by then, you won't be coming out."

"I'll need light," Thomas said. The Archivist nodded again, and the Elite captain handed him a portable glow lamp.

"Anything else?" the captain asked.

"A basic tool set wouldn't be unreasonable."

"I'm afraid not," the Archivist said. "Seeing that you can do a lot of damage with the contents of a tool kit, Thomas. I'm not a fool. If you need something, we will send it down to you. Until then, you have what you need."

Thomas pocketed the lockpick wires, in case the Archivist was inclined to take them back. And then he thought, *I'm free. If I can break through the soldiers and run . . .*

But truthfully? He didn't want to run.

He wanted to *know*.

Thomas placed his boot on the first step. He paused, listening. No sounds of machinery, not yet. He descended the staircase slowly, ready to plunge up or down at any sign of a trap.

But the stairs, at least, were safe.

He was not so certain of the floor, when he arrived at the last tread. It was not a large chamber, and there was nothing in it but gray flagstones, all identical as far as he could tell. This, he thought, was where Jess's speed and agility would have come in handy; his friend's reactions were supernaturally quick. Next to that, Thomas knew his size was a liability here. He crouched down and lowered the lamp, looking closer. As he did, he caught a faint, quick shimmer on one of the flagstones.

Moving the glow back and forth showed him that the stone had a very light coating of *something* on its surface. But whether that marked it as safe or dangerous . . . impossible to tell without experimentation.

Thomas reached into his pockets. The soldiers had, of course, confiscated almost everything; what he had left was a bit of paper, the twisted wires he'd used for lock picking, and lint. But he did have something else, he realized, and rolled up his sleeve to remove his golden Scholar's bracelet. For the first time, he remembered that the Obscurists could track locations. Had his been rendered inert? Or was it possible that Morgan could look for him? That rescue was on the way?

No way to be certain.

Thomas carefully tossed the bracelet onto the coated stone.

Nothing. No movement. No sound beyond the clink of metal on rock.

Now for the other test.

The glow lamp had a handle on top, and he held it by that as he slowly lowered it to one of the plain flagstones directly in front of the stairs.

He heard the hiss of steam. *Pressure release.* Thomas snatched the lantern back just as gleaming metal spears slammed down from the ceiling through openings that had been invisible in the dim light. They withdrew just as rapidly as they'd appeared, like a deadly mirage. By the time alarm ignited in his nerves, it was already over.

No bodies or blood here, so that meant that whatever tomb robbers had made it inside had managed to figure it out.

So that meant the coated flagstones were safe. It was a simple kind of challenge, meant for the careful and observant. Easy enough to avoid if someone knew how to reason it out.

He still tested the theory. The weight from the lantern on a coated flagstone got no response.

Was the floor considered the first trial? Or the second, after picking the lock? He couldn't be sure. Thomas balanced himself carefully as he rose and stepped onto the first safe stone and bent to retrieve his bracelet. The space on the stone was a narrow fit for his feet, and he realized that this was going to be harder than he'd thought. Ancient people had been smaller than average, and he was considerably larger. He'd need to go with great care.

Picking his way across the flagstones took time, but he had managed to avoid triggering any deadly surprises. The path led him to a blank wall. Completely, utterly blank. *Interesting.*

Thomas placed his hand on the wall. If the statue of Thoth had reacted to a Scholar's bracelet, perhaps this test did as well.

It did not. He nearly lost his precarious balance on the safe flagstone when he heard something moving behind him.

He had to suppress the impulse to recklessly turn, which would have surely killed him, and slowly looked over his shoulder. In an alcove that had been hidden before stood an automaton sphinx, but one that seemed sleeker, more well defined than the ones he knew from above in the city. *This was Heron's work.* He wanted to run his hands over the lines, get into the mechanism, see the wonders of this thing . . . and then he realized that this wondrous thing was likely going to kill him.

He froze, mind racing for any idea of how to battle an automaton while standing completely still on one small square. He didn't find any.

The sphinx's eyes slowly kindled to life, but instead of red, they were a pure, luminous blue. It didn't rise.

"What must I do to be worthy?" Thomas asked it, and said it in Greek, in the hope that was the language Heron would have taught it to recognize. The sphinx tilted its head up to look directly at him.

"Answer this: I have a mouth but do not speak. I have a bed but do not sleep. I run but go nowhere." It replied in Greek, but in archaic accents and usages that Thomas struggled to translate. He hoped he had it right. He'd be dead if he didn't.

Jess might know this, Thomas thought. *Or Khalila. Or Dario. Possibly even Morgan. I never paid attention to riddles.* That, as it turned out, was proving to be a liability. *Come on, Schreiber. Children play this game.* He couldn't be beaten so easily. It would be humiliating. And, secondarily, fatal.

I have a mouth. A bed. I run.

It came to him in a rush of giddy relief. "A river!"

The sphinx rose and walked out of its alcove. It padded toward him, and he looked for escape, but the careful, awkward hops he'd made to get to this point were impossible to replicate quickly. The sphinx didn't trigger the spears at all, stepping fluidly from one safe spot to the next, and he thought, *If I could get out of the way and trigger them myself* . . . but there was nowhere to jump to safety. He'd be killing them both.

He held his breath and tried to remember the lessons Jess had taught them about how to turn the sphinxes off in midleap; his brain, frustratingly, seemed cloudy on the finer points. He cursed softly in German and realized he ought to be praying instead, but surely God would understand.

The sphinx calmly paced right past him and put a sharply clawed paw to the wall.

The wall opened with a click and a creak, swinging back and off to the side. The sphinx crouched down beside it, ruffled its metal wings, and then went still again. Its eyes flickered from brilliant blue to empty black.

Thomas couldn't help the impulse to brush his fingers over the bronze skin. It didn't move. *Leave it,* he commanded himself, and ducked into the opening. On the other side of the short, dark hallway, another wall waited.

This one seemed perfectly understandable. A single stone stood out from the others in the wall, jutting at least an inch forward. It seemed obvious that it should be pressed.

That was alarming. The obvious was dangerous here. Thomas examined the stone from as many angles as he could, and finally, lacking any other answer, pressed his fingers to it.

The wall collapsed in a rush, and he froze because what was inside was nothing he expected.

It was a garden, underground. A garden of crystals: intricate structures and spires and squares, shapes that caught and reflected his lamp in a thousand subtle hues. Beautiful. So beautiful.

So sharp.

There was a path between the crystals, but it was narrow. Even Jess would have had trouble sliding through, Thomas thought, and he was as flexible as an otter. There was no chance someone of Thomas's size could move through without brushing against something delicate. *I don't want to damage them.* But there wasn't much choice. These crystals must have been slowly growing for ages.

The instant he brushed against one, it made a sound. A low, vibrating note. He wasn't musical; he couldn't possibly identify which note it could be . . . Surely that wouldn't be required.

The next crystal he brushed against made an entirely different note. Hmmm. *Please don't make this a musical puzzle. Engineering, yes. Music, no.* Or perhaps the notes had nothing to do with it at all.

As the second crystal sounded, the first sounded again. Atonal and strange.

The crystals now hemming him in on either side suddenly grew. He didn't quite believe his eyes; surely that hadn't happened. Surely the crystals he'd successfully avoided touching weren't now pointing sharp tips at him, like a row of knives.

He'd have to ease past them. Carefully. As he tried, one sliced easily through his coat and cut a thin line through his skin like a Medica's scalpel. It didn't even hurt, but he saw the blood staining cloth. The coat offered little protection.

Moving through had to be done in torturous, muscle-cramping increments. A second's inattention caused fabric to brush along another crystal. Three notes sounded, all out of key, louder than before.

The crystals grew. One drove straight into his palm, pinning him in place, and when he cried out in surprise the crystals cried out, too, a dirge of sound that vibrated through the cavern like a hellish chorus. Thomas gritted his teeth and carefully pulled his hand off the jutting, faceted spike. It glittered like false promises.

He was going to die here.

The crystal where he'd started chimed again. A single, pure note. He caught his breath and froze because he was afraid it would start the growth cycle all over again, but instead it seemed to slow down. Stop like a clockwork.

It is clockwork. It's a puzzle. You have to solve it.

He had no framework for this. There was no metal, no wire, no gears, no steam, nothing that an engineer could understand or dismantle. He could not come at this as an engineer. Heron had made musical instruments, too; he'd made a steam calliope that had rolled on its own cart from street corner to street corner, playing different tunes for the amusement of Alexandria's citizens. Heron saw music as a pleasing outcome of an engineering marvel.

Thomas knew Heron would be very disappointed in him right now.

The crystal chimed again. Thomas had the strange idea that it was trying to help him. He found himself humming and realized something: he *did* know something useful after all. A tone was just a waveform, no different than waves in the ocean, waves on a string. Sound traveled in waves. Frequencies were mathematical.

He lowered the note he was humming until he heard no opposing waves in the sound between that and the crystal's, and hummed it louder. He didn't dare sing it for fear of going off-key, but perhaps humming . . .

The first crystal chimed twice. It was a warning. He was going in the wrong direction.

Go back, he thought. *Start over. Think it through.*

Getting back was torture; he had to twist himself carefully, so carefully, around every jutting crystal so as not to wake any more vibrations. When he arrived back at the first, he took a moment just to breathe. The mask he wore was frustrating and confining, and he dripped with sweat; before he thought why he shouldn't, he pushed it up to gasp for breath.

The air smelled . . . fresh.

He waited, heart pounding, for any sign that he'd made a fatal mistake, but nothing happened. The air continued to taste, smell, and function just as normal. With a relieved sigh, he shoved the mask in his pocket, wiped the sweat from his face, and tried to compose his thoughts.

Sound was just mathematics. If he approached it that way, perhaps he could do this. Clearly, he was looking for *harmonics.* Waveforms that complemented one another.

He carefully tapped the first crystal, and a pure, singing tone sounded. It almost sounded encouraging. *Look at the forms.* These were organic crystals, yes, but at the same time they had been somehow planned. He tried to ignore the glittering facets, the deadly spikes, and unfocused his vision.

Something emerged out of the chaos.

Color. He'd noticed the variations, but there hadn't seemed to be a pattern; when he looked at the crystals without really *seeing* them, he realized he was looking at a rainbow. The first crystal he'd struck had a slight reddish hue. What did he know about red? *It has the longest light wavelength.*

This wasn't simply a puzzle of music. It was music and light, and the light was a clue.

The problem was, he'd never really noted the order of colors in a rainbow. Was it red, orange, yellow, blue—no, it couldn't be. Yellow and blue made green, green had to come after yellow, simple logic. Then blue, indigo, and violet. But the problem was that the hues kept shifting as he moved. From one angle the scheme was clear, but as soon as he moved, it vanished.

Move until it's clear again.

The hues gleamed again, and he looked carefully. *Orange.* He tapped it. The first crystal hummed in harmony with the second. He carefully edged around a particularly dense jutting of crystal and found the yellow. It added a rich tone to the chorus. Halfway through. Only three more shades to go.

But when he touched the green—or what he thought was the green—it hit a discordant note. Dissonance.

And the crystals shot toward him at a terrifying rate. *No, no, no, surely green comes after yellow, it has to . . .* but then he took another breath, steadied himself, and unfocused his eyes again. Looking at the blurry colors without looking.

Green was a trap. Green was being filtered through another, false crystal. The real green lay behind it.

He had to start over, edging past crystals that left shallow cuts all over him and tattered his coat to a ragged mess. His breath came in short, unconscious sobs. Despite his concentration, he was afraid. He started with the red crystal. Found the orange. The yellow. Edged oh so slowly and carefully to twist himself around the concealing clear crystal to the green behind it.

Harmony.

It was then he noticed the bones. Human bones, dry and white. They littered the ground around the green crystal. A skull sat impaled on a jutting clear spike.

Slowly. Go slowly.

It was terrifying, this puzzle, but he had the key now. Unfocus his eyes, find the color, make absolutely certain he was touching the right crystal. The last two fell without triggering another reset, though the violet crystal—the last—was located in a whole forest of disorienting, faceted fakes that he checked five times before deciding to risk his final choice.

The harmony blended, and the crystals' rich, pure chord rang through the chamber. It built and built to an almost painful level, and the colors flashed bright enough to blind.

The crystals retracted completely into small, gemlike stubs. One still dripped his blood.

There was another door standing beyond the last crystal outcropping. Another keyhole with no key in sight, but it had a very particular shape. He thought about trying the lockpicks, but then realized what it was. Obvious, really.

He went back and searched the crystals until he found the correct shape, and the instant he touched it, it broke off from its stem. He inserted it in the lock, and the wall rolled aside. With it came a powerful, awful stench.

The smell of death.

Thomas wasn't sure what it was, but he grabbed the mask from his pocket and put it on, in case there was something truly dangerous waiting for him. Like toxic gas, which seemed eerily likely.

Another sphinx sat beyond it, the identical twin of the last. Thomas, despite the pain in his pierced hand and the burning cuts, took a moment to simply admire it before he said, "May I pass?"

Its eyes turned blue. "Who makes me has no need of me. Who

buys me has no use for me. Who uses me cannot see or feel me. What am I?"

Thomas felt a jagged surge of real exhaustion and frustration. *Another riddle.* He hated this. His tired brain slid off the clues. *Who makes me has no need of me.* Plenty of things were made for others that their makers had no use for. *Who buys me has no use for me.* Why would someone buy something useless? *Who uses me cannot see or feel me.* Air? Oxygen? No, none of it made any sense at all. He wanted to shout at the automaton, tell it that he was doing this to save lives, just *let him through.* But he knew it wouldn't help.

He closed his eyes and thought for long moments, leaping from one thought to another. His nerves burned under his skin. He just wanted to smash his way through.

Who makes me has no need of me.

What did someone make, and someone buy, that neither one used? What did someone use who couldn't see or feel it?

And then he realized the answer: he was making the mistake of thinking the last person was alive.

Thomas opened his eyes and said, "A tomb. *Táfos.*"

The sphinx paused for long enough that it made him question his logic, but he refused to make another guess. He was right. He had to be right.

The sphinx moved, but its eyes were still burning that unearthly blue.

Behind it was a terrifying scatter of bones. *Many* bones, enough to be piled knee-high. Skulls rolling like marbles. And one body that had only half rotted, white bones cutting through the flesh.

Yet another test. The one everyone else failed. Had it been the riddle that had killed them, or the wall beyond?

Thomas stared at the wall, but it seemed utterly blank and featureless. He reached out but pulled back; surely touching it had been the first impulse of all of these dead people who'd come here before him.

He had to solve this problem another way. And standing here surrounded by the dead, he had no idea how to proceed. Every other puzzle had been logic and observation, or a riddle requiring viewing something from a different perspective . . .

A different perspective.

He crouched down and lifted his glow higher. There was something there, but so faint he couldn't read it.

As much as he hated the thought, he was going to have to go all the way down. Lie on the ground and look up.

Like a body in a tomb.

Thomas cleared bones away, stretched out, and looked straight up at the door.

There was writing on it that was visible only from this angle. Greek letters that spelled out, *What is lighter than a feather, but even the strongest cannot hold for long?*

This one wasn't even difficult. "Breath," Thomas said, and remembered to give the answer in Greek. *"Anapnoí."*

The wall slid away.

He rolled up to his feet and walked into the Tomb of Heron.

Someone was waiting, and Thomas stopped as the wall slid shut again behind him. He couldn't believe the evidence of his own eyes, because it seemed that someone was *alive* here.

No. Not alive. But lifelike in the extreme. A man wearing a Greek chiton and a draped robe. Older. Balding. With a kind face, a rounded belly, thin arms. Shorter than Thomas by a head.

Made of metal, but so cleverly done—even to the eyes—that it seemed more a work of divine hands than human. It had the texture of skin where skin should be, and metal that flowed like cloth. Even its eyes seemed real, and seemed to focus on Thomas as much as he did on the automaton.

"Welcome," it said. The voice sounded odd—real and not quite real at the same time. A human voice, captured through time. It spoke the same archaic Greek as the sphinxes. "I am Heron of Alexandria. You have come far to find me, but all you see before you is a ghost in a metal cage. I have inscribed the rhythm and tone of my voice on a wax tablet. What you now hear is a man long ago turned to dust, yet still I greet you." The voice shifted. Grew more stern. "If you have come for riches, know there may be a high price. If you have come for knowledge, perhaps you will find what you seek if you're clever and quick. Farewell, stranger. Find me in Elysium when your time on this earth is done, and tell me what use you made of what I have left for you."

The voice stopped. The statue went still.

Behind it a door opened, and gleamed on wonders. *Wonders.* Thomas caught his breath and, almost against his will, stepped forward. Was that . . . was that Heron's steam calliope? His automated puppet show that had drawn visitors from around the known world? And that fantastic machine in the corner . . . was that a *letterpress*? Like the one he and Jess had made, that started all of this? But of course Heron would have thought of such a valuable, important invention first.

They have suppressed it for so long. Not even Heron could be trusted with this, though there was no inventor the Great Library trusted more.

He hardly noticed when the door shut behind him. The air through the mask smelled fresh, and when he lowered the device, the air still seemed fine. He put the mask away—it was near the end of its useful life in any case—and walked to the steam calliope, a gilded array of tubes that rose in a fantastic swirl. Surely the boiler was dry now, and he didn't try the switch, but to hear it play would have been astonishing.

He wandered past a machine with a pointed stylus that was set to a wax tablet. "What is this?" he wondered aloud, and watched as the stylus printed the words he'd said onto the tablet. He'd spoken in Greek, and it had understood. The same fascinating mechanism that must have recorded Heron's voice before. A marvel that dated back to the very beginnings of the Great Library. He touched the delicate mechanism and thought, *Heron's hands made this.* It was like touching genius. He blinked away tears, took in a sharp breath, and felt a twinge inside. *I'm getting tired,* he thought, but that wasn't it. He coughed. Then kept coughing, a fit that racked him nearly double. He fumbled for the mask but couldn't keep it on. His eyes burned, and his skin, and he realized now that there was a smell that had been building in the fresh air, something foul and chemical and almost sweet.

And a green mist rising from the floor to curl around his ankles.

Heron's statue turned and said, "You have until the clock turns to find the answer and earn your discovery."

Thomas gasped for air against the constriction in his lungs, and looked up to see that the statue now held a water clock.

And the water in the top container was rapidly dripping into the bottom container.

Time was running out.

EPHEMERA

Message from the Archivist in Exile to Obscurist Vanya
Nikolin, discovered by Obscurists and destroyed before
delivery

It's all going wrong. This storm has driven off the ships. The surviving
Welsh and British have turned tail and intend to crawl back to the warm
embrace of the Great Library. The Spanish won't answer my messages.

To make things worse, my assassins have killed the new Archivist at
exactly the wrong moment. Santi's men are hunting down my Elites. I
need out of the city, and to do that, I need cover; the Russians have
agreed to provide that distraction at the northeast city gate.

I will have to abandon the riches of Heron's Tomb. As long as Schreiber's been inside, he's probably dead, anyway.

As the attack proceeds, dispatch the automata to find Santi's friends,
starting with Christopher Wolfe. I want all of them dead, including the
new Archivist if you can manage it. If not I'll settle for Wolfe, but that
must be done. Save Santi for last. I might yet find a use for him.

If he resists, I'll happily slit his throat.

CHAPTER FIFTEEN

GLAIN

She'd borne the visit to the Medica station with as much grace as she could, which was next to none. They'd cleaned and dressed the wounds left by the sphinx, and she'd been given leave to return to duty. The Medica's stern warning that she'd almost lost her life didn't much bother her. She was a soldier. Losing her life was an everyday risk.

Jess didn't earn the same dismissal from his sickbed. He was livid, of course, and it scared her a little how adamant he was that he could function well enough to leave. The Medica—a big, burly woman who could have wrestled Thomas into submission—glared at him until he fell into a stubborn silence. "No," she said flatly. "You're not going any-where. The damage to your lungs was bad enough before, I'm told; it's worse now, and more effort will make it fatal in short order. Keep go-ing, young man, and you will drown in your own juices. My orders are that you're restricted from any duties whatsoever. No arguments or I'll chain you to the bed."

"You probably would," Jess muttered. That earned another glare. "All right. I'll stay."

"And I'll order more treatments," she said, and turn to Wolfe, who lurked in the corner like a premonition. "Scholar? Can you stay with him and make sure he does as I say?"

"Yes," Wolfe replied, and crossed his arms. He looked severe, dour, and utterly remote. "I certainly will."

At least Glain thought she was leaving Jess in safety—as much as anyone had at the moment. As she nodded her good-byes to him and to Wolfe, she wondered if she'd ever see them again. So the nods turned, impulsively, into words. "Stay safe," she said, and was astonished that she'd said it. She felt her cheeks turn hot, and gods knew she hadn't blushed more than a few times in her life. She hated that it had happened now, of all moments. "Don't die on me. I need you."

"You're the one running out to fight," Jess said. "The worst I risk is an uncomfortable pillow. And . . ." He hesitated, and smiled. In it, she saw the old, cocky Jess. The one he ought to be now. "And I love you, too."

She felt a horrifying tightness in her throat. *Tears?* No. She wouldn't. "Well, I wouldn't go *that* far."

"I would," Wolfe said quietly. "May the gods look after you tonight. I want you back in the morning. You're precious to more people than you know."

She nodded. Not able to speak. She escaped before she could betray what that meant to her, but once she was outside in the furiously pounding rain, she had to stop and let it sluice cold over her. There. No tears possible now. They were invisible.

She allowed herself the luxury of only a moment to let the emotion have its way, and then she caught a passing transport rumbling toward the northern districts. If an attack was still coming tonight, it would be there, from the massed infantry forces that had been sitting so quietly and waiting for the naval invasion that had never landed. The Russians had marched a long way to get here. She didn't think they'd leave without a fight.

The High Garda presence was thick as the carrier approached the outer districts, and she jumped down and ran toward the northeastern gate, the one most likely to be attacked. That was where she'd find Captain Botha, she assumed, and her squad as well.

Botha, she was told when she encountered the first member of his company, was up on the ramparts. The walls of Alexandria were built in layers; the top was massively thick, but it was supported by inner rings that rose to various levels and provided ramps from one level to another. Botha, it seemed, had stationed his company on the top; they'd be in charge of firing down on any attackers rushing the gates.

And the Russians *would* be trying their mettle. She had no doubt. What she worried about was what else might happen in the confusion of the fight. She'd been in battles before; she knew how effective diversions could be.

Diversions. There was something in that, but she didn't have time to follow the thought. She joined the line of soldiers moving up to take their spots. Tonight, the ramps she climbed were slick with rain, narrow and ancient, and she held tight to the railing. A single misstep could send her crashing backward into the soldiers massed behind her, and that wouldn't do at all.

She was almost cheerful, which felt strange; it was cold and storming, there was an army at the city's gates that outnumbered the High Garda almost two to one . . . and she was *happy*. No getting around it: she was born for this. Her father would be scandalized. Her brothers would be jealous.

Her mother would be so proud.

Something whistled in the air far above her head, and she jerked her chin up to track its progress. Couldn't see the missile, but it must have been fired from the Russian army's positions. Greek fire? She couldn't see any fuse burning. And that sound . . . it seemed wrong. She'd grown accustomed to how ballista-fired bombs sounded. Those kind of missiles made an eerie whistling sound, too, but at an entirely different pitch; the whistle was attached to the bomb to create an unnerving effect on troops below. This seemed fainter, more as if the sound was a mere by-product of its flight.

"Move!" someone yelled behind her, and she quickly advanced up the ramp. She'd only made it half a dozen steps when the world exploded behind her. Not the awful gleam of Greek fire, but a hot orange like a forest set ablaze, and when she paused and turned, she saw devastation. Half a neighborhood blown apart, walls flung down, roofs shattered. Bodies running, falling. Burning.

That is not Greek fire.

She didn't know what it was, but it had a tremendous force to it, as bad as or worse than what they were used to seeing. This wasn't something the fire crews had prepared to handle. They needed water, and a lot of it. And no one had prepared to fight whatever this madness was.

More whistles overhead. The Russians were firing their strange weapons blind, trying to strike sheer terror, and it was working. She watched a temple crumble, a warehouse explode. *What if it hits a Medica facility? Homes? Schools?* She felt physically sick with rage, and her muscles ached with holding it inside. She didn't know if the Iron Tower or the Serapeum or the Great Archives could stand against this unknown bombardment. Whatever this awful stuff was, it held a horrible power, and it was entirely new to them.

"Squads to the wall!" Captain Botha shouted, and his voice carried even over the chaos. Glain ran to claim her spot, with her High Garda companions elbow to elbow. "Ready!" Beyond them other captains were positioning their own companies. Down on behind them, more soldiers fortified the gates. Others were readying ballistas to fire into the enemy forces. It was a massing of High Garda force that had rarely been seen, and never here in Alexandria. "Hold!"

Santi was up on the wall, Glain realized; she saw him standing with his captains as they spotted the Russian deployments. *He shouldn't be here. He should be safe in the Serapeum.* But that wasn't Santi; he, like her, needed to be in the thick of it. She looked around at the squad she'd

inherited from Tom Rolleson, now their lieutenant; she saw Troll farther down the row, watching the company's formations. "Blue Dogs!"
she yelled. "Get ready!"

They gave back the sharp bark of agreement. She watched Rolleson, not the enemy. What the enemy might do didn't concern her now.

More bombs came flying overhead. *What happens when they get our
range?* she thought suddenly, and imagined one of those landing here on
the terrace. It would be sheer carnage.

Whatever Santi was waiting for, it wasn't anything the Russians
were planning. And she almost missed it, except for the whisper of
wings above her in the darkness, and a sudden stop to the rain on her
head as an automaton flew over their position.

The mechanical dragon that Thomas had designed floated down,
almost invisible in the darkness. And then it breathed a horrifyingly
huge stream of Greek fire down on the army below. The light glazed
on the huge metallic wings as the dragon hovered, its snakelike head
bent forward. It was a nightmare come to life, and for the first time
Glain was glad to see it.

It was not targeting the soldiers, she realized, but some odd-looking
devices farther back, tubular and on wheels. The Greek fire hit those
structures and the metal melted in on itself with shocking speed. A series of violent explosions ripped the night apart, casting sharp fragments
through the opposing army in a bloody swath.

Glain couldn't help the cheer that tore out of her throat; she
shouldn't have been glad of their deaths, but she was. They'd have
cheered for hers.

The Russians turned their gunfire on the dragon, but it wasn't
alone. The smaller winged forms of automata sphinxes plunged out of
the rain and began to tear through whole columns of soldiers like paper.

It was sudden, total war.

"Free fire!" Rolleson shouted, echoing a command she couldn't
hear, and Glain repeated it for her squad as she aimed her rifle down at

the running troops below. They were coming steadily, and she respected them for that; it wasn't a panicked stampede but a measured assault. One of them threw something metallic at the gates. She heard the explosion. Felt it through her boots. Had they breached the barrier? It was hard to tell. She picked targets and fired, rocking the recoil with her shoulder and repositioning precisely for the next shot, and the next, and the next. Shadow targets, illuminated only by the light of the burning things—some new sort of ballistas?—that the dragon had torched. The darkness lit again with more explosions as ammunition ignited. Spectacular and awful. She averted her eyes briefly from the glare, then picked off three more attackers.

"Hold and away!" Rolleson shouted, and Glain roared it, too; she and the squad stepped back from the wall. "Cover!"

They all crouched, backs to the wall, as the ballistas fired and the shrieking Greek fire containers arced over their heads. If one of those went amiss, Glain thought, they'd all roast right here. But all the shots cleared their positions and shattered on the other side of the wall. Santi had aimed them precisely, she realized as she took her position again; he'd targeted four spots to divide the attacking forces and confuse their strategy. The ones down at the gate were now pinned in place; their explosives hadn't opened the way for them, and the High Garda, Glain's squad included, poured lethal fire down on top of them.

They were, of course, shooting back. She felt the impact of bullets on either side of her head where she was protected by the crenellations, and once a stunning impact to her helmet that made her see stars and blink in confusion for a solid few seconds. One of her squad—Sarven—fell and didn't move. She yelled for a Medica without pausing in her target selection and saw from the corner of her eye that he was dragged off for treatment. Men and women of the High Garda were falling, but not nearly as many as were being slaughtered beyond those gates. The Russians had come in force, but with their explosive weapons shattered, would they keep at it? Battering against an impenetrable wall, fighting mud, a dragon, bullets, Greek fire, sphinxes? Why wouldn't they re-treat?

She found out.

A massive carrier rolled relentlessly out of the midst of the Russian forces and headed for the gates. It was covered in spikes and metal plating, rolling on linked spinning tracks that churned through the mud at a shocking rate of speed. It was the size of small warship, and as the Russian troops retreated out of its way, it went straight for the gates.

It had one of those odd metal tubes sticking from the front of it, and as she watched, something exploded out of it in a rush of fire and smoke, and she felt stone crack and heave as the gates blew apart, flinging fragments into the city and into the ballista company below. Greek fire globes shattered, consuming the whole squad guarding them. "Gods," Glain breathed, and it was half a curse and half a prayer. She wanted to rush to their defense, but she looked to Rolleson. Rolleson looked just as anguished and conflicted, but Botha . . . Botha, and Santi beyond him, seemed unruffled. Santi gave orders she couldn't hear, but they came clear in the relay.

One company was withdrawing to fight on the ground, but Botha's company would stay on the wall. If they all rushed down, there was nothing to stop the Russians from regrouping and storming in behind the carrier. Santi was arranging forces to prevent them from taking advantage of a temporary victory.

The dragon landed in front of the gates where the carrier had entered and laid down a huge semicircle of fire. The Russians tried to rush forward, but automata lions leaped through the fire to take them down.

Santi reserved his vulnerable human soldiers for the next wave.

Glain aimed and fired at anyone stupid enough to try an approach. The rain droned relentlessly, and she felt her muscles beginning to ache from the strain. Chilled to the bone, hurting from constant adrenaline, and haunted by exhaustion. This would be a long night. A long fight.

She very nearly missed the attack, because it came from her side of the wall. A sphinx glided out of the darkness, and the only warning she had was the shadow cast on the wall, a moving, descending darkness that made her spin around to see what was coming.

The sphinx was gliding in talons first: a golden bird of prey about to pick off an unwary mouse.

I'm not a mouse.

She yelled, dodged, and dropped her rifle; it wouldn't do any good unless she was a far better sharpshooter. As the sphinx's sharp claws touched the stone and sparked, she rolled and lunged upward and beneath the biting jaws for where the switch was located. A split second later she remembered that the sphinx that had attacked them in the Necropolis *had* no off switch, and she realized that no one could save her if she'd just committed to the wrong plan; the other soldiers around her were backing off, confused and shocked, trying to continue firing on the Russians attacking the gate. No help. She had to do this alone.

Her fingers grazed a bump in the metal skin, and she pressed it hard as the sphinx screamed and raised both front paws to claw her from neck to legs.

It stuttered and froze, eyes dying to black.

She braced herself and kicked out, hard, sending it toppling in an uncontrolled crash over on its back. Glain stayed where she was as she gulped for breath and watched it for any sign of recovery, but it was utterly still.

That was when a shot shattered into the wall beside her head, and it took her a second to realize that the bullet hadn't been fired from the Russian side. It had come from *within the walls.* She threw herself forward, hiding in the bulk of the dead automaton, and felt the metal shiver as more bullets struck it. There was a pause, and she quickly slithered forward to try to locate the threat. For the trajectory to be so flat, it had to be someone on a rooftop, and likely close by—*there.* She caught a glint of metal. She rolled back just as another volley of shots came at her and hit the stone floor; the grit under her palms was fresh, scraped by the sphinx's claws. She was just able to reach her rifle, and pulled it toward her.

Whoever was shooting, they weren't aiming at anyone else. Just her. The other soldiers continued on, not oblivious to the threat but simply occupied. This was her problem. It was up to her to solve it.

She waited for another pause and mapped what she'd seen before. The glint of metal in reflected light. She calculated that to be the targeting glass on a High Garda rifle, which put her actual target the length of her forearm behind it.

The firing paused.

She came up on her knees and sighted. She caught the glare of the glass, but only for an instant because it was swinging *away* from her.

And toward the knot of captains where Lord Commander Santi stood.

She took a careful, even breath, held it, gauged her distance, and fired three times. She spaced the shots so that even if she missed with one, she was likely to land two.

No more shots came from that position, though she waited, still holding that breath until it turned stale and urgent. She was presenting a plain and perfect target.

But the sniper didn't take the bait.

She'd hit him.

Glain let the breath out and went back to her duties, firing at any Russian soldier who presented a target, until a sharp tap on her shoulder made her flinch. It was the lieutenant. "Sir?" she shouted. Her voice was too loud, but she was half-deaf from the din of battle.

"Take your squad to the streets behind the lines, Squad Leader. There's word of rebels down there taking shots at us. Find them!"

"Yes, sir!" she snapped and pitched her voice to carry to her squad, even over the never-ending rattle of fire. "Blue Dogs! With me!"

They barked the response and followed. She automatically counted heads; two missing, but the rest were uninjured. They took the ramp as fast as they dared, but Glain stopped and held them in place while she looked over the rail at the street below. The Russians' invading armored carrier had been caught on a row of angled steel caltrops the size of cattle; its treads still spun but it got no purchase. As she watched, a High Garda soldier scrambled up on the roof of the thing, found a hatch, and flung it open. He dropped a Greek fire grenade inside and leaped clear.

The screaming that erupted inside the metal monster was loud enough to be heard even over the thunder of battle.

Glain swallowed at the thought of the hell inside that vehicle, and led her squad the rest of the way down. Half the ballistas were in smoking ruins, thanks to the damage done by the carrier. The night air reeked of the stench of Greek fire and something new, a sharp and unpleasantly acrid smell she supposed was due to the new explosives the Russians had brought with them. She risked a glance at the gates.

There were no gates. Just a ragged hole in the wall where gates had been. A single iron hinge still hung limp from one surviving bolt. The only things that stood between Alexandria and the Russian forces were the High Garda, the Obscurists' automata, and the good favor of the city's gods. As many as they'd killed from the walls, it would not be enough. The Russians still had armored carriers and tens of thousands of soldiers to throw against these defenses, even if their new, deadly bomb throwers hadn't withstood the dragon's assault.

No help for that. She had a mission to carry out. The defense of the city was Lord Commander Santi's responsibility, not hers.

She led the Blue Dogs away from that fight. They dodged the ruins of the first building that had been leveled by Russian explosives, and as they got free of the noise of battle, Glain slowed them down and took her bearings. The sniper had been on the roof half a block away, and the shooter had almost certainly been connected to the saboteurs; most likely the rest wouldn't be far. This was what the Blue Dogs unit had been built to do: hunt down specific targets.

She turned the corner, setting the Blue Dogs on a standard fan formation, four going high and the rest staying low; their spotters would tell them where to turn, and she'd deploy the team to pick off their targets, one by one.

That was when she saw someone who seemed out of place peeping around a corner. A man she recognized, however vaguely; she never forgot a face, though it took her a few seconds to put him into place in her memory. She'd last seen him inside the Iron Tower. An Obscurist. He'd been one of those hanging back when Gregory and the Artifex had taken them all prisoner, and Wolfe's mother had given her life to save theirs.

What was an Obscurist doing out here, in the middle of a pitched battle zone, wearing common street clothing?

Nothing good.

She started to give a command, but stopped as a gleaming automaton stalked around the other corner and came toward him. It was a big Roman-style lion, and it was unnaturally large, this one; it made the normal Alexandrian versions look like lapdogs. It moved so quietly, too.

She thought for a moment it was hunting him, but no. It was *with* him.

She couldn't hear the commands the Obscurist gave the thing, but in seconds it responded. The lion let out a deep-throated growl and bounded off, running flat out toward the corner. Not toward them. Away.

Glain grabbed her second and said, "You have command. I need to follow the beast."

"Sir, what are you doing? You can't go alone!"

She didn't wait to argue about it; there wasn't time. She needed to stop whatever dire damage the lion had just been sent to inflict.

Though what she was going to do when she caught the thing, she had no idea.

Yet she had no choice.

She was no runner like Jess, but she was competent enough; she'd studied form and practiced hard, and though she got no joy in it, she could put on speed, if not his particular grace. The lion was moving fast, though. Too fast. Despite her best efforts, burning lungs and legs, she couldn't catch it. Couldn't even track it. Glain hated to admit defeat, but she knew she had to outsmart it, not outrun it.

She slumped against the wall of what would usually be a busy bakery but was silent as the grave tonight, and removed her Codex as she gasped for breath. Her legs were shaking with the effort, and she let herself slide down to a sitting position to brace herself for writing.

She sent the first message to Captain Botha, reporting what she'd seen. Then Wolfe, Dario, Khalila, Thomas, and Morgan, telling them where she'd last seen the creature and where she was. Not Jess; she didn't want to tempt him to leave the Medica building. Not Santi, who couldn't be distracted in the middle of this battle. She needed *everyone* on this; she had the feeling the automaton's orders would be something awful and very important. Having written it, she waited for messages back.

Morgan was the first, and she said, *I'm tracking it. Attempting to gain control.*

Glain concentrated on slowing her breathing and letting her body rest a moment. The reply came from Dario, too. He was heading out from the Serapeum. *Don't be a fool and do this alone. Tell me where you are.* Rich, coming from him. But she appreciated the sentiment. She dashed off a quick reply to give him the cross streets.

Nothing back from Wolfe or Thomas. Khalila wrote that she couldn't leave the Serapeum but that any resources needed by any of them that were not devoted to the battle at the gates were theirs to command.

Morgan's distinctive handwriting appeared as she began to acknowledge Khalila's message. She wrote, *It's coming for you, Glain.*

Glain read it, but before she had time to truly take it in she heard a low, rumbling growl. Not thunder this time. The rain was starting to slow, and she looked up to see the lion padding down the center of the empty street.

Glain stood up, slamming her Codex back in her belt, and readied her rifle. It was possible—dimly possible—to stop a lion with a precision shot to the eye, but in reality she wasn't quite that good. Worth a try, though. She knew she couldn't outrun the thing, and though she knew how to turn the regular models off, if this one had been modified it would be her last mistake. And this one seemed . . . modified.

Why was it stalking *her*? She just wasn't that important.

The lion came for her at a quick, straight trot. Even as much experience as she had with automata, *this* one had a special dread for her, and she couldn't even think why. Something in the proportions. The way it moved. The way its eyes gleamed, as if it was *hungry*.

Another explosion at the northeast gate. She felt it through the wall of the bakery, the stones beneath her feet, but she couldn't afford to turn to look.

She slowly let out her breath and fired for the thing's glowing red eye.

She missed. Not by much, a fraction of an inch. The bullet struck metal instead of the hardened glass of the eye. Didn't even leave a scratch.

The lion broke into a run. It was seconds away, and she fired again, but this shot was even less precise. She wanted to run, every instinct screamed for it, but she set herself like a mountain. *I will not move.*

Out of nowhere, she remembered something from a book she'd read back at Ptolemy House as a student. *The gods conceal from us the happiness of death, that we may better endure life.*

Oddly cheering, in this moment when she saw death coming straight for her.

"What the hell are you doing, just standing there?" a voice in her ear said, and a hand pulled her elbow and yanked her around the corner, out of the lion's sight. "Are you *trying* to get yourself killed?"

She knew the severe tone before she saw his face. Scholar Wolfe. *Of course.* That was why the lion had come this way.

It wasn't after her at all. It was locked on *him.*

She was just in the way.

"Run!" she said. "I'll keep it busy."

"Not alone you won't." That was Jess, who—she realized with a shock—was leaning with one hand on a wall not far away. She really must be slipping; she hadn't even noticed him at first. "We can work together. We have to."

"No time, it's coming!" She ripped free of Wolfe's grasp. "It's after *you.* Get out of here! Now!"

She felt a sudden burst of air from behind her, and felt a wave of heat simmer over her skin; for a horrible second she thought it was Greek fire and they were all dead, but then she saw Jess's face and knew exactly what had happened.

She turned and found Morgan had appeared behind her. She'd Translated in, though how that was possible without a configured Translation Chamber Glain couldn't even imagine. Pure power, most likely.

"Move!" Morgan shouted, and Glain did, diving out of her way toward Jess. The least she could do was stand between the walking wounded and the fight. Morgan stepped in front of Wolfe, who did *not* seem pleased by it.

The lion padded around the corner and stopped to assess the situation. Its massive head turned to regard Wolfe. Morgan, in front of him, looked very small in comparison.

Glain put a flat hand against Jess's chest as Jess tried to move forward. "No," she said. "She can do this."

The lion came toward Wolfe. Morgan stepped toward it, hand outstretched. Glain tensed as the lion's jaws opened, revealing a horrifying array of teeth. It could snap her in half, easily.

It simply . . . stopped.

"There you are," Morgan whispered. "Someone's rewritten you. Removed you from the system. They've made you their pet killer." Her fingers twitched, as if she were holding an invisible pen and writing on thin air. "He's very good, your master. But arrogant."

"What are you doing?" Glain asked. She didn't think Morgan would answer, but she had to ask it.

"Repairing her," Morgan said. "She's not meant to do this. Her mission is to protect the Great Library, not to hunt down Scholars. I'm sending her where she needs to be."

The lion slowly closed its jaws, and blinked, and its eyes faded to yellow. Still unnerving, and Glain didn't relax until it let out an ear-splitting roar, turned, and ran in the direction of the northeast gate.

Morgan had already turned toward Scholar Wolfe. "I'm glad you're safe," she said, and then looked at each of them in turn. Glain didn't like the shimmer in her eyes, or the feeling she got from her. Too . . . hot, somehow. Too full of energy, like power was about to burst out of her. "Scholar . . . the Obscurist who made these changes is still working for the old Archivist. I can track him. We need to stop him before he does something worse."

"He probably already has," Jess said. He sounded exhausted. "Do you know him? Who he is?"

"I can find him." She nodded. "He's close."

"What about the old man?" Wolfe asked. "Surely he can't be far away, either. He can't Translate out; Eskander's cut that off from him. Santi's blocking his way out from any of the other gates. His only chance at escape is through the chaos at the northeast gate."

"So he'll be close to the battle and looking for his chance," Jess said. "Or creating one if he can."

"Likely," Wolfe said. "We need to find him. Let's finish this."

"Khalila's offered us resources," Glain volunteered. "We should take advantage of that. We don't know who's with him, or how many guns he's got on his side. We need to find a spot and lure him into it. If we engage him in the middle of the High Garda army "

"Confusion," Jess said. "She's right, sir. We need to draw him to a place of our choosing, and be ready."

Wolfe looked to each of them, and finally, to Glain. "Very well," he said. "I'll place it in your hands, Wathen. Don't disappoint."

She touched her fist to her heart. "My pleasure, Scholar." She hesitated. "I'm not sure he'll fall for anything that comes from me, sir. Perhaps you could draw him in?"

"Probably not. He'd automatically assume it was a trap," Wolfe said. "I can't think of any of us he'd believe . . ." His voice trailed off, and though he didn't finish the thought, Jess did.

"Oh, I think you can," he said. "Because I'm thinking the very same thing."

And as if he'd been conjured up out of the rain, Dario Santiago rounded the corner and said, "*Dios*, what did I miss?"

EPHEMERA

Inscription on the wall of the Great Archives of Alexandria

In this place we burn the lamp of knowledge that never goes out. We light the world.

CHAPTER SIXTEEN

JESS

"You shouldn't be here," Wolfe said to Jess, while Glain wrote in her Codex and Morgan spoke to Dario. "I told you to stay in bed, boy. And you promised."

Jess shrugged. "Glain was in danger. Staying flat on my back there accomplishes nothing. Being upright with you might."

"The only thing it will accomplish is to get you killed."

Wolfe's voice was severe, but Jess didn't miss the pain hidden under it, either. He knew Wolfe was worried. But there wasn't any point. The entire Great Library could collapse before dawn; the Russians could prevail at the gate, could rumble through the streets in their armored carriers and crush the High Garda. The Iron Tower would close its doors, and so would the Serapeum and the Lighthouse and the Great Archives, but how long would that hold if Alexandria itself was taken? Eventually, the Great Library would have to submit. The city's residents wouldn't put up a fight; no one had ever trained them how. It had never been necessary.

He decided to be honest. Just with Wolfe, who he thought already knew. "I'm not going to make it, Scholar. Dying in a bed . . . that's not me. Getting killed for something worthwhile is better than dying alone. At the worst, I might buy you time to do what's needed."

Wolfe's expression flickered, but Jess didn't know what was underneath that mask. Anger? Anguish? Maybe both. "And what's that, in your opinion?"

"Kill that old bastard," Jess said. "Don't take him prisoner. Don't let Khalila tell you that justice must be impartial. She's right, but this is an exception. We've seen what damage he'll do as long as he draws breath."

He meant it. And he was honest enough, too, to know that part of the reason he said it with so much conviction was his own rage. He was hungry for revenge. And sick that he hadn't taken it out on Zara, who'd deserved it. Mercy was the effect of his friends, dragging him kicking and screaming into being a better man.

Jess didn't really think their good influence would last, in the end. He had too much of his family running through his veins, too much of his father's twisted, stunted outlook rubbed into him like a stain. It would take him a lifetime to unlearn it all. And here he was, barely eighteen, and dying, and all he could truly do was make one last mark. In a very real way, he thought, he'd already died in the arena with his brother.

Twins were not meant to survive alone.

Wolfe simply shook his head and motioned to Dario, who stepped away to huddle with Glain and Wolfe. That left Jess with Morgan, who was watching him with a frown. "You look dreadful," she said.

"Thanks."

"I mean it, Jess. You shouldn't be here."

She was seeing more, he thought, than just his generally awful outward appearance. He couldn't hide from her. It was something he both loved and feared about her. "You can't fix me," he said. "Can you?"

She shook her head. "It was your choice," she said. "I've been reminded that I can't save everyone, especially not if it's their own chosen path." She smiled, briefly. It hurt him. "I'm not even sure I can save myself, if I'm being quite honest."

Dario was shaking his head forcefully, and that caught Jess's attention. He left Morgan and walked to join that conversation. "No," Dario was saying. "I'm not doing this. I've had enough of intrigue. Let someone else—"

"No one else can make him believe it," Glain said. "Who do you think lies better, you or me?"

"*He will know!* I already double-crossed the Spanish; don't you think he'd have been told of that? I arranged for the slaughter of half his High Garda Elites! I'm the *last* person he'd believe just now."

"Dario. There's no one else." Glain sounded calm and patient, but there was weight there. "He's not going to believe Wolfe, or me, or gods know, Jess. Definitely not Morgan. Who else is there?"

Dario's brows drew together, and from Jess's viewpoint he could see the Spaniard *really* didn't like the suggestion he was about to make. "I . . . might have a solution," he said. "Jess, what about your father?"

"No," Wolfe snapped, at the same time that Jess said, "Yes." They looked at each other. Wolfe got to it first. "There is absolutely *no* way that I trust your father to do anything but betray our interests."

"Well, true," Jess agreed. He drew a breath harder than he meant to and was racked by coughs that grayed out his vision and turned his legs to jelly, and when he blinked his way back into the world, Wolfe was clutching his arm to hold him up. And they all stared at him with identical expressions of concern . . . no, not Morgan. Morgan's was sadder than the others. Tinged with the knowledge he was sicker than he pretended. "Sorry. Yes, my da is a snake who'll turn on anyone for a profit. But he won't turn on me. I'm all he's got left."

"Jess—" Morgan's voice was gentle, and more than a little appalled. "Jess, you can't do this."

"It's something I *can* do," he said. "I can beg. And he'll enjoy that." They all fell silent, even Dario, who in earlier days might have mocked him. Maybe they all knew the weight of what that meant to him. He ignored them. He took out his Codex and wrote to his father, in the family's code. As he did, he asked, "Where do you want to set the trap?"

A cough seized him at the end of that, twisted his lungs into knots, and reduced him to gagging blood on the ground. More than he liked. Wolfe held on to him, and he could feel the trembling of the Scholar's hands. See the horror, quickly covered again, on Dario's face.

After a long rain-drenched span of seconds, Glain said, "All right. You remember how to get to the ancient Serapeum, don't you? The one on our first day at Ptolemy House?"

The day they'd discovered just how potentially deadly the game of the Great Library really was. Jess caught his breath, but it tasted foul and didn't do him much good. "The old Archivist won't like it," he managed to say. "Too enclosed."

"Have your father say it's for his own safety. That's no doubt true; there's a standing bounty on Callum Brightwell's head all over the Great Library."

Jess didn't waste time or breath discussing that. He just wrote the message out. He wondered what his father felt, seeing his handwriting appear. Wondered if it brought relief or anger. Probably both.

The delay was agonizing. *What if he's so angry he won't reply? What if he's cut you off entirely?* That would probably be a personal blessing, but now . . .

His father's handwriting began to inscribe itself onto the page, bland words that hid the message within. *Are you sure?*

Yes, Jess replied. *Make it quick.*

The delay was longer this time. He tried to ignore his own weariness, the shakes that rattled through him, the bleariness of his eyes. *Come on, Da. For one time in your life, be useful to me without any gain for yourself.*

The message finally came through. *He took the bait. I've promised him escape and the funds to raise his own army to take back the throne. I told him you and Brendan both betrayed the family business and I wanted to make amends. He might not believe it. I wouldn't.*

Jess waited for something else, anything else . . . a simple *How are you?* or *Look after yourself,* or the impossible *I love you, son.* Anything but silence.

He finally closed the Codex and swallowed a bitter sense of loss. He hadn't actually lost anything.

But it still hurt.

"He's sent the message to the old man, and the old man's agreed. Whether or not the Archivist will show up . . . that's not certain."

"I'll go there," Wolfe said. "Glain? We'll need your squad. And to be cleverer than the old man thinks we are."

He glanced at Jess, just briefly, but Jess understood that to mean something. He nodded.

"I'll be fine; the Medica gave me a stronger mask and new medication on the way out," he said. He turned to Morgan, but seeing her face made him forget what he meant to say. She knew he was lying. "Can you help us with this?"

"Yes. I wish I could kill him for you. But . . . I can't." She lifted her hand so the ring was visible. "Eskander gave me this to help me control my . . . hungers. The ring won't allow me to harm anyone unless they're harming me first." She looked him straight in the eyes as she continued. "It also won't let me take away conscious choices people make. Such as making a deliberate decision to sacrifice themselves. Bear that in mind."

He nodded. He understood. And, in a strange way, he was grateful for it. Maybe he wouldn't be when this all came to an end and he was gasping for his last breath. But for now it felt comforting to know that his choices were his own, still.

"My clever father," Wolfe muttered. "Trust Eskander to find yet another way to make this more difficult. All right, then. Do what you can. Dario—"

"*I'm* not going to kill him," Dario said, and held up both hands in refusal. "I've got no wish to be cut to pieces by whatever automata he's programmed to avenge him. Or worse, murdered by his lackeys. That would be a commoner's way to die."

"We'll make sure everyone knows how royally you bled to death," Glain said, but she was smiling. Jess felt it, too: belonging somewhere. Belonging *here*, with *them*. It meant something more than just . . . usefulness.

He was fairly certain, though he had no good context for it, that this was what it felt like to have a real, genuinely loving family.

"Come on, then," Glain said. "My squad will meet us there. If I remember correctly, there's access to a sniper's gallery on the upper level. We'll position there."

"He'll know about it," Wolfe warned her. "Our sole advantage is that we get there first."

"Then let's move," Jess said. "I'll keep up." The looks they gave one another, if not him . . . It was irritating and warm at the same time. "Fine. Find me a ride, then."

"I happen to have a carrier parked just around the corner," Glain said, as if she hadn't been thinking about him when she ordered it up. "Dario, don't even think about asking for a nicer ride."

He shrugged that away. "Sadly, I'm becoming used to the hardships."

They did indeed get to the original Serapeum first; the carrier dropped them on the street near Ptolemy House and sped away, moving fast to some other destination. The rain was just a light drizzle now, and a bit warmer, or else Jess had just become accustomed to discomfort. The clouds still hit the moon, and even the streetlight glows couldn't make the streets look less than deserted and forbidding. From here, the sounds of fighting still echoed, but far away, as if they might not matter at all.

"Someone's still at Ptolemy House," Dario said, and Jess turned in that direction. Their old dormitory must have contained postulants for the upcoming year—unfortunate timing for them, he supposed—and he wondered who had been appointed as their proctor. Not Wolfe, obviously. For a moment he remembered what it had been like there. Dario, the peacock bully. Thomas, shy and quiet and unsure of his own genius. Khalila had changed the least, he thought; she'd always been so calmly self-assured. He and Morgan and Glain had probably shifted the most, each in their own directions. Each toward their strengths.

Had Wolfe changed? If he had, it was impossible to tell. He slapped both of them on the backs of their heads as he passed.

"Gawk later," he said. "Move."

The entrance to the ancient Serapeum, the very first public library of Alexandria—and in the world—seemed dark and deserted, until one of Glain's Blue Dogs melted out of the shadows. More followed. Not a magic trick, but it felt like one tonight. Jess nodded to those he knew, which was most, and from the way they looked at him, even the new ones knew who he was. "No one inside," Glain's lieutenant said. "You're sure about this. Once we're inside, we're rats in a trap."

"No," Glain said. "We're the cats. The rats are about to arrive, so let's get set up. Scholar, you, Jess, and Dario are the cheese. I'll keep Morgan with me."

Morgan started past but suddenly turned and enveloped him in a hug. Jess, surprised, returned it for just a few seconds before stepping away. "Not good-bye," he said. "You're not that lucky."

"I'm very lucky," Morgan said. "Look who I call friends."

Friends was a deliberate choice of word, he thought, and so was the hand she put so gently against his face. He swallowed a thickness in his throat as Glain, the Blue Dogs, and Morgan disappeared up a hidden set of narrow stairs. The space down here in the round chamber was empty; the scrolls were long since gone, and the stone shelves sat empty. It seemed ominously still.

Jess felt naked, cold, and suddenly very aware that he might end his life in this place. *Well,* he thought, *dying in an ancient library isn't the worst way to go.*

He just wished it had books on those empty shelves. Rare ones, the kind that smelled of the years they'd survived, written in the hand of their maker. He'd miss that. He'd miss a lot of things. Breakfast at their favorite sidewalk café with his friends. Thick Alexandrian coffee. The twisting streets of London. The taste of Spanish food. The smell of roses.

He closed his eyes and tried to hold on to those things until his brother's whisper said, *Don't die just yet. I'm enjoying my time on my own for a change.*

He almost smiled. Almost. Brendan felt so real, so present, that he thought he could touch him.

When he opened his eyes, Dario said, "They're coming."

He expected the Archivist, but instead it was a High Garda Elite captain, decked out in the red uniform. He, Jess thought, could pass even Lord Commander Santi's harsh inspection. Even his boots looked polished.

The captain hadn't even bothered to draw his gun, and didn't now. He also didn't look at all surprised. And . . . he was alone. No sign of the Archivist.

"Well," he said. "I didn't really expect much. But this is a nice surprise."

"Where is your master?" Wolfe asked. "Too afraid to show his face?"

"Too smart, Scholar. Far too smart. Unlike you. Really, did you think this simpleminded trap would work? That you'd convince the most hunted man in Alexandria to put his head in a noose just because a criminal whose sons already betrayed him *said so*? I'm curious."

"No," Wolfe said. "I really didn't think he would. But it's good he sent you. You'll do."

"Do for what? Did you forget about the observation level?" He looked up. So did Jess, and felt his stomach turn over.

He'd expected to see the Blue Dogs and Morgan. But they weren't there. He didn't know those faces at all.

Those hard, angry, unmerciful faces were aiming rifles down at him, Dario, and Wolfe. The trap they'd planned had closed on them instead.

"Any last words, Scholar? I'll be happy to record them and add them to your journal . . . Oh, sorry, the Archivist has ordered your journals burned. No one will remember you. Especially when we kill all your followers."

"I don't have followers," Wolfe said. He looked at his students. "Do I?"

"No, sir," Dario said. "I'm afraid not. You're too unlikeable."

"As I feared." He looked back at the captain. "You see? So leave my young friends out of this. Make it between adults, if you can manage that."

"I'm not interested in fighting you, *Scholar*."

"Well, in that case, I do have last words," Wolfe said. "If you wouldn't mind."

The captain drew his gun at last. He aimed straight at Wolfe. "Go ahead. Ten seconds."

Wolfe smiled. "I only need one. Morgan?"

From somewhere up above, she said, "Yes." And she dropped an illusion that must have cost her much, in terms of power and endurance.

Glain and her squad were standing motionless *behind* the Elite soldiers. The Blue Dogs barked in unison, and it was a guttural, eerie sound that woke chills down Jess's spine.

"Give up, Captain," Wolfe said quietly. "For the sake of your soldiers. Tell us where to find the Archivist and we'll spare all your lives."

Jess knew it wouldn't work. He lunged forward and grabbed hold of the Elite captain's hand as the man fired; the shot barely missed Wolfe's head and impacted the hard stone wall beyond. Gunfire erupted on the second level, but it wasn't coming at them. There was a battle going on between the soldiers. He could only hope Glain's squad was faster, if not better.

He managed to get the gun wide enough that the next shot the captain fired still went wide, but his strength was failing him. Dario came to the rescue, slamming a fist hard into the man's temple and rocking him off balance, and he, too, got a grip on the man, trying for the gun. Wolfe was moving forward, but everything seemed slowed down now. Jess shook with effort. His lungs burned. His whole body felt raw and empty and so very tired.

I'm losing. He could taste defeat. It was bitter, like the blood welling up in his lungs.

Wolfe took the gun away, went back a step, and without a blink of hesitation, shot the man.

The red-uniformed captain clearly couldn't believe it. Jess could almost read his rueful thoughts: *Felled by a Scholar.*

The man's knees folded, and the captain collapsed to the floor, bleeding. Dario stepped back, and pulled Jess away with him.

"Where is the old man?" Wolfe asked, and aimed his weapon at the captain's head. His voice sounded very quiet. Very calm. "You have one chance. Just one. Then I kill you."

"No you won't, *Scholar,*" the captain said, and bared his teeth. "I surrender. And you're not a murderer, are you?"

"Glain?" Wolfe called. Jess heard her boots on the stairs, and in the next instant she was beside them, smelling of gunpowder and blood. Her favorite perfume. "Status?"

"Six prisoners, sir, the rest are dead." She put her foot on the captain's chest. "Permission to execute the traitor?"

"No, Wathen. I don't think so. Take him to a Medica station and then put him behind bars." Wolfe let out an angry huff of breath. "We've failed. The Archivist is probably halfway to Russia now."

"Doubt it," Dario said. He had a cut on his head that was flooding crimson over his shirt; Jess hadn't seen it happen, and Dario hardly even seemed aware of it. "Glain. Step away." Glain did. Dario moved forward and put the point of his dagger against the captain's throat.

"Are we playing this game again?" The captain's teeth were gritted, but he seemed more irritated than frightened. "I'll tell you nothing."

"You said that when you were up against a good man. Look into my eyes, my friend, and tell me what you see. Am I a good man?" Dario grinned. It was one of the most chilling things Jess had seen him do. "I am going to kill you for the damage you've already done to my friends. And the only thing that will stop me is if you give his location. *The only thing.* And you have three seconds before I start stabbing you. I intend to see how many holes I can make before you die."

"You're a liar—"

"That took three seconds," Dario said, and moved his dagger. He plunged it into the man's side, and even Jess flinched; he hadn't expected it. Clearly, neither had the captain, who let out a choked cry. "It's a pity you chose this. Well, actually, it's not." He withdrew the blade and moved to the man's shoulder. He thrust expertly between bones, and the captain, pallid with shock, cried out this time. "Because I very much am going to enjoy—"

"Dario," Wolfe said. "Stop."

"No," Dario said. "You don't command me, Scholar. Not this time. I want this old man. I want this to be *done*, for all our sakes. He knows. He'll talk."

The captain, pale and silent, shook his head. Jess closed his eyes. He didn't want to see it, but he knew Dario had stabbed again when he heard the breathless scream. "Stop!" The captain's voice was raw with panic now.

"Talk," Dario replied. "Three seconds."

"He's going to kill her," the captain blurted. It was very nearly a snarl. Defiant to the end. "He's in the Serapeum, after your false *Archivist*. And he's going to make it hurt."

Dario froze. His blade was still in the man's body, and for a moment Jess wasn't certain what he meant to do. Then he slowly pulled the dagger out and said, "He's going after Khalila." There was no emotion to the words at all.

But all of it was in the blade he buried in the captain's heart.

Someone—Morgan, perhaps, still upstairs—gasped audibly, but no one else made a sound, not even Wolfe.

Jess felt an awful sort of emotion, something he could hardly understand that swept through him. Horror, yes, but also a kind of approval. *He would have been executed,* he thought. *Maybe that was cleaner than he deserved.*

Dario removed the blade, wiped it clean on the hem of his jacket, and said, "We need to go. Right now."

Not even Wolfe argued the point. But he turned to Jess and said, "Can you make it?"

"I will," Jess said.

But he knew his time was running out. And from the bleak look in the Scholar's eyes, so did Wolfe.

EPHEMERA

Text of a letter from Lord Commander Niccolo Santi to his lover, Christopher Wolfe, put aside in case of his death

I suppose it seems foolish to tell you now that I've loved you since the moment I first set eyes on you, Chris; that was self-evident at the time, and though I've never said it I assume you noticed.

Then again, you've always had a terrible opinion of your own attractiveness, so maybe you didn't. It doesn't matter now. I only meant to tell you that although I know my duty to the Great Library, it is a great struggle right now to not hand over my title, quit this battle, and find you. I want you safe. I want you always.

But I know that you'd just shout at me to go back to what I do best, even though I've lost an Archivist to assassins, even though I have little chance of holding this city against enemies inside and out. We've always had the odds against us, and God knows this is not my first failure, only my greatest.

I'll stay the course. And I know you will try to look after yourself, and those around you, because that's who you are.

I love you. Even if I can't be with you, I will never leave you.

I just wanted you to know that if you can't hear it from me tomorrow.

CHAPTER SEVENTEEN

THOMAS

The poisonous gas lapped around Thomas's lower legs now, and he felt frozen in place. He'd come so far, solved so many riddles, and now . . . now this.

It wasn't fair.

Thomas forced himself to *think*, not give in to the panic that stormed through him. This gas, was it the same that had so badly damaged Jess? Dragonfire, it was called?

If it was, then he had time. The smell was overwhelming, but it would take time to kill him. Minutes, perhaps hours or days. Certainly enough time to do what was necessary or there wouldn't have been any point in Heron's automaton warning him there was a puzzle to be solved.

His gaze raced around the room as he put the mask he'd been given back on. It wasn't of much use now—he'd exhausted the supply of whatever alchemical gas had been placed within it—but at least it helped a bit. It would buy him a few moments more.

Not the recording device, he thought. There simply wasn't enough there to exploit. What was left? Well, the automaton of Heron. The steam calliope that didn't seem to work. Piles of treasure. He lifted his glow to reach to the far edges of the room, and froze.

The back wall was full of *scrolls*.

For a moment he forgot that this room was trying to kill him, because the wonder of it overwhelmed him. These were *Heron's writings*, the secret works that he'd never shared with the Great Library. Things no one had seen. Discoveries that might well be greater than Poseidon rising from the sea. Valuable beyond anything else in this room.

Books were Heron's real treasure.

He had to force himself back to the practical work of survival. *You'll never know what's in them if you don't live.* That much was certain.

He said to the automaton, "Can you give me a clue?" It was worth a try.

The automaton was silent for a moment, and then it said, "What disappears when you say its name?"

Another riddle. Thomas barely checked a shout of frustration. The green mist was coiling up his legs now, nearly at his waist. If he was immersed in it, what would happen? How long would it take him to choke to death?

Fear, it seemed, was a wonderful focus lens, because the answer came to him almost immediately. "Silence," he said. "Silence disappears when you say its name. But is silence the answer or . . ." He stopped, because now it was obvious. "No. Sound is the answer. But what sound? The calliope? It doesn't work! I don't have time to—" He broke into ragged, tearing coughs. This gas would disable him before it ever reached his face, he thought. He had to *think*.

He looked at the water clock to see how much time was actually left. By the amount of water that had drained into the reservoir, and the space left to fill, he could only have a few moments to—

It's a water clock.

He lunged forward and took the mechanism from the automaton's grasp. It released it easily—as if it expected him to make that motion.

He looked at it from all angles and found an opening at the top that was fully sealed, which was why the water within it hadn't evaporated over the ages.

He grabbed a tool from a rack nearby and dug into the seal until it broke, and revealed a hole the size of the tip of a finger.

Thomas grabbed a funnel from the array of tools and raced to the calliope. It took precious seconds to find the opening; he jammed in the funnel and had to stop for another bout of horrible, painful coughs. His mouth felt too wet, and he tasted bitter foam he couldn't seem to swallow. The mist had risen to his chest now, a greenish sea of night-mares. His eyes burned and bled tears.

He had to have a steady hand to do this. He forced himself to be still and *focus*, and slowly poured the water from the clock into the funnel.

As soon as the clock was empty, he dropped it and slammed the lid shut. Now for the button, and then it would be done. A burner would ignite, heat the boiler; valves would release the steam in patterns and intensity to play the organ, and . . .

He couldn't see the button. The calliope's lower half was completely hidden in the mist, and it seemed to be rising faster now. His lungs hurt like they were filling with fire, and foam built in his mouth and nose, choking him. He could hear his strangled gasps, and his whole body was drenched in sweat.

His knees buckled. He grabbed for the steam calliope's frame and felt the whole thing rock unsteadily on metal wheels. *No, no, I can't go down. If I do I'll be dead.* Once his head went below that mist, he wouldn't survive.

Tears dripped down his face as he shut his eyes and once again summoned up focus. He'd seen this machine. He *knew* where the button was. Panic was blinding him, but he forced his mind to be still and show him what he needed to do.

The calliope drew itself in glittering lines in the pulsing darkness of his closed eyes, and there it was: the switch to flip the machine on. It was just a foot below the level of the mist.

He didn't open his eyes as he reached out.

His fingers closed on it, and he flipped it from down to up.

He heard the boiler begin to heat. It would take some seconds for the chemicals around it to heat it to boiling. He tried holding his breath, but it hurt too much, almost as much as breathing. *I am in a lake of fire,* he thought, *and burning from the inside out.*

Heron's automaton said, "Well done," and Thomas heard the hiss of steam engaging. The calliope was starting.

He opened his eyes as the notes sounded. The same notes as in the crystal cavern, but played in a beautiful, lyrical dance.

The mist continued to rise. It was at his chin. He wasn't going to make it out of this place.

And then there was a sudden, violent blast of cool air from somewhere above, driving down the mist, drying the tears on his cheeks. He turned his face up to it like it was the sun coming out from clouds, and tried to breathe. Even standing was too difficult now, and his knees failed him as the last of the gas was driven down into cleverly concealed metal vents that snapped closed.

He was on the floor. He didn't remember falling.

The automaton looked down on him with an expression almost of sadness. "You have done well," it said. "But your trial is not over. The gas will be fatal if you don't retrieve the antidote."

He coughed out a bitter mouthful of foam and rolled on his side to gasp, "Where?"

Heron's automaton pointed to the far wall, the one with the scrolls. A section of the shelves slid open like a drawer. Thomas stared at it in despair. It was too far away, and he was too weak. The idea of standing again, walking again, seemed as remote as the moon.

The automaton stretched out a hand.

He gritted his teeth and reached up for the help. Getting to his knees was agony. Getting to his feet made him spit blood. *How did Jess live through this?* he wondered, and he remembered the skull-like pallor of his friend's face. *Maybe he hasn't.*

Thomas made it to his feet, somehow, and caught himself against the worktable loaded with Heron's own tools. Pushed himself from there to the recording device. Then to the sphinx in the corner. Then, with a sob of pain, from there to the drawer.

Inside lay seven vials. He almost picked up the first one, and his blurry vision caught the colors of the glass.

The last trial.

He turned back to the automaton. "Is there more?"

"No. This is all."

"Can it cure two people?"

No answer. Perhaps Heron had never written that answer into the machine.

Thomas lunged away to the worktable, found a glass beaker, and poured the contents of the vials into it, in the correct order. Red, orange, yellow, green, blue, indigo, violet.

The mixture turned cloudy white.

I may kill us both, he thought, but better that than watching his friend die. He split the solution, pouring half into another vial and sealing it before he lifted the beaker to his lips.

He drank, and the taste of it was foul, but not as bad as the awful clinging horror of the Dragonfire gas. He felt it begin to work almost immediately, clearing the foam from his mouth and nose, opening up his throat. His lungs would take time, he thought; they seemed to be swollen and tender, stuffed with fluid.

But for the first time, he thought he would survive.

He took the vial and wrapped it carefully in fabric he tore from his ruined jacket. The pockets were still intact, so he stored the antidote there for Jess. *I have to hurry.*

Then he looked at the wonders around him and despaired, because they were exposed now, vulnerable, and he could not stay here. He'd opened the way for predators. For the evil old man to take *everything.*

He couldn't just leave it like this.

He found a scroll case among Heron's things and began to wrap as many scrolls as he could together to fit into the small, round openings inside. He managed to gather about half before the case was full. Then he found another empty chest hidden behind the sphinx and put the rest inside that.

He passed Heron's statue.

It said, "You are worthy of my legacy. Use my treasure well," and the gleam in its eyes went out. It was dead.

Its purpose had been served.

He went past the unmoving sphinx. Past the crystals, which stayed dormant. Past the next sphinx, too.

The anteroom beyond had bodies lying on the flagstone floor. Men and women in red uniforms. *He sent his people in after me.* That was foolish. He checked each of them but found them all dead—some, of wounds that could only have been made by the spears in the ceiling. Others, of wounds that looked like they'd been earned in battle.

He picked his way carefully on the safe path through the room, made the stairs, and realized that something was very, very wrong.

At the top of the staircase Thomas saw a flash of lightning split the sky.

The sky. He shouldn't have been able to see the sky.

But the temple that had covered this place was gone. Just . . . gone.

He emerged into a smoky pile of rubble, a broken god in pieces on the ground, and steadily falling rain. Fires were burning. Walls had been shattered.

The Archivist was gone. He wasn't among the dead; Thomas checked every body, no matter how torn and bloody. These were his soldiers, and two dead automata sphinxes who'd evidently attacked them.

No one to help here, and no one to stop, either. He was free. Free to go, with Heron's treasures.

"Stop," a voice said. He couldn't see anyone. Then lightning flared, and he saw Zara Cole crouched just ahead of him, aiming a rifle at his chest. Rain flattened her hair against her head, darkened her uniform almost to black. She must have been cold and miserable, but her aim was steady, her eyes calm.

Then she put her rifle down, raised her hands above her head, and said, "I surrender to you, Scholar Schreiber."

"Why?" Thomas asked. He didn't trust her, of course. He was looking for a trap, but the night didn't seem to hold any other soldiers, any other secrets. "Why would you give up *now*?"

She took in a deep breath and said, "I was wrong, Thomas. He never intended to save the Great Library. He intends to destroy it." She staggered and fell to her knees, and even though he didn't trust her, he carefully set down the boxes he carried and went to her.

Up close, he saw the holes in her uniform, and the blood that was pouring out of her wounds. She'd been shot. Several times.

"Lie down," he told her. "I'll find a Medica."

"No. No time," she said. "The Archivist shot me. *He shot me*, after everything—" She sounded more amazed than angry, and shook her head to dismiss it. "He thought you'd failed. He knew he was finished. He intends to take it all with him."

Thomas felt a surge of real fear at that. "What do you mean, *all*?"

"The Great Archives," she said. "He's set them to burn. Stop him. You have to . . ." She fell slowly, tipping on her side and then rolling on her back, staring up at him as he crouched beside her. She didn't seem to see him for a moment, but then she smiled. *Smiled.* "I knew you weren't dead," she said. "You're too hard to get rid of. So I waited for you."

"Yes, I see that," Thomas said. "Zara—"

"Go," she whispered. "I'm sorry. I thought . . . I thought he was the rightful leader of this city. But I was wrong. I was so wrong—"

"I have to leave you here."

"I know." In the next muttering thread of lightning from the clouds overhead, he saw her skin had gone chalky, her eyes almost luminous. "Tell Nic I'm sorry."

She died before the next lightning bolt split the sky overhead, and Thomas slowly rose to stare down at her.

Then he picked up the precious cargo of Heron's treasure, and ran.

EPHEMERA

Text of a letter from the Russian ambassador to the tsar of Russia. Available in the Codex after a twenty-year interdiction.

They've killed so many of us tonight. So many. And the old man has never come as he agreed with his magical inventions of Heron of Alexandria. You gave me the authority to prosecute this war.

Instead, I am ending it.

I am withdrawing our troops from this fight. Let the Great Library stand or fall as it may. We're far from home, and we have lost far too many of our sons and daughters.

The High Garda, it was said, was weak. The city was complacent and soft.

Neither of these things are true, and we cannot win this war without destroying ourselves in the process.

I, for one, hope that the Great Library survives. It has fought hard enough for that privilege.

CHAPTER EIGHTEEN

JESS

Khalila was in danger. There was no discussion on whether or not to go, only how best to get there before it was too late. Dario was just . . . gone, moving so quickly not even Glain could get in his way. Wolfe wrote quickly in his Codex, but even as his stylus was moving, he said, "We can't rely on security to stop the old man; he may still have allies inside the Serapeum, and he no doubt knows the place better than anyone."

The odds of the Archivist having a secret way into the Serapeum were good, and Jess realized with a chill that no matter how careful Santi had been, he couldn't know all the modifications and specializations the old man would have made during his reign. "His office is the most likely entry point," Jess said. "He'll have some way in and out that he kept secret. He could go in that way."

"But Khalila isn't using his office," Glain said.

"Wasn't," Wolfe corrected her. "Now that she's been elevated, she might. She *was* using a small desk in a storage area, and last I saw she was in a conference room with the Curia. But we don't know what's happened since."

"Sir," Jess said. "Send the warning to Dario. He'll get to her and defend her to the death. You know he will."

Wolfe glanced at him, then nodded and kept writing. "Yes. You're right. But we still should hurry. This is his endgame, I think. And we don't know what he's got planned."

"The old Archivist doesn't have his Elites anymore," Glain said. "We've killed most of them. So what could he possibly have left?"

"His pet Obscurist." Morgan had been silently watching, but now she stepped forward. "Vanya Nikolin. He's very good at staying out of sight. I'm not certain how powerful he is, but if he can assist the Archivist in any way, it's by making him undetectable to most."

"Can you find this Obscurist?" Wolfe asked. "If you can, then it's very possible that we can find the Archivist along with him. If I know the old man, he'll keep his Obscurist close and try to use one of the Serapeum's Translation Chambers to escape once he's done."

"After he kills Khalila, and does God only knows what kind of damage," Jess said. "We can't wait for a transport." *And I'll slow you down,* he thought, and felt a surge of frustration and despair. It stung, but he had to be practical. He wasn't well enough to run, or even walk. And they all knew that.

Morgan nodded. "Hands," she said. They all looked at each other uncertainly. She rolled her eyes. "Stand in a circle and hold hands. I'll get you inside the Serapeum."

"Morgan," Wolfe said. "Are you sure—" He glanced significantly at Jess. What he really meant was, *Can he survive the trip?*

And Jess wasn't at all sure he could, but damned if he was going to say it. Not with Khalila's life and the entire Great Library in the balance.

"Is there a choice?" Morgan asked quietly.

Wolfe didn't like the answer; Jess could see that. But he held out his hands, and Jess clasped his left, Morgan his right. Glain stepped up and completed the circle.

Glain looked to her Blue Dog second, who was watching this with real worry. "Go straight to Lord Commander Santi," she said. "Tell him we're tracking the old man to the Serapeum, and Khalila is in danger. What are you waiting for? Go!"

"Sir." He saluted

Then the room dissolved around them in a flash of light, and Jess was falling, flying, flailing, in an ice-cold hell of darkness until suddenly it was done and he was collapsing to the floor. Translation. He *hated* Translation. And this time, he felt the damage it did to him, pulling at him in all kinds of horrible ways. It felt as if he was dying, as if he'd never draw in another lifesaving breath again . . . and he heard himself gasping over and over like a landed fish. Felt hands turning him over. Heard a confusion of voices smearing the air.

Then he was able to breathe a little, and the fog parted. He blinked and focused. Morgan was kneeling over him. And Wolfe. Glain stood apart, staring down.

"You didn't even let us say it," Jess managed to whisper.

"*In bocca al lupo,*" Morgan said. Her voice was gentle, her eyes full of grief. "The wolf hasn't eaten you yet, Jess. I've helped you a little, but . . ."

"But you can't save me," he said. "I know. It's all right."

The walls above him looked familiar. So did the looming bulk of a desk. Gods in niches.

They were in the Archivist's old office, and Jess felt a sudden shock of horror. The smell. The acrid, awful smell of the gas was everywhere. "Poison!" he gasped. "Get out!"

"It's no longer effective," Morgan said, and wrinkled her nose. "It's foul-smelling, but that's the worst of it. The part that made it so dangerous can only survive for an hour before it breaks down. I read the account in the Black Archives. We'll be all right."

Wolfe turned to Morgan. "Can you tell if the old man has been here?"

Morgan nodded. Her eyes were closed, but when she opened them Jess saw that shimmer again. Unearthly and wrong. "He has," she said.

"But he's gone. I don't know where he is now. We should get to Khalila, quickly."

Jess tried to get up, but he couldn't. The smell of the gas made him feel sick and weak all over again. He coughed and concealed the blood by hacking it onto his sleeve. Dark cloth concealed everything.

Wolfe checked the time. "She may be in the prayer room. There's one set aside in the Serapeum near the conference room where I last saw her. Can you locate her? Or Dario?"

"Yes," Morgan said. "But"—she looked at Jess—"he can't come with us."

"I know," Jess said. "I'll follow." That was a lie. He had nothing left.

Morgan put a gentle hand on his brow, and he was shocked at how cold it was. Or how feverish he felt. He didn't know which of them was worse at the moment. "Stay here," she said. "Please."

He couldn't do anything else. His lungs were a ruin of pain, every breath agonizing. Blood bubbled at the back of his throat. *I'm coming apart.*

He didn't want to die in the Archivist's office. After all this, not here.

Wolfe said, "I'll stay—"

"No," Jess gasped. He managed to sit up and put his back against the desk. Smiled. "No, Scholar. Go. I'm all right. Just *go!*"

Wolfe's face told him everything he needed to know about how painful the decision was, and how inevitable.

His friends left him behind. He was glad. This wasn't something he wanted any of them to see.

He coughed out a mouthful of blood onto the carpeting and realized that it was already stained. *Neksa's blood?* She'd died here. Then he frowned, because he clearly remembered that the Archivist had replaced that carpet. He touched the stain, and his fingers came away bright red.

Fresh blood. And not his own. What could that mean? Had someone caught the Archivist here and been injured or killed for their trouble?

Jess pulled himself up and followed the drops of blood across the carpet to the silent automata gods. There was a bright pool of crimson at the feet of Anubis, as if someone gravely wounded had been here and . . . touched what? He looked at everything twice and finally saw a smear of blood on the flail in the god's hand. He touched it. Nothing happened. He wrapped his hand around it and tried to pull it. That wasn't right, but he felt it give slightly.

He turned his wrist and twisted.

The god stepped down and away from the opening, and the panel behind him slid open. Jess watched the automaton closely, ready to dodge should Anubis use that flail . . . but it seemed passive. He stepped up onto the pedestal and through the open doorway.

Anubis climbed back up to its former position. The door slid closed again.

Jess turned to see . . . a library. A room full of books, rich with the smell of aging paper, leather bindings. A hint of dust. Just the kind of room he would pick to die in, he thought, and felt a flicker of relief. He could feel the end coming. And this was a good place for it, at last.

The library was full of originals. Illegal, hoarded originals, just like home. The irony of it tasted bitter as the tainted blood at the back of his throat.

There was an old man in a chair, and he was bleeding all over the brown leather.

"Well," the old Archivist said. "I see that neither of us has outrun our destinies, Brightwell." He laughed a little, and gasped. His face turned the color of the palest of papers, so pale Jess could almost see the sharp lines of the skull beneath. "Irony of ironies. I came to die in the company of my oldest friends, and here *you* are. I can't seem to get rid of you."

"What happened?" Jess asked.

"Do you really care?" The Archivist smiled a little, but it failed after an instant. "Going to call someone? Medica? High Garda? An executioner? I fear you're too late."

"Who did it?"

"In the end? Zara managed one last shot as I was leaving," he said. "I stretched her loyalty too far. 'Tis not so deep as a well nor so wide as a church-door, but 'tis enough, 'twill serve.'"

"Don't you dare quote Shakespeare."

"I like Shakespeare, boy. I like everything. I read everything. Well, *have* read. All new things are now behind me." The Archivist reached out for a book and opened it—not one of the rare originals on the shelves, but a simple Blank. His fingers were bloody and shaking. "Can't damage the books by staining them. I thought I'd read something familiar now, if I could. Would you load one for me?"

In this moment he was just an old man afraid to die. All that he'd been, all the cruelty and power and fanatical zeal, had been dropped somewhere on the other side of this door. He wanted comfort.

And he did not deserve it. Jess thought of Brendan, dying in his arms. Thought of Neksa murdered on this vile old dictator's command, and the people killed in the arena he hadn't even known. Thousands of deaths to hang around this man's neck. Tens of thousands.

Including his own, because he knew the poison would get him yet. One last, fatal gift from the grave.

He opened his own Codex. "What do you want?"

"I think Aristotle's *Poetics*. One of my favorites."

Jess tapped the title and held the Codex to the Blank. Aristotle's flowing Greek filled the pages, and the Archivist smiled a little. "I will be the last to read this book," he said. "Isn't that a great and terrible thing?"

"You mean, it's the last thing you'll read."

"No," the Archivist said, and met his eyes. Jess had been wrong. Pale, weak, dying, the old man was still himself. Still full of spiteful power, and something worse. "I will be the last to read *Poetics*. The last to read *any* of the books stored in the Great Archives. So it's fitting that I will savor it before it's gone."

Jess's mouth went dry. He remembered being a child, locked in a carriage with a madman who ripped pages from the world's rarest book only to eat them. There was some of that evil pleasure in the Archivist's eyes now. He *enjoyed* taking something out of the world. He intended to be buried with his possessions, like an ancient Pharaoh. Only the Great Archives never belonged to him.

"What have you done?" he blurted.

"Blame Archivist Nobel," the Archivist said. "He never imagined a day when destroying the Great Library was a choice we could really make; he intended the system as a deterrent for any enemies willing to attack Alexandria. But that's purely his lack of imagination. It only takes the will to act."

Jess forgot his own weakness. He grabbed the old man by the front of his jacket and dragged him up and out of the chair, but the Archivist was deadweight, hardly able to stand. His head lolled drunkenly on his neck. He was bleeding so badly it fell like rain around him.

"This place is mine," the Archivist said. He sounded faint and exhausted. "And I will take it back. I bind it in blood and ashes and flame. Tomorrow I will be gone, but so will the Great Library of Alexandria. It's done, boy. It's done."

Jess let go and stepped back. He couldn't comprehend what he was hearing.

"What have you done?" he asked again.

"I've killed it," the man said. He smiled.

And then he collapsed.

Dead.

EPHEMERA

Excerpt from Brendan Brightwell's personal journal,
never transcribed into the Great Archives

I had a dream once that I was an only child, and I woke up from it crying. I was just a wee lad then, and when Jess asked me why I was crying I hit him until he went away.

Because that was the moment I realized that although I thought I hated my brother, hated the whole idea of there being two of us identical on this earth . . . I couldn't do without him, either. I needed him.

And, yes, I loved him.

By the time we were old enough to form these thoughts properly, and adult enough to talk about them, we weren't really talking at all. Jess had turned bookish and hated everything about his life, including me. I can't really blame him for it. Da had made our lives a living hell the whole time, and I'd been the one Da favored.

I wish I'd made things right.

I hope I still can someday.

I don't want to be alone.

CHAPTER NINETEEN

Khalila

Khalila was in midsentence when Dario burst into the conference room, a full dozen High Garda soldiers in his wake. She paused, shocked, and he sent her a quick, apologetic glance and turned to the soldiers. "Close the shutters and secure the doors," he said. "No one comes in or out without my approval."

"Hold!" Khalila said sharply. "Scholar Santiago doesn't speak for me. What is this?"

"The old man is here," Dario told her. She saw the very real worry in his eyes. "He means to kill you, *querida*, and I will not let that happen. These are Santi's picked troops. They're loyal."

The Curia members—only three in the room just now—had come to their feet. Litterae Magnus Vargas had drawn a concealed High Garda weapon. And Khalila felt the cool reassurance of the dagger she kept strapped to her forearm. It was no defense against a bullet, but what was? She wore an armored jacket beneath her summer blue dress, and a thin layer of flexible mail under the hijab to protect her head. It was practical. It was not perfect.

"Thank you for your concern," she said, "but we are in the middle of coordinating—"

"I don't care," Dario interrupted. "I need you safe."

She drew herself up to her full height and met his gaze squarely. "Scholar," she said, and kept her voice calm and quiet. "What I need from *you* is obedience. Take these soldiers and leave the room. You may secure it from outside if you like. I will order the shutters closed. But *you must go*. Now." She turned to the lieutenant in charge of the High Garda. "And you need to understand who to obey. You obey *me*, the members of the Curia, and only after us, a full Scholar, no matter what his relationship to me might be. Do you understand this?"

He seemed shocked, but he nodded and composed himself quickly. "Yes, Archivist. My apologies. I believed there was a direct and immediate threat to your safety."

"Not in this room," she said. "And I trust you to prevent any from reaching it. Scholar Santiago? A word."

She turned and walked toward the farthest corner of the room, and heard his footsteps follow her after a few seconds of silence. She didn't turn until he reached her. "This will not happen again," she told him. "Dario, *I am not your* querida. I am the Archivist and Pharaoh of the Great Library, and you will not do this again. Do you understand?" She leveled a stare on him, and knew he felt it. She saw him flinch from the deep cut she'd just delivered. She didn't like it, but she knew it was necessary.

"I was just—"

"I know what you were doing," she interrupted. "I love you, Dario. But I will not be ordered about, or silenced, or overruled. In private, we are equals. Here, we are *not* and we can never be. Do you understand?"

He held in whatever anger he felt, though she saw a muscle clench tight along his jaw. "I understand." The words were quiet and very clear. "My apologies, Archivist. I am yours to command." She waited for the *but*. He managed to avoid it. She gave him full credit for it; she wouldn't have thought he could. "We questioned the captain of the Elites. He said that you were to be killed here, in the Serapeum."

"Lord Commander Santi authorized additional guards," she said. "Do you not think I am kept aware? Dario. My love. You must trust that I know what I'm doing, or this will not work between the two of us. I'm honored by your passion, but—"

"But I undermined your authority," he said, and bowed his head. "I'm sorry. I only meant to guard you."

"I've taken the highest office in the Great Library. That entails risk. And I can't be seen to be afraid of it."

This time, he didn't speak at all. Only nodded. And that was when she knew he understood.

"Thank you," she whispered, and gently kissed him. "For knowing when to stop."

He smiled a little, but there was a bleak distance in his eyes she didn't fully understand. "Oh, I don't," he said. "Not where your safety is concerned. But I'll be more careful." He bowed. Not even a trace of mockery. "With your permission, Archivist, I'll withdraw from the room. I'll be right outside when you need me."

She nodded, and hoped the warmth in her gaze was enough to bridge the distance.

Dario straightened and headed for the door. The last soldier in the room was at the windows, cranking down the metal shutters.

He was killed by a sphinx as it glided in through the opening, silent on its metal wings. It speared him through the chest with talons as long as an eagle's, and flung him across the room in a spray of torn flesh and blood.

Dario's hand went for a sword that was missing from his belt, and then he drew his dagger.

Litterae Vargas shouted, "High Garda! Defend the Archivist!" And the doors that had just shut flew open as they rushed in.

Khalila had a knife that was already in her hand even before the shock hit her—shock that immediately vanished like mist under the sun, with determination and anger taking its place. *They dare to kill here again.* High Garda soldiers ran to her and surrounded her in a wall of bodies, and the Curia members dived for protection behind an overturned table—but the sphinx wasn't coming for them.

It turned its Pharaoh's head straight toward her, and shrieked.

Dario stepped out of the protection of the High Garda. "No!" Khalila cried, but she knew what he was doing, and why. *I can do this. I don't need you to do it for me.* But that wasn't true. When she was just Scholar Khalila Seif, she would have risked herself freely. But the same position that meant he couldn't command her meant that she couldn't order him not to protect her, either.

He gave her a flash of a smile, cocky as ever, and she saw for the first time that he had blood in his hair, blood on his shirt—how had she missed it before?

Then he was moving.

He ran at the sphinx, dodged a swipe from a taloned paw, and then another. He buried his sword in one of the thing's eyes, and as it lifted its head and let out another violent scream, he twisted in close and jammed his fingers up under the thing's chin. Then he rolled under it, between the slashing paws, and curled into a ball with his hands covering his head. He was helpless if it hadn't worked, if it turned on him . . .

But it stopped, midturn, with its claws hovering a few inches above his body.

Khalila didn't dare breathe. She heard the hiss of steam, the ticking of the clockworks inside the automaton's body.

Dario opened one eye, saw the claws looming over him, and flinched.

"Move!" Khalila snapped, and the soldiers stepped away from her. She ran to Dario, grabbed his hands, and pulled him out from under the dead automaton. Then up and into her arms. "What idiocy was *that*?"

"Heroism," he said, and gave her a shaky smile. "Pure heroism."

She only sighed. Then she stepped back, folded her hands together, and said, "Thank you for your bravery, Scholar Santiago."

He stopped smiling, but she saw the glow in his eyes nevertheless. He bowed deeply. "Archivist. I'll be outside. Just in case there's another chance to prove my worth."

He walked to the door, and a guard looked at her for a nod before he opened it for Dario's departure.

Khalila caught her breath on something that might have been a laugh, or a sob, or both, and turned to the lieutenant of the High Garda soldiers. "Please see to your fallen man. What is his name . . . ?"

"Reyansh Bannerjee."

"I will personally inform his family of his sacrifice, and that he gave his life for mine."

"Yes, Archivist." The lieutenant signaled his men, and four of them broke away to carry Reyansh Bannerjee—a man she had never known, a man with a life and a family and a reality now ended—away. *I owe him my life. I will do him honor every day I must shoulder this responsibility.*

She'd only just caught her breath and retrieved her fallen dagger when a knock came at the door. Dario's voice said, "Archivist? Scholar Wolfe is here."

"He may enter," she said. "Members of the Curia, are you all right—?"

"Fine," Litterae Vargas reported, and helped the older members to their feet. "We'll continue our business when you're ready. Personally, I could use a drink."

Once they were out, Wolfe entered, and once she'd given permission the soldiers also allowed Glain, Morgan, and Dario to join them. Just her friends now, and for the first time she let her guard down. A little.

"You're all right?" Wolfe asked her. At her nod, he continued. "We were told there was a threat to your safety. We came as soon as we could." He cast a sidelong look at Dario. "Though I see he managed to get here sooner."

"I commandeered a carriage, and then I ran," Dario said flatly. "Like the devil was after me. Where's Jess?"

"Resting," Morgan said. "In the old Archivist's office. He couldn't make it the rest of the way. We'll go back for him, but we needed to be sure—"

"I'm fine," Khalila said, and managed a smile. "And you, Morgan?"

"Yes. I'm well enough. Do you know where Thomas is?"

"No," Khalila said. "The High Garda's been on the hunt when they can, but . . . You don't think something's happened to him, do you?"

"I think Thomas wouldn't disappear at a time like this unless he had no choice in the matter," Wolfe answered. "And he was last seen leaving the Lighthouse, on his way to the workshops—"

Wolfe's Codex shivered in its holder at his belt. So did Glain's. So did Morgan's. And Dario's.

And Khalila's, too.

They all opened them at about the same moment. Wolfe was just a fraction faster to the meaning.

"It's from Thomas. He says the Great Archives are in danger. The Archivist intends to destroy them."

For a blank instant, Khalila looked at him, waiting for him to give some order, and then she remembered. No. This was her duty, not his.

"Who's the best expert on the Great Archives available?"

"There are special Scholars who maintain the collection," Wolfe said. He was already writing in his Codex. "And a special company of guards dedicated to its protection."

"Summon the Scholars, if they're not already inside the facility," she said. "We'll require their expertise. Do it on my authority."

She quickly wrote to Lord Commander Santi. *I will need your troops stationed at the Great Archives to be under my immediate command. Secure the facility. No one goes in or leaves unless I grant permission. Kill anyone who attempts entry without my approval.*

Understood, Santi wrote back. *The battle is winding up here. Russians retreating. I will come myself.*

She hesitated, then wrote, *Hurry. We need you.*

Then she looked up and said, "Now. We all go. If the Great Archives are in danger, we can't wait here."

Wolfe bowed slightly, and put his fist over his heart. A High Garda gesture. "In your service, Archivist." She listened for any hint of mockery. But he was completely sincere.

I am the Archivist of the Great Library, she thought. *If only for this one night.*

But for this one night, the Great Library will survive. At whatever cost.

Insha'Allah.

EPHEMERA

Text of a letter handwritten by Obscurist Alfred Nobel,
kept and handed down to each Archivist in turn until
the reign of Archivist Khalila Seif

I am writing to give you a burden so great that our minds can scarcely grasp its significance. I am sorry, but you must read this, keep it, and share it only with your trusted Curia and the Lord Commander of the High Garda, all of whom must be sworn to secrecy in this matter.

After much debate, we have installed four controls in the Greek fire system beneath the Great Archives. A saboteur might find the controls. To that end, we have taken a lesson from the writings of Great Heron, and carefully concealed what to do in the event of an unwanted activation of this system.

The drawings below show precisely what must be done.

Do not fall prey to the trap we have set, or all is lost.

CHAPTER TWENTY

JESS

Jess looked down at the dead Archivist for a frozen eternity of seconds, and then fumbled the breathing mask from his pocket and dragged down breaths, as many and as fast as he could stand. It helped a little. Working out how to leave the library room took long minutes, but he finally found the switch that moved the god out of the way. The walk from the Archivist's office to the formal entry area seemed to take forever—an endless hallway, and he moved on leaden legs.

But he made it to the hub at the end of the hallway. From there, a steam-powered lifting chamber took him up to the fourth level of the pyramid. He stumbled out as soon as the doors opened on the right level. He wasn't sure how much strength he had left, but there was no time to waste. He had to use it all.

High Garda were *everywhere*, and as Jess approached they shouted at him to stop. He was forced to obey at the point of guns. He looked for a friendly face, found nothing but death staring back.

"Archivist," he gasped. "I need the Archivist—" He nearly fell, and braced himself against the wall. "Archives are in danger. Tell her."

"She knows." Lord Commander Niccolo Santi's voice came from

behind him, and Jess turned to look. Santi was a terrifying sight: exhausted, red-eyed, smoke-stained, and his expression was absolutely bloody murderous. "Thomas sent word. He's coming, too. Where have you been?"

No point in wasting his breath explaining. Jess doubled over coughing, and fumbled for his mask. Took a couple of breaths and tried again. "The old Archivist said something about Archivist Nobel."

Santi grabbed Jess by the shoulders and stared at him, and Jess had never seen the man so shaken. "What did you say?"

"He said—Nobel had never imagined destroying the Great Library, but he'd made it possible."

"Where is the old Archivist?"

"Dead," Jess said. "In his private library."

"Jess!" He heard Khalila's shout, and he looked up and saw her pushing past the soldiers toward him. She was flanked by his friends, and he saw her expression shift when she saw him, but she didn't ask him what was wrong. She came straight to the point, moving her attention to Santi. "Lord Commander, I'm glad you're here. We believe the Great Archives are in danger. According to Thomas, who is on his way there."

"Something Jess just said made me realize he's right. The old man has a way to do something unthinkable."

"That's a word I've never heard you use before," Wolfe said. "Nic, what's happened?"

"About to happen." Santi took in a deep breath. "Khalila, you should have been briefed on this; Archivist Murasaki was, but there hasn't been time to meet with you. The Great Archives have, for more than a full century, had a fail-safe system. It was installed by Archivist Nobel during his reign—a bluff meant to terrify nations into compliance at a time when many wanted to take Alexandria for themselves. In the event of an attack, should any nation seize control of the source of knowledge—it would be destroyed. Everyone would lose. Only the

Archivist and the Lord Commander knew about this fail-safe." He shook his head. "The awful thing is that it's worked. It's kept most countries from testing our resolve."

"That's ___" Jess saw the horror dawn in Khalila's eyes, just as he felt it dawn inside him. "That's *monstrous*."

"It kept the peace. It was never meant to be used, only as an apocalyptic threat."

"Nobel's great secret," Wolfe said. "There were rumors, but—they actually *installed it*?"

"Yes," Santi said. "A massive series of Greek fire sealed in tubes running beneath the Great Archives. Only the Archivist or Lord High Commander can activate it. Only the Archivist can stop it once activated."

"How?" Khalila asked tensely. "How can I stop it?"

"*You* can't," Santi said. "Your name has yet to be written in the official record. You haven't been fully confirmed. The fail-safe can only be countermanded by an Archivist written in the history."

"You're missing the obvious. She only needs to be written into the official record," Wolfe said. "Immediately. We do that, and this is over."

"We can't," Santi said. "It has to be done after a Scholars' Conclave. She hasn't had one."

"Does a formality matter *now*?"

"No, Scholar, he's right," Khalila said. "The records can't be amended. They're locked. Unless Morgan can—"

Morgan, Jess saw, was already trying. She was looking into a strange middle distance, eyes unfocused, and her hands were moving in odd patterns. "Give me your Codex, Archivist."

Khalila handed it to her. Morgan opened it, and patterns of shimmering, incredibly complex lines formed between her hands and the book. Part of it seemed to waver. Lines disappeared. But then it all just . . . vanished.

Morgan flinched and dropped the Codex. Her hands looked red, as if she'd been burned by it. She gasped and pulled them close to her chest. "I'm sorry," she said. Her voice shook. "I can't. I'm not even sure Eskander can do it. That's something . . . the protections on those documents were done by someone *much* more powerful than I am. Or ever will be."

Khalila took a deep breath and abandoned that hope. She cast about for an instant, then said, "Thank you for trying. Scholars, it has to be run by some kind of machine. Can the machine itself be stopped instead? Dismantled, perhaps?"

Santi looked at her. "I don't know."

"Then we'd better damn well try," Wolfe said. He started to speak, then stopped and looked at Khalila. "Archivist?"

"Yes. We must find a way inside, locate the machine, and stop this from happening. There's no time for anything else, if Thomas and Jess are both right."

"Archivist, you can't risk yourself—," Santi started to say. Khalila turned to look at him.

"If I lose the Great Archives, there is nothing left to risk," she said. "I don't intend to lose them. I'm coming."

Morgan said, "Hands," and held hers out. This time, they didn't hesitate, and Santi joined the circle.

All together now. Together at the end of things.

All except for Thomas. Where was he? What had happened to him? Jess hated not knowing. His friend needed help; that much was clear. And he couldn't give it.

Translation.

Jess came through it alive, but he knew it would be the very last time he could endure it; his whole body felt twisted with the effort, and he resorted to his mask again to force air into his failing lungs. Morgan held his hand, and he knew she wanted to help him. He also knew that she couldn't, not much. But maybe . . . just maybe . . . enough to get him through this.

After this didn't really matter.

They stood inside the Great Archives. He knew this chamber; he'd been here before, a vast and vaulting space where he, Wolfe, and Morgan had ended up after Translating from his father's estate. The beginning of this strange road they were running.

"Well, this should be easy," Dario said as he looked around at the incredible *size* of the place. Impossibly, he'd retained a sense of humor. "Please tell me there's a simple off button."

"Quiet," Morgan said. "Thomas is outside. I'm bringing him in."

And in the next blink, there Thomas stood—smeared with ashes and dust and blood, ragged as if he'd been in a fight with a room full of knives, loaded down with two massive cases. He staggered and caught himself on a massive pillar.

"How—," Thomas said, and checked what he was going to say. He looked at Morgan. "You brought me here."

"You were at the door, arguing with soldiers," she said. "I just . . . moved things along."

Khalila nodded, smile sparking wide. "You're alive!"

"Only just," he said, and stepped forward to greet her—and then hesitated. "You're wearing a crown. The Archivist's crown."

As if she'd forgotten, Khalila touched it where it sat atop her hijab. "At the moment," she said. "But I'm still your friend, and I'm happy to see you, Thomas."

Thomas nodded and looked at Wolfe. Santi. Glain. Dario. Last, at Jess. Jess felt something cold and knotted ease up inside him. They might all be doomed, but at least they were, for the first time in a while, *together.* And together, they were powerful.

"We don't have much time," Thomas said. "I'm sorry. Zara said that the Archivist was going to burn the Great Archives. We have to prevent that."

"We know," Wolfe said. "Alfred Nobel's hideous fail-safe device. But we don't know how to control it."

Khalila said, "Perhaps the old man didn't actually activate it . . . ?"

"No," Morgan said. "He did. I can see the power gathering. But it takes time to charge."

"Like the Ray of Apollo," Thomas said. "The batteries have to be charged before the process can begin. We can still interrupt it."

"How?" Wolfe demanded. "Where?"

Morgan pointed at each of the four distant wings of the building. "It's gathering at the entrances to each of those openings. There must be some central control at each point. Something to relay the power on."

Khalila had her Codex, and she read something from it. "The Senior Research Librarian of the Great Archives is unable to leave; he was injured and is in a Medica facility. But he confirms that there are four control points. There are manual shutoffs to each wing, in case maintenance had to be done. But he doesn't know how to access them without opening a sealed document kept inside his office."

"No time for that," Morgan said. "The devices are inside something. Marble."

"Under the floor?"

"No. Above it. Inside—" She suddenly smiled. "Inside the base of a statue."

"There are statues of Zeus at the entrance to each of the wings," Santi said. "In the base of those?"

"Yes."

"How much time do we have left?" he asked.

Morgan shook her head. "I don't know. But maybe . . ." She turned her head, as if she was listening. "Break the seal."

"What?"

"Break the seals." She blinked and looked at him. "I don't know what that means. It's what the ring tells me."

"What ring—"

Morgan shoved that aside with an impatient gesture. "Just *do it*. Now! We're running out of time!"

They were standing in a deathtrap of monumental proportions, Jess realized. And no time to ask more questions. He looked to Wolfe, and Wolfe said, "Nic, go south with Khalila. Thomas, north with Jess. Dario, with me to the east. Glain and Morgan, west. Look for a Great Library seal on the statues; that must be what she means. *Go!*"

They scattered, moving fast. Jess kept up with Thomas, though he knew it was costing him the last of his endurance, and they spotted a vast archway to the north. Over it was a Latin phrase: *Sapientia melior auro.* Wisdom is better than gold.

Zeus's massive seated form sat carved in marble beside that entrance. At any other time the sight might have awed him; the statue stood ten times his height, a breathtaking work of art in perfect marble. But just now he only cared about one thing: the seal of the Great Library embossed in gold on the base of the throne.

He pulled his sidearm and hammered at it with the butt of the gun. It cracked but didn't break.

Thomas moved him aside and slammed the point of his elbow into the seal—once, twice, three times.

The seal broke, and beneath that lay a lever. Thomas turned it.

The entire statue rolled aside on noiseless wheels, and behind it stood a closed door.

Locked. Jess was too sick to even try to pick it; he shot the lock away, and Thomas swung the door wide.

He could hear ticking the moment the door opened.

The room held a simple metal console with a clock embedded in its surface. As Jess watched, the second hand swept backward. It was counting down.

"Do you see an off switch?" he asked. Coughs were boiling at the back of his throat, and he felt his lungs filling with foam and liquid.

"No," Thomas said. He pulled a panel from the front of the thing and bent down. "Yes! I see it!" He bent down and tried for it. Grimaced and shook his head. "I can't. My hand is too large to fit. Jess, here.

Here!" He grabbed Jess and pulled him down before Jess could move, and pointed. Jess followed his pointing finger and started to reach for the red valve.

It was too easy. He rested his fingers on it, hesitated, and shook his head.

"Turn the valve!" Thomas shouted.

"That's wrong," Jess said. His brain was cloudy, but he pushed that away. Pushed all of it away. He'd seen this before; he'd seen Great Library traps all his life, meant to catch thieves and smugglers. The valve was bait, like a mockup of a rare book left within easy reach. It was there to catch the unwary.

He looked to the other side. There was another Great Library seal, glass cleverly painted to look like metal.

Break the seal.

He smashed his fist into it, ignored the pain as the glass shattered, and found another valve under the shards.

He turned it.

The ticking stopped.

"*Mein* Gott. Thank you. I should have seen that," Thomas said. He was visibly shaken. "The others—"

"The others might fall for it," Jess said. "Go. Tell them." He couldn't get up. His mouth was full of foam again. He couldn't gag down a breath; his lungs felt filled with concrete. He spat the foam out, coughed, and managed to croak out, "Go!"

Thomas looked at him for an instant in agonized indecision, then took something out of his pocket and pressed it into Jess's hands. "Drink it!" he ordered, then turned and ran as he shouted a warning. Maybe he would reach the others in time.

Jess looked at the lump of tattered cloth that Thomas had handed him, and slowly began to unwrap it. There was a glass tube inside, full of liquid. He tried to remove the stopper. His fingers kept slipping. *The air is burning,* Jess thought. But it wasn't the air. He was gasping but getting nothing from the effort. He was suddenly and tremendously tired. *I'm dying in a room full of books after all. The biggest collection of all,* he thought. And that felt right, even if he was afraid and in pain and angry that it had to be this way, that he had to do this alone, that he wouldn't get to say good-bye.

He'd forgotten about the vial. It was still in his hand, but it no longer really mattered.

He let it roll away across the floor.

He let his eyes drift closed, and time drifted.

Something's on my face. He came awake with a gasp, and realized it was his breathing mask; he could barely draw in the next, choked breath, but he tried. It cleared his lungs enough that he was able to manage desperate, shallow gasps.

I think I was dead. Was I?

Khalila. She was weeping, tears streaming down her cheeks.

She was dragging him across the marble floor, and in the next blink Dario was there, too, dragging him faster.

Something was wrong with the light.

The light flickering behind the two of them was green.

The Great Archives were burning.

Dario and Khalila dragged him to the center of the vast chamber. Three of the Archive wings were silent and safe.

The entrance where Morgan and Glain had been working was a hell of green flames. The inscription above that arch said, *Scientia ipsa potentia est.*

Knowledge is power.

Knowledge was burning.

Wolfe was shouting something, but Jess couldn't make it out. Nothing made sense anymore. They couldn't lose. They *couldn't.*

Books were *burning.*

Morgan was standing at the burning entrance with her hands flung wide. The Greek fire inside was trying to break past her, trying to consume everything. Every scrap of knowledge in the entire Great Library.

Glain stood there ashen, helpless, shaking. "My fault," she said. "I should have known."

Thomas put an arm around her. "No, Glain. *My* fault. I should have been faster to tell you."

"Morgan!" Wolfe shouted. "Morgan, let go! We have to get out!"

"No," Khalila said, and walked forward. She stood next to Morgan, looking at her, and turned toward the rest of them. There was something different about her now. Something . . . regal. Not Khalila, Jess realized. She spoke as the Archivist of the Great Library. "We haven't copied everything. We will lose all if she lets go. She knows what has to be done." She put her hand on Morgan's shoulder. "We will remember what you do. I love you, my friend. But you are the only one who can accomplish this."

Morgan looked over her shoulder, directly at Jess. In that moment, he loved her with all his heart and soul. And he wanted desperately to take her place, to let it be him instead. If he'd had the slightest chance of doing what she could, he would have plunged in no matter what it cost.

He didn't have that power. She did. And he had to let her make her choice, just as she'd let him make his own.

But he could make sure she didn't die alone.

She saw it in him, somehow. And as he stumbled toward her, he felt a sudden gust of wind push him back, sliding him across the marble floor and right into Thomas's grip. "No!" he shouted, and tried to fight free. "No, let me—" Coughing caught him again, doubled him over. Blood poured out of his mouth in a sick wave. He tasted bitter foam and copper.

"Did you drink it?" Thomas asked him, and yanked him upright. "Jess! Did you drink what I gave you?"

He just shook his head. "Left it." Thomas dropped him and headed for the shattered statue.

"Jess," Morgan said, and he focused on her with an effort. "You have to live. Live for me. Tell Glain it wasn't her fault. I'm the one who turned the valve." She smiled, just a little. "I'm glad I loved you."

She stepped forward into the hellish inferno.

They all cried out, Jess thought, all of them, denying what she was doing, but they couldn't stop her. None of them dared. The blaze wrapped around her, and it started to burn her, and then the fire just . . . stopped, as if it had never erupted at all.

Because she cut off the oxygen that fueled it.

"Morgan!" Wolfe rushed forward, hit an unyielding barrier, and battered against it. Beyond that lay a melted ruin where the wing of the Archives had been, a hellish slurry of melted stone and ash. And Morgan, burned and shaking, who was killing herself along with the Greek fire that sizzled, hissed, tried to burn but was starved of its fuel.

Jess tried to watch, but his eyes had blurred again, and the foam bubbled up from his lungs. Bloody froth in his mouth. He coughed it out and kept coughing. Santi and Wolfe were trying to get to her. But he already knew it was too late. She'd make sure it was too late. She'd only let go when the last of the Greek fire had no chance of re-igniting.

The barrier collapsed at last, and so did he, hitting the floor as Santi and Wolfe lurched over the line where Morgan's power had been. The Greek fire liquid had turned into a thick brown sludge running over the floor, but it didn't burn now. Harmless.

Morgan had saved the Great Archives.

She lay limp and blackened in Santi's arms as he picked her up, and Jess whispered, "No," and lunged forward.

When he fell, it was like dropping through a trapdoor of the world, into absolute darkness.

"Easy," a voice said. "Jess. Swallow."

There was an awful metallic taste in his mouth. Liquid. He tried to spit it out but a huge hand covered his mouth, and he had no choice but to swallow it. He gagged and coughed as the hand pulled away, but the taste faded, and what was left was a soothing weight that worked its way down his burning throat and into his chest. Heavy and cool. Comforting.

"That's the last of it," Thomas said. "Stay still. It should work soon. You might still need rest."

Jess licked his dry lips and said, "What is it?"

"The antidote," Thomas said. "I found it in Heron's Tomb."

Jess lay on cool sheets in a brightly lit room, and the lingering stench of Greek fire seemed to cling to everything. His head ached. His lungs burned. He felt tender all over. He just wanted to rest.

Then he remembered.

Morgan.

He pushed the mask aside and tried to get up, but nausea and weakness shoved him down again. *I dreamed it. She's all right. She has to be.*

"Jess." That was Anit's voice. He looked over and found her sitting at his bedside next to Thomas, and she was holding his hand in hers. "Welcome back to the land of the living, my brother."

"I—" His throat ached, and it would barely form words, but at least it wasn't a bloody mess of foam now. He fumbled for the glass of water on the table beside him. Anit held it to his lips and fed him sips. "How long?"

"Days," she said. "That's the third dose of the antidote; Thomas made it himself from the sample he brought. The Medica were afraid you'd never wake."

He didn't want to ask, but he made himself. "Morgan?"

Anit looked away. "I'm sorry," she said. "She was badly burned, and she died inside the Great Archives."

He looked at Thomas and read the truth on his best friend's face. Thomas didn't speak. He didn't need to.

It hadn't been a nightmare. Morgan was dead.

He expected grief, but even so he wasn't prepared. It hit like a storm, ripping through him in convulsing waves. *Gone. She's gone.* Like his brother.

Everything he loved left him.

Despite the pain, he didn't feel any urge to weep. His eyes burned, but it felt angry, not sad. "She shouldn't have died for it," he said. "The Great Library never did anything for her. It took her freedom away. And now it took her life."

"She chose to save it," Thomas said. "She could have run. She didn't."

He knew he had to honor what she'd done. It had been the bravest thing he'd ever seen.

But he hated himself for not stopping her.

Thomas cleared his throat. "Jess, the Archivist is here. We should let her speak with you alone."

His brain was sluggish, and for a moment Jess thought he meant the bitter old man he'd left dead in the Serapeum . . . but no, of course it was Khalila. A more serious Khalila, dressed in plain black, with only the crown with the seal of the Great Library atop her hijab to show her status. She exchanged a hug with Anit—when had they become friends?—and claimed the chair beside Jess's bed. "I've prayed for your recovery," she told him. "Insha'Allah, they think you'll be back to normal in a few weeks."

"Weeks," he repeated. He was glad to see her, but he felt . . . numbed, as well. Oddly distant. *I survived.* He'd never expected that. Never expected to have to live through all of this.

He'd been chasing down death. He'd actually caught it.

And somehow it had slipped away despite all his best efforts.

"I expect you'll convince them to make it sooner," Khalila said. She took his hand in hers. "My friend, I'm so very sorry."

"About Morgan?" He shook his head. "Thomas says she made her choice." *And I'm angry with her. She should have run. She should have never been there at all.*

"She chose to save books that would have otherwise vanished from this earth," Khalila said. "Her name's being carved into the Scholar Steps. She's going to be honored among the highest heroes of the Great Library."

"I don't think she ever wanted that," he said. "I think she just wanted to be free."

"She was free, ever since the arena; she could have gone at any time. She *chose* to stay. Obscurists are free now, free to live outside the Iron Tower, to have families, to do anything they wish. I've made sure of that, in her honor."

"I wish it had all burned," he said, and closed his eyes. "If she was the price of winning."

"You don't mean that."

He didn't. He couldn't imagine a world without the Great Library. Without books. Without knowledge at his fingertips when he needed it.

It struck him suddenly that every book he read now would be a gift. A gift from Morgan.

And that was the moment that grief truly broke inside him, and the angry, painful tears came. It didn't last long, and Khalila just held his hand as the storm passed, then silently handed him a handkerchief. He wiped his face and took a careful breath. It hurt, but it was only a shadow of the pain he'd felt before. "She didn't have any family left," he said. "Her da tried to kill her. He was the last of them."

"She's been laid to rest in the Necropolis," Khalila said. "We put her in the old Archivist's miniature Serapeum, and buried him in a pauper's hole instead. It seemed appropriate."

He'd missed her funeral. *No.*

"Your family's arrived," she said. "They asked to see you, and they want to take your brother's body back to London. I refused to allow any of it until you were awake and I knew what you wanted to do."

His da, here, in Alexandria. Well, that was a terrible idea. "Brendan would want to go home," he said. "He liked Alexandria, but he'd want to be in England. Let them have him."

"I was afraid we'd have to give them two sons," she said. "I'm glad I was wrong."

She took the handkerchief back from him and folded it neatly before slipping it into a pocket of her dress.

"I don't think I've ever seen you wearing plain black before," he said. "You're wearing mourning?"

"Yes," she said. "For Morgan. She was part of my family. As are you, my brother."

"I've already got Anit; you don't need to adopt me, too."

"But I *want* to. And since I'm the Archivist, you really can't object." She gave him that charming, slightly wicked smile.

"If you're the Archivist, you ought to be wearing all the gold robes," he pointed out.

"I'm a Scholar, Jess. And I'll continue to act like one, despite my responsibilities." She added her other hand on top of his. "You did all you could do. You and Thomas, you saved the Great Library, too. And I expect you will keep on doing that in whatever form you choose. Thomas has requested that a new Curia position be opened. He is calling it *Liberius*. Publisher, I believe that would be. It would oversee the installation of his printing machines, and I think he wants you to be part of that."

That woke some warmth in places that had gone cold inside. *Books. We'll make books.* He remembered the feel of an original, the hand-cut paper, the binding and stitching. *We'll sell them. Openly. To people who want to have them in their homes.*

"No more raids?" he asked her. "The books will be legal to own?"

"Legal to own," she said. "And that promise has made the Burners lay down their bombs, it seems. At least for now."

"The Russians?"

"Withdrawn, and making peace now that the old Archivist is dead. The Spanish ambassador is petitioning to make a new treaty." Her smile grew big enough to reveal dimples in her cheeks. "I'm keeping him waiting. A little."

"That's strategically wicked of you. I like it." Books. Thomas had the authority to print real, original books. That . . . that would change the world, surely. It had certainly changed his. "I should get up. Get dressed."

"No, you should not," Khalila told him. "Save your strength. Your father wants to come to see you in the morning. But only if you agree, of course."

"Might as well get it over with," Jess said sourly. "Say a prayer for me, will you?"

"You are always on my list," she said. She bent and planted a warm, gentle kiss on his cheek. "My brother."

"Two sisters I never had. So strange."

"Oh, I think you'll find you have more siblings than you can handle." She looked at the time. "I'm sorry to leave you, but I have a meeting with the kings of Wales and England, and I must make a decision about what to do with France; it's ghoulish to continue to operate it as a memorial to our own power, and I'd like to hand it back to the rightful French citizens. But there are treaties to negotiate there as well. I'll see you as soon as I can, Jess."

She left, and six High Garda soldiers formed up around her at the doorway. He'd just been kissed farewell by the Archivist of the Great Library.

His life had gotten complicated.

He slept, woke, demanded a bath and a meal, and got them. When his parents arrived with the sun, they found Jess up and walking, if carefully and slowly.

Both his parents wore black. Jess accepted his mother's silent embrace, and thought she looked sincerely worried about him.

Callum Brightwell didn't bother with any pleasantries. He swept Jess with a look and said, "You seem better than I expected."

"Thanks," Jess said. "Don't tell me you came all this way to smother me with parental love."

"Jess," his mother murmured. "We do love you."

One of you might, he thought. But his mother had never stood up to his bully father, so that didn't really count for much, either.

"We're only here to claim Brendan's body," Callum said. "The damned High Garda won't let us have him until you sign a release to allow it. Here."

He thrust out a Codex, and Jess read the document inscribed on the page. An agreement allowing Callum Brightwell to take the body of Brendan Brightwell from where it lay in state in the Serapeum with the others who'd fallen in the conflict, and remove it for burial to England.

Jess said, without looking up, "Where are you going to bury him?"

"Does it matter to you?"

"Yes."

"On a hillside on the castle's grounds," his mother said. "He liked it there. He sat sometimes to read and watch the sea."

A lonely, windswept hillside in England. Maybe she was right; maybe it was what Brendan would have wanted. He didn't know. They'd never talked about it. Never thought it could happen.

Jess closed the Codex. "I'll think about it," he said.

His father's face flushed a deep, ugly red. "No, you'll do what you're told. He's lying dead inside that great bloody pyramid *because of you!* The least you can do is let me get him decently buried and not gawped at by half the librarians in the world—"

"Honored, you mean. By people who loved him."

"Don't you dare, boy. I loved Brendan—"

"More than me, yes, I know."

"Sign the form!" His father's fist was clenched. Jess watched it, but he wasn't afraid. Or surprised. He wasn't sure if he was strong enough to fight the old man—or, at least, to win—but he'd damn well try.

It caught him by surprise when his mother stood up and said, in the sharpest voice he'd ever heard from her, "Leave him alone, Callum!"

It seemed, from the look on his face, that his father had never heard that tone, either. "What?" He recovered smoothly. "This isn't your business. This is between—"

"Shut up," she said. "I've had more than enough of your cruelty and arrogance. I *will not* let you do it a moment longer. Not to my last child. *Go away.*"

Jess's mouth was open, but he didn't really know what to say. He just watched this woman he'd always loved but never known change before his eyes into . . . someone else.

A person. A real, live person instead of a silent statue.

"My dear, you can't really think—" Callum was trying a new technique. Wheedling. It didn't work.

She stalked past him to the door and opened it for him. "Leave," she said. "Now. We'll discuss this later."

"You can't—"

"She can." Jess kept his voice level, and he was surprised to find it hardly hurt at all to feel the rage coming off his father like a mist. He'd grown a shield against it, finally. So had his mother. And he felt that Brendan would have liked that. "The High Garda will escort you back to where you belong. You can wait."

"I'm not going anywhere!" Brightwell roared, and raised that clenched fist.

A black shadow flashed through the doorway, as if it had been waiting, and caught his father's arm. Shoved him back with such force Callum Brightwell hit the wall, stumbled, and fell flat.

Jess's mother didn't come to her husband's defense. She crossed her arms and glared down at him.

Scholar Wolfe stood over him, smoldering like the coals in a barely covered fire, and said, "Get up, you miserable bastard. Don't come back unless Jess asks for you. You're lucky you're not in chains, but I promise you, it can still happen."

"He's my son!" Brightwell shouted, and scrambled to his feet with his fists clenched. "*Mine*, not yours!"

"Wrong," Jess said quietly. "On both counts. I'm not your property. And I'm more his son than I ever was yours."

Callum Brightwell was at a loss for words, finally. And he seemed small, and bewildered. A bully robbed of victims.

He left without another word.

Jess's mother drew in a deep breath and extended her hand to Wolfe. "Thank you," she said. "For loving my son as much as I do."

He kissed her hand and held it for a moment. "I can't imagine the strength it has taken you to get to this moment," Wolfe said. "And I'm glad I saw it."

"So am I," she said. She smiled. "I don't think we've ever been properly introduced, Scholar Wolfe. I'm Celia Brightwell. Jess's mother. And I intend to be a true mother to my boy from this moment on."

Jess didn't altogether trust it, this fragile feeling blooming inside. He'd been living in a desert so long that finding a rose in the sand seemed impossible.

But he said, "I love you, Mum."

And when her arms went around him, he knew he meant it.

Brendan's body had been carefully preserved, and he almost looked alive. Almost. Jess didn't touch him, though he pulled up a chair to look down into the mirror of his own face. He thought how close he'd come to occupying a bier beside his twin, and some part of him still thought that might have been right. But he could almost hear his brother's reply. *Plenty of time. I'll wait.*

"So, Scraps, do you want to go home? Let Father bury you and raise up some monument in your honor? Pretend like he ever cared about either one of us, except for what we could do for him?" Jess asked the question, but he knew he'd have to answer that for himself. "Yes, I suppose you would. You'd like to be back there, I know that. And getting Da to waste his money on a monument? You'd enjoy that, I'm sure. The larger, the better."

He half expected Brendan to turn his head, laugh, tell him it had all been a brilliant prank. But his brother was gone, and he needed to finally accept that.

It was going to take a lifetime to understand it.

He'd been sitting for a while when he heard footsteps. He didn't turn. He'd heard other visitors come and go, murmurs and whispers. None of them had disturbed him.

"You should be in bed," Thomas said from behind him.

"I know," he said. It wasn't just Thomas who'd come. It was everyone. Dario, dressed in darkly glittering richness. Archivist Khalila, holding a small bunch of English violets. Wolfe and Santi, standing together with clasped hands. Even Glain in her sharp High Garda uniform, hands clasped behind her back.

Everyone present but Morgan. The spot where she should have been felt like a new wound, and he looked away, back to his brother.

"He'd be honored," Jess said. "To think all these important people have time to come visit him."

"And visit you," Khalila said. "I'm sorry it took as long as it did."

"Well, you were signing treaties and negotiating the return of France," Jess replied. "I think he'd forgive you. I know I do." He stood up. For a moment they all simply looked at him. No one seemed to quite know what to say.

So of course, Khalila went first.

"I brought these," Khalila said, and handed him the flowers. "I hope they are appropriate—"

"He'd like them," Jess assured her, and put them on top of his brother's still chest. "Thank you. All of you. You didn't need to come."

"We did," Glain said. "Don't be daft."

"Glain," Khalila reproached her, but it was gentle.

Glain was the first to hug him. He was surprised by that; she hardly ever showed that side. It was a warrior's embrace, all muscle, and a sharp clap on the back as punctuation. "Don't follow him," she whispered. "We still need you here with us." She left just as quickly, head high. Off to rejoin her squad.

Dario came next, and he offered his hand. Jess ignored it and embraced him, too. "I'll stop calling you Scrubber," Dario said as he slapped his back. "Eventually. Maybe."

"I'll look forward to that. Your Royalness."

After Dario, Khalila. Her hug took his breath away, and he felt something crack inside, just a little. "I'm proud of you," he said. "And a little afraid of you, too. I heard they've confirmed you. Youngest Archivist in history, so they say."

She gave him another kiss on the cheek. "And you have to listen to me when I tell you that you'll be all right," she said. "We're all going to make sure you are."

Then it was Thomas, and a very careful embrace from arms the size of healthy young trees. "Khalila told you about the press? The new publishing operation? We're going to replicate the Great Archives! People will be able to *own* books, Jess."

"Yes, I heard," Jess said. "I'll join you when I'm able."

"Your office is already being built. I've made you Chief Printer."

"Do I get paid?"

"We'll discuss it. But it comes with all the books you can read."

"Then I'm in," Jess said, and smiled. "See you tomorrow."

When Thomas was gone, it was just Wolfe and Santi. Wolfe said, "Are you in fact all right? Be honest. You've seen me at my lowest. Don't be afraid to admit it if you need our help."

"I know, and I promise, I would. But I'm . . . better," Jess said. "More than I expected. This is . . ." He took in a careful breath and glanced down at Brendan. "An ending. I don't know who I am without my brother, but I suppose now I have to learn. He'd demand that."

"Well," Santi said, "let me be the first to tell you that I've released you from contract to the High Garda. You get full salary for the rest of your life, by the way. Orders of the Archivist." He embraced Jess. "You're not just Wolfe's son, you know. I love you, too."

"I know that, sir. Thank you."

Perhaps it was worth surviving, after all.

Anit was waiting in the hall when he left; the High Garda stationed there were eyeing her with real mistrust, and her own guards gave it back in full. His gaze caught on the tall form of Katja, who nodded back. "Condolences," Anit said. "I hear you're a great hero now."

"I'm not," he said. "But thanks."

"So heroic you won't be in the family anymore, perhaps?"

"Oh, I'll always be a cousin," he said, and cast a smile at Katja, who raised a lofty eyebrow. "Just not one who runs books. I'll be printing them instead."

"So I heard," she agreed. "Come on, my brother. Let's have coffee. I understand the day is beautiful, the sun is shining—"

"And you have an interesting proposal for me?"

"Of course. I'm thinking of opening a bookshop. The first of its kind in Alexandria. And I'd like you to be my partner."

"Fifty-fifty?"

"Seventy-thirty."

"We'll discuss it."

He opened his Codex, signed the release form, and let his brother go at last.

EPILOGUE

"Thank you for letting me be here," Wolfe said, and his father nodded. "I haven't been in the Iron Tower of my own accord for . . . quite a while."

"*Ever*, I think is the word you're searching for," Eskander said. "But you're always welcome."

"I'm surprised you haven't left. You're not required to stay, you know."

"Funny thing. I've spent so many years behind these walls that I can't imagine living somewhere else. But I think the new Obscurists will find it easier to come and go."

Wolfe stood awkwardly in the open lobby. The Iron Tower stretched out above him, quiet for now. High Garda still manned posts at the front entrance, and the burn marks still on the floor indicated why. Alexandria wasn't quite what it was. Not yet. And maybe it never would be again.

Nic thought that would be a very good thing, a sign of progress after centuries of stagnation. Wolfe reserved his judgment.

He felt he needed to say something more to his father, but he wasn't quite sure what. Finally, he just blurted out his real question. "Where is Morgan?"

"Her body is in the Necropolis, as you were told," Eskander said. "With all the proper rites and funerals."

"I know that, but—" Wolfe struggled with the words. "I can still feel her presence. I needed to ask why."

"Does Niccolo know you're here?"

"No, I—I didn't know what to tell him." He swallowed. "Am I going mad?"

"Not at all." His father's eyebrows rose. "I confess, I didn't expect this. You never had talent."

"Thanks."

"*Obscurist* talent, Christopher. It was always latent in you, but it never manifested before. How is it you can sense her?"

"Maybe I'm imagining it. Wishing it to be true."

"Or maybe what you sense is this." Eskander reached into his pocket and took out a large amber ring. "Put it on."

"I—"

"Put it on."

Wolfe slipped the ring on his finger, and for a moment, nothing seemed any different. A vague sense of unease, of sensing someone standing just out of view.

Of being watched.

And then Morgan's voice said, "I was wondering if you'd find out."

He turned, looking for her, but saw no one. He had not, he realized, actually heard her. The words were not in his ears, but in his head. "Morgan?"

"I'm inside the ring," she said, and laughed. It felt bright as sunshine on skin. "It sounds like I'm trapped, doesn't it? But I'm not. I'm free. There's so much here! Endless expanses that become whatever I want them to be. I'm part of the Imperishable."

"Apeiron," Wolfe said. "The ring is made to contain and channel apeiron. Is that—where you are?"

"I'm everywhere," she said. "I'm with all of you. And you're with me. It's what I always was, Scholar. Just . . . free." Her voice grew a lit-tle sad. "But not in the form you knew me. I'd like to tell Jess that I'm sorry."

"I'm not telling him a voice in a ring talked to me," he said. "And he's better off not knowing *this*."

"Yes. That's true. He's got a path now. Knowing I was here—it might pull him away from that. It's a good, strong path. A long one."

"You see futures."

"I see everything," she said.

It was on the tip of his tongue to ask what she saw for him, but he resisted. He'd never wanted to know the future. If he didn't know storms were coming, it was easier to enjoy the sunshine.

"You sent for me, didn't you? Why?" he asked.

"Because of this."

His world opened. His body burned, tingled, and *woke* with sensa-tions he'd never known, never imagined in his life. He saw the flow of life, the bones of the universe, the building blocks of *everything*, and it was the most beautiful thing he could imagine.

"You were meant to be an Obscurist," she said. "Something went wrong in your body, but only just slightly. The talent was always there; you just couldn't reach it. And now you can be what you were supposed to be. If you wish. You could be very, very powerful."

He let out a raw sound and put his back to a wall to hold himself steady. He'd been a disappointment to his parents, a failure rejected and sent to find his own way beyond these iron walls. And she offered to give him *that*.

For an awful moment, he wanted it more than anything.

Then he caught his breath and said, "Give it to someone who needs it. I don't."

Another silky, cool voice in his head said, "You see? I told you. He has his own path. Let him walk it, Morgan. I am interested to see what he makes of it."

"Who is *that*?" he blurted.

"Archivist Gargi Vachaknavi," Morgan said. "Dead thousands of years, but alive in the Imperishable. Don't mind her. She thinks you're better off as you were."

"I am!"

"Are you sure?"

"Yes! I don't want to be—this!"

"Then I'll take it all back," she said, and the power faded out of him. All the brilliance and beauty and breathtaking wonder, gone.

He was back in his own skin, his own world, and he was achingly, shatteringly grateful.

"Morgan?"

"Yes?"

"How much power do you really have?" He wasn't sure he wanted to know. He caught his father's eye. His father, he thought, wasn't surprised by any of this. It was as if he could hear the conversation. That was irritating, and a bit comforting.

"I don't know," she said. "I'd rather not know, to be honest. I'd rather just watch over the Great Library," she said. "It's what I'm supposed to do. And it will keep me out of trouble, I think."

"Morgan—"

"We won't speak again, Scholar Wolfe. Be kinder to yourself. And to Commander Santi, too. I loved you both, and in here, I always will."

And then he felt her go. Her presence that he'd sensed, however dimly . . . vanished, like mist under the sun.

He ripped the ring from his finger and handed it back to Eskander. Glared at him. "Why did you do that?"

"Interesting, isn't she?" Eskander said, and put the ring back in his pocket. "She terrifies me. But I think we may need her in times to come. The problem of ending one era of oppression is that we all have to decide what comes next. And we should discuss that, at length." He started up the long, winding steps. "Come on, then. I've made tea."

"Why me? We hardly know each other."

"Yes," Eskander said. "But I think we also know each other very well, Christopher; you and I, we're far too much alike. Your apprentices have torn up the roots of the world—and I am glad they did. But we're going to have a job of it if we intend for the Great Library to survive the next thousand years. We have plans to make. Are you coming?"

Wolfe hesitated, and then said, "Yes."

AFTERWORD

I had the idea for the Great Library a long, long time ago, but it was just too big, too complicated to attempt. I waited ten years to finally try . . . and fail. And another five to try again. The world of the Great Library, and all the characters I loved writing so much, is one that's rooted in the very real history of libraries, of knowledge, of the battle over who owns it, distributes it, controls it.

In this world today where knowledge is everywhere and yet nowhere . . . I think this story is more timely than ever.

Thank you for being part of this epic journey.

Now go out and build the world the way you want to see it, bit by bit, day by day.

Word by word.

It's in your hands.

—Rachel Caine

SOUND TRACK

As is my usual custom, I created a sound track to help me through the writing of this book. Each song listed contains some theme or mood that reflected either events or characters within the book, and I hope you'll enjoy the playlist. Please remember: streaming music services are great, but musicians earn little from them, so if you can, invest in their music and own it for yourself. It helps keep them creating!

"Rise" (feat. the Word Alive)	League of Legends, the Glitch Mob & Mako
"Alone in a Room"	Asking Alexandria
"Every Step That I Take" (feat. Portugal, the Man and Whethan)	Tom Morello
"Mantra"	Bring Me the Horizon
"Dead Man Walking"	WAR★HALL
"For the Glory"	All Good Things
"All My Friends"	The Revivalists

"You Should See Me in a Crown" — Billie Eilish

"Natural" — Imagine Dragons

"Church" — Fall Out Boy

"What If We Run" — Bart Van Bemmel

"Glitter & Gold" — Barns Courtney

"Ashes" — Von Grey

"Burn It Down" — Fitz & the Tantrums

"Hit the Ground Running" — Alice Merton

"My Reflection" — Von Grey

"Friction" — Imagine Dragons

"Nina Cried Power" (feat. Mavis Staples) — Hozier

"Poison in the Water" — Von Grey

"Be Legendary" — Pop Evil